FALLOUT ZONE

Stephen Rodgers

Prologue - The day it happened

BBC Radio 4 shipping forecast
Biscay, Trafalgar, Fitzroy – south westerly gale eight, rising to nine. Visibility poor.
Sole, Lundy, Fastnet – south westerly severe gale nine, rising to ten later and possibly violent storm eleven in parts. Visibility poor.

Bristol Channel

Mischa Balan always enjoyed listening to the morning shipping forecast on his way to work at the Thorpehead nuclear power station. He told himself it was mainly because he was about to spend the next 12 hours in the reactor control centre with absolutely no clue as to what the weather was like outside. But it was also because he was still adjusting to living on the coast and at the mercy of the elements. He had been in West Tyneford for less than a year but in that time he had experienced the full gamut of Atlantic weather conditions. This was a remote part of the West Country that sat on a ledge between wild moorlands and the Bristol Channel and for Mischa, it was like a new world.

Arriving from Bucharest with his parents as a baby, he grew up in Hertfordshire where Berkhamstead was probably as far away from the coast as you could be. During a four-year degree course at Leeds University it's fair to say he never really got his feet wet either, so the move west for his first job at Thorpehead was the beginning of an entirely new experience. And he had embraced it. Some of the friends he made at the pub in Holmbeach worked on the fishing boats that still operated from the harbour and the tales they told about their daily travails over a pint were always far more riveting than his accounts of a shift in the control room. He'd really caught the surfing bug and was surprisingly good at it. His work schedule alternated between three day and three night shifts with three days off between each. It did not respect weekends – nuclear power generation was 24/7 – but the downtime meant there was plenty of opportunity to go surfing on the wide sweep of Tyneford Bay.

The biggest difference between him and his new friends in Holmbeach was that he earned considerably more money. Even though he was still classed as a trainee and wouldn't be fully qualified for another year, the money was far above the average wage in this part of the world. So much so that he was able to rent a converted cottage set on a promontory above Holmbeach and with probably the best view anyone could wish to wake up to. That's as long as you looked directly out to sea and didn't turn your head to the right. Because at the far end of the bay stood his place of work – Thorpehead Power Station. Officially opened just over 12 months ago, Thorpehead was the first nuclear power station built in the United Kingdom for 20 years. And it was the first of a revolutionary new design of SMRs – small modular reactors. These operated in the same way as traditional pressurised water reactors or PWRs but their big advantage was the cost. The reactor was built off-site in modular form and then put together at the power station. Many of the last PWR's were beset with construction delays and cost overruns to the extent that the benefits of producing nuclear energy were largely negated by the high infrastructure costs. The new modular alternatives had rekindled the British Government's love affair with nuclear power and it was once more being viewed as the country's primary response to the energy security question. Thorpehead was the trailblazer in what would be Britain's new nuclear era – a network of small, single reactor sites built around the country at a fraction of the usual cost yet developing almost the same amount of energy. There was even talk that future developments of SMR reactors would also be able to deliver hydrogen as a byproduct of nuclear fission.

It was only a short drive to work each morning. Sometimes it could be in glorious weather with the sun shining and the sea shimmering turquoise. On other days, the Atlantic rollers would be rising majestically before crashing to the shore in an explosion of white foam, making Mischa wish he was going surfing instead. But today it wasn't just windy, it was wild. Spray coming off the waves was indistinguishable from the torrent of rainwater heading in the same direction. And the incoming tide was driving the Atlantic Ocean like a conveyor belt towards Tyneford Bay. In all the time he had been listening to the weather forecast he had yet to hear Violent Storm 11 being used in relation to Lundy and he was already struggling to keep the car on the road as he drove along the coast. The lads at the pub had already said they were confined to port for the coming days and even then, there were concerns about unusually high Spring tides. The area had one of the highest tidal ranges in the world and this morning they were expecting high tide to reach just short of 15 metres.

Most of the people who worked at Thorpehead arrived from the other direction or were bused in from Riverbridge, the largest town of any significance, lying around eight miles further up the estuary. Mischa's daily routine always snapped into work mode the minute he left the coast road and joined the queuing traffic at the security gate. Although still junior in rank, his role as a control room operator was one of the more senior in a power station, and it came with the added perk of a reserved parking space almost adjacent to the second security gate. He was grateful for that when, on opening the car door, he needed both hands to prevent it being ripped from the chassis thanks to Storm Hilda – that's what the Met Office had named it. The wind almost blew him to the turnstile and inside to the temporary building which housed the body and baggage scanners. Today somehow, it really did feel temporary. But the moment he passed through the next set of doors into the hermetically sealed environment of the control building the wild Atlantic was left behind. The next 12 hours would consist of LED-lit systems monitoring.

There was just time for a coffee before he made his way to the control room. After a year, the surroundings were now more than familiar to him. In front of the horseshoe-shaped control panels sat two operators, Toby and Jim, the latter readying himself to vacate for Mischa. He had just seen Giles at the cafeteria, who would be on his way to take over from Toby. Immediately in front of where they sat were the control switches for the pumps, while above were the monitors and screens for the reactor control, coolant and secondary cycle systems. Across the top of the rig sat the annunciator or alarm panels. Behind Toby and Jim, on an elevated platform,

Micha's supervisor, Gordon Lanseer, was receiving his handover briefing from his predecessor on the night shift.

'They say there's a fair old storm brewing out there,' Jim said to Mischa. His heavy Glaswegian accent still took Mischa by surprise sometimes, besides having grown up in Berkhamstead and been at university with students from all over the country.

'Yes, Storm Hilda is an angry lady. I almost lost control of the car on the coast road coming in and the forecast is for even stronger winds to come.'

'Aye, and the tide's going to be testing our sea defences for the first time as well.'

'I'd be more concerned about falling trees on the road if you are heading back to Riverbridge. Take care.'

'Och, I'll do that. But if ye don't see me the night, you'll know something dreadful has happened,' Jim responded, raising his voice in dramatic style as if a prophet of doom.

'Don't tempt fate. I'll see you at the end of the shift,' said Mischa as he logged-on to the system while Jim and Toby made for the door.

In Holmbeach, the cafes and souvenir shops which surrounded the harbour were closed, many of the shop fronts shuttered. The harbour wall, built in the 18th century at the height of the iron ore industry, provided perfect cover for the boats against prevailing south westerly winds. While even the mightiest force of the Atlantic was no match for a four-metre-thick wall of granite and slate, the waves which pounded against it could throw up walls of water some ten metres high. And it wasn't just water which would drench the harbourside houses and shops. The flotsam picked up in the waves could be fatal and spectacular as it may look in a selfie or on Tik Tok, when storms were forecast for Holmbeach, locals stayed indoors and shuttered their windows.

At the back end of the town, Brad Ackford had no need to shutter the windows of his flat against the waves but the wind was still finding its way and howling through every single gap it could find. It wasn't just the badly fitting windows that Storm Hilda was exploiting, but around the doors and even between the floors. This was social housing Holmbeach style. Brad, along with his partner Cheryl and three-year-old daughter Lucy, lived in a small block of flats built over retail businesses on the ground floor. It was a common design, built by local councils around the country in the heyday of pre-cast concrete. A flight of steps at the rear of the shops led to a first-floor open terrace with half a dozen separate front doors. The flats themselves were in fact duplexes with a lounge, kitchen and bathroom on the first floor and two bedrooms on the second.

If there was one advantage to their age, it was that these flats were designed in accordance with the Parker Morris minimum space requirements which were applied to all council house building from just after the Second World War until 1980 when Prime Minister Margaret Thatcher declared them a barrier to development. But the disadvantage of their age was that concrete was later discovered to have a shorter lifespan than originally thought and after so many years, insulating them just proved an impossible task, even without the best endeavours of the Atlantic. But it was a home and even though it was no longer a council house per see, Brad and his young family did enjoy some security. Although Holmbeach Council sold the flats to a housing society some years ago, a covenant was attached to the sale to ensure they would be maintained for rent to local people. This followed mistakes learnt from a previous sale of an identical block of flats at the other end of the street. There, the tenants had exercised their right to buy and purchased the flats at a heavy discount. Within a couple of years, all of them had seized on the boom in the housing market to sell their flat at full market value, often pocketing the profit to put down a deposit on a new build development just on the edge of Holmbeach. With the flats now in private ownership, they were all holiday lets today and on the odd occasion when one did come onto the market, the asking price was way beyond the means of anyone working locally.

For Brad it was largely academic in any event. The chances of even getting a mortgage in the first place were next to zero because of his job as a fisherman. Even though Cheryl had a steady job as a nurse at Riverbridge General, Brad worked on one of the boats which made up Holmbeach's small and declining fishing fleet. What was once a thriving industry in this part of the world, Holmbeach had gone the way of many smaller ports with industrial scale competition, regulation which didn't end but actually got worse after Brexit and simple market forces. Larger vessels which fished the same waters were increasingly landing their catch, either directly in France or Spain, or at ports in this country where there was infrastructure for the fish to get to market quickly. Holmbeach was miles from the nearest motorway and most of the catch landed by Brad and crews from the other boats was sold locally into the restaurant trade and fed to tourists.

Brad had come from a long line of fishermen but even his father had decided to call it a day five years ago, selling his boat and opening what was now becoming one of the best-known fish and chip shops in the area. But for Brad, fishing was all he knew and he didn't want to be involved in the new family business. Although he was lucky to be taken on by one of the other crews, he was self-employed and his earnings came from a share of the catch. Sometimes that could be a lot, other times not so much. But on days like today, it was nothing. With Storm Hilda uprated to potential Force 10 or 11, they had returned quickly to port yesterday and it was unlikely they would be moving for the next 48 hours. With nothing to do and no money coming in, Cheryl had left him to look after Lucy. Normally, she would be at the nursery but child care cost a fortune. At least if Brad was at home, Cheryl said, they could save on some of the outgoings. To be honest, he always enjoyed this arrangement. When he was working, tide and weather controlled his hours which meant Lucy was often asleep when he got home or at the nursery when he woke up. So having one-to-one time with her was a bonus for Brad, and usually meant that Lucy could play whatever games she wanted and eat and drink all the things her mum said she couldn't. This morning, after a breakfast of chocolate and banana and a game of hide and seek they had settled down on the settee for some quiet time with CBeebies on TV.

Other than the howl of the wind and the splash of rain on the windows, there was very little traffic noise outside. The shop on the ground floor had been turned into a Chinese takeaway so there was no longer the regular to and fro of customers during the day and the smell of ginger and cooking oil didn't usually waft up until early evening. But as they sat watching the TV there was a loud bang, as if the starter cannon had been fired at the gig races. The settee was against the lounge wall and at that same moment, Brad and Lucy both felt themselves jolt forward. Brad instinctively put his arm across his daughter to protect her from falling and the noise of breaking glass came from the kitchen.

'What was that, Daddy?' asked Lucy.

'I don't know love, I really don't'

Everything was still again. Brad got up and looked at the settee. It hadn't moved, but it was as if the wall had. He went to the kitchen to find Lucy's glass in pieces on the floor. She must have put it back on the edge of the draining board when she finished her orange juice. But otherwise, everything was just as they left it after breakfast. A quick look upstairs and there was nothing different in any of the bedrooms or in the bathroom when he came back down.

'I've no idea what that was but it was certainly weird,' Brad said as he sat back down next to Lucy. After a while, he took out his mobile phone to see if there was anything on social media about the loud bang. As soon as he opened the Connecting Holmbeach community group on Facebook the first post he read was 'Did the earth move for you too!' Several more posts appeared, asking if anyone else had heard a bang or experienced their house shaking. More posts appeared, some asking the same questions, others offering puerile and not particularly funny explanations until one regular contributor to the site posted a link to the BBC News website:

Earth tremor in Bristol Channel causes buildings to shake

An earth tremor measuring 4.5 on the Richter Scale with its epicentre in the Bristol Channel has been reported by the British Geological Society (BGS) this morning. The quake occurred at 9.32 am at a depth of 3 miles, almost midway between Tyneford Bay and Penarth in South Wales. People have reported homes shaking and unstable objects falling in locations as far away as Newport and throughout the South West although there have been no instances of any exterior damage to buildings or roads. According to the BGS, small quakes are not uncommon although at 4.5 on the Richter Scale, this is the highest ever recorded in the Bristol Channel. The previous highest was 4.1, which occurred south of Taunton in 2018.

Mischa was a couple of hours into the shift when Gordon Lanseer stepped down from the platform and came over to him and Giles.

'High tide is at ten o'clock. It's the highest Spring tide since we came on stream but it's still well below the sea defence. Keep an eye on the monitors though.'

'How high exactly?' asked Giles.

'They're saying fourteen-point-seven-metres in some places.'

'But the sea wall is only fifteen metres high, Boss,' Mischa said.

'It's still within tolerance but the reactor is over two hundred metres further back and another five metres higher than the wall. They were well aware of the tidal range when Thorpehead was built, but I just want to keep an eye on things as we haven't seen a tide this high before.' With that, the supervisor returned to his platform where a Teams call was ringing through.

Just under two miles off Thorpehead, two intake heads sat on the seabed. Their purpose was to draw almost 60,000 litres a second into the tunnel which lay 25 metres below the surface. This fed the cooling system for the new, state-of-the-art mini reactor at the Thorpehead Power Station, the start of the process which produced the steam to drive the turbines. After the cooling process, the water which had been sucked in at such a rate through the inlet pipes was then returned to the Bristol Channel via the outfall head of Tunnel 2 situated a mile closer to the shore.

At 9.32 am, the seabed shook momentarily. To the naked eye, the energy released by the quake would hardly have been noticed on the surface where the sea was already being whipped up by the storm force south-westerly and incoming Spring tide. But 25 metres below the seabed the effect of the quake was catastrophic. Less than three years earlier, Tunnel 1 had been hailed by construction firm Bicarel as a "significant step forward" in the British Government's plan for a new generation of low-cost nuclear power stations and a "testament to Bicarel's expertise in delivering groundbreaking and complex projects." With the same type of tunnel boring machine that was used in the recent cross-London underground line, the intake tunnels had been sprayed with over 5,000 cubic metres of concrete in what was considered by civil engineering experts to be a breathtakingly short period of time. When the last of the traditional pressurised water reactors had been built off the Suffolk coast almost 20 years earlier, the water intake construction was estimated to have taken over 2 million man-hours. Bicarel's project at Thorpehead used less than half that. But at 9.32 am, a large crack appeared along the tunnel floor. Water always finds the path of least resistance and with 60,000 litres of water a second coursing through the tunnel, it was only moments before the integrity of the structure was compromised. At 9.33 am, Tunnel 1 simply collapsed in on itself.

Back in Holmbeach, Brad was trying to explain to Lucy the strange experience of the earth tremor that had not long taken place. Suddenly there was another loud boom, this time more like an aircraft breaking the sound barrier, and the floor trembled.

'Another one!' yelled Lucy excitedly.

But Brad knew immediately that this was different. Braving the elements, he stepped out of the front door of the apartment onto the terrace. Although he could not see the headland or the power station from here, he knew the thick black cloud of smoke he was looking at was coming from Thorpehead. But even through the driving rain Brad could clearly make out in the heart of the smoke cloud, the bright red sparks of molten metal rising into the air like a volcanic eruption.

Part One

2 - Twenty years earlier

Oxford

'I think it best that you all leave now and without a fuss,' the manager said. In his hand was the roll of £50 notes he had just been given.

The Boatman was one of Oxford's best-known riverside pubs, alongside the Thames and in season, a popular haunt for the college rowing teams whose boathouses were located close by. Although 'pub' might not be the correct description. These days The Boatman was more of a restaurant with roms that also sold beer. The staff all wore blue and white striped polo shirts with Crew Member on the back. The manager had Coxswain on his as he looked around the private dining room. On one side of the room were two Crew members comforting a third girl who was sitting on a chair in tears, her striped polo dishevelled. On the other side, around twenty male students in varying states of dress and levels of inebriation, some with food on their clothes and in their hair. In between, the oval dining table with the detritus of their dinner, empty wine bottles and glasses. Around the walls, where framed pictures of the River Thames in years gone by, trophies and commemorative half-sized oars hung, splatters of mashed potato and red wine could be seen dripping. Clearly not all of the booze had been consumed but used as part of some boarding school bun fight. The dining room had been booked by the Oxford Bugs Rugby Club to celebrate their last match of the Michaelmas Term. Although to call it a match was rather like calling The Boatman a pub. The Bugs didn't actually play any matches, just took part in the post-match celebrations. During 0 or Noughth Week, the Bugs attended several events, offering Threshers a club that believed in the amateur principles of rugby – a game that could be played regardless of shape or size where camaraderie on the field extended to the clubhouse afterwards. Naturally, any new student actually interested in rugby already had a traditional pathway through their college team to a Blue for the very best of them. The Bugs played no matches because there were no potential opponents. But more significantly, the four-figure annual membership fee made it clear that this was no sports club but a drinking club, accessible only by a certain type of student with financial means.

The Bugs usually only had two 'fixtures' a term and with colleges about to break for Christmas, this was not only the highlight of the year but the first time they had visited The Boatman. In fact, the Bugs never held more than one event at any venue as the evening always ended with not only a lot of food and wine being ordered but untold breakages and damage to property. At the end of the Trinity term, one member attending his last match before leaving Oxford had emptied a decanter of Haut-Brion onto the carpet and proceeded to replace it with his own urine. The main reason membership of the Bugs cost so much was to have a fund ready to pay for the damage they caused and avoid any police involvement.

'For God's sake Ellers, why did you have to do that to the waitress?' Roly said once they were all outside The Boatman. 'We were just beginning to have fun. Now we're out in the cold and we hadn't finished the booze.'

'Fucking whore,' Mark Ellrington replied. 'Bitch was asking for it. Been giving me the eye all night. They're all the fucking same. Give you the come-on then burst into fucking tears when you actually give them what they want.'

'Well, what are we going to do now, it's bollocking cold out here?'

'I know,' said Viktor, one of the last of the group to leave the pub. He was balancing three bottles of champagne on a tray. 'Let's find a quiet spot on the river where we can do justice to these bad boys.'

'Perfect Viktor, lead the way.' Hands appeared from all directions to claim a bottle each as the group headed off across the bridge to the tow path opposite The Boatman.'What's with the tray?' one of the group called out.

'I thought we would need something for this,' replied Viktor, holding aloft a small, transparent packet containing fine white powder.

'Not here, you idiot!' James grabbed Viktor's arm and brought it back by his side. 'At least wait until we are out of the street lights.'

It was cold but thankfully not raining tonight. A soldier always makes the most of his situation, and as Matty pulled his sleeping bag as far over his head as he could, he decided that he actually quite liked his new home. It was now just over six months since he arrived in Oxford and most of that time was spent sleeping rough on Christ Church Meadow, alongside the River Thames. The gates were shut each evening on the stroke of 8 pm but Matty had found a way in through the fence behind the boathouses and a sheltered spot between a clump of trees which was not overlooked. He had the park to himself as long as he was up and gone by 8 am, leaving no trace of his presence by the time the wardens opened up. Unusually for a homeless person, Matty actually enjoyed the discipline his nightly routine required. It was in no small part due to his military training but it also ensured that each day had a purpose. He had seen so many homeless men and women over the last 18 months who simply tried to mask the pain of living rough with drugs or alcohol, one day merging into the next until they simply gave up on life.

For Matty, life still had a purpose, even if he still needed time to process what the next stage in his journey would be. It had never been easy growing up in Ashington in the aftermath of the pit closures. Like his dad and his grandad, Matty had been destined to follow them down the mine but at 17, he and his best mate Eric left school and joined the Army. They had money, travel and adventure right up until the posting to Iraq. The two were billeted together and had turned the corner of their quarters into a Newcastle United fan zone. Team photos adorned the wall and an "Always a Mag" banner was draped between their two bunks. When Eric's patrol hit an IED, he and six other soldiers lost their lives. Matty had been on a night surveillance op and only heard when he got back to the compound the following morning. Trying to digest the news, Matty went to their quarters, only to find Eric's locker had already been cleared and even the Magpies banner removed. That's when the dam burst emotionally. Within a week, he was sent home to his battalion in Yorkshire and within six months, was medically discharged from the Army. Life back on civvy street wasn't any easier. He couldn't hold down a job for more than a few weeks and was dismissed as a barman at his local in Ashington after assaulting a customer who had madesome comment about the armed forces. His mood swings became too much for his mum, who had already gone through the same situation with his dad's depression and drinking after losing his job at the colliery.

So Matty left home and headed for the streets of London. His military training helped him survive living rough in the capital, but wherever he went he found so many others in the same situation. There was always competition for the best begging pitches or the least inhospitable places to sleep and eventually he decided to look for new territory. With a shower and change of clothes provided by the Salvation Army and enough money for a single ticket, he managed the journey to Oxford looking little different from the other passengers on the bus. And life in the city of spires had been, if not enjoyable, surprisingly regimented. Carrying his home on his back, Matty was still a soldier when it came to his sleeping bag and his rucksack. Everything was neatly rolled and folded each morning when he left Christ Church Meadow and went to work. Work in this case was Cornmarket Street where bank ATMs and food outlets provided several profitable pitches to beg. Just like London, it was surprising just how much loose change you could collect in a day. Tourists were always more generous than locals, and foreign tourists in particular had no sense of the value of the loose change they were collecting each time they made a purchase in one of the city centre shops. Some of the students were a bit up themselves, making insulting comments but Matty, after more than a year on the streets, had now learned not to react. By contrast, many of the female students would engage with him, charmed by his Geordie accent, and if he didn't get money there was an endless supply of coffees, sandwiches or sausage rolls being offered. Regularly fed and watered and as much as £100 in loose change on a good day, Matty's regimented lifestyle on the streets was easily survivable. At least the days were. The nights were a different matter. Despite securing a secret hideaway that was peaceful, the cold and the damp always permeated his sleeping bag and clothes, even in summer. Sleep seldom came naturally and he always craved something to take the edge off his physical and mental state. He had seen what alcohol had done to his father and to so many of his acquaintances in the homeless fraternity. Smelling of booze was also a turn-off when asking shoppers for loose change. But with his earnings, Matty was often able to buy something stronger. With Oxford's student population there was no shortage of people to buy from; the hardest part was finding clever ways to convert his loose change into denominations the dealers required. When he could do so, Matty was able to deaden the pain to get through the night. In summer, the nights were shorter and the pickings richer from the tourists in Oxford. But the situation reversed as winter drew in, and it was now December. What's more, his secret arrangement on Christ Church Meadow had been rumbled. Last week, he discovered that not only had his access behind the boat houses been boarded up, there were signs on all of the park gates warning the public that CCTV was now in place.

But Matty had not had to travel far to find his new nighttime home. Just across the bridge on the Abingdon road was a small island in the Thames. It housed a cricket pitch and pavilion and a derelict manor house. A notice attached to the fence detailed a planning application which had been lodged to demolish the interior of the Grade II listed building while maintaining the façade and creating six luxury apartments. Matty had heard that the building had stood empty for a number of years and this being December, nobody would be in the cricket pavilion. He had found a gap in the panel fence just off the tow path and just inside was a clear patch of grass sheltered by the trees. This was now his new overnight home. With no substance to take his mind off things tonight, Matty started thinking about what lay ahead in his life. He had needed to get away from everything he knew or that was familiar to his old life. But he no longer had nightmares about Iraq and now found himself remembering Eric for all the good times they had together, whether in the army or at St James Park. Even those privileged, knobhead students who had no idea about his past when hurling abuse at him, failed to make him snap. Perhaps the trauma from Iraq was out of his system. Maybe it was time to go home and be with his mum for Christmas. Tomorrow he would start collecting for a National Express ticket to Newcastle.

'Shots fired, shots fired, take cover.' Matty cried, waking from his fitful sleep and sitting bolt upright in his sleeping bag. Was he dreaming? No, three pops, possibly small arms fire. He leapt to his feet and began to survey his surroundings. Now he heard voices close by.

'Viktor, you commie bastard. You're a star,' called Roly as he took a swig out of each champagne bottle opened before passing it around the group.

'And don't forget I still have this!' said Viktor, removing a giant silver hipflask from his jacket pocket. 'It's Beluga Gold, vodka from my uncle's presidential reserve. My 'end of term' present. Arrived this morning. I tried it of course, before decanting it, and can thoroughly recommend.'

'No wonder you're more pissed than the rest of us, if you have been pre-loading on that', quipped Roly.

Matty quickly realised what was happening. He was outnumbered and they were all pretty pissed. There was no way he could simply ask them to move on and have their party somewhere else. He decided the best option was simply to sit tight, but as he turned, he was caught in the light of a mobile phone torch. Mark and a couple of others were using their phones to prepare the lines on the tray Viktor had liberated from the pub when he sensed movement off to his right. He lifted his phone and shone it right in Matty's face.

'Well, fucking well, what is this? Looks like someone has come to join our party. Pray come in sir,' his voice adopting a mocking, deferential tone. 'Have a seat by the river, would you care for champagne, vodka, or perhaps some blow. It's fresh in from Kyrgmanistan actually!'

'No problem, lads. I'm fine. Just been trying to get some kip. I'll leave you's to it.'

'Sorry, Mr Crusty,' Mark's tone now more threatening. 'You've gatecrashed the Bugs Michaelmas party, but we are a very sociable bunch. It would be very rude of you to just leave again. I tell you what.' Mark withdrew a twenty-pound note from his pocket and proceeded to roll it up. 'Why don't you try out our blow?' Three lines of the white powder were now neatly lined up on the tray. 'And if you do the first line, you can keep the twenty. Call it my Christmas gift to the poor unfortunates of Oxford.'

At any other time, Matty would have needed no second invitation but he had just that night decided his life on the streets was going to end, and all his military instinct was telling him to exfiltrate.

'Nah, really, I'm fine. Thanks for the offer like, but I'll just be away back to me billet. Happy Christmas t'y'all.'

But as he turned, Mark sprang upwards. 'Fucking peasant. You don't refuse my hospitality when it has been so generously offered.' He made a grab for Matty but stumbled, his head connecting with Matty's stomach. Matty's legs gave way and he fell backwards from the bank and into the river. His training had taught him not to panic and his first reaction was to turn and swim the short distance back to the bank. But while in his mind he knew what to do, his body was not responding. The water was freezing and in those first few moments, his body was paralysed. He tried to open his mouth to cry for help, but no sound came out. The Thames was not only freezing but in fast-flowing spate following the recent rain. At first, he could see the group of men standing motionless and watching him. But they soon disappeared into the gloom as the current carried him downriver. The students were soon lost in the dark. Matty could see no stars; the sky was ink black, and then simply everything else went blank.

The Bugs stood frozen on the riverbank. By the time the realisation of what just happened began to sink in, the rough sleeper was already drifting out of sight. Roly made a move towards the water but James pulled him back.

'Don't be an idiot, Roly. You won't last five minutes in there. Just look at the current.'

Nobody moved or said anything for what in reality was a few moments, but seemed like an age.

'I didn't do anything, the crazy bastard must have jumped

to get away from me,' pleaded Mark. 'It wasn't my fucking fault.'

'We have to do something to help him,' countered Roly. 'I'm calling 999.'

'No, you are not. No way we're getting involved. He'll be dead before anyone manages to find him and it'll just mean one fucking beggar less in Oxford tomorrow. Who's going to miss him or even fucking care!' Mark was becoming animated. Viktor had snorted one of the lines and was now well into the hip flask of his uncle's vodka. Sensing that things could get a lot worse than they presently were, James decided it was time to take control.

'Listen, all of you. We have not been here for very long. Let's make our way back to town and make sure we are noticed. Chances are that nobody knew the poor sod was here, but if they do find his stuff, they may just assume he had an accident. Let's pick up the bottles and get rid of that,' he said, pointing at the remaining lines of coke on the tray. 'Once we get back across the bridge, we can go along St Aldates where we will be picked up on CCTV. With any luck, nobody will ever know that we've been down here.'

Once they were safely back across the bridge, they dropped the tray over the fence outside the pub and made their way noisily up St Aldates, singing and passing around the bottles of champagne. To make sure they were noticed, they offered a special rendition of the 'rugger, bugger' Bugs team call which normally preceded some act of wanton behaviour during their meals, as they passed in front of the police station. When they reached High Street, it was time for the group to split up and head home to their respective colleges. Viktor, by this time was being kept up by two of his so-called team mates, having hardly shared but done some serious damage to the contents of his hip flask. Only Mark and James were heading for Balliol, so they split from the rest of the group and made their way towards Broad Street, probably the earliest end to any Bugs event since the club was founded. As they walked along Cornmarket Street they passed another rough sleeper, curled up in the doorway of Boots.

'You know, I think I've seen that tramp before, begging along here with the rest of them,' Mark said.

'You didn't see anyone, Mark. We were thrown out of the pub and made our way back here, remember?'

'Yeah, sorry mate, you're right. All we did was a bit of blow and then we went home, officer! You're fucking amazing, Jimmy. We were all shit-faced tonight but when the fucking chips were down, you were ice-cool, mate. Fucking nerves of steel. Stick by me, Jimmy. Together we'll go far.'

3 - Seven years earlier

Holmbeach Town Hall

'The number of ballot papers rejected was as follows: want of an official mark – one; voting for more candidates than entitled to – 32. The total electorate is 52,450. There were 35,210 ballot papers issued with a turnout of 67.1%. And as returning officer, I do hereby declare that James Whitleigh-Howse is duly elected as Member of Parliament for Holmbeach and West Tyneford.'

It was just gone two o'clock in the morning. The auditorium was full of activists from all parties and assorted members of the national and regional media to witness the result of the by-election caused by the shock resignation of Alistair Howden a few weeks earlier. The son of a fisherman, he had grown up in the area and represented Holbeach and West Tyneford for more than 25 years. A loyal party member in both government and opposition during this time, Howden was until recently, chair of the House of Commons Committee on Standards. Then, stories began circulating about an established MP who was leaking government procurement plans to outside companies in return for financial and sexual favours. The Honourable Member for

Holmbeach and West Tyneford was named on social media and despite repeated denials, the story went viral. The more the government attempted to spike the accusations, the more they gathered momentum. In the end, Alistair Howden was true to his title of Honourable, and in an emotional statement to the press, he continued to deny being the subject of the rumours but accepted that the story had become too big a distraction for his party and the Government. He therefore took the only option he felt he had and resigned as an MP. On the same day the date of the by-election was announced, Alistair Howden was found dead at his London apartment from a suspected barbiturate overdose.

James Whitleigh-Howse was invited forward by the Returning Officer to make his acceptance speech.

'May I begin by expressing my deepest gratitude to the residents of Holmbeach and West Tyneford for the faith they have placed in me tonight. I am grateful to the Returning Officer, police and count staff who have given up their time to uphold our magnificent democratic process. I would also like to thank my opponents for standing up for their beliefs and conducting their campaigns with dignity. And, of course, I have to express my heartfelt appreciation to my campaign manager, Robert Frost and his team of volunteers for their tireless efforts over the last six weeks.

'The circumstances which have led to the calling of this by-election were unfortunate and the consequences for my predecessor, tragic. Alistair Howden was a good man, a West Tyneford man and someone who fought tirelessly for this constituency. So may I assure not just those who have kept faith with my party but all of the constituents of Holmbeach and West Tyneford that I will continue to honour that legacy. To that end, one of my priorities upon taking up my seat in Westminster next week will be to push for Thorpehead Nuclear Power Station to be chosen as the first location in this government's programme of small modular *reactors. It was a promise I made on the doorstep throughout this campaign, and I keep my promises.*

'I don't want to keep everyone from their beds after such a long day already, but I do want to say a special thank you to my wife Charlotte, who is here with me and our two young children, who are home in bed for agreeing to share me with the people of Holmbeach and West Tyneford. Thank you and good night.'

Although each of the main parties put up candidates, Holmbeach and West Tyneford was always considered a safe seat. It nevertheless marked a significant step forward in the career of James Whitleigh-Howse. Leaving Balliol with a First in PPE is usually a direct route into politics – think tanks, researcher or parliamentary assistant, then candidate.

But James joined his father, who was a successful hedge fund manager in the City. It meant plenty of travel and maintaining client relations before ultimately, he branched out, finding his own clients and establishing his own fund which was registered in the Cayman Islands. What to most outsiders would simply look like spread betting on the stock market was actually a computer-generated system of algorithms to make trades in thousandths of a second. Armies of analysts and programmers seemed to do the work while James simply needed to keep the clients happy and make them richer than they already were. And as their wealth grew, so did James's 2% for managing the fund and 20% of the profits. When asked by friends or colleagues why he hadn't gone straight into politics from Oxford, his response was always unequivocal – 'because I can't afford to!' He knew he would end up in politics, and one day in government, but there was no way he was going to make do on a basic £90,000 a year MP salary.

His father's reputation had helped James make his first

serious money just twelve months after leaving university. When he began to develop his own clientele his old Balliol pal Mark Ellrington and family were among the first to invest. Not long after, the fund grew significantly with investments from the personal accounts of, among others, the President of Kyrgmanistan together with those of his nephew, Viktor Baliyashvili.

After four years, he felt he had a big enough nest egg to be able to consider stepping back and living off the meagre earnings of an MP. And when the Holmbeach and West Tyneford by-election was called, he had another reason to be interested. His wife's family was a major landowner in the area. James had been born in Surrey and since he began working in the City, had been living in a new apartment complex in Chelsea. Charlotte was a year younger than James and had graduated from St Hilda's College. Their paths had not crossed during the years they were at Oxford together and thankfully, she had never even heard of the Bugs Rugby Club either. They met at a political do at Westminster. Her father was a party donor and had secured her an internship at party HQ while James was there as a guest of one of his clients. After a short romance, the two were married at St Peter's Church overlooking Holmbeach and moved into a property on the family estate, just outside Riverbridge. Children quickly followed and James was soon spending the working week in London, returning to the West Country at weekends. Charlotte was in her element, raising a family and enjoying the country life, riding out with the hunt and opening fetes as the representative of the squire. As the only child, both the house and several hundred acres of farmland on the Bristol Channel coast would one day belong to her and James.

The party faithful began to file out of the town hall to either continue the celebrations or drown their sorrows, council workers started to break down the trestle tables and stack up the empty ballot boxes ready to be put back in storage. Charlotte approached James at the foot of the stage and threw her arms around him.

'My MP! I'm so pleased for you, darling. Ma and Pops are over the moon too. It feels like you're really a part of this community now.'

'Thank you, sweetpea. You know I could never have done this without the support of a good lady. You have been an absolute rock, as always.'

'It will be so exciting to tell the children in the morning. Not that they understand what being an MP is but they know Daddy has been working hard for something these last weeks.'

'Ah. Well actually, Robert was just saying that perhaps it would be better if he and I head straight back to London. There's still plenty I have to do on the fund because I will need to be stepping back, then it's over to Westminster for the induction.'

Charlotte looked like all the air had suddenly been sucked out of her. 'You've been awake for almost twenty-four hours. You can't drive back now. And Ma and Pops are looking forward to seeing you tomorrow.'

'I'm sorry sweetpea. Needs must. I'm an MP now. Robert and I can share the driving and as soon as I have tidied up everything in London, I'll be back for the weekend. We can have a family lunch together on Sunday. I promise.'

With little or no traffic on the road, they were back at James's Chelsea apartment just as the sun was rising over the

Thames. A few moments later, Robert emerged from the shower wearing a silk bathrobe and towelling his hair to find James staring out through the floor-to-ceiling windows of the lounge. Deep in thought as he watched the winter sunlight reflecting off the windows of the tower blocks on the opposite side of the river, he didn't notice Robert until he was standing almost behind him.

'No time for second thoughts, you're a Member of Parliament now.'

'No, I was just thinking of Charlotte. Something she said tonight. Am I tying myself too much to Holmbeach?'

'God no. You're not going to be stuck in that shithole like the previous incumbent. Howden was a dinosaur and bound to become extinct. Call it natural evolution, even though I might have interfered with the natural process just a tiny bit. But you're an MP now and that's what matters.'

'You never explained just how you managed to get the sleaze story to stick.'

'It's what you pay me to do. You have your skills when it comes to market manipulation, setting hares running and selling short. Well, so do I in my line of business.'

'Yes, but nobody dies as a result of what I do. Howden was a good man. Charlotte's parents thought the world of him.'

'Listen, that wasn't my intention, but it happened. Who knows, perhaps there was some smoke after all. We'll never know now, but Howden is the past, you are the future.' Frost moved closer behind the new MP.

'But this is the present and perhaps you should be thinking right now about the other thing you pay me for?' And with that, he let the silk gown fall off his shoulders to the floor.

4 – Five years earlier

Whitehall, London

Roland Smith was alone in his office on the second floor of the Old Admiralty Building, overlooking Horse Guards Parade. Since his appointment as Minister for Energy he had decided there would be changes around here, starting with the décor. While he could do nothing about the oak panelled walls, the oil painting of the Battle of Trafalgar which dominated the wall immediately opposite his desk had been returned to the National Gallery. Busts and statuettes of various admirals and prime ministers which adorned the built-in porticoes had also been removed to the basement store. In their place hung a giant seascape painted by a Cornish artist and modern sculpture pieces from an up-and-coming potter from North Yorkshire.

The Ministry for Energy was a new creation of the government in response to the turbulent events in Russia and the Middle East which had had a catastrophic impact on oil and gas supplies. Roland Smith's job had been to steer the country towards energy security so that it was never again susceptible to shortages or price hikes as a result of world events. He had been given a mission for change and that started with his choice of artwork for his work environment.

It was a minister's privilege after all. His Permanent Secretary, Sir William Potts almost had a heart attack when he first saw the changes, but to Roland, drab historical scenes of a past glory being replaced by bold colours and abstract art shapes represented a move forward, just like the Ministry for Energy ushering in a new and bright future for the country. And today was to see the first major step in that journey; a policy to create cheap and clean energy from a new generation of small, modular nuclear reactors.

Next door in the Private Office meeting room, civil servants and advisors were gathering for a briefing to advise the Minister on the department's choice of the best bidder to build what could eventually be a network of ten nuclear power stations around the country. In a few moments, Sir William would arrive to usher him into the room and begin a process that could transform the country's economy and its standing on the world stage. But in these last moments of calm in the rare solitude of his own office, Roland gazed out onto Horse Guard's Parade and reflected on the journey that brought him here.

Unlike his friend and alumnus James Whiteliegh-Howse, Roland had followed the well-trodden path from Oxbridge First through political think tanks and special adviser to an MP. With a father in the military, Roland's upbringing had been one of boarding schools with holidays spent in whichever exotic location his father's posting happened to take him. While at university, Roland spent most holidays working as an intern at the party headquarters, so by the time he came down from Oxford, he was already a familiar face at central office in London SW1. His first role as a Spad or special adviser was for the Secretary of State for Defence, from where it was a seamless transition to candidate in an ultra-safe seat in Berkshire at the General Election just over 12 years ago.

There had been women in his life but any relationship ended whenever the prospect of commitment emerged. It may have been his family's military background but Roland's driving ambition was simply to serve. He was wedded to his career and just as his father had served King and country, Roland was there to serve his constituents, his party and the Government.

His career path at Westminster also followed a similarly straightforward path. Backbench MP, Parliamentary Private Secretary, Junior Minister and finally, his own Ministry. So now here he was, about to take a decision which would have a major impact on the country's economic future as well as directly benefit two of his old pals from university. Viktor and Mark were the owners of Bicarel, the preferred bidder. Should he have declared an interest or recused himself from the process? The truth was that he had not had any contact with either of them since Oxford, fifteen years ago. He knew they had begun working together but was unaware of what their business actually involved until he took up this post at the Ministry for Energy. With James it was different. They had both been members of the party, even if James had only recently ascended to the rank of MP. He was lobbying for his constituency to be chosen as the site for the first reactor which obviously meant supporting the Bicarel bid. But MPs lobbying a minister was part and parcel of Westminster life and far more transparent. No, Roland Smith was appointed Minister for Energy with a brief to bring about energy security and today was his first opportunity to set the country on a path towards a more prosperous future. This was not another case of cronyism like the ones which had plagued his predecessors and almost lost the party the last General Election. This was an opportunity to make real progress. The Bicarel bid was streets ahead of the competitors and the consultants' report recommended it, albeit with some qualifications. Now he needed to ensure the decision was ratified without any further conditions or delay, not for the sake of his old university mates but for the sake of the country.

The unmistakable three short knocks on the door preceded the entrance of Sir William Potts.

'Minister, we are all present and correct. If you would be so kind as to join us?'

Roland followed his permanent secretary through the double doors into the panelled committee room on the other side of the Private Office. The windowless room was brightly lit, due in no small part to a giant LED 'living sky' installation on the ceiling which ran almost the whole length of the boardroom table. Roland had first seen these in use when visiting his father in hospital. They could almost bring daylight rather than neon light to dark, and sometimes drab surroundings and the moving cloud scenes could be switched with others, such as cherry blossom or ocean waves by a simple keyboard command. Not only did they brighten up a windowless room, the hospital staff were convinced the ceilings reduced stress and anxiety for both patients and relatives. When Roland had first seen the committee room at the Ministry of Energy, he knew this was another of the changes he had to make. To Sir William, it was just another piece of modern art, although he did need some persuading when he discovered where the panels were to be installed.

Around the table sat around a dozen people, only half of which Roland could actually name. There was Michael

Barlow, the Under-Secretary and Sir William's deputy. Next to him sat the Assistant Director Amelia Longstaff. Roland's Parliamentary Private Secretary, Ewan Hartley MP sat at the far end of the table alongside his special advisor, Hugo Phelps. A small huddle of two men and a woman sat close together, halfway along the table and while Sir William would make the introductions, Roland assumed these were from the firm of consultants which had been brought in to evaluate the bids and produce the report that he had read the previous week. On the other side of the table sat two ministry staffers who he sort of recognised but could not name. But they were clearly going to be recording the minutes of the meeting. Those who were not familiar with ministerial briefing began to rise from their seats as if at school before Roland dismissively waved them down and took his place at the head of the table. Sir William welcomed everyone and the Minister, confirming to Roland through his introductions that the strangers were indeed from the consultancy firm.

'So, Minister,' he began. 'The purpose of this briefing is to update you on the department's recommendations as to the preferred bidder to build a new generation of small modular nuclear power stations, henceforth to be called SMRs, in the United Kingdom. For context, whereas our neighbours in France have just embarked on a similar path to build SMRs, they have just signed a contract for a company to construct a power station which the French government, via its state-owned electricity generator, will then operate. His Majesty's Government has adopted a different approach, looking to enter into an agreement with a third-party operator to both build and operate the power station in return for an undertaking from the government to purchase the electricity generated at a guaranteed price, henceforth to be known as the strike price, and for an agreed number of years.'

'Thank you, Sir William. Yes. I have read the submission and I am aware of how our deal is different from the French. Particularly that the government has no responsibility for the development costs and no exposure to losses as a result of any delay.'

'Precisely, Minister. On that basis, and as you are no doubt aware, our department has spent the last twelve months reviewing the competing bids before consulting with our friends at Fieldhouse and Elcock, who are here today,' nodding to the woman and two men whose names Roland had already forgotten, 'on our choice of the two shortlisted contenders, General Power and Bicarel. As you will also be aware, Fieldhouse and Elcock have recommended the latter, primarily on the basis of the strike price and the timetable for delivery. Bicarel's strike price is less than two-thirds of General Power's and crucially, the proposed build time of five years is half that of their competitor. This, in turn, reduces the number of years that the government would be required to purchase electricity under the guarantee. General Power is proposing to build the new reactor alongside an existing one in Northumberland which is due for decommissioning in the next five years, while the Bicarel power station would be a brand-new development on the Bristol Channel.

'Fieldhouse and Elcock have expressed some concerns about the deliverability of the Bicarel scheme. General Power is a well-established operator with a sound record on safety whereas Bicarel are very much new to the sector. While they have indeed just signed a contract with the French

Government, the fact remains, they have no track record. They have assured us that they will have shovels in the ground within days of signing if we do select Bicarel, and they own the site at Thorpehead as well as much of the surrounding land. Our colleagues in France are understandably not prepared to share any information with us regarding their own dealings with Bicarel, save to say that we have not picked up any negative vibes coming from across the Channel.'

'As Minister for Energy, my mission is to wean this country off imported fossil fuels and secure our future energy needs. To me, Bicarel is a no-brainer. The strike price represents best value according to your submission, Sir William, and the shortest lead time. The government has no financial exposure until the power station starts generating electricity, so if Bicarel have got their figures wrong, they are the ones who will carry the can if there are any delays. The decision will ultimately need to go to the Home Secretary for sign off but I am minded to award the contract to Bicarel unless there is more anyone wishes to say?'

'There's the issue of waste too,' Hugo Wilks, Roland's Spad cut in. 'As you know, the Greens have been making a lot of noise about the nuclear waste storage facility in Cumbria and want to see measures for the long-term storage included with any decision on more nuclear power stations.'

'Yes, I have received an urgent written question from their party leader. Sir William, can you explain what they are getting so agitated about? Ten MPs and they act like they're the government. I always thought they were in favour of nuclear.'

'Thank you, Minister. I believe their position on nuclear is supportive, particularly if it reduces carbon emissions. It would appear from the Honourable Gentleman's urgent question, there are environmental concerns over the storage of our legacy nuclear waste amid safety issues at the storage facility in Cumbria. Previous government administrations have looked into the long-term storage in underground chambers but little progress has been made over the last twenty years. I should say that since the establishment of a Ministry specifically devoted to energy, that rather thorny issue now falls within the remit of this department.'

'If I may, Minister,' Amelia Longstaff raised a finger. 'My understanding of the Bicarel proposal is that spent fuel rods will be kept on site for the short to medium term until they are safe enough to be transported to another facility.'

'So basically, we are discussing a hypothetical situation which may or may not occur in the next generation?' Roland snapped.

'The Greens want assurances that detailed plans for nuclear waste storage and disposal are included in any contract the government signs for SMRs.' Hugo the Spad responded.

'With all due respect, Minister, I think we risk conflating two issues. The government is about to enter into an agreement with a nuclear energy supplier to buy electricity at an agreed price. This department is also responsible for framing a policy to safely store nuclear waste, it must be said, for many thousands of years. That is, by its nature, a long-term process and it would be very difficult or nigh on impossible to have such arrangements in place before we even build another nuclear reactor. Can I suggest that we do not let the parliamentary urgent question get in the way of today's business but that my department formulates a response for you once the meeting is over.

'Thank you, Sir William. As lucid as always. Agreed. I am therefore making my decision that we accept the proposal from Bicarel at the strike price and duration agreed and that the Home Secretary is requested to sign off on the contract. Thank you, ladies and gentlemen for your attendance today and the work you have put into reaching this decision.'

With that, Roland got up and left the room, quickly followed back into his office by Sir William, his Under-Secretary Michael Barlow and Assistant Director Amelia Longstaff, to draft a response to the urgent written question from the Green Party.

******

City of London

The guests made their way out on the balcony from the lavish reception room. The lights dimmed and the pulsing electro-beat music began. Not club music but more the sort which accompanies the opening credits of a TV news programme. This was not a club after all, but Paternoster Street in the heart of London's financial area and home to the London Stock Exchange.

It was 7.59 am. The traditional ringing of the bell to signal the start of trading on the market floor had ceased in the 1980s when Big Bang saw the armies of traders in their multi-coloured jackets replaced by an installation of 500 LED screens around a giant illuminated cube. But the Market Open ceremony remained a key part of the daily routine at the London Stock Exchange and today the honour of placing the glass tablet on the console fell to Bicarel, the latest company to float its shares on the market.

With all the guests in place, the music ramped up and a

large LED screen behind them on the terrace began the digital countdown from 20. Standing on either side of the dais and holding the specially engraved glass tablet between them were Viktor Baliyashvili and Mark Ellrington, President and Chief Executive respectively of Bicarel. In the front row, among the invited bankers, lawyers and accountants were two members of Her Majesty's Government, the Minister for Energy, Roland Smith and West Country MP James Whitleigh-Howse. All were alumni of Oxford University, as well as members of the infamous Bugs, so-called rugby club. The intervening two decades had seen each of them pursue different career paths which had nonetheless intertwined, culminating in their presence today to celebrate the transformation of a once Soviet-era power company to a world-leading developer of small modular reactors or SMRs, which were about to transform the nuclear power industry.

Everybody joined in the countdown to zero, at which point Viktor and Mark put the tablet in place and the words 'Market Open' appeared on the screen behind them. Ahead, the giant LED installation sprang into life with graphs and tables as share prices of listed companies made their way along the ticker set high up on each side of the exchange walls. Bicarel was now trading on the London Stock Exchange and all indications were that the price would exceed initial forecasts due to unconfirmed reports of a major government announcement due soon.

Viktor Baliyashvili had never known his father. He died when Viktor was just a few months old. Since then, he had been taken under the wing of his uncle, Alexander, the President and supreme ruler of Kyrgmanistan. The mineral-rich former Soviet state had declared independence in 1990, but by that time, Alexander Baliyashvili was already a wealthy man. Like all the other oligarchs, he had purchased state assets from Boris Yeltsin at a time when the Soviet President was desperately in need of cash. Baliyashvili not only acquired rights to coal and nickel mining but even managed to buy Kyrgmanistan's electricity generating company with a loan from the Russian (i.e. Yeltsin's) State Bank.

With no children of his own, Alexander treated Viktor as his son and heir who wanted for nothing. Except perhaps love. It was several years before he finally had confirmation of his suspicions that Alexander's feelings for his mother were far more than simply his widowed sister-in-law. It was probably why Viktor was seldom at home in Kyrgmanistan. Boarding school in Scotland until he was 13 and then Eton. Summer holidays would often involve camps in the States and on the rare occasions when he did manage to go home, his mother or his uncle would often be away on business. He more or less drank his way through Oxford yet somehow managed to leave with a Third in Economics and Social History. In his final year at college, the President handed over the ownership of the Kyrgelektrik, the state power company to Viktor.

So, at the age of 22, Viktor Baliyashvili found himself in Ganirvan, the capital of Kyrgmanistan, a city he barely knew and president of the state-owned power company, a position and a business for which he held no qualification or relevant experience. As far as he could see, the company did what it had always done during the Soviet era, supplying power to the factories and keeping the lights on for the citizens of Kyrgmanistan. It ran, just as it had done so for the previous 60 years, thanks to managers who had seemingly been there for almost as long and a variety of committees that met regularly to discuss issues such as staff welfare and recreational facilities for workers' families. Whether it made any money, Viktor had no idea. The basics he had learned at Oxford about profit, reinvestment and efficiency were certainly never on the agenda of any of the management committee meetings he had attended before becoming tired of the whole process.

Kyrgmanistan was now an independent and autonomous nation and Viktor's uncle, a recognised head of state with all the trappings that came with it. State visits, speeches at the United Nations in New York and frequent visits to London, where the British government was desperate to channel money, regardless of its origin, through the city of London. And whether as a guest at a Mansion House banquet or a press conference on the White House lawn, Alexander Baliyashvili was increasingly seen with Viktor's mother Rovshana by his side. Viktor was finding himself increasingly alone, bored and with no idea what the future held. Money had never been an issue during his student days. His uncle simply provided whatever was needed. But the funding ceased with the gift of Kyrgelektrik. His uncle's bestowing Kyrgmanistan's power generation company to Viktor was intended, not just to provide financial independence but to ensure he was sufficiently occupied so as not to cause any further distraction to the newly proclaimed president and his soon-to-be wife.

If Viktor needed money he simply had to ask, no tell, Alana, the dour fifty-something accountant who also seemed to have been at Kyrgelektrik from the beginning. Her mousy hair was kept in place by a black band; she had next to no make-up and seemingly wore the same clothes to work every day. At least she always looked that way on the days Viktor went to the office. He had no idea whether she was married or had a family. She never engaged in conversation with anyone in the office and never smiled. The Soviet Union may well have broken up, but for many working at Kyrgelektrik, little had changed in the new, independent Kyrgmanistan. When Viktor demanded money, Alana was always courteous but short. She would make the necessary bank transfers or provide cash from the safe. It was usually enough to cater for Viktor's only pastimes living in Ganirvan - vodka and women. But the day he decided it would be nice to have a yacht and moor it at a Black Sea resort, or perhaps have it sailed around the Mediterranean during the summer, the accountant's face showed some reaction for the first time. She didn't refuse as such, but simply explained in very basic terms that Kyrgelektrik had never or would never have such large financial reserves to even contemplate such a venture.

Watching a news report on state TV one night of his uncle and his mother at a meeting with the Governor of the Bank of England, Viktor's thoughts quickly turned to his Oxford days and Mark Ellrington in particular. They hadn't seen each other since graduation and despite the usual promises to keep in touch, had only exchanged the odd message at birthdays or if another alumnus they both knew was in the news for some reason or other. Viktor knew that Mark had joined the family firm and they had backed him shortly afterwards in his own corporate restructuring venture. Without knowing too much of the detail, he understood Mark had earned a reputation for stepping into struggling companies, stripping out the assets and then letting the original company fail. Viktor missed Oxford and the Bugs, and he was bored. Mark Ellrington could remedy that particular malaise and maybe, at the same time, help

Kyrgelektrik to provide him with the lifestyle he was used to.

He had sent Mark a message inviting him to come to Kyrgmanistan for a holiday with the chance of some paid consultancy work thrown in. Ellrington was on the next flight to Ganirvan and after a few lost days of drinking, women and a few 'Bugs style' antics in restaurants, Viktor announced to the Kyrgelektrik management committee that the company had engaged the services of a British management consultant to advise on 'efficiencies'.

It soon became clear that when he wasn't partying, Mark Ellrington knew what he was doing. Viktor was spending more time at work too as he was the only one capable of translating Mark's habitual colourful language to the factory managers. Even when translated, some of the recommendations might just as well have been in a foreign language for the staff who had never before had to contemplate words like targets or redundancy.

But Mark's plans went much further. 'Fucking simples, mate' was his response to Viktor's quest for cash he could splash on luxuries. Before long, Kyrgelektrik was a corporation with Viktor owning all the shares. Its asset value was such that when Mark negotiated the sale of just 10% of the shares to a Malaysian wealth fund, Viktor hit the jackpot. Mark had plenty of other plans for property investment and factories to develop new energy technologies, starting with nuclear. Mark had a plan and the ambition to see it through while Viktor had cash, penthouses and yachts. Kyrgelektrik was merged into a new company, Bicarel, with Viktor as its figurehead chairman and Mark as chief executive. Within four years, Bicarel had undercut all competitors to land the contract to build a new reactor for France Electricité on the Normandy coast. The modular reactors were being built at a new factory just outside Ganirvan, creating more jobs than had been lost at the old Kyrgelektrik site and sparing President Alexander Baliyashvili any embarrassment after gifting the company to his nephew. The component reactor parts were being shipped to France and then installed on site, a method projected to save both time and construction costs and reducing the payback time for the power station. The nuclear industry worldwide was now looking with interest at Bicarel.

With the Stock Market now officially open for the day, the assembled guests returned to the reception room to enjoy a champagne breakfast and the customary speeches. Viktor had been due to say a few words of introduction, but Mark had already realised when they placed the ceremony tablet to launch the day that Viktor's orange juice was two parts vodka.

James Whitleigh-Howse eased through the guests to tap Mark on the shoulder.

'Roly has gone back to Whitehall. He was uneasy about being here for the launch but his secretary had recorded it in the diary as an event with old college friends. Sends his apologies but thinks it best if he's not here for the speeches.'

'Probably for the best. Viktor's fucking pissed already. I'm going to tell him we have to be out of here by nine so there's no time for his speech. He probably won't care. Thank fuck the press aren't allowed in for these things.'

A couple of minutes later, Mark stood behind the dais, gently tapping the microphone as the chatter in the room.

'Ladies and gentlemen. For those who don't know me, I am Mark Ellrington, Chief Executive of Bicarel. Thank you for being able to join

us on this auspicious occasion. When Viktor Baliyashvili first approached me about plans he had for Kyrgelektrik, I did not think we would be launching a company on the London Stock Exchange just under five years later. That we are here today is down to a lot of people, but mainly to the vision of one man who I have had the pleasure of knowing since university days and working alongside during this journey. So can I ask you all to raise your glasses to Viktor Baliyashvili?'

'*Viktor Baliyashvili*', came the chorus from the room, followed by polite applause. Viktor, who had moved on from screwdrivers to champagne, nodded graciously and raised his glass in return.

'What Viktor saw while running his country's power company was that the future was in clean energy. But while nuclear energy offered most of the answers, it was beset with high start-up costs and long lead-in times. How could you persuade countries such as Kyrgmanistan to abandon its own plentiful supply of fossil fuels in favour of alternatives that cost more? By looking closely at why nuclear power stations were so expensive in the first place, Viktor and Bicarel have come up not just with a solution, but a new manufacturing industry which is currently employing more people in his homeland as well as other sites around the world. But crucially, where the level of investment previously needed to build power stations could only come from governments, the Bicarel Small Modular Reactor is a game-changer. Now, it is possible for much smaller energy projects to be completed in sites around the world, which are both more realistic in terms of investment and with a much clearer and faster route to financial returns. As such, nuclear energy is ripe for private investment and today, ladies and gentlemen, we are delighted that you are here to witness its birth.'

The invited guests left to make their way to work elsewhere in the city, leaving just Mark, Viktor and James in the room as catering staff cleared away the plates, glasses and table cloths.

'So when do we have press conference?' Viktor almost shouting now. Completely pissed at nine in the morning.

'Shut the fuck up will you', snapped Mark. 'You're a rich fucker already. If you didn't notice all those figures on the screen in there, Bicarel's trading at well over the offer price already. You should be grateful the Stock Market doesn't allow the press in for these events. We do not want any awkward questions just now. Just let the price do its own thing for fuck sake.'

'Yes, it won't be long now,' added James. 'Roly said Thorpehead is on the Secretary of State's desk right now and he doesn't think there is anything likely to make her go against the minister's recommendation.'

'Just as fucking well. Apparently, I own a fucking farm down there.

******

Finance Matters newspaper

GOVERNMENT GREEN LIGHT FOR NUCLEAR POWER STATION

The government has this week confirmed Thorpehead on the Bristol Channel as the site for the first nuclear power station to be built in the country for more than a decade.

A deal has been signed with the multi-national Bicarel to build the first of a new generation of small modular reactors (SMR) in what is hoped will kick-start nuclear energy production in this country. The deal commits the Government to purchase electricity from Thorpehead at a fixed price and is worth £10bn to Bicarel. A memorandum of understanding is understood to have been agreed for a further eight sites around the United Kingdom to be built over the next three decades. The government says the move will ensure the country's energy security for future generations and end future reliance on fossil fuels.

The £10bn price tag represents a major saving on previous nuclear power projects, with the last one to be built on these shores at Bursleham finally operational 10 years late and costing almost £30bn, twice the original budget. Crucially, the Bicarel SMRs are not only cheaper than the old pressurised water reactors (PWR) but build times are considerably shorter. Thorpehead is planned to be operational within five years of the first shovel in the ground.

Bicarel was formed less than five years ago out of Kyrgelektrik, the former state power company of Kyrgmanistan owned by Viktor Baliyashvili, nephew of the country's president. Three years ago, it won the contract to build the first SMR for France Electricité, the French state electricity company at Torteville-les-Plages in Normandy. The SMRs are constructed in parts at a factory outside the Kyrgmanistan capital, Ganirvan and then transported and erected on-site. Despite some initial delays, the Normandy reactor is due to go live within the next two years.

This week's news comes as a further boost to the former Soviet power company which has undergone a complete transformation under Baliyashvili, together with English Chief Executive Mark Ellrington. The son of James Ellrington OBE, founder of global management consultants Chieveleys, he headed a successful corporate restructuring business before joining forces with fellow Oxford student Baliyashvili to turn around the fortunes of the floundering state company. The pair privatised the business and, under its new name of Bicarel, set about diversifying into the nuclear sector. Hard on the heels of the French government contract, Bicarel recently floated on the London Stock Exchange. Buoyed by rumours of an impending deal with the UK Government, shares far exceeded the offer price, netting Alexander Baliyashvili an estimated £6bn for his 70% stake. Investors continue to be infatuated with Bicarel and this week's news has seen shares continue to rise by a further 12%.

Speaking after the announcement, Ellrington told Finance Matters that the government had made an important statement for the future of nuclear energy production: "Ending reliance on fossil fuels has always been at odds with achieving energy security. What Bicarel has achieved with its production of small modular reactors finally resolves that issue and I am delighted the British government has followed France in reaching that conclusion. Crucially, Bicarel's reduced start-up cost model means that nuclear energy is now a realistic option for private finance and this is clearly reflected in the rise in our share value in recent times."

Junior Energy Minister Roland Smith said the Bicarel deal was a game-changer for the future of the nuclear industry in the United Kingdom.

5 - Three years earlier

Holmbeach

'Right, everybody, can you all look this way. I'll take the pic but then please stay where you are so I can take your names and roles afterwards.'

Having got the attention of the assembled members of the West Tyneford Rotary Club, Jack Makepiece took out his iPhone and captured the cheque presentation being made to the manager of the Tiny Tots club. This was journalism Holmbeach style. Just one person, a notebook, an iPhone set to 24 megapixel pro-raw and a fundraising donation from local business leaders to a nursery operating out of the church hall. It's not what he imagined when he first decided he wanted to be a journalist. Nor was it the life he was actually leading twelve months earlier.

With a university degree in journalism, Jack was one of the very few lucky ones who landed a place on the graduate scheme at one of the country's leading dailies. What's more, he had been assigned to the financial investigations team and, within only a few months, had his byline on a potentially explosive article. Thanks to Jack Makepiece, the paper broke an exclusive which not only rocked the City but the corridors of power in Westminster. The finance desk was the perfect home for Jack. His initial career ambition before journalism had been an accountant and he was perfectly at home with balance sheets and shareholder reports. But his scoop owed less to his investigative powers than to a whistleblower.

The story involved a certain Rajan Singh, originally from India but more recently a well-known playboy and socialite in London. He featured regularly in OK Magazine, played polo with some of the royals and had over 100,000 followers on TikTok, drawn mostly to his regular posts from lavish parties and in the company of famous faces. His business interests were in IT and telecoms, more usually acting as a broker between governments of emerging nations and commercial organisations in the West. It was after a deal between an American telecoms firm and an African nation for a 5G phone network that the paper's news desk was contacted by a source within the company with concerns about commission payments. It seemed that, in addition to the fee which was shown quite clearly in the contract documents being due to Singh's company, the American company had made additional 'facilitating' payments to a company based in the Bahamas. Where Jack had earned his salary was in following the oblique payment trail across several other accounts in tax havens to finally identify Rajan Singh as one of the ultimate beneficiaries. What really added fuel to the fire, and catapulted a finance story into the national headlines, was that shortly after the 5G African deal, Singh started to make political donations to the British party of government.

But before Jack could publish any of his follow-up work to identify other beneficiaries of this mysterious offshore account, the paper received a letter before action from Singh's lawyers claiming defamation and libel. Rajan Singh certainly was well-connected. The lawyers hired were Bartram and Fripp, renowned rottweilers in the legal profession and the go-to firm for any celebrity looking to keep their names out of the headlines and, more recently, rich moguls and oligarchs pursuing a new trend of issuing strategic lawsuits against public participation, or SLAPPs.

To make matters worse, Singh was not only donating to the party currently running the country, he was a friend of the Home Secretary. While it was not uncommon for 10 Downing Street to be on first-name terms with the national newspaper editors, Jack's editor received a call the day after the article was published, which was far less friendly than usual. Bartram and Fripp were contending that the documents originally supplied to Jack by the whistleblower were false and that the newspaper had failed to carry out due diligence prior to publishing accusations about their client. At the same time, the whistleblower had simply disappeared. Jack's calls and emails were not answered and when they sent someone from the paper's New York office to the last address they had, the house was empty and neighbours said the family had just up and left.

A solution to the legal case was quickly found. A retraction and apology, given the same prominence as the original story and payment of Bartram and Fripp's fees would be sufficient for Mr Singh (soon, it was rumoured to become Sir Rajan Singh) to waive any claim to damages and compensation. The newspaper's reputational damage was another matter, but without the original source, the cost and likely outcome of defending Jack's story in court was not even an option. For Jack of course, it was the end of his days as a journalist at a national newspaper. Having been asked to resign, he knew no other title was likely to consider him.

So, in his early twenties, single and unemployed, there was only one option open to Jack Makepiece – go home to mum and dad. Home was Holmbeach and the Boar's Head, or at least the three-bedroom bungalow his parents had built last year just 50 metres down the road. Jack had grown up in the Boar's Head where his parents were first managers, and then later, owners of the popular pub. Originally, it had been a typical workers' pub, frequented mainly by fishermen and supplemented by tourists during the summer months. The brewery, realising the decline in trade as first the fishing fleet dwindled and then the fish market closed, was keen to offload the Boar's Head before it became a financial millstone and Mr and Mrs Makepiece were keen to take it on at the below market value price they were offered. What they had foreseen but the brewery hadn't, was the change in people's dining habits, particularly in tourist areas and the growth in gastro pubs. With a bigger mortgage, they had been able to extend the Boar's Head behind its traditional façade to add a kitchen, restaurant and a small number of bedrooms, while retaining the public bar as near as possible to the original. In the years that followed, the Boar's Head built a reputation for its seafood and the hotel rooms achieved year-round occupancy. So last year, Jack's parents made the decision to vacate their (and Jack's) living space to convert it into more letting rooms and build what would ultimately be their retirement home further down the road.

And this was Jack's home now while he worked as chief reporter on *The Moorsman* – a weekly newspaper which had served the West Tyneford area for the last 50 years. That he was working at all and still in journalism was largely down to a friendship between his parents and Barney Jones, *The Moorsman* editor and a regular at the Boar's Head since even before they took on the management of the pub.

The Moorsman had been the brainchild of Barney's dad, Ben Jones, an acerbic scribe at the Mirror in the days when Fleet Street was the place that housed newspapers cheek by jowl, rather than today when the term is just a collective noun for the national press. But he ceased to be the scourge of politicians and wealthy industrialists when Robert Maxwell, someone regularly in Ben Jones' crosshairs, purchased the Mirror and set about moving his empire out to Wapping. Ben was one of the early cohort to find their services were no longer required and used his pay-off to move his family out of London to the West Country to enjoy an early retirement. But it wasn't long before he got itchy feet, or fingers in this case, so set about starting his own weekly newspaper. Being a long way from the capital it was clear there was no room, or indeed subject matter, for the traditional Rory Jones style journalism. Even if there was, he also realised that he would be living next door to and drinking in the same pubs as his victims, so *The Moorsman* became a weekly celebration of rural life and a champion for causes which affected this part of the world. As such, the newspaper became the established voice of the West Tyneford area and the go-to publication to find out what was really happening. So it was a natural progression for his son Barney to join the family firm on leaving school, and he had remained there long after his father's actual retirement and sad passing only a few years later.

The Moorsman had continued in much the same vein as Ben Jones had created it but in the last decade it had suffered the same effects as much of the printed press across the country. Younger generations were getting their news from other sources and those online alternatives were also hoovering up a large chunk of the advertising revenue that had previously been taken for granted. *The Moorsman* was still a going concern, but profits were falling year on year. When Barney was approached a couple of years ago to sell the title to a large national media organisation, the money was not particularly good but a more secure future became the deciding factor. Another attraction was that *The Moorsman* could continue almost with no change. Hollingsworth Media owned more than 200 papers around the country and all of them operated independently with their own branding and identity. The economies of scale came in the actual production of the newspapers and the accounting services which were handled centrally. What this meant for Barney was that *The Moorsman's* office in Holmbeach was run on a shoestring.

The team consisted of Barney and a reporter, a role which fortunately became vacant just before Jack Makepiece returned from London. Susie had been responsible for the advert sales for almost as long as Barney had worked there and with revenue figures falling each year, had decided to reduce her hours commensurately. The only other person employed by *The Moorsman* was an apprentice, Duncan. He was actually doing an NVQ Level 3 in business management but his role at the newspaper seemed to cover anything from coffee maker to delivery van driver. Whatever he was learning on his day-release at West Tyneford College, when in the office it looked as if Barney was treating Duncan as he had himself been tutored by his father.

For Jack, where there were once press conferences at the Bank of England for interest rate announcements, lunches with the PR manager at a city investment firm or in-depth analysis of FTSE 100 company accounts, now there were just village fetes, charity cheque presentations and contentious planning applications. If there was a whiff of scandal anywhere, Jack's natural urge to dig further in the hope of an exclusive story would often be dampened by Barney's caution and desire to keep everyone in the community happy. He believed negative stories did not sell newspapers and could put off potential advertisers. But Jack had quickly accepted that he couldn't rewind the tape and this was the life he now had in West Tyneford. His salary was a pittance, even compared to his relatively junior ranking in London, but he was living at home in a part of the country where he had grown up and been happy. And he was still a journalist, doing a job which didn't tie him to a desk and which changed from day to day.

Today, having said goodbye to the staff at the nursery and members of the Rotary Club he was next on his way to Burford, a village midway between Riverbridge and the Holmbeach, for a protest meeting held by the campaign group against the building of the nuclear power station at Thorpehead.

Burford, West Tyneford

John Forster drove his 20-year-old Landrover Defender into the square at Burford and drew up as close as he could to the village hall. It was a journey he had made innumerable times in his lifetime but never before for the reason tonight. The first public event organised by WATER (West Tyneford Against Thorpehead Energy Reactor), the campaign group he had played a part in founding to oppose plans for the Thorpehead Power Station.

He was born and grew up at Coombe Farm, the fourth generation of the family to own, but not in his case to farm the land. An only child, it was clear to his parents from an early age that John's skills were cerebral rather than agricultural. A scholarship at a boarding school just outside Taunton led to Oxford and a First in Economics and Management. From there, he followed a well-trodden path to the civil service and a career as a Whitehall mandarin. Time in the Diplomatic Service included a couple of uneventful postings abroad but John had largely just kept his head down and attended to the job at hand. He never married. His first real romance was during the final year at university but it ended when she told him she preferred John's best friend and roommate. It was not as if that drove him to a life of celibacy. There had been romances, including one during his time in Central America that almost cost him his job. But he was simply content with his life and his work, while his leisure time was largely given over to his passion for birdwatching.

When his father died suddenly, John arranged to lease much of the land to neighbouring farmers, leaving his mother with the house, a modest income and a small holding from which she was almost self-sufficient. But when she died a few years ago, it was time for him to retire from the civil service and return home. His family had never been wealthy, but they were asset-rich, especially in the eyes of Her Majesty's Revenue and Customs. The only way to pay the Inheritance Tax they had assessed and keep the family home was to sell the fields his father and father before him had farmed for so many years. And little did he know when he received an offer from a wealthy industrialist, just what purpose the fields would eventually be put. When Mark

Ellrington bought the land, there was talk of building a holiday retreat for him and his family. There had been rumours of a luxury hotel for shooting parties but likewise, no planning applications had ever been lodged with the local council. In fact, for more than a decade, the land lay untouched and had become something of a haven for wildlife – a particular bonus for John and his love of the local fauna.

But then, just around two years ago, everything changed. Thorpehead had been selected as the first site for a new breed of nuclear power stations being developed by the multi-national company Bicarel, and Mark Ellrington was its owner. West Tyneford Council had granted planning permission for an access road to serve the construction of the power station, along with the temporary construction of workers' accommodation and plant and equipment storage on the land which Ellrington had purchased from John Forster all those years earlier. Already, the habitats which had been home to such an array of wildlife during the farm's fallow years had been mercilessly bulldozed and fencing erected. Now, instead of waking up each morning to the sound of birdsong, it was the reversing alarms of lorries and workmen's voices. And this was just the early stages of preparation for the access road. There was still much more construction work to be done.

When John Fortser walked into the Burford village hall, he was pleasantly surprised to see that very few seats remained empty. They hadn't been able to do much publicity. A few handbills and posters plus a small advert in The Moorsman had pushed the limits of their marketing skills and the group's budget. Marjorie, the self-appointed secretary of WATER came over to John, her face beaming.

'It's not just us who are concerned,' she yelled. 'Look at the turnout, it's virtually standing room only. Time to do your thing, John.'

At 7 pm on the dot, John mounted the stage and moved towards the dais. Unfolding his prepared speech, he tapped the microphone and gave a cough as the audience came to order.

'Good evening. May I first thank you for turning out in such large numbers. My name is John Forster. I was born in West Tyneford and after a career in the civil service, I returned to live in the family home.

Like many of you in the hall tonight, I am concerned that the Thorpehead Nuclear Power Station project is being forced on us without proper consideration of all the impacts. The need for "energy security" seems to have taken centre stage and is being used to drown out any other argument, whether on cost, environment or the wishes of the local community. Tonight, I want to share two of my own major concerns. Without wishing to trivialise them, I am going to call them my two worries – because, like the name of our group, they start with the letter W.

'The first W is, naturally enough, water. It's no coincidence that we have used that as an acronym for this group. Yes, we live by the coast and power stations are usually built by the coast because they rely on water – lots of it. You will no doubt already have read about the inflow pipe to be built under the seabed, which is going to draw in up to sixty-thousand litres a second to cool the reactors. But that's not all it will draw in. Bicarel have stated that the number of fish potentially lost would be no more than a small fishing boat catches in a year. Have they not been to Holmbeach Quay recently? Our fishing fleet numbers fewer than ten vessels. Are they really saying it's alright for it to continue declining by one a year?

'But salt water is not on its own sufficient to run a power station. When it comes to actually cooling the reactor and the irradiated fuel once

it has been removed, only fresh water will do. And in equally vast quantities. They may be using trailblazing technology with the proposed SMR at Thorpehead, but it will still require in excess of eight hundred thousand litres of fresh water a day. And where is that coming from? Perhaps rivers which run from the moors to the coast and from underneath the soil many of you still farm?

'The Environment Agency is already predicting that in just ten years after Thorpehead is due to start operating, some counties in England will already be suffering a water deficit and will require supplies to be pumped from elsewhere. The simple fact of the matter is that we do not know where Thorpehead will get its fresh water from. It is a question I have been asking Bicarel and our MP James Whiteligh-Howse for the last two years without a response. I am worried with a capital W.

'So, let's turn to my second W – waste. As you all are already too painfully aware, this government has fallen in love with nuclear energy once more. And the reason for this renewed enthusiasm is new, and as yet unproven technology that will remove the previous cost constraints and time delays of building the power stations in the first place. So, let's just for one moment, accept that government line that this is the way we decarbonise our energy supply. What this new technology does not change is the question of what we do with the nuclear waste.

'Let's not forget the legacy we are living with today from the ten Magnox power stations from the 1950s and the advanced gas-cooled reactors that replaced them between the 1960s and 1980s. The present government policy is to leave these stations for between eighty and one hundred years after they close before they can be safely decommissioned, even though the physical condition of many is deteriorating rapidly.

'As for the spent nuclear fuel, we have to keep it under water to cool before it can even be moved. Strontium 90 and Cesium 137 have half-lives of around thirty years but Plutonium 239 will need twenty-four thousand years to halve its radioactivity level. The Nuclear Decommissioning Authority has named this country's waste storage facility in Cumbria one of the most hazardous sites in the world, while keeping it running already costs us over two-billion pounds each year.

'The answer, we are told, is to store all our nuclear waste underground. Excuse me, but doesn't that sound very much the same solution proposed by our forefathers for dealing with household waste a century ago? The main difference of course is that nobody wants a nuclear waste dump under their own home. The government has been busily pursuing plans for three different sites for the last ten years but how many do we actually have at the moment? Yes, that's right, none.

'And if we did have the sites, the latest estimates for storing the waste and decommissioning all our old nuclear power stations are a staggering three-hundred-billion pounds. And yet with no plan and no likely means of being able to pay for it even if we did, this government continues to plough blindly on, convinced that nuclear power is the only possible way forward. It is not. We need to adopt a more holistic approach to renewable energy that this same government junked at the last election because it believed we could not afford such a policy. I say we need to remind the country that we cannot afford the true cost of nuclear, either economically or morally. Is this really the best legacy we can leave our children and the generations to come?

'We're delighted to see so many of you here tonight. It shows that not everyone thinks Thorpehead represents the best future for West Tyneford in the way the government and our MP would have everyone believe. Now, we need your help in getting the message out. I am going to open the meeting now for questions from the audience, but please make sure, before you leave, that our secretary Marjorie – she's at the desk by the door there – has your details so we can keep you up to date with our next planned actions. Thank you.'

After the warm applause had died down, a succession of local people stood to voice their own concerns about the power station. A fisherman feared for his future, and a Holmbeach resident worried about the town being swamped by workers contracted during the construction. There were fears raised about traffic volumes, security, environmental impact, pressure on schools and health services.

Jack sat at the back with his iPhone on record but also using his shorthand to take notes. He hoped John Fortser would have a transcript of his address. It was clear from the public participation that the local reaction was set against Thorpehead itself rather than the nuclear power industry as a whole and he would ask Forster about that when they got the chance to have a chat shortly.

When the hall eventually began to empty and the ever-efficient Marjorie began stacking the chairs against the walls, Jack approached John Forster to introduce himself.

'Hello John, I'm Jack Makepiece from *The Moorsman*. That was an interesting speech and you seem to have a lot of support. Have you got a few minutes to answer some more questions?'

'*The Moorsman*? Well, blow me, you took your time. I've lost count of the number of emails I have sent you lot about Thorpehead. Looks like we had to pay for an advert in your paper about tonight for you to finally take note.'

It was true that Jack only knew about tonight's event via Susie who had sold WATER the advert. Barney had never mentioned the group before, and he would have received the press releases that Forster presumably sent.

'I'm really sorry.' Jack replied quickly. 'My editor must have received your emails but I came because I had seen the posters and leaflets in my pub – we'll, my parents' pub. They own the Boar's Head in Holmbeach.'

'Makepiece, of course, I should have recognised the name. So, you're working on *The Moorsman* now?'

'Yes, not long back from London so I'm keen to get across

as many of the local issues as quickly as I can.'

'Well, welcome home, Jack. Why don't we go back to your pub and I can bring you right up to speed on how Thorpehead is affecting not just my life but everyone else's around here?'

Back at the Boar's Head, the two sat either side of a pint, and then another as John Forster relayed his own story of how his family legacy had been trashed and the fields his father and grandfather had farmed, turned into a construction site. He also expanded on his concerns raised in his speech earlier that evening about nuclear power generally.

'But surely if we are going to stop using fossil fuels for energy, we can't do without nuclear?' asked Jack.

'Aggh, you swallowed the 'what happens when the wind doesn't blow' bollocks too! The nuclear industry has successfully sewn that narrative into the debate for the last twenty years or more. The whole renewables argument needs a holistic approach, not just wind or solar versus nuclear. And if we had devoted the same resource and time into battery storage or tidal power as we have into nuclear over the last fifty years, the future for places like West Tyneford would look a lot better than it does currently.'

'But our MP and the government are saying Thorpehead will transform the economy down here,' said Jack, playing Devil's advocate.

'Transform the economy for who exactly? Yes, the construction project will bring inward investment. Places like this pub may well see a benefit but will it create jobs for local people? And once it's operational – I still like to say 'if' it's operational – most of the employment will be high-skilled and won't really benefit fishermen who have lost their livelihoods. No, the people who will really benefit are the likes of Mark Ellrington and his mates in high places.'

The pub had almost emptied by the time John Forster had reached a natural conclusion. Jack's notes ran to several more pages than he had first imagined at the start of the evening and he had received the email with John's speech at the village hall.

As they said their farewells, John headed out into the pub car park and clambered, rather unsteadily, into his Defender for the short drive home. For Jack, however, the evening was not finished. Deadline for this week's issue of *The Moorsman* was less than 24 hours away and it looked like he had a new front-page lead to write.

******

The Moorsman newspaper

THREATS TO FISHING INDUSTRY AND WATER SHORTAGES LINKED TO POWER STATION

By Jack Makepiece

West Tyneford could see its fishing industry completely wiped out and suffer water shortages once the Thorpehead Nuclear Power Station is operational. That's the message from West Tyneford Against Thorpehead Energy Reactor (WATER), the protest group trying to have the major infrastructure project cancelled.

Over 150 people packed the Burford village hall last Wednesday evening to hear local resident and organiser of WATER. John Forster warn of dangers he says are being kept from locals as construction work on the site gets underway. Mr Forster, who lives at Coombe Farm, told the packed meeting that the power station will use up to 800,000 litres of fresh water a day in addition to salt water for its cooling and storage and that this can only come from underground sources, so valuable to the area's farmlands. What is more, the saltwater intake pipes being built deep into the Bristol Channel will not only draw in millions of litres a day but also tonnes of fish, putting what is left of the fishing fleet in Holmbeach at severe risk. Mr Forster said: "Bicarel have stated that the number of fish potentially lost would be no more than a small fishing boat catches in a year. Have they not been to Holmbeach Quay recently? Our fishing fleet numbers fewer than 10 vessels. Are they really saying it's alright for it to continue declining by one a year?"

Two years ago, Thorpehead was announced as the location for the first a new breed of small modular nuclear reactors (SMR) being commissioned by the government in partnership with Bicarel, the multi-national conglomerate run by British entrepreneur Mark Ellrington. Factory building the reactors in sections and erecting them onsite is designed to reduce both construction costs and delivery time compared to traditional nuclear power stations, therefore reducing the cost of delivering energy. The government is investing heavily in SMRs as its major strategy in decarbonised energy security, ahead of renewables such as wind and solar. A prototype SMR will shortly come on stream at Torteville-les-Plages on France's Normandy coast.

But WATER believes that residents of West Tyneford, and the rest of the United Kingdom, are not being told of the real costs of this strategy - in particular, dealing with nuclear waste. John Forster told last week's meeting that the government has yet to put any plans in place to dispose of spent nuclear fuel from power stations decommissioned in the last century and even if storage sites did exist, the costs are estimated to be in excess of £300bn. Speaking to The Moorsman after the meeting, Mr Forster said: "Successive governments have kicked this problem down the road for years. The storage facility in Cumbria is a potential accident waiting to happen and is costing about £2bn a year to keep running. Spent fuel rods can't be moved for several years but so far we don't have one underground site ready. This government can't even deal with our nuclear legacy of the last 50 years and yet it wants to plough ahead with a new programme of nuclear power stations just because they are cheaper than they used to be."

Reacting to the WATER's accusations, a spokesperson from Bicarel, the company behind the Thorpehead project, told us: "The government has quite rightly decided that energy security can only really be achieved through nuclear power as we move away from fossil fuels. Renewable energy can only answer part of the problem while nuclear is regular, carbon-free, and now, thanks to our revolutionary modular design, remarkably cheaper and quicker to bring online.

"We have had, and continue to have, a positive dialogue with the community of West Tyneford and enjoy the positive backing of the local MP. We are convinced that Thorpehead will bring continued and long-standing economic benefits to the area and its residents and look forward to a continued and fruitful relationship."

The Moorsman contacted MP James Whitleigh-Howse, but at the time of going to print, had not received a response.

If you would like to support WATER or find out more about the organisation, then visit: www.waterwesttyneford.co.uk

Jack had finished his first draft at around 3 am and emailed it to Barney. At the same time, he fired off emails to the press office at Bicarel UK and to James Whitleigh-Howse's constituency office in Holmbeach. He wasn't expecting a response but hopefully they would provide comments he could add to his article later in the day.

He'd gone to bed, but just like when he had worked in the City and on a roll with a big story, it was difficult to switch off and actually get any real sleep. This was probably the first time since returning home that he had had such a sensation. So, not surprisingly, he was at his desk in *The Moorsman* office shortly after 8 am. Already, there were two emails waiting for him. One from Barney to say he was on a train to London – Jack had forgotten that this was Barney's monthly visit to HQ. The only real contact he had with the owners was a monthly catch-up on sales figures, distribution and overheads, followed by a convivial and liquid lunch in the company boardroom. Susie said they used to send out the menus (including wine selection) in advance to all the local newspaper editors in the group who were summoned.

Barney messaged that he had quickly read the piece and was happy to lead with the story, as long as it had balanced comments from Bicarel. The second email was from Bicarel's head of communications in London. Boy, they didn't sleep much either. Jack inserted the quote into the article and left the stop-gap 'we asked MP James Whiteligh-Howse for a comment' in place, hoping to replace it with a quote before finalising the page and uploading it onto the Hollingsworth Media file transfer protocol portal in time for the 6 pm cut-off. In the end, no comment was received from the MP and the message left on Robert Frost's voicemail went unanswered.

So that was it. Susie had uploaded the classified ads pages and Barney had signed off and submitted all the other news pages, including Jack's cheque presentation story at the nursery, the previous evening. Jack had the honour of confirming the last page uploaded on the system and this week's *Moorsman* was on its way.

Sleep came much more easily that night. An evening in the Boar's Head where he didn't have to refrain from excess because he was writing a story, probably helped. As he woke, refreshed the following morning and headed for the office, *The Moorsman* was already on the newsstands – and the phones were ringing off the hook!

Barney appeared at his office door before Jack could even drop his messenger bag on the desk. He had received calls from Bicarel, James Whiteligh-Howse's agent, Robert Frost and the head of communications at Hollingsworth head office, with whom Barney had shared almost a whole bottle of Malbec less than a day earlier.

'Thanks, Jack. I'm out of the office for one day and the shit hits the fan. Really good of you.'

'Sorry, Barney, what's the problem?'

'The problem is I leave the lead to you for the first time and before the ink has dried, I have complaints from head office, our MP and the biggest employer in the area. Apparently, *The Moorsman* is in bed with a bunch of crackpot conspiracy theorists looking to disrupt the best chance we have for future economic prosperity in West Tyneford!'

'Who the fuck is saying that? My article was fair, balanced and reflected the views of a large part of our readership,' Jack fired back. In that moment he was right back on the finance desk in London when the letter from Rajan Singh's solicitors landed.

'Come on, Barney, just step back and think for a minute. You read the draft and thought it was fair as long as we included comments from the other side. Bicarel gave us a response; our MP didn't, despite my trying. So again, where's the problem?'

'Bicarel think we have taken sides and have threatened to pull their advertising. Whiteligh-Howse thinks we should not be publishing negative stories about the area at a time when future prospects should be positive. He reminded me of how hard he worked to make sure West Tyneford was chosen as the pilot for the SMR project. And it seems our MD has been getting calls from the Minister about rocking the boat on their flagship nuclear policy. You may well be used to this in Fleet Street, Jack but this is West Tyneford where we all get on well and the only controversy is the judging at the local flower show!'

'Barney, please just take a breath and think. First and foremost, this is a local interest story. That hall in Burford was packed the other night. They are not crackpots. There are genuine concerns among our readers about what's happening at Thorpehead. This may not be what usually happens at *The Moorsman* but it is our duty to report those concerns. John Forster told me he had given up sending us press releases because nothing ever appeared in the paper. And if you have had the reaction you say and it's only 9.30 am on publication day, don't you think we may have touched a nerve somewhere?'

Barney blew through his teeth. Jack got the distinct impression that even as a newspaper editor, this was the first time he had ever had his work challenged.

'I don't know,' he uttered after exhaling a few more deep breaths. 'Bicarel want me to print a retraction next week. I have a few days to think about what to write. But in the meantime, please stick to reporting village fetes and planning committee meetings, Jack.'

Barney turned back into his office and closed the door behind him – something Jack had never seen in his albeit short time at *The Moorsman*.

A week is a long time in politics and 24 hours is a long

time at a weekly newspaper. Barney had barely spoken to Jack beyond 'good morning' or 'good night' but elsewhere, there were significant happenings at *The Moorsman*. First, Barney's email – editor@themoorsman.co.uk – saw a lot more activity than usual with the subject bar Letters to the Editor. Reaction to *The Moorsman's* lead article on Thorpehead was both supportive and contrary – although significantly more the former. But half a dozen letters about a lead article within 24 hours of publication was unheard of. Normally, the biggest area of contention was dog poo on the Holmbeach promenade.

It was too early to have sales figures for this week's edition but Barney had never before had requests from the wholesalers for more copies because some outlets had sold out. While sales were still holding up generally, there were always unsold returns at the end of each week. This week, it seemed that some newsagents and supermarkets had already sold their allocations. And although Barney paid only passing attention to online activity – this was very much young Duncan's domain – the daily stats he received from him were hard to ignore. He had to admit to only an arms'-length appreciation of 'hits', 'page impressions' and 'time per page', but the figures Duncan was emailing him about *The Moorsman* website were at least twice what he was used to seeing.

Susie had been quick to seize on the stats, too. She was already using the increased print and digital readership figures – albeit as yet unverified – to return to some advertisers who had previously considered *The Moorsman* not sufficiently relevant to their target audience. Presumably, she had been able to push against an open door because those advertisers themselves had read or been aware of the lead story in the paper and were now willing to chance some of their budget on the publication. Susie wasted no time in drawing Barney's attention to the new space orders for next week's edition from local companies he had previously told her were never likely to lower themselves to advertise in their little publication.

Barney also took the opportunity to ask Susie how much advertising *The Moorsman* was getting from Bicarel and its associate companies involved in the Thorpehead construction, as well as from the local MP. She was happy to confirm that other than statutory notices during the planning stages for the power station, most news about Thorpehead had come via press releases, which Barney had simply published as news in the paper. As for the MP, despite all the expenses he claimed and the costs for running a constituency office at which he was seldom present, the advertising spend with *The Moorsman* over the previous 12 months was a big fat zero.

So, in a little more than 24 hours since having the future of his local newspaper threatened by powerful forces, Barney was looking at the prospect of increased cover sales, advertising revenue and, thanks to his hot-shot reporter from London, a newspaper that had some relevance to the local population.

He sent a quick email to Jack. *Reference: WATER. and Thorpehead. Don't think we need to publish a retraction or apology. Got a really good Letters page for next week. Perhaps we can do some more in-depth research on the claims WATER are making about the fishing industry?*

6 - Thirty-three months earlier

Holmbeach

It was early evening and Jack was alone in *The Moorsman* office. Susie had left at 5 pm on the dot and Barney was having dinner with the rep from the insurance company. They were old friends as much as business contacts and would probably be in the Boar's Head all evening. Today was Duncan's college day and Jack still had 800 words to write for this week's planning news.

Holmbeach might be the back of beyond, but thankfully, the local council had embraced technology a few years ago and webcast all its committee meetings. The main reason was so that members of the public living in some of the remote villages across West Tyneford could be spared a long drive or perilous journey on the county's intermittent and erratic bus network in order to witness local democracy in action. While Jack had no such problems with transport, the council offices were a 15-minute walk tops; it had been raining all day so he could simply watch the machinations of the Holmbeach Council planning committee (rather grandly named the Development Control Committee) from the comfort of his own desk. Sometimes, it was good to actually be present at committee meetings – he could interview members of the public and he was learning quickly that councillors said one thing in the debating chamber but were far more forthcoming during a quiet chat in the corridor. But today's agenda was pretty routine. Often the committee had to decide whether to grant planning permission for a new barn on a farm, or a building extension to what was originally a Victorian labourer's cottage. Sometimes the meetings provided good copy, especially if a neighbour objected. Then there were the applications to turn old, or even derelict rural properties into what would clearly become luxury holiday lets, pricing local people out of the housing market – this was one theme that *The Moorsman* had been running with long before Jack arrived back on the scene. And of course, there were often planning applications linked to the construction work at Thorpehead. Applications for temporary buildings for equipment or access roads for the lorries still had to pass through the hands of Holmbeach Council's Development Control Committee, even if they were already agreed in principle with the Ministry for Energy in Whitehall.

But today, like the weather, the meeting was pretty bleak with nothing remotely controversial. In fact, not only was Jack struggling to stay focused on the screen, at one point, it looked as if one or two of the erstwhile committee members were having a similar problem staying awake. Having decided that approval of a new temporary classroom at the local primary school was going to be the lead for this week's column, he was on the last paragraph when his email pinged – it was John Forster.

Hi Jack. Just been reading this month's Civil Engineer magazine online. There's an article about delays to the new reactor at Torteville-

les-Plages in France. You probably know that there were loads of problems with the previous reactor there but this one is the first of the new design they are planning for Thorpehead. The article doesn't go into specifics but I thought you may be able to find an inside track through your contacts? Catch up later. J

Jack brought up the *Civil Engineer* website on his screen and soon found the article.

Delays at Torteville 2 in France

The company building the nuclear reactor at Torteville-les-Plages in France says the recently announced construction delays are nothing like the problems which beset its predecessor.

Bicarel, the engineering company run by British industrialist Mark Ellrington, announced last week that it had discovered some anomalies with pipework delivered with the latest section of the reactor. It is confident that the issues can be resolved on site without the need to supply new pipes from its factory in Kyrgmanistan.

A spokesperson has said that checks and remedial work will take 'a few weeks' but that the project is still on target to go live by the original deadline.

Torteville 1, which was developed by France Electricité and not by Bicarel, was 10 years late going live and rumoured to have cost €9bn, triple the original estimate.

John Forster was someone with seemingly endless knowledge on matters that concerned him – particularly Thorpehead – yet little concern for other issues which troubled him less. Jack surmised that by 'your contacts' Forster simply assumed that all journalists knew one another, whether they worked on professional magazines like the *Civil Engineer* or rural rags like *The Moorsman*. As it was, the online article was simply attributed to a 'staff reporter' and the editorial style suggested it had more likely just been copied and pasted from a press release. So he went looking closer to the source and a Google search for local newspapers in France featuring the power station at Torteville-les-Plages brought him to *La Voix de la Manche*. There too was an article about a small delay in construction, and through the filter of Translateme.com it was pretty clear the article was almost word-for-word the same as the one in *Civil Engineer*.

Despite his disadvantage with the language, Jack easily found the search facility on the *La Voix de la Manche* site and went looking for any other articles about the new reactor at Torteville-les-Plages. The first one he found was written three years earlier by a Christophe Lejeune.

New era for nuclear power

A new era in France's nuclear power history looks set to dawn following the signing of an agreement between France Electricité and construction company Bicarel to build a new nuclear reactor at Torteville-les-Plages.

The new generation reactor is, according to the state-owned electricity company, smaller, less expensive and quicker to build yet capable of producing almost as much energy as the older pressurised water reactors.

The major advantage is in the reactor itself, which is built in sections and then transported by sea rather than built from scratch on site. This means fewer workers are required at the construction site and crucially, that the build time is up to a third less than normal. The resulting saving on infrastructure costs means the reactor, Torteville 2, will start generating energy much sooner than its predecessor.

Torteville 1 finally began operating 5 years ago, a full decade after its original deadline. The construction was beset with problems and safety concerns as well as two explosions, one of which killed three workers. Although France Electricité never published the final cost, experts calculated that, taking into account the days lost through strike action by construction workers worried about safety, the final bill was almost

€9bn.

Instead of managing the construction of Torteville 2 itself, France Electricité has signed an agreement with Bicarel, the multi-national engineering company headed by British industrialist Mark Ellrington. Speaking to reporters at the official signing ceremony in Cherbourg yesterday, Ellrington said: "This is not only a big day for France but for the nuclear power industry worldwide. While nuclear energy is both efficient and carbon-free, historically it has been hindered by high build costs and long lead-in times. Torteville 2 will be the first of a new generation of reactors which will make nuclear power easy to obtain almost anywhere in the World."

Reacting to the news, Jacques Dumarrin of the union Syndicat Technique said: "When Torteville 1 was built, three of our members were killed and we had to go on strike to ensure the safety of others. Now we are being told that Torteville 2 will need fewer of our members to be involved. What makes that worse is that the company the government has contracted to build it is British-run – a country renowned for putting cost ahead of safety."

Jack found other articles by the same reporter and decided Christophe Lejeune may be someone worth talking to. It would have to wait though. If it was early evening in Holmbeach then France would be another hour ahead. But looking at the website, it was clear that *La Voix de la Manche* was no comparison to *The Moorsman*. This was a large regional, covering an area from Calais right around to the south of Brittany – and it was a daily. Alongside almost every story on the website, there was a telephone number, email address and social media tags to contact what was clearly the newsroom. So Jack picked up his phone and called the number. It was answered after two rings.

'Rédaction'

'Good evening. My name is Jack Makepiece. I am a

journalist from a newspaper in England. Do you speak English?'

'Yes, of course, Jack. How can I help you?'

'That's great, thanks. I work for a local paper close to Thorpehead, where they are building a nuclear power station similar to the one at Torteville-les-Plages. I have found some articles on your website written by Christophe Lejeune and I would really like to get in touch with him.'

There was a short silence and when the French voice returned, Jack noticed that the warm, welcoming tone of just a second or so earlier was now far more formal.

'I am afraid Monsieur Lejeune no longer works in this department. He is now in the petites annonces.

Jack didn't know very much French but was sure he had seen 'petites annonces' before, and it meant the classifieds.

'Do you have a number for him by any chance?'

'Non. Send an email. It's Christophe_Lejeune@vdlm.fr. Good evening' With that, the line went dead.

How does an obviously well-respected journalist reporting on major infrastructure projects for one of the biggest daily newspapers in France end up working in the classified ads section? But then Jack quickly asked himself the same question. How does a graduate entry journalist working in the financial section of one of Britain's best-known dailies end up writing stories about planning applications for a zombie newspaper in the middle of nowhere?

Still, he wasn't likely to be able to answer that question tonight, so he resolved to fire off a quick email to Christophe Lejeune before uploading his completed planning story for Barney to sub in the morning. Chances were that his boss would still be at the pub by the time he got home in any event.

But before he could log off, his email pinged again with a response from the mysterious French reporter.

Cannot help you. Do not email me again and do not try to call. Speak to Michel Bernadetti in Cherbourg.

It looked like being bought a pint by his editor for working late would have to wait. Why such a brusque response? The message read as if the guy was really spooked. And who was Michel Bernadetti? Jack began searches the way he always did, with just a name to go on. But this one was obviously French so Facebook and Google were unlikely to be as much help. So he started with LinkedIn, apparently with over 20 million users in France. There were six Michel Bernadettis – Jack was relieved, there could have been hundreds. Then all he had was a name. He knew nothing else about the person he was looking for. His only chance was to look for a geographic link to Torteville-les-Plages, or at least Normandy. And there was just one. Michel Bernadetti, born in Cherbourg, studied Physics at Rouen University and working as a building inspector for the county council. So far, so good. But then nothing. Everything was there in detail and the account obviously very active until two years ago, and then everything came to a halt. Nothing since. No updates, no messages, no new friends or colleagues added.

Jack felt this had to be the man, but he would try to pick up the trail with the county council and some of Bernadetti's contacts in the morning. Before calling it a day, he sent a direct message from his own LinkedIn account.

Hi Michel. I hope I have found the right person. I'm a journalist in England working on a story about the new nuclear power station at Thorpehead. Someone at La Voix de la Manche suggested I contact a

Michel Bernadetti regarding the project at Torteville-les-Plages. If this is indeed you, please respond or email me at jack.makepiece@themoorsman.co.uk. Apologies for the inconvenience if it is not the correct Michel.

Jack decided to call it a day. Walking back through the near deserted streets of Holmbeach, the weather had not improved. Sometimes it could be really wild and windy here with the harbour regularly the first port of call for the gale force winds which swept across the Atlantic. When the sun shone and the sky was cloudless and blue, you would wonder why anyone holidayed in the Caribbean. But today it was that other weather phenomenon which regularly afflicted Holmbeach. That combination of mist and drizzle which simply soaked you to the skin – locals always called it 'mizzle'. By the time Jack reached the Boar's Head, he was cold, wet and didn't really feel like sharing a pint with Barney and the insurance rep who would by now be several ahead of him. He carried on down the road to his parents' house and went straight up to his room. Before finally turning in, he did what all journalists did at 11.30 pm – he checked his emails.

There was one message. From an encrypted mail account.

Please do not use LinkedIn to try to contact Michel. Create your own Proton encrypted account and correspond only with this email address. I will pass on messages between the two of you.
Elodie.

7 – Thirty-two months earlier

Cherbourg, France

Jack could see the Normandy coastline approaching fast. He never considered himself much of a sailor. Not that he had a lot of experience, despite growing up on the coast.

But standing on the deck of a cruise ship as it enters an iconic port is an unforgettable experience. For Jack, that arrival into New York will never be surpassed. What a way to start your gap year after graduating from Oxford. His parents' surprise graduation present. They bought him a ticket to join them on their anniversary cruise so they could spend a few days together before he embarked on his American adventure. A shift as a summer camp assistant in New England, some time for travelling and then a 6-month internship at the New York Post before returning to London as a graduate entrant at one of the best-known national dailies. It was a memorable 12 months but gliding slowly into Manhattan on that crisp, cloudless morning was still one of the most vivid recollections of that time.

Less luxurious but almost as spectacular was that ferry trip from Rovinj to Venice when he and his girlfriend at the time went to the Greek islands during the university summer break. Her mother had done the same thing, almost a rite of passage for bohemian spirits in the 60s, and she wanted to see the islands and experience the life that had been the subject of so many tales throughout her childhood. But this was the second decade of a new millennium. The Hydra of Leonard Cohen and Marianne was now just a day trip for tourists and cruise passengers out of Piraeus and she and Jack had performed a rapid U-turn, deciding instead to seek new adventures travelling home overland. Not only had his girlfriend's dream evaporated once they reached Croatia, but so had her feelings for Jack. By the time they reached Venice, they were barely speaking and she phoned her parents the minute they arrived to buy her a one-way ticket home from Marco Polo airport. But sailing in front of St Mark's Square and the Doge's Palace as the ferry came into dock remained the one positive souvenir from that student romance.

But now, watching the port of Cherbourg and its post-war, Soviet-style tower blocks, emerging through the grey morning mist didn't have quite the same effect. Standing on the small observation deck on the catamaran at least meant he could get some fresh air after a couple of very queasy hours since leaving Poole at the crack of dawn. Travelling at over 40 knots meant you couldn't go outside and sit on deck so you were forced to remain within the confines of the 'air-conditioned' public areas. The ship had the words 'wave piercer' emblazoned along its side, that didn't mean a thing. Although only a slight swell in the Channel that morning, the corkscrew motion of the vessel made the journey more like a ride inside a tumble dryer and increasing numbers of passengers reacted the only way they could. For the last hour, the air conditioning vents simply circulated the back-of-the-throat aroma of sick bags.

It had only been a couple of weeks since Jack received that first Proton mail message from Elodie and while he had indeed created his own account and begun exchanging messages, he was still not entirely sure why he was here. But Elodie had said that Michel Bernadetti was indeed involved with the power station at Torteville-les-Plages and had lots he wanted to tell Jack – but only in person. The shuttle bus from the ferry terminal deposited him at the Place de la République and he followed the very brief instructions he had received to find the Rue Henri Dunant. With the time difference, it was now approaching midday but there seemed little sign as yet of any mass exodus of office workers bound for their favourite lunchtime restaurant, as was his long-held image of French life. In fact, the few restaurants and cafes which weren't shuttered seemed to be Vietnamese, Lebanese or take-away sandwich joints. So it was hardly surprising that he would find his ultimate destination here – O'Brady's Irish Bar.

As he pushed open the heavy door, he was greeted with the blast of 'Zombie' by The Cranberries, but nothing else. No drinkers and no staff. Making his way to the bar, the sound of Dolores O'Riordan's voice immediately reduced to background levels and a man in his late twenties appeared from a back office.

'Sorry, I didn't hear you come in.' he was greeted in English.

'I'm not surprised.'

'It's still early and normally I have the place to myself for a while. You must be Jack.'

'Is it that obvious? And you're Michel? I assumed I would be meeting with you here but not that you worked here.'

Michel gave the ubiquitous French shrug of the shoulders. 'It's a long story. Let's sit in the corner over there. I don't expect we will get any customers for a while but I can keep an eye on the door as we speak.'

Jack moved to the low table and Michel returned from the back office holding a pink A4 folder and a glass of Guinness, which he had begun pouring when he first appeared behind the bar.

'Welcome to France. I can't join you in a drink, just in case a customer does come in.'

'So how does a building inspector with a degree in Physics end up working the graveyard shift in an Irish bar on the Normandy coast?'

'Like I said, it's a long story and one I can probably only tell you face-to-face.'

'I'm all ears,' replied Jack. 'And does it also explain all the cloak and dagger in trying to track you down and setting up this meeting?' Michel took a deep breath.

'If you have read my LinkedIn profile then you will know that I do have a degree in physics. And I was lucky to find a job here where I could use it. I grew up here and I love it, but it was always likely that to continue with my career I would have to move to somewhere more industrial like Lyon. It's mainly farming and tourism in this part of the world but with Torteville just around the corner, there was always a chance I could find something that suited me.'

'But your profile says you worked for the county council.'

'That's right. It was my parents who suggested I apply to the *Département*. The pay might not be as good as the private sector but the pension and benefits more than made up. My Dad said if I worked for the Département it would be a job for life. Well, I proved him wrong.'

'So how's that connected to the power station at Torteville-les-Plages?'

'The county council had teams of people there almost all the time. Occasionally, I would be involved with a road project or the building of an apartment block, but with all the major construction at Torteville, I was mainly there, particularly when they began installing the new the water intake tunnels and the mini-reactor.'

The background music had moved on from the Cranberries to the Waterboys as the pub door suddenly opened. Michel leapt to his feet to greet the enquiring visitors, only to wish them 'bonne journée' after confirming that the pub did not serve lunch.

'I was in charge of one small team looking at the containment vessel and I had concerns about some of the prefabricated parts. I went to my boss who called a meeting with Bicarel.'

'Bicarel?'

'Yes, the same company that you must know. Bicarel is the construction firm working for France Electricité, which is government-owned. They are building the reactor in parts at a factory in Kyrgmanistan then are shipping them here to install on site. It is supposed to save a lot of time and cost but I was becoming concerned over the strength of some of the components being delivered.'

'What type of problem?' asked Jack.

'As far as I could see, some sections didn't meet the safety pressure standards set down by the National Atomic Safety Service, but several sections had already been installed before I started working there. The vessel is a key part of the reactor, about 10 metres tall and weighing over 300 tonnes. You can't simply take it out and fit a new one.'

'Bicarel simply did not want to hear what I was saying and said the parts had already been tested before leaving the factories and complied with the standards. But when I asked to see the test reports – nothing.'

'So they just went ahead? But wouldn't the council have to sign off on that?'

'Well, that's when it got interesting,' Michel replied, removing a photocopied sheet from the pink folder. 'I knew they were trying to cover it up and I didn't trust my boss to stand with me against the French Government – so I went to the press.'

He handed Jack the sheet of paper. It was a copy of an article from the local newspaper *La Voix de la Manche* headlined: *Catastrophe nucléaire?: de graves défauts découverts lors de la construction du réacteur (Nuclear catastrophe at Torteville-les-Plages? Serious faults discovered with reactor build).* The article described the discovery that Michel had made, crediting an unnamed source within the construction site and went on to consider the cost of replacing the vessel in time and in euros. Jack read the article in silence.

'When did this article appear? I found quite a few pieces from *La Voix de La Manche* during my research but I have never seen this before.'

'It never made it into print. That's a screenshot from the online version. Bicarel acted quickly. It wasn't on the website for twenty-four hours before they had it removed and the article never made the print edition. The journalist I gave the story to ended working on obituaries and the classifieds at the paper and hasn't spoken to me since. The company then put out a press release saying they had discovered some anomalies within the pipework which would need to be repaired. There would be a further delay and a slight increase in the costs as a result.'

'But did they not replace the vessel?'

'Not at first, but it does seem they took my warnings seriously. The last I heard, some of the construction crews were being stood down while new components were being sourced from a company in Finland. If that's the case, they will virtually be building a new reactor from scratch and it will cost them at least three billion euros more.'

'But I don't think any of the problems with Thorpehead have centred around the safety of the concrete or steel,' said Jack, scrolling through his notes on the iPad.

'I'm not surprised. Bicarel, or should I say the French Government, really did a good job of shutting this down. Anyone who did see the article while it was briefly in the public domain would have accepted the Bicarel response and put it down to a particular problem with the French site, not a design flaw.'

Jack blew through his teeth,

'Jeez, I can see why you wouldn't discuss this other than face-to-face.'

'But that's only part of it, my friend. They didn't just shut the article down, they closed me down as well.'

'How do you mean?'

'You won't be surprised to learn that I lost my job after that. The council couldn't prove that I was the source of the article but my boss and Bicarel knew it was me. So only a week later, I was called into the boss's office and told about the council budget pressures and the need to make cost savings. Everything they did was legal and I was properly compensated for my loss of office, but like I said, I managed to prove my papa wrong about working for the council being a job for life.'

'But you are qualified and experienced. Couldn't you find a job somewhere else?'

'Don't you think I tried? I sent my c.v. to almost every other département in France, to the major builders, even energy companies.'

'And?'

'And nothing. Not one département even responded and the larger corporations that did reply were all sorry, but they weren't hiring at the moment.'

The background music loop had now reverted to more traditional tones and what sounded like a Planxty classic from the 70s. The door then opened and the first real customers of the day entered the bar. As Michel attended carefully to their Guinness, Jack re-read the article from *La Voix de la Manche*. He had had numerous conversations and meetings with John Forster back in Holmbeach about the location of the Thorpehead power plant, the fresh water supply and concerns about the waste, but there had never been any mention of design failings or the integrity of the reactors. Michel's pink folder was still sitting on the table. He gently opened to see what else he might have to say. While obviously all in French, it looked like Michel did indeed have facts and figures to back up his concerns about the strength of welds and their safety under pressure. He promptly closed the folder as Michel returned from the bar with another Guinness for Jack.

'I assume you are going back on the catamaran later this

afternoon so you have time for another Guinness?'

'So, did you use your redundancy money to buy the pub then? Lots of people used to do that in England. My parents have run a pub for thirty years and they always think people who do that have no idea how much work it actually involves.'

'I wish my pay-off was big enough to be able to buy a bar, but no. In fact, without being able to find another job, it's been paying the bills while it lasts. This bar belongs to a man from Guernsey. He was a fisherman and regularly came into Cherbourg to unload his catch. After Brexit, it became much harder for him so he ended up selling his share in the trawler and bought this place instead. Bicarel and the council have made sure I can't get a job in Cherbourg but this guy wasn't really here when the Torteville business kicked off. He trusts me but I'm paid on the 'black'. Is that how you say it?'

'And what will you do next?'

'I don't know, to be honest. This is alright for now but my money is running out soon and I'll have to find something else.'

Jack was quiet for a moment while Andy Irvine began the second verse of "The Blacksmith."

'As you know, I have been working closely with a campaign group who want to stop the Thorpehead station from going ahead. I really think you could help them with your background and information. It would be great if you could meet them.'

'Not here. I haven't told you yet, but I am fairly sure Bicarel has not finished with me.'

'How do you mean?' Jack asked, now a concerned look on his face.

'Just small things. Sometimes I think I am being followed, strange things happen on my phone and I am certain my laptop has been hacked.'

'Hence all the difficulty in getting hold of you.'

Maybe I'm paranoid, but I am just being careful. We can't meet again in Cherbourg. If we meet, it should be in England and we still need to be careful how we communicate. It's why you received messages from my friend, and even then, she uses encrypted email.'

'But surely they won't suspect me?'

'Why not? If they find out we have been in touch, it will be easy to work out why. You need to be careful with your online research history. Try to use different IP addresses, go to public libraries or internet cafes and always have one computer which is never connected to the internet to keep your findings on.'

'So would you consider coming to England? My parents have a pub in Holmbeach. I don't know what the situation is but they are often looking for staff. They have a couple of live-in positions too.'

'The way things are going here, it may well be I need an escape route before long. Let's keep that in mind,' Michel said as he rose to serve the next round of the black stuff for the Cherbourg locals who were clearly enjoying "the authentic *Oirish* experience". They said their farewells just as the tape loop had returned to 'contemporary', if that is how you can describe The Corrs. Fearing that next up would be U2, Jack decided it was time to walk back to the ferry terminal so that he could at least enjoy some fresh air before the hermetically sealed journey inside the 'wave-piercing' catamaran bound for Poole.

As he settled into his seat on board, the phone rang. John Forster.

'Hi, Jack. Just curious to know how things went with our contact at Torteville?'

Jack was about to bring Forster up to date before he remembered Michel's parting words about who might be listening.

'OK. Not what I was expecting. I'll explain when I see you tomorrow.'

8 – Thirty-two months earlier

Holmbeach

The following morning, Jack went into *The Moorsman* office to catch up on his emails and finish a couple of local items he had promised Barney for the next edition. He called John Forster, saying he had a couple of follow-up questions for his next article about the WATER campaign and suggested they met on the coastal path. He said he was still suffering from his cross-channel ferry experience and could really do with some fresh air. When he met John at the cliff top car park he explained the real reasons for the subterfuge and relayed Bernadetti's warnings about the need for discretion.

'Bit over the top isn't it?' said John. 'We may be against nuclear power but this is Britain. Opposing government policy was still allowed the last time I checked.'

'You didn't meet him, John. He's no crank and he's genuinely scared for his safety. I haven't had the chance to speak to my parents yet but I want to get him over here to work at the pub. You can meet him then and decide for yourself, but I do think he could be very useful to us if we are going to move this thing forward.'

When Jack got home that evening, he went to see his dad at the Boar's Head and yes, one of the students who had been working there all summer was about to return to university. There would be a vacancy for a general bar person with extra duties in the restaurant if he fitted in. Jack wasted no time in sending a message back to Michel in France via Elodie using his Proton Mail account.

A few days later, Jack was at the National Express bus stop in Riverbridge with John Forster, waiting for the arrival of the service from Bournemouth via Poole. The bus pulled in on time at 6 pm and the three of them piled into the old Defender and headed for Coombe Farm before delivering the new employee to the Boar's Head. Sitting in John Forster's lounge, Michel told the same story he had given Jack the previous week but with one specific addition. Since Jack's visit to Cherbourg, the owner of O'Brady's Irish bar had received a visit from an inspector from the *Ministre du Travail et de l'Emploi*, following a report that he had been paying staff off the books. It seemed that Jack's job offer had come at just the right time, but Michel was convinced it was no coincidence that his work 'on the black' had been discovered.

John explained the background to the WATER campaign group as well as his own concerns over the future for nuclear energy while showing Michel copies of the media coverage they had received to date – effectively Jack's articles in *The Moorsman* and some of the Letters to the Editor which had followed. Michel held the paper out in front of him, gripped between his thumb and index finger at arm's length as if he had just fished it out of the toilet bowl.

'That's it? This is how you plan to stop one of the most

powerful industrialists in the world from building a nuclear power station in your backyard?'

'We really don't have the resources to do much more. We have no wealthy backers like Bicarel and quite honestly, if it wasn't for Jack's paper taking an interest I don't think we would even have the profile we have locally.'

Michel was quiet for a moment and then turned back to John Forster.

'The way I see it, there are two battles to be fought. Locally, you want to prevent a nuclear power station being built at Thorpehead. Nationally, you John Forster, want to see the British government stop pursuing nuclear energy, full stop.'

'In a nutshell, yes.'

'Then I think we adopt different strategies for each. For Thorpehead we target Bicarel and their false claims about cost and efficiency.' He pulled out from his backpack the pink folder that Jack had seen at O'Brady's in Cherbourg.

'There is plenty here that we can use to highlight Bicarel's corner-cutting and dubious practices in the construction of their "revolutionary" reactors,' Michel said, using finger quotes.

'As for the government and your anti-nuclear stance, we should focus on the waste issue. It's not the same argument in France because there we already have the facilities in place for underground storage, whether you agree with it or not. But here, especially with the problems in Cumbria, which everybody knows about and no chance of building any storage facilities anytime soon, then we do have a message which can resonate.'

'That sounds great,' Jack cut in. 'But how do we get that

message across? *The Moorsman* can handle the local issues but my editor will not be the slightest bit interested in mounting a national anti-nuclear campaign.'

'I get that,' replied Michel. 'You are right that your paper should stay focused on Thorpehead but we are going to need social media to get the national message across.'

'That's easy for you to say!' chortled John. 'It took me five years to even get to grips with Facebook, and don't even bother saying social media to Marjorie!'

'No, this needs an expert,' said Michel. 'And fortunately, I am one!'

It wasn't just Gallic arrogance that prompted the statement. Michel was calm and reflective as he explained how they would launch a coordinated awareness campaign across media platforms, the names of which meant nothing to John Forster, and even Jack would have struggled to explain how they worked. But it was clear Michel was comfortable in this milieu, even though he was probably older than Jack. Within a quarter of an hour, he outlined clearly and coherently how he would go about increasing awareness of the dangers associated with treating nuclear waste while Jack and John discussed possible target articles and public meetings to raise concerns about Bicarel's low-cost energy promise. With the dying embers of a late summer's day bathing the Bristol Channel in a glow of blue and sodium yellow, Michel had one final statement to make before rounding off for the day.

'While I am happy to drive all this from behind, the campaign has to be fronted by you, John and your newspaper, Jack. There is no way anyone can know I am involved. Bicarel have long tentacles and hopefully they won't detect my involvement. For now, they think I have gone into hiding in France. The longer they think that, the better.'

With that, the 'meeting' broke up and the three jumped back into the Defender for John to drop them back at the Boar's Head and for Michel to meet his new employers.

It was less than three months since Jack's article about the WATER meeting at Burford appeared in *The Moorsman*. The next editions had carried a more in-depth follow-up about John Forster and how he came to launch the WATER campaign, and then an article on fears for the future of the Holmbeach fishing fleet. It included a personal testimony from one young resident, Brad Ackford, who worked the boats while his pregnant wife was a nurse at the local hospital.

Jack was now working through the file Michel had brought from France on the build specifications for the modular reactor at Torteville-les-Plages, but it was not only in French but highly technical. It did give him other leads for his own research, though and he had begun putting together the chain from the other end – the association between Bicarel and the factory in Kyrgmanistan which was building the modular reactors.

Michel settled quickly into life at the Boar's Head. A popular and welcoming barman to the locals and using his French charm on the diners when working shifts in the restaurant. His downtime was spent either designing the website and message pages on an old laptop with no internet that John Forster had given him, or in John's study at Coombe Farm if he needed to work online. WATER now had its own website which had a link to another one – *"What Do We Do with Nuclear Waste?"* Michel taught John the basics of WordPress and he was quickly able to keep the WATER site up to date with the latest news of campaign meetings, petitions and protests, as well as posting links to Jack's articles as they appeared in *The Moorsman*. On the other site, Michel had uploaded many of the research papers John Forster had written about the problems of storing legacy nuclear waste in the country and the lack of any clear plan to deal with the government's much heralded policy to develop SMRs. Other than using some of the figures in his speech at the village hall in Burford, he had not had the opportunity of sharing any of this information.

So, using www.whatdowedowithnuclearwaste.com as a reference point, Michel had set in motion an awareness campaign with accounts created across numerous social media platforms to drive traffic towards it. John Fortser's knowledge did not expand far beyond Facebook, X and Instagram and Michel had said these were important, particularly as politicians seemed to spend most of their days looking at them. But he also showed him a whole palette of different platforms which Michel said were the way that younger generations got their news. The aim was simply to get more people asking the question "what do-we-do with nuclear waste?" and make politicians and decision makers aware that the question was being asked. Michel had also asked John if he knew of any high-profile celebrities who were known to be 'anti-nuclear'. Bringing them on board would not only heighten the profile but adding their own followers would boost awareness of the site considerably.

Like it or not, John Forster was also becoming something of a celebrity himself. While it was never his intention when he started the WATER campaign, people were beginning to notice him, and not just while out and about or in the supermarket. Jack's articles in *The Moorsman* had been picked up by the BBC locally, who had filmed an interview on the clifftop with the Thorpehead construction site in the background. As sometimes happens on a slow news day, part of the package also made it onto the BBC national news broadcast that evening. *The Observer* had also come down to interview John for a magazine piece while, not to be outdone, ITV's regional news had followed up on Jack's story about the Thorpehead water intake pipe and the threat it posed to the fishing industry. A reporter and film crew had come to Holmbeach and at least had had the courtesy to acknowledge The Moorsman as the source, including an interview with Barney in their report.

******

Having just endured a very long, sometimes fractious meeting of the West Tyneford Council, Jack decided to stop off at the Boar's Head before going home to read through his notes. Despite some personal attacks across the floor of the council chamber, very little was actually decided and Jack was not sure how he would fill the 700 words Barney had given him when he went back to the office in the morning. Sitting at the bar, he noticed the familiar Defender pulling into the car park. Michel was supposed to be on duty that evening but had no doubt been at Coombe Farm with John during the afternoon. John often dropped him off but tonight he was coming in and both of them seemed far more animated than usual.

'You two look like you have won the lottery. Has the Government decided to scrap its nuclear policy while I was incarcerated in the council chamber?'

'Not quite,' answered John. 'But we may be a lot closer than we were this morning. Time for drinks, I think.'

'Not me, I have to relieve Mike behind the bar. But you tell him,' Michel said as he went off to the back room to get changed.

'We have a new follower on X, and it's only bloody Mike Danvers! Michel had never heard of him but said he had millions of followers and the like.'

Mike Danvers was not quite a national treasure in the David Attenborough mould but he was considered a celebrity and loved by young and old. Originally a stand-up comedian with some pretty borderline material, he got a lucky break about 15 years ago, landing a part in the country's most popular TV soap. From that, the face of Mike Danvers graced TV chat shows, quiz shows and more recently as a wildlife presenter. It was this role which brought him the affection from younger audiences with his wacky yet often acerbic coverage of environmental issues. Wisely, during his rise as a TV star, he had kept many of the political views which formed his early stand-up routines hidden from the public. But more recently, having reached the point where he was seen as 'establishment' by many, and financially secure so as not to have to worry so much for his future, he had become more openly radical. While the BBC might not want to risk hiring him to host a quiz show, his social media comments had drawn massive followings and he was rumoured to be earning seven-figure sums from the main platforms alone.

'So Monsieur Danvers is a bit of a coup, no?' Michel said as he re-emerged behind the bar, now dressed in chinos and a black open-neck shirt together with name badge.

'There was a direct message from him this morning when Michel came in this morning,' explained John. 'He said he'd read the article in the *Observer* and then found the waste website. Wished us luck with our campaign and that he would like to help wherever he could. Next thing he has posted about us on his social media and Michel said he had over 10 million followers on X.'

'There's over a million on Instagram and TikTok and some of his YouTube environment videos are watched by more than that. If he shares and retweets our posts, that is going to be massive,' Michel added as he poured a pint of bitter for John and a Peroni for Jack. The bar was beginning to fill up, mainly with locals who all seemed to know Michel well already. John and Jack took their drinks to a seat in the bay window so they could continue to talk in peace.

'You know, I think we really can make a difference with all this,' said John, still flying high at the news that Mike Danvers had reached out. 'Michel is a wizard with all this internet stuff but it certainly looks like it's working. Marjorie didn't get it all when he started but even she was jumping up and down when I told her about Danvers. It's not been bad for *The Moorsman* either, has it?'

'I think it took Barney a while to get on board, but having had TV crews in the office and The Observer picking up our stories, I think he is starting to realise that we can be more than just a local gossip rag. The last two editions have sold more than any week over the last five years, apparently and Susie is certainly seeing the benefit in advertising sales.'

John drained his pint and with two his limit, even though Coombe Farm was almost around the corner, he said his farewells to the locals he knew and nodded to Michel, still busy behind the bar. Jack accompanied him out into the car park and as the Defender rattled and roared its way along the coast road leaving a puff of black smoke in its wake, he strolled down the road to his parents' house where he would have to put any euphoria to one side and decide how he was going to write up his report tomorrow on one of the most tedious council meetings he had ever attended.

As John approached the driveway to Coombe Farm, the work compound appeared to have more heavy plant and equipment parked up than he had noticed previously. No doubt he and Michel were too distracted by the day's major event to have noticed on the way out. The earth mound that had blocked his view of the hills and cast a shadow over the farmhouse had now become so familiar he was used to it. He parked on the drive and as he approached the front door he noticed an envelope poking out of the letter box. It was addressed to John Forster but had no stamp. It had been hand-delivered. John turned his key in the door and instinctively reached for the light switch just inside. Nothing. Using the torch on his phone he moved on into the kitchen, but the light didn't come on there either. The red power light on the fridge was extinguished too. He checked the fuse cupboard under the stairs. Perhaps all the additional computer use had blown something. But the trip switch had not been thrown so he must have had a power cut. He took the two portable lamps out of the cupboard. There was a time when the whole farmhouse had been lit by lamps, but thankfully they were now battery and not paraffin-powered. He sat in the kitchen and called the electricity company's emergency number which was answered promptly and efficiently. When he gave his address, the initial reaction was that there was no known outage in the area but as his property was remote, they would need to carry out a manual check.

It looked like John would have no power until the morning at least. He wanted to check the traffic levels on the campaign websites and social media accounts since Danvers's endorsement, but with no electricity and no means of recharging his mobile, that would have to wait. Thankfully, the stove was powered by Calor gas so he could make a cup of tea before an enforced early night. As the kettle boiled he sat down and opened the letter which had been pushed into his letterbox. It was a Notice from West Tyneford Council informing him that Bicarel had applied to amend the planning consent for the temporary Thorpehead construction road to become the permanent access route to the power station. The original plan had involved a shorter route about two miles further along the coast but according to the latest application, this would have involved blasting through an area of solid granite which had not previously been identified. The resulting cost and time delay would have compromised the timetable for the opening and consequent operation of Thorpehead, and so the company now proposed to make the longer route being used for the construction traffic a permanent feature. The landowner, Bicarel's boss Mark Ellrington, had given no objection and as all planning matters concerning Thorpehead were now being decided by the Minister, planning approval was therefore deemed as consent.

John sat in the gloom, digesting the news that, far from stopping the development of nuclear power stations there was a strong possibility that he would be living alongside the access road to one. Then his mobile rang, it was the electricity company. They would be sending engineers to check in the morning, but it looked on their system as if the power to Coombe Farm had been cut, literally. The location, as far as they could tell, was adjacent to the entrance to Coombe Farm, just where work was starting on the access route.

With what John Forster thought was remarkable efficiency, engineers from the electricity company were at Coombe Farm shortly after 8 am the following morning. They had already identified the problem – one of the posts carrying the overhead cable had been struck, presumably by a construction vehicle, and would not need replacing. Colleagues were in the process of reconnecting the cable and power would be restored within the hour. True to their word, a few minutes later, John heard the electric motor of the fridge launch into action and the hall light he had tried last night came on. He popped a couple of slices of bread into the toaster and booted up his computer while waiting for the kettle to boil. Reviewing the WATER group emails had become a regular feature of breakfast time in the last few weeks and the increasing volume of mail meant this task was eating further into the morning routine. Among this morning's messages was a request from a researcher on the BBC's flagship daily *News Review* programme for a live interview. Although the email had been sent at 9.30 pm yesterday, when he dialled the number the call was immediately answered by a bright, cheery voice.

'Good morning, this is Rebecca from *News Review*. How can I help?' John introduced himself and said he was responding to her message.

'Oh, thank you so much for calling, John. I was about to call you again as things have moved on since I reached out to you last night. We were very interested in the recent attention you have been getting for your campaign but Ed, you know Ed Jacobson, he's the BBC Political Editor and one of our presenters? We'll he's been in touch with the Government and they've agreed to put the Minister for

Energy up for an interview. We thought it would be really great if we could get you in to put your concerns directly to the Minister.'

'That's fantastic news. I'd be delighted to take part. When do you have in mind?'

'Well, the interview would be tonight, right after the 10 o'clock news. But you don't have to come up to London. The Minister will most likely be in the Westminster studio and we were thinking you could join down the line from our Exeter studio.'

Before John really had the chance to gather his thoughts or ask further questions, the charming Rebecca talked him through the running order for that evening's broadcast and took his personal details and car registration so she could advise security at BBC Exeter. And she was gone, presumably making arrangements for the next segment of the programme.

John immediately dialled Jack at *The Moorsman*.

'You'll never guess what just happened? I'm doing a live interview with the Energy Minister on tonight's News Review!'

'What Roland Smith? I think he's an old college mate of Whitleigh-Howse though I have yet to find anything incriminating. Well, that's brilliant, John. I guess that piece of theirs that made it onto the ten o'clock news probably helped but given the timing of it, I bet they follow Mike Danvers on X.'

'Well, fortunately I don't have to go up to London for the interview. They are going to film me from the Exeter studio.'

'I'm sure you will be fine. It's not like you need to rehearse anything. You've got all the ammo you need at your fingertips. Give him hell, John, I'll be watching and writing an article about your appearance for next week's edition.'

The old Defender was far more suited to country roads and tracks than urban driving or commuting so John normally used public transport on the rare occasions he had to go to places like Taunton or Exeter. But at this time of evening the streets of Exeter city centre were relatively quiet and he made good progress to find the converted Georgian building which now housed the regional offices of the BBC.

The security guard showed him where to park and then told him to come back to the cabin to be issued with a visitor pass. Someone would then come to collect him and take him to the newsroom. Just before 10.30 pm another security guard arrived and took John across to the main building. The large, open-plan newsroom contained upwards of 30 desks with computers while television screens mounted on the walls each displayed the output from rival television channels. But it was late at night and while news might be a 24/7 phenomenon, this was regional TV. There was literally nobody in the room. The desks were unoccupied, the glass-walled break-out rooms empty and the televisions on mute. John was shown to a comfortable red velour sofa and asked to wait while somebody would come from the studio to attend to him. Before he could even look at the various newspapers spread out across the coffee table, a petite lady with mousy hair and a broad smile, who he recognised from the local news broadcasts, came out from the door marked Studio 1.

'Hello. You must be John. I'm Sarah and they've asked me to look after you. I have just finished the late bulletin and we have about five minutes until your live link.'

Rather than leading John back into the studio, she led him to a small corner of the newsroom where a typist's chair sat opposite a filing cabinet. On top of the cabinet sat a single fixed camera lens about 15 centimetres in diameter encased in black steel and resembling an old cinema projector.

'Oh, so no make-up, camera, lights, action,' said John, rather nervously.

'Afraid not. It's all rather homespun here these days. Even my late bulletin in the studio is just me and an automatic camera.'

She clipped an earpiece and lapel mic onto John and led the audio cable down the back of the chair.

'I'll just explain. It's very simple. The chair is fixed in position and all you have to do is look directly into the lens. You will hear the live stream of the News Review once it starts and the producer will also speak to you through your earpiece. It's a little disconcerting at first that you can't see who's asking you questions but just remember to keep looking right into the lens. I'm just finishing up and will be around to uncouple you when the interview is over. Just relax and good luck.'

With that, the delightful Sarah headed back to the studio and the next voice he heard through the earpiece was the *News Review* producer. After checking sound levels, he told John that the interview would be the first item on the show and that Ed Jacobson would make the introductions before asking the first question. With that, John heard the familiar theme music and the stilted, slightly Scottish intoned voice of the BBC's Political Editor.

EJ   First tonight, the Government's decision to renew its nuclear energy programme after the disastrous

Burselham power station experience a decade ago has been heralded as a major boost to the economy and an end to concerns over Britain's future energy supply. A ten-billion-pound deal with a Kyrgmanistan company to build small modular reactors quicker and cheaper is the key to this strategy, but not everybody is convinced. At Thorpehead on the Bristol Channel, where the first new power station is being built, residents are questioning whether the project will really achieve the benefits being promised or if the sacrifices they are being asked to make are too great. Joining me tonight from our Westminster studio is Energy Minister Roland Smith and in the West Country, John Forster, spokesperson for the campaign group WATER – West Tyneford Against Thorpehead's Energy Reactor. John Forster, your group is called WATER and there's more to the choice of that acronym. Am I right?

JF   Good evening, Ed. Yes, you are right. For all the supposed benefits of SMRs …

EJ   Small modular reactors

JF   Yes, sorry, small modular reactors. Whatever benefits there may be in building them, the fact is they still need a lot of water to operate. In fact …

EJ   Isn't that why they have chosen Thorpehead? It's by the sea.

JF   Yes, it's by the sea and yes it will draw in millions of litres of sea water each day, as well as thousands of fish that the fishermen of Holmbeach rely on for their living. But sea water is only part of the cooling process. Fresh water is also a vital part of the process and the estimate is that Thorpehead will need up to eight-hundred-thousand litres a day. You have to remember that in our part of the world, hosepipe bans are common and with the tourist influx every summer, demand for water already puts a strain on the system. Where are we going to find eight-hundred-thousand extra litres a day?

EJ Minister, your power station is going to take all their water and kill the fish!

RS Good evening Ed, thank you for having me on your programme tonight. Can I just start by reminding viewers of the reasons why we have decided to kick-start our nuclear energy programme? We have a climate emergency. If we have been slow to accept it, we do fully understand that we cannot rely on fossil fuels in future. Nor can we rely on foreign powers for the supply of those fossil fuels as events in recent history have clearly demonstrated. Nuclear power has always been a potential source of plentiful and clean energy, but we have fallen short previously due to the cost and long lead-in times to create it. The deal we signed two years ago resolves both of those issues in one. Generating nuclear power in less than five years from starting to build is simply incredible. Thorpehead will be operational in just two years' time, and as we complete more SMRs we will even be able to export power rather than import it. As to the water, yes, these power stations do need fresh water as well as sea water for the cooling process. We have commissioned reports into the impact of the sea water intake on local fish stocks and while some loss is unavoidable, the consultants tell us this will be negligible.

EJ And what about fresh water? eight-hundred-thousand litres a day?

RS I don't have the precise figures in front of me, I am afraid. Yes, fresh water is needed. I am not sure how

Mister Forster has arrived at that figure but I do know from the geological surveys carried out before commissioning Thorpehead that the area is rich in underground springs fed from water running off the moors. Very little of that is used currently, although I think some rural properties, including where Mister Forster actually lives, receive their water directly from a spring. The rest just finds its way to the sea.

JF That's disingenuous and arrogant if I may say so. Yes, as it happens, my house is fed by spring water, as are many of the farms in the area. One of the key effects of climate change is going to be a global shortage of drinking water. Yes, I know we still use drinking water to wash our cars and water our lawns, but things are going to have to change over the coming years. To simply brush it off as if you will be taking water nobody else uses and that's the problem solved, is short-sighted and frankly, naive. Don't forget, the spent fuel rods from Thorpehead will need to be stored on site in fresh water for more than 30 years until they're safe enough to move – that's if you have anywhere to move them to by then. The need for fresh water at Thorpehead will last for years after the station has stopped generating power. And you really think we will have enough water for all of that in fifty, or sixty years' time?

EJ Yes, your campaign is concerned about the legacy of nuclear waste as well, isn't it?

JF Too right it is. We are forever being told that nuclear power is cheap and clean but nobody ever wants to talk about clearing up the mess it creates. Once power stations reach the end of their useful lives, they have to stand idle for decades until they are safe enough to decommission. Spent nuclear fuel rods from the Magnox reactors from the 1950s are still sitting up in Cumbria in deteriorating conditions and costing the Government as much as three billion pounds each year. Now this Government wants to build even more nuclear power stations when, for the last forty years, it hasn't known what to do with the waste. Can I ask the Minister, 'What are you going to do with waste?'

EJ Minister?

RS I have to say, it's very dangerous if we allow alarmist commentary to enter the debate over nuclear energy. As far as Cumbria is concerned, it's a large and complex operation but everything is and always has been under complete control. The long-term plan for the safe storage of spent nuclear fuel is in underground chambers and the Government is in ongoing consultation over potential sites.

EJ How many sites do you actually have in the pipeline and what are the likely timescales?

RS Discussions are at a delicate stage at the moment and it would be wrong of me to ………

EJ So you have no sites actually in build or at planning stage to house the existing waste. A report published last year estimated the total cost of decommissioning all the old nuclear power stations and storing the waste underground at three hundred billion pounds. Nuclear power isn't that cheap after all, is it?

RS I'm afraid that is not a figure I recognise. The Government is fully committed to the safe storage of spent nuclear fuel just as it is to the new programme of SMRs. It is the safest, cleanest and cheapest option available to us.

JF I worry that government ministers still use the word 'cheap' in the same sentence as nuclear safety. As we have seen in France, where the first Bicarel SMR is being built at Torteville-les-Plages, the Government there took the cheapest bid and then had to delay the project because some of the units delivered were not up to standard.

RS That is absolute rubbish. I'm not here to defend the French Government but it is my clear understanding the delays were caused by some welding issues on site. I must say I think it is shameful that the BBC allows people to come on to this programme and make baseless and misleading statements just to cause alarm …

EJ Gentlemen, I would love to continue this discussion, but sadly we are out of time. Thank you, Energy Minister Roland Smith and from our Exeter studio, John Forster. Now, there have been further demonstrations in Israel's West Bank after four Palestinians were shot at a roadblock yesterday. Joining us now from Tel Aviv is our Middle East correspondent ……

'Thank you, John, that was excellent,' the producer's voice came through his earpiece. 'Sorry we had to cut you off earlier than planned but we had the satellite link from Israel and didn't want to lose it again.

And with that, Sarah appeared behind him to dismantle the sound equipment and a security guard appeared to escort him back to the car park. Exeter city centre was actually busier than on the way in as the pubs closed and young people, mainly students John assumed, made their way homewards or onwards to further their entertainment. He was soon out of town and heading north. Pulling up at Coombe Farm just after midnight, he was relieved to find the lights still working.

9 – Twenty-six months earlier

Switzerland

Slats of sunlight played across Robert Frost's face through the half-open blinds of the chalet. He eased himself out of the bed, not wanting to wake James who was gently snoring beside him. They had arrived late the previous evening when everything was in darkness. While the partially shuttered bedroom window had given him a taste, Robert was keen to see the full splendour of this chalet's location. It belonged to Alexander Baliyashvili, President of Kyrgmanistan, and was a particular favourite of his new wife Rovshana, Viktor's mother. As well as a base for skiing holidays, the chalet was also a well-known location linked to the annual World Economic Forum at Davos, just a few kilometres away.

While the media descends on the resort every January to interview world leaders, it is away from the glare of the TV cameras, in places like the Baliyashvili villa that meetings which really matter take place. James had told him the place was originally some kind of sanatorium until the Swiss Government took it over during the Second World War as part of the defence network to secure the country's borders and neutrality. It was then used as a military training facility before standing empty for a few years. The Kyrgmanistan President is said to have bought it unseen during a boozy lunch in Zurich with a Swiss banker and a government official. Nobody knows, perhaps not even Viktor's uncle, just how much had been spent on its renovation and while the chalet's decor did not have the ostentatious gold trappings and kitsch that oligarchs often prefer, it was clear that no expense had been spared.

Robert tiptoed out of the bedroom and into the lounge. Making himself a drink from the largest barista pro coffee machine he had ever seen, certainly nothing like the Nespresso at his flat in Chiswick, he slid open the French window and took a seat on the balcony. The digital display on the hot tub told him the outside temperature was 2 degrees but in the dry atmosphere, at high altitude and the sun beating down, Robert felt no cold at all, wrapped in his thick towel robe. If the temperature was not Mediterranean, the blue sky certainly was. He thought of the print he had on his lounge wall back in Chiswick - Window at Tangiers - bought from a gallery around the corner for £150. But the cobalt blue of Matisse's sea was the colour of the sky here. He sensed movement behind him and turned to find James, bleary-eyed and dressed in an identical towel robe.

'Not a bad view, eh?'

'I'm sure it's worth every penny. I'm sorry, I didn't want to disturb you but my mind was already racing over today and the meeting.'

'No problem,' answered James. 'And don't worry, we've plenty of time to relax. The housekeeper told me last night that Viktor and Mark are due this afternoon but Roly has a select committee this morning and is unlikely to make it until dinner. So, we could go skiing or perhaps go down into Davos for lunch. But before that ....' James loosened the belt of his robe and let it fall open. 'I think I have other needs requiring the attention of my private secretary.'

*****

Although the sun had dropped behind the mountains some hours earlier, the village and valley beyond were still clearly visible through the floor-to-ceiling glass of the chalet lounge. A full moon had risen with its light reflecting off the snow-covered meadows. The five men sat in a semi-circle looking out across the landscape, each sitting in a high-backed, white leather armchair and nursing a heavy cut crystal glass. Dinner had included the ubiquitous fondue and wine had flowed freely. Unusually, it was not Chateau Haut-Brion but a local red wine from the Rhone Valley. Equally unusual for when these protagonists had normally come together around a table, none of the food had ended up on the walls, nor had the waitresses had to endure a hand up their skirts while serving or clearing away dishes. Spirits were high and impressive quantities of alcohol consumed but the 'Bugs' had grown up and clearly had more serious matters to consider. That thought had clearly occurred to Mark Ellrington.

'Do you fuckers realise, the last time we were all together doing this was back in Oxford - the night we launched that fucking crusty down the River Thames?'

'I wouldn't go so far as to say "we"', James cut in.

'Whatever. Fact is, we've never really had a reunion until now.'

'That's just as well,' said Roly. 'This meeting has been logged in my ministerial diary as a college reunion.'

'Anyway, night is yet young,' boomed Viktor. 'Plenty of time for fun later. But business first.'

'Viktor's right,' said Mark. 'Let's just take stock of where we are. Perhaps our Cayman Islands consultant can bring us up to date?'

'No need for that,' said James. 'Yes, I realise Bicarel is paying handsomely for its management advice, but as to who owns the particular brass-plate company you are referring to, I really couldn't comment!'

'Oh fuck off, you posh cunt, just give us the update so we can get on with Viktor's play time.'

James let the comment pass over him, retaining the genteel and non-committal smile that he had perfected for whenever he was asked a difficult question by journalists or indeed, MPs in the House.

'Overall, it's very good news but with one caveat on which perhaps Robert will be able to give us more information later. Obviously, Thorpehead is on track for completion and it's on time and within budget. Plenty of brownie points for governments that deliver on their promises. As you probably know, His Majesty's Government has drawn up its shortlist of eight more potential sites and has entered into negotiations on commissioning the first two of those. Roly?'

'Yes, we have had to go through a competitive tender process, but I am due to sign off on the Suffolk site next week and I have a final meeting with the boffins about North Wales right after. The PM favours announcing both at the same time but I would think Bicarel will have its next contracts in the coming weeks.'

'Hear that Viktor,' said Mark. 'You need to hang on to

your shares for a bit longer, you Russky bastard. Viktor has decided he wants to alter his fucking work-life balance,' using finger quotes. 'He wants to do even less of the former and enjoy the latter, and selling off more of his shares to pay for it. The share price is riding high at the moment but two more power stations in build will really send it into orbit.'

'Well, Viktor, our UK-based company will be more than happy to handle the arrangements for you once again. And of course, if you wish to increase your personal investment in our wealth fund as a result, we will be delighted to help.'

'For the usual fucking fee, of course,' snapped Mark.

Viktor, by now, had lost interest and was busy refilling his Napoleon brandy.

'There is one fly in the ointment I should warn you all about,' continued James.

'As you are aware, the local campaign group at Thorpehead have been quite vociferous and been getting quite a lot of media attention recently. When it was local, I was mainly able to deal with it in the constituency but of late they have been making the national press and TV.

'Tell me about it,' said Roly. 'I had to do an interview with that bloke Forster on *News Review* not long ago. He started talking of a cover-up at the Bicarel site in France.'

'What the fuck,' shouted Mark. 'Where did that come from?'

'I think I might know,' said Robert. Not a former member of the Bugs, indeed not even an Oxford alumnus, Robert had remained detached through dinner, drinking only mineral water. As James Whitleigh-Howse's permanent secretary, albeit private lover at the same time, he had so far not taken part in the after-dinner discussion. But the subject had now landed in his domain.

'We looked into WATER right at the start and didn't really have many concerns. Your man Forster is a retired civil servant, but in no way a big hitter and he seems to have got into bed with a mildly awkward journalist. A bloke called Makepiece. Looks like he was set to be a big Fleet Street sensation but he got over-excited on his first big scoop and got his fingers severely burnt. Went running home to mummy and daddy with his tail firmly between his legs. He's not stupid though and we have had to deal with him on other constituency matters. Generally, he's firm but fair but we couldn't see that he was the source for much of the stuff that appears on the WATER website and campaign material. He's basically a decent journalist with perhaps a few contacts, nothing more than that.'

'So what's the problem?' said Mark, slightly irritated.

'It looks like they may have information relating to Torteville-les-Plages and neither Forster nor Makepiece have that sort of knowledge. There had to be someone else. And there is. There was a council building control officer, Michel Bernadetti, who supposedly found some problems and threatened to blow the whistle when none of his superiors would listen. Electricité de France managed to persuade the council to sack him and employed private detectives to keep an eye on him afterwards. They thought he might have held on to some documents and they didn't want him going to the press. He was doing casual work in and around Cherbourg for a while but they lost track of him altogether about twelve months ago. Electricté de France is owned by the French Government and James managed to pull some strings with the Foreign Office. French security services went digging and the last record they have of him is boarding a ferry in Cherbourg for Poole just under a year ago. Working backwards from the constituency, it didn't take long to find him. Bernadetti is working in Holmbeach at the Boar's Head pub, which is owned by Makepiece's parents.'

'We did have a problem with the French project,' said Mark after a short pause. 'There were some stress issues with the first modules from the factory in Ganirvan. We said we would replace them but the fucking French said no, they would source the units elsewhere, and they did. Now the cunts are refusing to pay the final instalment. The only saving grace is that they don't want to admit they made a mistake so put out the story about faulty welding needing to be re-done just to save face. But if some cunt has got that story, we could have a fucking big problem.'

A pin had just pricked the buoyant atmosphere which had been building in the lounge since dinner. Viktor filled his crystal glass one more time and declared, 'Would be no problem in Kyrgmanistan. We have very simple way of dealing with problem.'

'Quite so, Viktor,' said James. 'But Bicarel is a listed company on the fringes of the FTSE 100. We need to handle matters slightly more diplomatically. There are three avenues of this WATER campaign that we need to shut down. The easiest is the journalist. I only need to make a couple of calls and I think we can gag Makepiece, especially if the alternative threat is to shut down the newspaper. John Forster is slightly more tricky. He is a law-abiding citizen but an individual. I think a well-briefed law firm may well be able to blunt his enthusiasm, especially if it potentially involves expensive litigation. The French chap will be more difficult, but hopefully if we can deal with the first two, he will have nowhere to take his story.

'I wouldn't worry too much about Forster. If he reaches

the stage where he has to sell his house to pay his legal fees, he may just find that his fucking house isn't actually worth very much,' said Mark. 'Who would want to buy a bothy with no fucking power or water sitting in the middle of a fucking building site?'

'And I wouldn't worry too much about our Frenchman,' added Robert. 'If all else fails, I think I have a plan for him too.'

10 – Twenty-five months earlier

Holmbeach

John Forster woke to a bright sunny day at Coombe Farm. Well at least that's what he'd assumed. The land all around his smallholding, land that used to belong to his family before his decision to sell, now resembled an Iron Age burial ground. Conical mounds of earth as high as 15 metres surrounded his farmhouse, ensuring that almost no sunlight actually fell on his lounge or kitchen during the day. While his driveway still provided unhindered access to the lane, his journey to and from the main road almost always involved giving way to some piece of heavy plant or a delivery lorry. The drivers either didn't care or had been instructed not to engage with John, who had been brought up around these parts where a wave or greeting was obligatory between passing motorists or pedestrians. There had been minimal contact with the site management although the chief engineer had been courteous and even sympathetic after the first incident with the power cable. But it was fair to say that Coombe Farm and Bicarel Construction were not the best of neighbours. On mornings like this, John used to take a long walk with his binoculars before breakfast, but those days were long gone. And he doubted they would ever return, even if Thorpehead was finally completed – something he most certainly had not yet resigned himself to accepting.

As the kettle boiled for his first cup of tea for the day he heard the thud of the mail dropping through the letter box. It was not that long ago that he would have been able to see the postman's van approaching from his kitchen window but now he assumed that the postie also had to negotiate the lane with oncoming lorries and diggers. Gathering up the post from the doormat John returned to the kitchen to sort through it. These days, the bulk of the letters were for WATER and he would separate those off from his personal mail and give them to Marjorie to deal with. But in amongst them was a rather thick foolscap envelope bearing the logo of Bartram and Fripp, a London law firm. Intrigued, he opened it and sat down to read through the six pages of tightly packed text. Messrs. Bartram and Fripp were issuing a letter before action, not to WATER but to John personally on behalf of their client, Bicarel. Cutting through the veiled threats and legal terminology, it appeared that Bicarel believed John, through his public statements and media interviews on behalf of WATER, was potentially harming the reputation of the company at a crucial time in its business activity. Having successfully launched on the London Stock Market and recently won significant government contracts, negative and untrue stories about the company and safety of nuclear power could deter future investors and have a damaging impact on its share price. The fifth and sixth pages of the letter contained an annexe detailing each of the articles published about John and the relevant quotes on which Bartram and Fripp's contentions were based. This included the recent BBC *News Review* interview in which John had referred to the Bicarel power station in Normandy. At this early stage in proceedings, the solicitors were advising that their client was prepared to drop its action as long as the campaign group WATER was disbanded, that he undertook to make no further public comments about Bicarel and issued a statement (drafted by Batrtam and Fripp) about the safety of nuclear energy. The client would not seek damages as long as the legal fees were paid, but refusal to agree these terms would result in further and expensive legal action through the courts. John picked up his phone and called Jack.

'Hi John. How's life on the building site?' came Jack's cheery voice.

'Where are you? Something's come up. I need to speak to you and Michel straight away.'

'I've just arrived at the office. What's the problem?'

'I can't talk on the phone. There is something you both need to see.'

'OK then, no problem. Michel is working this morning so let's meet at the Boar's Head in half an hour.'

John left his tea, gathered up the solicitor's letter and jumped into the Defender. He slammed it into first and shot out of the drive and into the lane, totally oblivious to the low-loader which had to perform an emergency stop to avoid him.

Jack and Michel sat quietly in the pub lounge as they read through the detailed accusations in the letter.

'You know what this is, John?' said Jack. 'A SLAPP – a strategic lawsuit against public participation. Effectively, it's what rich people do to silence others who can't afford to defend themselves. That's what happened to me in London following my African telecoms story and it's the same bastard firm of solicitors. They are hired guns for any oligarch or crook who wants to keep their dirty secrets secret. Usually, it's journalists or publishers who they target. Even the Murdoch empire, with all its millions, has been known to give in rather than risk losing and picking up the tab.'

'So, they sue us for damages and WATER has no money to pay. Where's the problem?' asked Michel.

'It's what happened at my old newspaper. Our solicitors advised us that if we lost, the damages would not have been all that significant – judges are fairly restricted in their powers. But it's the cost awards that really hurt and Bartram and Fripp are renowned for that. There was one case which they won and were paid costs amounting to ten times the damages awarded to their client. And that's why the SLAPP is against John personally and not the campaign group.'

'So that's it then, we're screwed,' said John.' There's no way I can afford to defend a libel case.'

Michel was about to explode. 'You can't just wave the white flag at the first sign of opposition. We've obviously got Bicarel rattled. Let's look at what they are accusing you of in this letter,' he said, waving the weighty tome from the solicitors in a dismissive manner. 'All the statements they have listed here where you have supposedly been negative about Bicarel are backed up with facts. You haven't just dreamt up figures about water use or the damage to fish stocks. The costs of dealing with nuclear waste come from experts in the field and you have simply referenced them. And you didn't say anything about Torteville-les-Plages in your TV interview that could be traced back to the information that I have. This is what you call a fishing exercise, isn't it? They want to shut us down, I understand that. But they have nothing I can see in this letter. In fact, if they went to court, Bicarel would probably have to disclose more than we have so far in our campaign. I say 'fuck them'. Let them take it further.'

'That's easy for you to say, Michel,' said John. 'You're very much in the background of WATER and if it all goes belly-up, you can move on. I'm the one who lives here and I'm who they have got in their crosshairs at the moment.'

'I'm not sure how Barney will react either,' added Jack.

'If you've only just received that letter this morning John, who knows if they haven't sent something similar to *The Moorsman*. That business all but broke me when I was in London. I don't think I could go through it again, and Barney certainly doesn't deserve it.'

'But from what you say, this is what big companies do in order to silence opposition,' Michel responded. 'Are you really saying that after everything we have achieved so far. All the publicity, not just about Thorpehead, but people are beginning to question the need for nuclear power stations at all. Now, after one letter from a firm of fucking lawyer shysters, we just roll over and give up?'

'I'm not really sure that we have any alternative,' John said very quietly.

'*Je m'en fous des ces cons*,' shouted Michel. 'Of course we have an alternative. Jack, I am grateful for everything you and your family have done for me but honestly, I would not have come here if I thought this was how you would react when things get difficult. I had enough of that in Normandy. Everyone was too scared to challenge what was happening and in the end, I had to run and hide for my own safety. Bicarel are worried. That's all this letter tells us. We must stand up to them. Don't just give in. Show them we are not scared and let them decide what to do next. We know they cut corners with Torteville and there's no reason to believe they are doing anything different at Thorpehead. The question is whether they are prepared to risk that becoming public knowledge. We have to be strong.'

Jack and John remained silent for more than a few moments.

'I guess I need to check with Barney first to see if *The Moorsman* has had any contact from Bartram and Fripp,' said Jack.

'I'll have a word with Leonard at Baddock Associates in Riverbridge,' John added. 'They are your typical country lawyers, more used to farm sales and rights of way disputes than libel cases and SLAPPs. They would probably freak if I asked them to defend me but I have known Leonard since we were teenagers. He'd be happy to give me some advice over a pint. I'll give it some more thought before formulating our response to these solicitors.

'That's a relief. I'm on duty for the lunch shift in a while so let's agree to meet again tomorrow and discuss the next steps,' Michel said as he headed behind the bar into the staff quarters to change for duty.

Jack and John said their farewells. Jack was eager to see what sort of reaction he would get from Barney once back at *The Moorsman* and John navigated the Defender at a more sensible pace back towards Coombe Farm. When he walked back into the kitchen, this morning's cup of tea was still sitting on the breakfast bar, now stone cold and unappetizing with the tea bag still floating on the surface. Starting afresh, he tipped the brown liquid down the sink and went to refill the kettle. But when he turned on the cold tap, the trickle of water that came out was almost the same colour as the tea he had just jettisoned. He went to the bathroom and tried the tap there. The pipe vibrated and made an awful noise but nothing came out. Outside, just a sprinkle of water emerged from the garden hose when he turned on the tap there. Clearly, it was just the water which was left in the hosepipe from its last use. He had no cold water. For anyone else, it would have meant a call to the water board emergency number but Coombe Farm was fed by a local spring. There could only be one answer. John went back inside and called the construction company's site office. He got straight through to the manager he dealt with after the electricity supply had been 'accidentally' cut when one of the diggers collided with a post and the cable was cut.

'Hello again, John Forster from Coombe Farm here. I don't seem to have any fresh water. Is there anything you might be able to help me with?'

'Ah right. Coombe Farm, of course. I guess we should have thought of that. We've been working on the fresh water supply for the reactors and have begun laying pipes in the fields up around your way. That may have affected your supply.'

'What do you mean 'may have?' If you have tapped the spring then of course it's affected my supply!'

'Yes, I suppose you are right. Obviously, the water supply isn't needed until the reactors are operational but we had instructions to lay the pipework this week in preparation. The water is just diverted for now. We won't be connecting it to the power station for a while yet.'

Exasperated, John tried to remain calm. 'Yes, but in the meantime, you have cut off my water supply. That spring has served my land for generations. I want it reverted as soon as possible.'

'I'm sorry Mister Forster. I understand the spring has

been serving your farmhouse through a local pipe system for many years but the spring is actually located on our land. Land you sold a few years ago. Our workers had to remove your pipes this morning in order to lay our new system.'

More exasperated but no longer calm, John burst out.

'But I haven't even been consulted about this. Fresh water is a basic necessity for residential premises. How can you possibly do such a thing without even advising me? I demand you reconnect my water supply immediately!'

'I'm sorry Mister Forster. It seems our lawyers have been all through this. The spring is on our land and since the time you sold it to us, you have been tapping the water without our permission. Between you and me, there should have been some kind of agreement in the sale but head office says there definitely isn't. You may want to get yourself a lawyer to check things out from your end, but our guys are adamant.'

'But why on earth have you done the work today if you didn't need the water? If there was some sort of disagreement we could have resolved it without simply cutting the supply?'

'I can't tell you the answer to that Mister Forster. We receive our work schedules from head office and laying the new pipes was added to it just a couple of weeks ago. I am afraid you will need to speak to someone up there to find out why.'

John of course knew why. So it wasn't just solicitors' letters Bicarel were reverting to. They were playing dirty and cutting off the water was the latest part of the harassment, which began with the creation of earth mounds all around Coombe Farm and the ability to play fast and loose with the electricity supply. John picked up the letter from Bartram and Fripp and switched on his computer to compose his reply:

Dear Sirs,

I acknowledge receipt of your letter of 15th inst.

Having studied its contents carefully, I have the following comments:

In respect of your accusations detailed on pages 2 and 3 and items i to vii contained on the annexe (pages 5 and 6) …

GO FUCK YOURSELVES

Yours faithfully

John Forster

WATER

John printed the letter and signed it and just as he folded it into an envelope to post the next morning, the lights went out and the radio fell silent.

11 – Twenty-four months earlier

Holmbeach

Jack emailed the pictures he had taken of the overturned milk lorry on the A366 to Duncan back at the office. The road between Riverbridge and Holmbeach was blocked and the police were saying it was likely to remain so for the next three hours. Diversions were already being put in place and Duncan was busy updating *The Moorsman's* website and social media so readers would be aware. It would be old news by the time next week's paper came out and would probably only merit a picture story by then, but at least with social media there was immediacy and still a need for Jack's journalistic skills. He would usually upload stories like this to the website directly but out here, where the moorland hills dropped sharply to the coast, 5G was non-existent and the images were taking a long time just to send to the office. He wrote a brief 150-word summary and messaged Duncan so that he had everything to post the story. Duncan usually acknowledged receipt with a quick one-word reply or a thumbs-up emoji but when Jack's phone pinged, it wasn't him but the editor, Barney.

Can you come right back to the office pls? Important.

It was unusual for Barney to be following the news as it broke and even more unusual for him to be using text messages to contact Jack. *On my way.*

Michel was on the early shift today. There were no customers in the bar for morning coffees as yet but as he entered the room, he bumped into Mrs Makepiece coming in the other direction, holding the morning post.

'Perfect timing, Michel,' she said. 'You've got mail! Hope you haven't been breaking some local girl's heart!' she joked, handing over an envelope addressed to him at the Boar's Head.

'Thank you, Madame Makepiece. I have no idea who would be writing to me here.' Michel stuffed the envelope into his back pocket and went to take up his position behind the bar. But with no one to serve, he quickly removed it again. The envelope was handwritten and the postmark local. When he opened it, the message was typed and in French. It was from Elodie, the only person back in Cherbourg he had been able to trust and the one who had acted as gatekeeper, passing messages between him and Jack when they first met.

My dear Michel,

Excuse the unusual approach but this is probably the safest way to contact you. Things settled down after you left but just lately there have been people asking after you at your old apartment and at O'Brady's. I was also contacted out of the blue by someone who used to work at Electricité de France who says he knew you at the time you were with the council. He gave me a document which, if it is genuine, could be dynamite for the Torteville-les-Plages project. I didn't know what else to do so I have brought it with me to England. I arrived yesterday and I need to see you so that you can compare it with the other files you have.

I'll explain how I found you when we meet but please come to the Costa Coffee in Holmbeach tomorrow (Thursday) at 2 pm. Bring your files. If you cannot be there, find a way to leave a message for me there with an alternative arrangement. I am afraid to contact you any other way because I am almost certain my calls are being monitored. A demain. E.

Jack put his phone and iPad back into his messenger bag and, fortunate enough to have parked on the Holmbeach side of the road closure, was back in town within 15 minutes. He knew something wasn't right the minute he walked in the door. Duncan was head down, focused on his computer screen and refusing to look up. Susie said nothing, unusual in itself, and her eyes were red, as if she had been crying. Barney was at his office door, beckoning Jack in.

Jack started speaking as he sat down. 'I hope Duncan has got that story up. Traffic is going to be crazy. The police say there's no way any of the Thorpehead delivery lorries will get through and they are going to have to hold them at the motorway services.'

'Yes, everything is fine but that's not what I want to talk about. I have to tell you that I am retiring as editor of *The Moorsman* and there are going to be some major changes affecting both you and Susie.'

'What sort of changes, Barney?'

'Well, without beating about the bush, I am afraid that both of your positions are being made redundant. I have had head office on the line for an hour this morning. They are restructuring the way their regional titles operate, "rationalising management functions" is the term they used.'

Jack was still taking in Barney's statement. 'What exactly does that mean, Barney?'

'Well, up to now every one of Hollingsworth Media's local papers has operated independently. Now the bean counters have been looking at the costs and are worried about all the duplication across the group, so want to make savings.'

'But *The Moorsman* is doing well, isn't it?'

'Better recently than it has in the last few years but as you know Jack, newsprint is struggling everywhere with falling revenues, and Hollingsworth is no different.'

'So what does "rationalising management functions" mean for me then?'

'In short, instead of each title producing its own editorial and selling advertising, those roles will be handled by regional hubs. *The Moorsman* will be produced alongside other Hollingsworth titles in Devon and Somerset from an office in Taunton. They have already identified the staff they want to put into the Taunton hub and I am afraid that for you and Susie, they are offering redundancy. It's more than your statutory rights but I am afraid they have made it clear there is no point in you applying for a reporter post in Taunton. It looks like Duncan is being kept on to work on digital and social media, but he'll be working from home as the office here in Holmbeach will close. At least he will be able to finish his apprenticeship, so that's something I suppose.'

Jack was still too shocked to react the way his journalist training dictated he should, but gradually the news began to sink in.

'But *The Moorsman* is a key part of this community, Barney. We are the voice of West Tyneford. Look how the area has got behind us over Thorpehead. They trust us, they believe in *The Moorsman* and rely on it to find out what is really going on around here. How can anyone do that from an office in Taunton? *The Moorsman* will become nothing more than an admag full of press releases and puff pieces.'

'You don't think I have already said as much to head office? Believe me, I had no inkling this was going to happen. The last Hollingsworth editors' meeting I went to in London was only a couple of months ago and yes, they said things were not easy but there was no mention of rationalisation. This has come out of the blue, but believe me Jack, my hands are tied. I am so sorry for you both. Susie has been here almost as long as I have and you have been a breath of fresh air. Someone from Hollingsworth Human Resources is on their way to discuss your packages and they should be here by midday – assuming they can get through the road diversion.'

'And what about you, Barney?'

'Do you think I want to be part of a future *Moorsman* run out of Taunton? I don't for a minute imagine they want me either but at my age, early retirement is probably the easiest option.'

'So, when is this all supposed to happen?'

'Well, that's the thing, Jack. The next edition of *The Moorsman* will be produced in Taunton. When the HR guys arrive, you will need to hand over your keys, phone and iPad. I'm afraid, despite all your first-class journalism over Thorpehead, Jack Makepiece's last byline will be an overturned milk lorry on the Riverbridge road.'

What Jack, nor Barney for that matter, were aware of was the role played in the decision to close *The Moorsman* office by Sir Ian Davison, Chair of Hollingsworth Media. He had worked his way up from political reporter to editor of Hollingsworth's flagship daily, *The Clarion* and while in that role, was one of the standard bearers of the campaign to take Britain out of the European Union. Davison used his position of privilege to berate "unelected bureaucrats in Brussels" in regular leader columns. Few loyal readers of The Clarion were aware at the time that the pugnacious Scottish journalist also owned an enormous cereal farm covering a large swathe of Norfolk. Although the land was purchased with the rewards of his seven-figure salary as editor of the paper, the farm was profitable in no small part to agricultural subsidies running into several hundred thousand pounds a year and granted by those same unelected bureaucrats in Brussels. With Brexit secured, Davison was elevated from his role at *The Clarion* to the main board of Hollingsworth Media and was knighted shortly afterwards for services to journalism.

Prior to becoming a journalist, Ian Davison studied at Oxford University where he became friends at the debating society with a certain Malcom Whitleigh-Howse. Although both followed completely different career paths, they remained close friends long after graduating. So much so that, a few years later, Davison was honoured to be godfather to the Whitleigh-Howse's firstborn, James. He took a keen interest in his godson's development and educational achievements and when James branched out of the family business to create his own wealth fund, it proved to be the perfect place for the newspaper magnate cum cereal farmer to squirrel away some of his excess income.

So, several years later, it only took one phone call from the Honourable Member of Parliament for Holmbeach & West Tyneford about a bothersome newspaper in his constituency to spring an action plan at Hollingsworth Media. In truth, rationalisation of its regional newspaper group was already being considered seriously. It was widely known that *The Clarion* was haemorrhaging money in a spectacular fashion. Daily sales had plummeted to almost half the three million figure of pre-Brexit days, but the regional titles were also feeling the pain of dwindling sales and falling advertising revenue. Plans to cut costs, mainly by reducing the workforce, were a regular feature of Hollingsworth Media board meetings and the rationalisation plan Barney had just explained to Jack was indeed real. But what neither of them knew was that, rather than a nationwide roll-out of the group sales and editorial hubs, Taunton was actually the only one.

Duncan took a call from the Hollingsworth HR guys to say they were clear of the roadblock and would be at the office shortly. Barney called the team together for one last time. Choking back emotion, he addressed Susie, Jack and Duncan.

'As you know, *The Moorsman* has been my life. My father started it and while I had no one to leave it to, I must admit that I could see it being in safe and younger hands for the time when I was no longer around. Perhaps I should have walked away when I sold it to Hollingsworth but as virtually nothing changed, I admit I probably became complacent about the future. But now it seems they have chosen a future that is not to my liking, and obviously not to yours. I am sorry if I have let you down but please believe me when I say *The Moorsman* today would not be the paper it is without your involvement. You should be very proud of what you have achieved and whatever the future holds for you, please look back at your time here and be happy. When the Hollingsworth guys arrive, they want to speak to me and then they will go through arrangements for the future with you,

Duncan. One of them will then sit down with each of you, Susie and Jack. At that point, I will leave and take Duncan with me to the Boar's Head where we will wait for the two of you to join us. What happens for the rest of the day, I have no idea, but let's not forget we work in the newspaper industry and what that traditionally means when pubs are involved!'

Mutual hugs and kisses were interrupted by the arrival at the door of two well-groomed men in suits carrying briefcases. Later that day, while the Boar's Head was in full wake mode, two men locked the doors of a Holmbeach office on their way out, having turned off the lights of *The Moorsman* for the last time.

Michel walked down into Holmbeach town centre at 1.30 pm and took up a window seat in the local café on the opposite side of the road from Costa Coffee. In his messenger bag was the file of council documents he had brought with him when he left Cherbourg. Despite Elodie's explanation, receiving the letter had troubled him. The note was composed on a computer and only the address was handwritten – and then in block capitals. She had only signed herself 'E' so he had no clue as to her handwriting. Michel had not been in England for long, but it was long enough to notice the tell-tale differences between English and French handwriting styles. But in truth, he probably wouldn't have been able to recognise Elodie's own handwriting as the only non-verbal communication between the two of them had either been text or email. He decided to keep an eye on the Costa opposite to see if anyone arrived before the appointed hour or whether, when Elodie turned up, there was anyone following her. Unusually, Costa was virtually empty today and the only customers who arrived had bought takeaways and left again shortly afterwards.

At 1.59 pm Michel crossed the road, ordered an espresso and sat at a table at the rear of the cafe and kept his eyes on the door. Somehow the English even managed to make espresso coffee taste like dishwater but by the time he had drunk it, there was still no sign of Elodie. He asked at the counter whether anyone had left a message for him but the barista only confirmed what he already knew. It had been a quiet day. After another five minutes, Michel went back to the counter and engaged the barista in conversation, initially by describing his own job and where he worked. He then explained he was due to meet someone but had come out having forgotten his phone. Could he possibly borrow the barista's phone to call his friend and find out where they were? The young man obliged immediately as they were now clearly brothers in the same business. Michel knew Elodie's number by heart and while calling her would have gone entirely against her instructions, by now Michel was only seeking confirmation that his misgivings since receiving the letter were well placed. Holding the phone close to his ear so that the barista would not hear the continental ringing tone, he listened to the first three rings, then, 'Allo?' He recognised the voice immediately. It was Elodie, and she wasn't anywhere near Holmbeach. He cut the call but then pretended to have a conversation with a friend who had clearly forgotten their date.

Michel thanked the young barista, returning his phone with a shrug and suggested he come up and see him at the Boar's Head sometime. He then casually left Costa Coffee, but as soon as he turned the corner he sprinted down a narrow alley. He needed to be as far away from here as possible, and probably as far away from Holmbeach as he could get. But first, he needed to get back to the Boar's Head, if only to hand over his folder for safekeeping and to collect his passport.

He walked at a brisk pace so as not to arouse any suspicion, but as he reached the shortcut from the edge of the harbour, up the steps to the cliff top, a black VW Vito van came screeching to a halt alongside him. The side door opened and two pairs of hands expertly gripped each of Michel's shoulders and lifted him off his feet and into the back. The Vito was already heading off up the coast road before the side door had even closed.

The following morning, John Forster drove into the Boar's Head car park just before noon. He was taken aback to find Jack on the customer side of the public bar and already nursing a pint.

'Bit early for you. Are we celebrating something?'

'No, just me coming to terms with the fact I used to be a journalist.'

'Hair of the dog? You look like you've been here since yesterday.'

'You're not looking that great yourself,' Jack cut back before taking another swig of his beer.

'You try washing in bottled water and see how you would look. But that's not what you messaged me about is it? So what's the problem, Jack?' Jack brought him up to date with what had happened at *The Moorsman* the previous day, but now there was another problem too.

'It's Michel. He's missing.'

'How do you mean?'

'I mean missing. He's not at work and he's not in his

room. No one has seen him since yesterday. He didn't show for the evening shift but as we were all having our farewell party for *The Moorsman*, nobody really noticed.

'He can be a funny chap from time to time. Couldn't he have just met someone and decided he was having a better time than going to work? Or he's got pissed and is sleeping it off somewhere. We weren't due to meet again until this evening in any event. It's a bit soon to be getting worried about him, don't you think?'

'I said something similar to Mum, although to be fair, even that would have been out of character. She asked me to check out his room this morning so I went upstairs to have a look. His bed's not been slept in but there's a load of cash and his passport in his bedside table. The laptop he uses for the website is there, and so was this.' Jack pulled the letter from Elodie out of his pocket and handed it to John.

'Read it. It's from Elodie, the person we had to liaise with in Cherbourg. She said she had important news and wanted to meet. I went down to Costa Coffee this morning and spoke to the guy who was on duty yesterday. He says Michel was there but the person he was waiting for didn't show. So I called Elodie. She's in France, John and she didn't send Michel any letter. Didn't even know he was here.'

'The letter says to bring the file.'

'Yes. I didn't think about it when I first looked in his room but I came right back and searched thoroughly. Unless he had a secret hiding place, the folder's not there.'

'OK. I don't think we can do anything else but report this to the police.'

'Well, there are a couple of problems with that, John. First, Michel's an adult and he's not been missing 24 hours.

They're not going to do anything yet. But the bigger problem is nobody even knows he is here. I didn't know but Mum just told me he has been working off the books.'

'I didn't think for one minute that your parents did things like that.'

'They don't. Well, they didn't. Apparently, Michel was adamant. He didn't want to show up on any records. Normally they would have sent him packing at that but they were concerned for me. They knew I wanted him here, even though they weren't sure what for at the time.'

John was quiet.

'So, we have someone who is possibly being pursued in France and is living here illegally. He is in possession of sensitive and confidential material and involved with a campaign group trying to stop a government-backed nuclear power project. He goes missing and we can't involve the police. If they weren't before, things have just become very serious indeed, Jack.'

The *Marianna* was a converted bulk carrier contracted by Bicarel as part of the Thorpehead construction project. Ultimately, it would transport some of the modular reactor units on the last part of their journey from the factory in Kyrgmanistan to a specially built pontoon at the power station – thus avoiding any potentially hazardous journeys on the narrow roads of West Tyneford. But for now, the *Marianna* was acting as a supply ship, bringing down bulkier pieces of construction equipment from the Port of Bristol and taking away large quantities of ballast from the tunnelling to be disposed of further out at sea. The vessel's timetable was dictated by the tides and so it was no surprise to see its lights off the coast at Holmbeach at any time of night. Tonight was no different, other than for the Zodiac craft which launched off its starboard side and headed for the harbour. Holmbeach was asleep. The fishing boats had either set off for the night or were berthed alongside and both tourists and locals had long left the pubs and were tucked up in bed. The Zodiac's pilot cut the engine as he approached the harbour entrance and glided smoothly up to the slipway.

At that point, three men appeared from the black VW Vito which had been parked up on the harbour wall and removed an object from the rear doors. They carried what looked like a cylindrical tube about two metres long and around 80 centimetres wide down the slipway and carefully loaded it on board the Zodiac. The cylinder could have been any component for the massive water intake project still underway and if it had not been so dark, anyone watching this strange transfer of goods from land to sea would probably have noticed the two feet sticking out at one end of the structure. With the cargo safely on board, the Zodiac pilot pushed off and paddled the craft out beyond the harbour wall before starting the engine once again. While the black Vito made its discreet exit from Holmbeach, the Zodiac was winched back on board the Marianna which itself weighed anchor a short time later. With a hold of dredged mud, the ship was headed out into the Bristol Channel on one of its regular runs to the agreed dumping ground for waste from the tunnel construction.

12 - Twelve months earlier

The Moorsman front page article

THORPEHEAD GOES LIVE

This week will see the Thorpehead power station come on stream, heralding a new age for the nuclear industry and the country's energy security for decades to come.

The Prime Minister is travelling to Holmbeach this Friday, where he will perform the ceremonial commissioning of the revolutionary reactor, accompanied by the Minister for Energy and local MP James Whitleigh-Howse. The Holmbeach and West Tyneford MP lobbied hard for Thorpehead to be chosen as the first location for the new breed of Small Modular Reactors (SMRs) in the country. Two further sites have since been confirmed in Suffolk and North Wales and the Government expects to have as many as 10 new reactors in operation within the next decade. SMRs are factory-built in parts and then assembled on site, drastically reducing build times and start-up costs. Thorpehead opens this week, just five years since it was first announced.

A Ministry of Energy spokesperson told The Moorsman: "Thorpehead represents a new era for fossil-free energy generation in the United Kingdom. It has been built on time and within budget at a fraction of the cost of previous nuclear power projects. The country can look forward to many years of cheap, clean energy which is not at the mercy of political uncertainty in other parts of the world."

Holmbeach & West Tyneford MP James Whitleigh-Howse said: "I am so proud to be able to attend the official opening of Thorpehead. Apart from the clear and obvious benefits for the country, this project has already reaped rewards locally. The local economy has received a terrific boost in recent years while construction took place and we can look forward to new employment opportunities once the site is up and running."

Jack finished reading the article and then folded the newspaper back into its rack in the bar of the Boar's Head. He wondered briefly what sort of story he would have written if he was still the chief reporter at *The Moorsman*. Instead, the so-called editor in Taunton had simply copied and pasted the press release that either the ministry or Whitleigh-Howse's office had sent them. The weekly paper had been out for 48 hours already and today was actually the day that the bigwigs from London were in town to officially commission Thorpehead. It was still early and the public bar was not very busy. Jack continued tidying up in between serving the odd customer. Since being made redundant last year, working for his parents at the pub was the only job Jack had. The sudden and unresolved disappearance of Michel had at least created a vacancy.

The television mounted on the wall in the far corner of the bar was tuned to *BBC News 24* with the sound muted. But he didn't need sound, nor the rolling ticker across the bottom of the screen to tell him when the programme cut to the live broadcast of the Prime Minister at Thorpehead. Jack looked up at the screen and saw several familiar faces. On one side of the Prime Minister was the Energy Minister

Roland Smith, the one with who John Forster clashed during that live News Review broadcast. On the PM's other flank was James Whitleigh-Howse, smiling like the cat who got the cream. How long before a ministerial position came his way, Jack thought. There was even talk of him as a future party leader. In the background, Jack recognised Whitleigh-Howse's right-hand man, Robert Frost and another person who Jack assumed must have been Mark Ellrington from Bicarel. From what he understood, this was the brains behind the operation, the original owner and nephew of the Kyrgmanistan President having seemingly taken a back seat in the nuclear power station development.

Jack had to break off to take a food order at the bar from a couple who had come in earlier, and when he looked up again, the Prime Minister was pressing, or supposedly pressing the button which would pull the control rods partially out of the reactor, and thus commence generating nuclear power. So that was it. The moment Jack, Michel and John had dared to hope could have been prevented by the WATER campaign just a couple of years ago, had finally arrived. Was it just a pipe dream that they could have stopped it and with the public's support, make those in authority think again? Whatever it was, they had failed, and the people smiling at the cameras on the screen had got their way. As the BBC reporter handed back to the studio, a large family group walked through the door of the bar and Jack was immediately brought back to job in hand.

John Forster sat in the sunshine at his usual table and waited for his coffee. Of the various options in Reinosa this was his favourite spot for a morning caffe con leche during his weekly visit. The delightful old town nestled in the foothills of the Picos de Europa in Cantabria, one of the autonomous regions of Northern Spain. John was living in a cottage only a few kilometres out of town but at the top of a steep and winding track. Once a shepherd's hut, the stone-built structure was warm in winter and cool in summer, having been entirely renovated with every modern convenience by the municipality just a few years earlier. John was renting his two-bedroom retreat from the council for a mere €200 a month. While it had running water and electricity (something that was missing at Coombe Farm) the phone signal was almost non-existent, and so a major part of his weekly trips down into Reinosa also included a chance to catch up on the online newspapers on his tablet thanks to the café's Wi-Fi. If his coffee tasted a little bitter today, it was probably due to all the reports he was reading about the opening of Thorpehead. From *The Clarion* to the *Finance News*, all were gushing in their praise for bringing the power station online so quickly and for the future prospects for energy security. Even titles which had been sympathetic to the WATER campaign at the time appeared to be jumping on the bandwagon in support of the government.

After telling the law firm Bartram and Fripp to stick their cease and desist letter where the sun didn't shine, things had taken a turn for the worse. The London solicitors did not heed John's advice and proceeded with the next steps in their threatened action on behalf of Bicarel. Coombe Farm came under repeated siege from the Thorpehead construction work. Even after the phase of the building work involving the access road was complete and the mechanical diggers had moved on, mounds of spoil still regularly appeared overnight outside the farmhouse. The electricity would be 'accidentally' cut off on a regular basis, causing John to wait for 24 hours to be reconnected. He had given up using his freezer and the digital clocks around the house (oven, microwave, TV) all told different times or simply flashed as John could no longer be bothered to reset them each time. Even the legal action against Bicarel, taken by the electricity company, failed to have any impact. They simply paid whatever fines or compensation sought by the power provider, but never a penny to John. The water problem was unresolvable. Bicarel owned the land where the spring rose and refused him permission to tap it. The cost to connect Coombe Farm to the mains was almost as much as the property was worth in its current state and John had even reverted to joining the local gym in Holmbeach. He had never used a treadmill or an exercise bike in his life but the monthly subscription gave him access to a shower and a flushing toilet. And then there was Michel. He had vanished into thin air. There had been no signs he was unhappy or frightened, quite the opposite in fact. It was clear nobody in France had seen him so he hadn't gone home. As they hadn't alerted the police, there had been no search for Michel. But if he had had an accident or fallen on a cliff path it wouldn't have been long before he was discovered. There really wasn't any other explanation, other than something sinister had happened. When John launched his WATER campaign the intention was to mobilise public opinion against the plan for Thorpehead. At no point did he anticipate being in danger. But then came litigation, his house under siege and, he was sure, threats to his own safety.

So enough was enough. He told Batrtam and Fripp he would wind up WATER if they took no further action. He put Coombe Farm on the market, knowing that the only likely purchaser of the house and small holding in its current state would be Bicarel. Although only a fraction of its true value before construction work began, they made a reasonable offer for the property even though when the cheque finally arrived, the lawyers acting for Bicarel, Bartram and Fripp had deducted their own sizeable costs. But it was enough for John, along with his civil service pension, to live comfortably somewhere else. He loaded two suitcases of his most valued possessions into the Defender and boarded the ferry for Spain. Arriving in Santander, he headed south and up into the Picos de Europa.

It didn't take long to find his perfect retreat, the cottage where he could return to the sort of life he was enjoying at Coombe Farm before anyone mentioned Thorpehead. Now he could set out each morning with his binoculars and camera in search of snow finches or wallcreepers while high above, he was regularly supervised by Egyptian vultures circling on the thermals. Although the coast was less than an hour away, here the scenery was positively alpine. At around 1,000 metres above sea level it was cooler than the coast in summer and not as severe as higher up in the Picos during winter. But there were distinct seasons and corresponding changes in the fauna to enjoy. His weekly jaunts down to Reinosa to stock up, catch up on the news and enjoy a leisurely lunch provided about as much company as John craved. For the rest of the time he was at ease with his thoughts, his camera and the wildlife. But today, he was not in Northern Spain but, on reading all the British newspapers online, he was back at Thorpehead and the morning sun had turned to chill.

In the Thorpehead operations centre, hardly anything appeared to change once the Prime Minister had supposedly pushed the magic button to start the withdrawal of the control rods. Initialising nuclear reaction was actually a lengthy process which had taken up much of the preceding three days and the control staff seemed totally unfazed by their VIP photo opportunity.

But once the obligatory pictures had been taken and the media teams had been ushered out, the visitors began to separate. The Prime Minister was whisked off to board a waiting helicopter while Roly Smith's private secretary was waiting to escort him to the ministerial car. Robert and James were in the next car in the convoy, following the minister's security detail while Mark Ellrington brought up the rear in his chauffeur-driven Range Rover Sentinel. As they reached the security gate at the Thorpehead exit, a single protester stood outside holding a placard. On one side it read Everyone needs WATER, on the other, Thorpehead equals alongside an image of the radioactive warning trefoil. As the cars drove by, Marjorie twirled the placard to ensure the occupants saw both messages.

Part Two

13 - The day it happened

Thorpehead

The first flashing red light and alarm in the control room was the feedwater pump. The second was the reactor temperature alert. In all his time at Thorpehead, Mischa had never seen the gauge at anything other than 315oC. Suddenly, the reading was 750oC and rising.

'Coolant alert,' Gordon Landseer announced calmly. 'Either the pump generators have tripped or we have steam bubbles in the reactor. Reboot the pumps for Tunnel One.'

This was a standard operational drill that Mischa had performed several times as part of his final year of on-the-job training. But after depressing the switch for more than 15 seconds, nothing was happening and another bank of red lights glowed menacingly. The reactor temperature was over 1,000°C.

'We'll have to switch to the back-ups but we're going to have to do something about the temperature,' said Landseer, a little more urgency in his voice now. 'Giles, switch to back-up pump generators, but if we can't cool the reactor the fuel rods will become exposed and the pressure level will reach critical. We'll have to prepare for venting.'

Venting is the controlled release of gases from the reactor into the atmosphere in order to reduce the pressure and is only ever considered a last resort. With everybody in the control room's attention focused on the pump functions and the reactor temperature, nobody was watching the screens monitoring the outside cameras. For the last two hours the camera pointing out to sea had been feeding back images of a grey sky and a grey sea, whipped up by the gale force winds as it moved closer to the shore and higher up the Thorpehead sea defences. The power of the ocean as it advances on an incoming tide is an intoxicating sight. The irresistible force had been meeting the immovable object of the 15-metre-high sea wall with increasingly spectacular results as high tide approached. The defences had been winning until, shortly after 9.30 am, shock waves from the tremor three miles below the surface gave the onrushing Atlantic Ocean even more momentum and suddenly waves started to break over the wall at Thorpehead. The nightmare scenario that some had feared, but was convincingly dismissed by Bicarel as such an unlikely combination of natural and atmospheric events as to be almost impossible, had just come about. The sea defences were not sufficient and Britain's great white hope for the future of nuclear power was now at the mercy of the elements. Gordon Landseer was right. This breach was too small and too far away to be a threat to the reactor, but the power plant at a lower level was not so immune.

Giles had completed the start-up process for the emergency cooling pumps – but nothing was happening. A check on the input levels showed not thousands of litres per second but zero.

'It's the intake pipes, Boss. The pumps are running but

there's no water coming in,' he called out the Landseer.

'Prepare to open the vents. We have to cool the reactor.'

'What about contamination?' shouted Mischa. The reactor temperature reading now was at 2,200°C.

'Should be mainly Xenon and it will be easily dispersed in this weather.' Gordon Landseer decided to take control of the venting process in any event but before he could key in the command to open the vent, the next alarm started to sound.

As waves continued to break over the sea wall, once inside the perimeter the water had nowhere to drain away. First port of call was the electricity sub-station in front of the reactor building. In the control room, the screens went blank and the overhead lights went out, leaving the red flashing alarms as the only source of illumination until the diesel generators kicked in. As the systems slowly started to reboot in the gloom of the emergency lighting, the first thing Mischa noticed was the reactor temperature which was now showing at 2,760°C.

'The fuel rods will melt if we don't start cooling now,' he shouted.

'We're on emergency power, boss,' said Giles. 'It's only driving the system. It won't be enough to open the vents.'

Gordon Landseer spoke as he acted. 'We're shutting down the reactor. It's the only option we have left.'

With emergency power back on, the phone lines were ringing. The Bicarel operations centre in Milton Keynes wanting to know what was going on, then the foreman from the reactor building warning of strange noises coming from the core. Mischa kept his eye on the temperature readings which were still rising. But with no venting until power was restored and no water being pumped, the fuel rods in the reactor were still in grave danger of melting. There was still no explanation for the lack of water being pumped, but now that the external camera screens were back on, it was easier to explain the loss of power. Waves were no longer breaking over the sea defences but the Atlantic Ocean was now over a metre deep on the inside of the wall.

Mischa kept watching the temperature gauge. It was now 3,000°C and an eardrum-splitting alarm sounded in the control room. Without any pumps working, there was no more coolant and all the remaining water was turning into steam, increasing the pressure even further. Mischa felt the walls of the control room starting to shake. Then, inside the reactor the build-up of hydrogen reacted with the oxygen from the steam. The last thing Mischa heard was the tremendous roar of the explosion before masonry began falling from the ceiling and the supposedly airtight door to the control room was blown off its hinges, sucking in a metallic grey cloud of steam.

Without any coolant, the uranium fuel rods inside the reactor had raised the temperature almost to the surface of the sun. The remaining water had been turned into steam and the pressure between the reactor and the outer concrete shell had increased off the scale. When the outer wall was breached, the hydrogen bubble reacted with the oxygen with devastating effect. The reactor building, along with anyone who had been working in it, were simply vaporised while the walls of the adjacent control building collapsed, bringing the ceiling crashing down on the Thorpehead nerve centre.

The explosion in the reactor reduced the control rods, uranium fuel and zirconium casing into tiny particles which were sucked into the air and carried away on the gale-force south-westerly wind. The cocktail of gases included iodine 131, cesium 137 and plutonium 239. The core of the reactor continued to glow bright red as it burned at over 3,000°C. The torrential rain being dumped onto Thorpehead by Storm Hilda did nothing to extinguish the fire but simply added steam, laden with radioactive aerosols, to the rising plume of black smoke and orange sparks.

With wind speeds of over 110 kilometres an hour and driving rain, the plume did not rise very high into the atmosphere but was carried inland quickly before falling as radioactive rain. Local residents, at home and sheltering from the storm, soon noticed the raindrops crashing against their windows taking on a greyish black hue. Meanwhile, radionuclides continued to boil in the reactor core.

They didn't need the alarm to sound at Thorpehead's own fire station. The crew on Alpha watch had heard the roar and felt the blast of air at almost the same time. With dedicated appliances and crews, having 24/7 fire and rescue services on site was a legal requirement but in reality, the job was little different from any other fire station. In the first twelve months of operation, call-outs had mostly been to deal with diesel spillages from heavy goods vehicles, small electrical fires in the administration block and one 'rescue' of a staff member who had accidentally locked himself in a store room.

Martin Walsh, the watch commander had ordered they wear their Tyvek suits as they set off from the station, just inside Thorpehead's perimeter fence, towards the source of the black billowing cloud. He knew this was what he and the team had trained for and why their posting was different from any other fire station. But at the same time, if this was what he thought it must be, he had no idea how one fire appliance would make the slightest difference. The driver was struggling to keep the engine on the road against the wind and the windscreen wipers were fighting a losing battle against the driving rain. The job was made even more difficult by the black smears the wipers were leaving on the glass, almost as if it was oil and not water that they were driving through. The one piece of non-standard equipment this fire appliance had on board was a radiation detector. No one had ever paid much attention to the dial. Since the power station had opened, the reading had always indicated normal levels of background radiation around 0.5 roentgen per hour. But no sooner had they left the garage and the appliance became soaked in the driving grey coloured rain, the red light was flashing and the reading had leapt to 200 roentgen per hour.

'Shit, look at that!' said Martin. 'If this reading is correct, we are only going to have 15 minutes' exposure before we need to retreat.'

When they reached the administration block, the crew could see almost every window and blown out and internal blinds being blown through the gaps by the gale-force wind. Staff were emerging from the main entrance, many with bloodied faces or helping colleagues who had clearly been caught by flying glass. But immediately beyond the building lay the confirmation of all of watch commander Martin Walsh's fears. The dome-shaped structure which housed the reactor simply was not there anymore. In its place was a roaring cauldron belching out spark-tinged black smoke and steam. Between that and the fire engine stood the remains of the control building, like a half-fallen house of cards.

'What do we do now, boss?' one of the crew called from

the rear of the cab.

'Breathing equipment and we carry out search and rescue in the control building,' Martin replied calmly. 'But we have 10 minutes max. Then we are all out of here.'
The Geiger counter inside the cab was now reading 1500 roentgen per hour.

The breakfast room at the Boar's Head was usually empty by 9 am but today, every table was still occupied. The walking group which had booked every room at the hotel, had clearly had to abandon their plans to walk the coastal path once they had received the weather forecast. So, instead of rising at first light and heading off on what is normally a demanding but nevertheless rewarding trek south along the Bristol Channel to Moretenshaw and the bus back to Holmbeach, they were embarked on indoor pursuits. Last night's hastily arranged quiz evening was adjudged a triumph and many of the group remained in the bar chatting and drinking into the early hours. Despite this morning's later-than-usual start, all were in good spirits and Jack had already set up the digital projector in the bar for one of the group to give a talk on the fauna of the area which they would not be able to see in person on this occasion. Jack was in charge for a few days. His parents, grateful for the way in which he had settled back into the family business, had decided to reward themselves with a few days away.

Jack and one of the waitresses were collecting empty breakfast plates from the tables when they heard the blast. At almost the same time, the building shook as a violent blast of air hit the Boar's Head. The hotel had been under the cosh of a gale force storm for the last 24 hours, but this was different. It was far stronger and faster than anything that had preceded it and the outside benches and tables in the pub garden which had so far resisted Storm Hilda because they were bolted into the ground, were lifted and carried way down the road. Everyone stopped talking and looked inquisitively at one another.

'What was that, Jack?' the group organiser called out.

'No idea Mister Beresford. Looks like the storm is intensifying, but as for the bang? Sounded as if it was coming from Thorpehead.'

Jack took his phone from his back pocket to see if there was anything on social media or if the Met Office had upgraded the storm threat. But as the force of the explosion had carried away the 5G masts in the area, all Jack could see on his phone was the 'No internet service' message. He turned on the TV in the bar area and switched to the BBC local channel to see if anything would be announced there and then went back to clearing away the breakfast plates.

Within a few minutes, the walkers sitting at the front of the hotel began to hear a siren and the sound of a loud hailer announcement. At first, the sounds were muffled against the roar of the Atlantic winds but the message, which was being repeated, became louder and clearer. Jack returned from the kitchen into the breakfast room just as a police Landrover with its blue lights flashing emerged onto the coast road outside the Boar's Head.

"THERE HAS BEEN AN INCIDENT AT THE THORPEHEAD POWER STATION. PLEASE STAY INDOORS AND KEEP ALL WINDOWS CLOSED. STAY TUNED TO A RADIO OR TV. WE WILL PROVIDE MORE INFORMATION AS SOON AS WE HAVE IT, BUT DO NOT GO OUTSIDE UNDER ANY CIRCUMSTANCES."

At that precise moment, a ticker appeared across the bottom of the TV screen repeating the same message, although there was not yet any interruption to the programme and so some minor celebrity was still demonstrating how to make the perfect pancake.

'Listen to that, "stay indoors"', said one of the walkers. 'Do they really think we would be going outside or opening a window in this weather!'

'It's unusual though. Especially if it involves the power station,' Jack replied. Life had settled back into some sort of routine over the last twelve months since *The Moorsman* and the campaign against Thorpehead. But he was lost for a moment as he remembered all the concerns over the construction and Michel's stolen files from France. The colour drained from his face and a sense of panic kicked in.

He told all the guest to return to their rooms and check that they hadn't left any windows even slightly open and set about doing the same in the public areas, shutting the main door to the hotel, the kitchen service area and bar cellar. Still checking that he had no service on his phone, he returned to the bar and the TV to wait for more news.

Shelley Marsden had woken during the night at the noise of the rain smashing into the bedroom window. They had warned that the storm was coming and that's why school was cancelled today. The fourteen-year-old pulled the duvet up over her head and, doubly cocooned against the elements and no prospect of an alarm going off on her phone, slept soundly until gone 9 am. She put on her dressing gown and went downstairs. Unusually, there was no sound of breakfast TV coming from the kitchen. Mum always watched Good Morning West while she made their breakfasts and packed lunches for school. But today, there was just a box of cereal and an open carton of milk on the work surface. On the settee in the far corner of the room, Evan, her nine-year-old brother was perched with a bowl of Cocoa Krisp on one knee and his mobile on the other. Headphones on, he was oblivious to anything else other than what was on the screen, so much so that every other spoonful of cereal had failed to make it all the way to his mouth, creating an abstract pattern on his pyjama top instead. Shelley yanked the headphones off, causing Evan to spill yet another part of his breakfast.

'What do you think you're doing?'

'I didn't want to wake you, that's all.'

'Didn't want anyone to know you are on TikTok, more like. Mum will go mad. You know you're not supposed to watch it.'

'Yeah, well Mum's not here. There's a note.'

Shelley went back to the breakfast bar and picked up the scrap of paper resting against the toaster.

Hi, you two,

Sorry, was asked to go in during the night. Somebody had called in sick and they were short. I know there's no school today so said OK. Make yourselves breakfast but don't please go out, the storm is really blowing up. I'll wait until Dad finishes his shift and we'll come back together in time for lunch.

Be good and Evan, do what your sister says.

Love Mum xxx

P.S. No TikTok Evan!

'See what she says, Evan? No TikTok!'

'Yeah, well she's not here and you're not my mum!'

Shelley thought about enforcing the "do what your sister says" part of the message but knew from past experience that it would be useless. The last thing she wanted on a day off from school was to be fighting with her brother. It was happening quite regularly since she turned fourteen that her mum would leave her in temporary charge of her younger brother. Dad worked at Thorpehead Power Station. He was some kind of engineer and they had moved to Holmbeach last year from Cumbria when the new station opened. Mum was a whizz with computers and had all sorts of qualifications. She hadn't been working before they moved but had found a part-time position at Thorpehead doing something in the operations centre. They must have thought she was good, as they kept asking her to do shifts and cover for other people. With Dad mainly working nights, she tended to fit her work around when Shelley and her brother were at school, but just recently she seemed to be getting calls to help out at all times of day, and night. It was gone nine now, and when Dad finished his shift he was usually home before midday, so she only had to put up with Evan for a couple of hours, So probably better to let him carry on watching TikTok and feign ignorance when Mum got home. The alternative would be to take his phone away and then find something else to entertain him for the next two to three hours.

Just then, there was a gust of wind that rattled all the windows, and it was far worse than anything Shelley had heard during the night. It was followed by a loud explosion. Evan stopped watching TikTok, not because he was distracted by the noise, but because his screen went blank.

'What's happening, Shel?'

'I don't know Ev. Thunder maybe?'

'It was much too loud for thunder. And my phone has gone dead.'

At Furzebrook House, just outside Burford, Charlotte Whitleigh-Howse was seated in front of her computer in the study, anxious to finish writing this month's newsletter for the local hunt. With the primary school closed due to the bad weather, daughters Daisy and Margot were busy with their assignment. Charlotte had promised them if they both painted a picture with the theme of a stormy day, then the rest of the morning would be spent baking cupcakes. They all heard the roar and the whole house shook a second later as the air blast hit. Charlotte leapt from the desk and headed downstairs to the lounge to find the girls looking out of the window.

'What was that, Mummy?' Daisy asked.

'I don't know, dear. Please come away from the window though. It's not safe.'

The sound outside had returned to the howl of the gale-force wind, and Charlotte knew that the air blast coming so close behind the boom could only mean an explosion. And she knew instinctively where it had come from. With that, the daylight started to fade and the sky darkened.

'Carry on with your painting, girls. I am just going to call Daddy.'

But Margot, the younger of the two girls was still fascinated by what was happening outside.

'Look, Daisy, it's snowing and the snow is black.'

The rain had been unrelenting since they went to bed the previous evening. But now it was falling as large, grey flakes. Irradiated graphite particles from the disintegrated core, together with radioactive cesium and xenon particles were coating any surface the rain fell with a black film.

Charlotte rushed back upstairs to the study and grabbed her phone off the desk. No signal. She ran into the bedroom and tried the landline on the bedside table. It was still working. She got straight through to James's office at Westminster and the call was answered by Robert. James had a select committee this morning and was going directly to Prime Minister's Questions from there. Charlotte told Robert about the blast coming from the Thorpehead direction and he told her not to worry, he would make enquiries and call her back. With that, she went back downstairs to the lounge, but the girls were not there. Two half-finished paintings of people with umbrellas battling against the wind were strewn across the table. She tried the kitchen but they weren't there either. Then she heard the joyful screams and cries coming from outside. As Charlotte looked through the window, she saw Daisy and Margot in their raincoats and wellies jumping up and down in puddles of black water and covered in grey flecks of ash.

14 - One hour later

News 24.com

10.20 am: Incident at nuclear power station

We are receiving news of an as-yet-unspecified incident at the nuclear power station at Thorpehead, located on the Bristol Channel.

Emergency services are in attendance following reports of an explosion. Local residents are being told to remain indoors and the Government has convened a meeting of COBRA. Little else is known about the extent or the source of the explosion at this stage and the area has been battered by gale-force winds over the last 24 hours as Storm Hilda makes landfall in Britain.

Earlier this morning, BBC Western reported that a tremor measuring 4.5 on the Richter Scale had been recorded with its epicentre in the Bristol Channel with shocks felt in Holmbeach, the nearest town to Thorpehead. It is not known yet whether there is any connection between the seismic activity and the incident.

Thorpehead opened just 12 months ago in the vanguard of the Government's policy to develop nuclear energy using a new breed of small modular reactors.

More news to follow …

Cabinet Office Briefing Room, Whitehall

The Cabinet Office Briefing Room sits below the Cabinet Office at 70 Whitehall with underground access from 10 Downing Street. Its name gave birth to the adjusted acronym, COBRA, now commonly used to describe meetings of the Civil Contingencies Committee. COBRA is a key part of the national security framework and its work within the Cabinet Office is to assess risks to national security and coordinate cross-government resilience and response to catastrophic emergencies. Today's COBRA meeting had been convened following news of a nuclear incident at the Thorpehead power station. The room was subtly lit, allowing the glow from the large multi-screen array on the far wall to dominate. Weather maps and charts were displaying on the different screens while to one side, a freestanding TV monitor was blank for the time being. A large, oval boardroom table took up most of Briefing Room 1 while alcoves set in the side walls housed members of the Civil Contingencies Secretariat either working at their laptops or in hushed conversation on their phones.

Seated around the table already were the Home Secretary Nadia Yadav, Defence Secretary Nicholas Stanley-Hutchinson, Field Marshal Leighton Parks, Chief of the Defence Staff and Mark Brooks, Permanent Under Secretary to the Cabinet Office and Director of Civil Contingencies. They were joined by Bridgette McAndrew, Deputy Director of MI5 and Professor Derek Beaumont, the Government Chief Scientific Officer. Two seats at the centre of the table remained unoccupied until the briefing room door was opened to usher in the Prime Minister Gordon Strathyre and his cabinet secretary Archie Wilkes. Strathyre took his seat, slamming a folder down on the table in front of him.

'This meeting of COBRA has been called in response to an incident at Thorpehead nuclear power station this morning. Mark, can you please tell us what the fuck has just happened?'

All eyes turned towards the Civil Contingencies Director who was seated at the end of the table nearest the display. By this time, the freestanding screen had come to life as Deputy Chief Constable Oliver Merton, the Gold Commander based at Exeter had joined the meeting via Zoom.

'At nine-fifty-eight this morning, the core reactor at Thorpehead exploded, causing catastrophic damage in the immediate vicinity and releasing radioactive steam into the atmosphere. The severe weather in the area is carrying that steam and other radioactive particles in an easterly direction at speeds in excess of 60 miles per hour. There are fire crews on site but they are already encountering high levels of radiation around the reactor and have withdrawn to a safer distance. The fire in the reactor continues to burn. The major threats we are currently faced with are containment of the fire, public safety in the area around Thorpehead and the radioactive cloud which is travelling across England as we speak.'

'What's the position on the ground, Gold Command?' the Prime Minister asked.

Oliver Merton's face filled the screen closest to where Mark Brooks was seated.

'We have fatalities and injuries at the power station itself. The control centre has collapsed and everyone working there is either trapped beneath the rubble or presumed dead.

Further from the reactor, the administration block has been severely damaged, with casualties on their way to Riverbridge Hospital. Injuries are mainly from flying glass and debris but the hospital has declared a critical emergency. The fire chief says it is impossible to get close to the reactor due to the high levels of radiation. Even with full protection, firefighters would be limited to a few minutes at most and given the likely heat, it would need a concentrated response with an army of firefighters that currently we don't have. Local residents are being told to stay indoors and close all windows until we know more. But at the same time, we are putting measures in place to evacuate Holmbeach and Burford. We are setting up reception centres in Riverbridge and to the south to house those evacuated temporarily. Riverbridge itself is eight miles south of Thorpehead and appears for the moment to be unaffected by fallout. We will be taking regular readings but radiation levels are currently not causing concern. If the situation changes then we will have to consider evacuating Riverbridge and the hospital, which is currently our primary response centre.'

'What about this cloud?' asked the Prime Minister.

'If I may, Prime Minister.' Attention focused Professor Derek Beaumont.

'You should all be able to see the weather map on the screen. The Met Office are updating wind speeds and direction on a minute-by-minute basis. Overnight, there were storm-force winds battering the coast from a south-westerly direction. As we go through the morning, these have been abating and the direction has changed slightly. We don't as yet know the cause, but it does appear that pressure has built up within the core reactor to the extent that it has overwhelmed the containment vessel. This will have sent a plume of steam containing radioactive elements from the core, together with debris, into the atmosphere. Not only is this being carried by strong winds but it is falling as contaminated rain along its path.'

'How big is this cloud likely to be?'

'Well, that's the problem we have. For as long as the fire continues to burn in the reactor, radioactive particles will continue to be released in the steam. We don't know yet what temperature the fire is burning at, so we can't rule out China Syndrome as yet either'

'China Syndrome? That was a Jane Fonda film, wasn't it?'

'It was. But while the story was fiction, the phenomenon is real. A severe nuclear core meltdown can theoretically burn through the containment structure below the reactor and continue through the Earth's crust. We will need to monitor the situation very closely in the coming hours.'

'And you are saying that in the meantime the fire will continue to fuel a radioactive cloud which will cross the country?'

'What about us? Will it affect London?' the Home Secretary speaking for the first time in the meeting.

Mark Brooks took over. 'If we can enlarge the weather map screen you will be able to see the Met Office modelling that Professor Beaumont was referring to. You will notice the vectors changing very slightly now. The situation has settled to a degree over the last thirty minutes or so, and you can see the wind direction indicators are plotting a defined path across the country. As the Gold Commander has said, we do not know at this stage how long the fire will continue to throw up radioactive particles, but based on the predicted wind speeds over the next twelve hours you can see what the worst-case scenario looks like.'

There was a collective gasp around Cabinet Office Briefing Room 1 as, on the central screen, a red ribbon was superimposed on the map of the British Isles. Highlighted beneath the red band were white dots and the locations they represented on the map. Bristol, Swindon, Harlow, Chelmsford, Harlow, Felixstowe.

'There must be a million people living in those places,' the Home Secretary said. 'We'll never evacuate them all before the cloud reaches them.'

'Probably closer to two million, Home Secretary, once you factor in the towns and communities between those major population centres. Likewise, we don't know at this point how wide the affected area may be. The band on the map here is purely an estimate at this stage. These are gale-force winds and it's quite likely that particles will be dispersed over a wider area. The Met Office says that areas to the south of the line are less likely to be affected, but if you take a parallel line north,' Mark clicked the mouse on his laptop.

'You can see what other areas could be affected.' With that, an orange band appeared across the map, sitting adjacent to the red one.

'Cardiff, Newport, Oxford, Luton and Ipswich are all at risk. We are setting up monitoring along the route as we speak, but the truth is, at this early stage, we have no idea how far the radiation will travel or how wide the contaminated fallout zone will be.'

'I should remind you of two important factors,' Professor Beaumont added. 'The first is that as we speak, radionuclides continue to boil in the reactor at Thorpehead and particles are being released into the atmosphere. That will continue until such time as the fire is under control. The second is that while those particles continue to be carried on the wind, in many areas they are falling as rain and contaminating anything they land on – not just fields but buildings, vehicles and people.'

'Tell me this is not happening,' Strathyre murmured. 'We have no other option than mass evacuation, starting with Bristol.'

'Agreed, Prime Minister. We have civil contingency plans for evacuations within cities but this is beyond anything we have ever been tasked with modelling. The Bristol city area has four-hundred-and-fifty-thousand inhabitants before you count the suburbs. We'll need to make similar arrangements for other towns and cities along the route, even if only precautionary until we know more about the contamination.'

'And we don't know yet if this is an accident or an attack?'

'We have not ruled out terrorism at this stage, Prime Minister.' MI5 Deputy Director Bridgette McAndrew replied. 'The Director is in a briefing with CCHQ as we speak, but there has been no chatter picked up in recent weeks which would indicate any immediate threat to our nuclear facilities. We are continuing to monitor traffic and the security level raised at our other power stations.'

'Right,' said the Prime Minister. 'I am going to call the Palace to inform the King I intend to invoke the 2015 Civil Emergencies Act. Mark, you are to commence evacuation procedures in the Bristol area with the support of the military. COBRA will remain in session and we will re-convene in three hours.'

With that, Prime Minister Gordon Strathyre rose and left Cabinet Office Briefing Room 1 along with Archie Wilks to return to his office and a phone call to the King.

In 10 Downing Street, having put the phone down following a lengthy conversation with His Majesty, in which he was reminded that the King's private residence possibly lay along the path of the radioactive cloud, Gordon Strathyre sat back in his leather chair and gazed out into the Rose Garden below. This really was not what he had signed up for when he went into politics. Every MP talks about serving their country and serving their constituents. Indeed, he had said something along similar lines on the steps of 10 Downing Street only a few months earlier when, after a fairly bloodless coup had deposed the previous incumbent, he had come up hard on the rails to win the election for party leader.

Unlike the previous Prime Minister, Gordon Strathyre was the poster boy of his fellow MPs and party members as well as the country's first unelected leader for more than two decades. While that fact annoyed the opposition and what little remained of the liberal-based media, it didn't bother him. For Gordon Strathyre, politics was a means to an end. He only scraped into Oxford thanks to his father's influence, thus maintaining the generational heritage of male Strathyres at Keble College. He left with a degree of sorts but no real plans until a friend got him a job at a London PR firm. Here, Gordon was in his element. His magnetic personality and natural gift of the gab ensured he was the centre of attention in any room and he always had a tale to tell – even if it was not actually based on truth. It didn't take long to build up strong, and in many cases, personal relationships with key journalists and editors and he became the go-to man for fashion brands and celebrities looking to bolster their image. When, ten years ago, his company won the contract to manage the party's general election campaign, he was the natural choice to lead it and, following a landslide victory it was not long before they wanted their poacher to become a gamekeeper. A by-election the following year ushered Gordon Strathyre MP into Westminster, where his natural charm and wit soon made him the darling of the party. But while others sought to serve or to work their way up the political ladder, he was more interested in the influence and opportunities that came the way of a personally ambitious and media-friendly member of His Majesty's Government.

He had not been involved in the internal squabbling and backstabbing among his colleagues which had led to the vote of no confidence in the previous Prime Minister, and had not even considered running in the leadership campaign that followed. But it was in a secret meeting with party grandees in a private room at the Courtauld Club that Gordon Strathyre began to see an even more appealing pathway unfold. Prime Minister with a place on the world stage, grace and favour accommodation, the phone numbers of presidents and other prime ministers, not forgetting the memoir and limitless earning potential when he finally became a 'former Prime Minister'. And thus far, that was how things were working.

He never really had time for red boxes and reading reports, but he hired very good and expensive advisers like Archie Wilkes to do that for him. His perceived policy of giving his Ministers full rein in their duties was not only popular at Cabinet meetings but seen externally as innovative and progressive. In reality, he just didn't have the ability or the inclination to do otherwise. But now the plan to "retire" from politics ahead of a General Election in order to give someone else an opportunity to serve was threatened. Now,

Gordon Strathyre was facing a national emergency and the country would be looking to him for leadership. This was definitely not part of the plan and not something he immediately had any idea of how to deal with.

News 24.com

11.40 am: Update

Emergency declared at Thorpehead Nuclear Power Station

The Prime Minister Gordon Strathyre has invoked the 2015 Civil Emergencies Act in response to an explosion at the Thorpehead Nuclear Power Station which has destroyed the reactor core.

Emergency services have confirmed there have been fatalities, although cannot give precise numbers yet. A number of casualties have also been transferred to Riverbridge General Hospital, eight miles away. The fire continues to burn in the reactor core and authorities are concerned about the leak of radioactive particles following the blast.

Following a meeting of COBRA earlier this morning, the Prime Minister has informed Buckingham Palace that the Government is invoking the 2015 Civil Emergencies Act to better coordinate its response to the incident. The Act specifically allows for decisions to be taken without waiting for the approval of Parliament and it is understood this includes plans for mass evacuation in the event of radiation being spread from the site due to the gale force winds of Storm Hilda. People living in Holmbeach and Burford, the two towns closest to Thorpehead are being evacuated to temporary facilities at Riverbridge and beyond but News24.com understands that arrangements are already being put in place for wider evacuation in Bristol, some 80km away.

A Government spokesperson has just briefed the media, stating: "The COBRA committee met for the first time this morning following an explosion at the Thorpehead Nuclear Power Station on the Bristol

Channel just after 9.30 am today. The priorities are currently containing the fire and the safety of staff at the site and those living close by.

"Precautionary measures are also being put in place for wider evacuation should the situation require it and to this end, the Prime Minister has informed the King of the Government's decision to invoke the 2015 Civil Emergencies Act. This will mean the Government agencies can work more effectively with emergency services, the military and other category one responders and take rapid decisions where required. This remains a fluid situation, COBRA continues in session and further announcements will be made as soon as we have more facts."

Asked whether the incident was terror-related, the spokesperson told News24.com: "At this early stage we have ruled nothing out but our immediate concern remains dealing with the aftermath of the explosion."

And asked about the earth tremor in the Bristol Channel earlier this morning: "Again, it would be unwise to speculate on possible causes while we are still seeking to ascertain the full impact of the explosion. The Prime Minister is due to meet with COBRA imminently, after which we expect to be in a better position to make a detailed statement."

Asked if the Prime Minister would be addressing the nation, the spokesperson said again that such a decision would depend on the outcome of the COBRA meeting.

Bristol

Erika sat at her position at the checkout, trying to avoid the gaze of the customer whose cans of vegetables and packets of rice she was busily scanning. She wasn't being rude but didn't want to give the lady an opportunity to engage her in conversation. It wouldn't deflect her from the job in hand. How hard was it to scan barcodes? But she knew her manager Janosch was watching the CCTV monitors in the back office. When she tried to make a fuss of the toddler with the young mother she had served a few minutes ago, the instantly recognisable Polish voice had sounded through her earpiece, telling her to keep focused on the job.

Even though she had only recently arrived from Budapest herself and Janosch had been living in Bristol for 10 years, there was no mistaking his accent. She was precisely halfway through this morning's shift, having started at 6 am by helping to unload the Pinto Foods delivery lorry which had arrived overnight. Then there was an hour or so of stacking shelves before the store opened, followed by turns on the checkout or assisting customers using the self-service lane. Sometimes it was both. Pinto Foods had introduced self-checkout supposedly in response to customer demand, but everyone knew it was to reduce staff numbers. And even though it seemed that one in every three customers needed assistance with anything from age verification for alcohol to weighing loose vegetables, there weren't always staff stationed there to help.

So, in the middle of scanning customers' goods at the checkout, staff would regularly have to get up when they heard the "approval needed" message and go to help at the self-checkout. And if they didn't react quickly enough, the heavily accented voice of Janosch would be heard through the earpiece of their internal comms device. It was a standing joke between the staff that Janosch never had time to actually help with situations like that because he was too busy in the dingy back office watching the monitors. He had told them once that as manager, his bonus was impacted by any losses from shoplifting and that was why he spent so much time on surveillance. But when somebody pointed out that the whole point of staff wearing internal radio mics was so that they could communicate effectively on the shop floor, Janosch just grunted and went back into his office. For Janosch, the internal comms existed so that he could order staff to stack shelves if the checkouts were quiet or to keep them on their toes if he thought they were interacting too much with the customers.

Just as Erika began scanning the next customer's goods, she heard a chorus of shrill alarm bells ringing, seemingly from every corner of the shop. It was not the store's fire alarm, that was unmistakable and ear-shatteringly loud. This was like a series of small alarm clocks going off in harmony. Customers all around her began by looking confused but an instant later, realised the sound was coming from their phones, all of their phones. At the same time, Erika felt the vibration in the back pocket of her jeans. Staff were not allowed to use their phones on duty and Erika's was on silent. As she fished beneath her tabard and took out her phone, it too was ringing with the same alarm tone. As customers answered the calls on their phones, others started receiving similar ringtones on theirs. Erika looked at her phone and read the message:

ISSUED BY THE UK GOVERNMENT

A CRITICAL ALERT HAS BEEN DECALRED FOLLOWING AN INCIDENT AT THORPEHEAD NUCLEAR POWER STATION AT 9.58 AM TODAY. YOU MUST RETURN IMMEDIATELY TO YOUR HOME AND REMAIN THERE WITH ALL WINDOWS CLOSED. AS A PRECAUTION, A FULL-SCALE EVACUATION OF THE AREA IS BEING PREPARED. YOU MUST PACK CLOTHING FOR UP TO A WEEK AND IF YOU ARE TAKING ANY MEDICATION, ENSURE YOU HAVE SUFFICIENT FOR AT LEAST THIS PERIOD OF TIME. ENSURE YOUR PHONE IS CHARGED AND DO NOT FORGET TO PACK YOUR CHARGER. YOU WILL BE CONTACTED IN THE NEXT 12 HOURS WITH

FURTHER INSTRUCTIONS REGARDING THE EVACUATION IF THE SITUATION REMAINS CRITICAL. THIS IS NOT A DRILL. THE SITUATION IS SERIOUS, BUT THESE MEASURES ARE PRECAUTIONARY AT THIS STAGE. YOU MUST CEASE ANY ACTIVITY NOW AND RETURN HOME TO PREPARE FOR EVACUATION. MORE INFORMATION WILL BE POSTED AT: HMGOV.UK/ALERTS AS IT BECOMES AVAILABLE AND YOU ARE REQUIRED TO AWAIT FURTHER ALERTS ON THIS SYSTEM FOR INSTRUCTIONS REGARDING YOUR AREA.

Janosch could hear the chorus of ringtones outside in the store before noticing on the monitors that the customers were all standing still, many reading their phones. He went out to the tills and saw Erika, phone in hand.

'What's happening? Why are you on your phone?'

'I don't understand,' Erika cried out. 'Everybody is getting this on their phone. Look.' She handed her phone to Janosch who began reading the government alert.

'We have to go, Janosch. Everybody has to go home.'

Janosch finished reading the message and simply froze. He looked around the shop, back at the phone and at Erika. His mouth opened but no words came out. For the customers in the store, the message was beginning to sink in. Some without phones were asking those who had received the message what the hell was going on. Meanwhile, others were beginning to receive the alarm ringing tones on their own phones. If time had stood still, it was probably only for seconds but then the panic started. Many simply dropped their shopping and headed for the car park. Others left without thinking, their trolleys still full of shopping they had yet to pay for.

While everyone was heading for the exit, one or two people started coming in the opposite direction, pushing empty trolleys and then proceeded to fill them with tinned goods and booze before joining the mass exodus. Janosch snapped back to life once he realised what was happening.

'Stop. You can't let them leave without paying! This will cost me a fortune!'

But there was no one left at the tills now. No customers or staff.

'Janosch, you idiot,' Erika shouted as she ran past in her coat and with her backpack. 'We all have to go home and prepare to be evacuated. Just lock up the shop for God's sake and go home.' And with that, she was gone. Everyone was gone, even the opportunist shoplifters. As Janosch went back towards his office, he heard a faint ringing which was growing louder as he got closer. As he opened the office door, his phone was sitting on his desk with the familiar ring alert that he had heard just minutes earlier.

Janosch checked that no further customers had come in to stock up on free provisions and gradually went about switching off the lights and bringing the shutters down. Locking the staff entrance behind him, he was surprised at first to see that the car park was not already deserted. It soon became apparent why; customers were in their vehicles with the engines running but were struggling to exit onto the main road where traffic was already gridlocked. Horns were blaring, drivers were shouting and swearing at each other through open windows. One customer, seemingly frustrated by the wait to get out of the car park had taken it upon herself to drive along the pavement as far as the next junction, only to meet another car head-on.

Above and beyond the chaos in the immediate vicinity, a

siren began to sound. It was actually a common sound in this part of Bristol. With a chemical works located at the docks nearby, the alarm which signalled for everyone to stay indoors with windows closed was tested regularly. It sounded, followed by the all-clear signal at 2 pm on the second day of each month. But it wasn't 2 pm, today wasn't the second and there was no all-clear signal to follow. With that, the rain which had eased slightly during the morning, began to fall more heavily, spotting all the gridlocked vehicles with oily black globules and particles of greyish ash.

Holmbeach

The guests were all in the lounge of the Boar's Head. Jack, the kitchen staff and the hotel receptionist were there too. As the police had instructed just twenty minutes earlier, they were ready and waiting to be evacuated to Riverbridge Leisure Centre for their own safety until such time as the "situation" was clearer. The guests had packed all their belongings and vacated their rooms but the hotel staff were more or less wearing their work outfits. The bus pulled up in front of the hotel and two police officers rushed into the reception area.

Everyone was told to ensure they had personal identification and any medication they required for the next 24 hours and to make their way quickly onto the waiting bus. Questions about whether they would be coming back to the hotel and what to do with their vehicles were all batted away with assurances that all would be explained once they reached Riverbridge.

'You're coming too, Jack,' said one of the police constables. Jack recognised him as a regular in the Boar's Head bar.

'I can't. I need to make sure everything is secure here. My parents are away at the moment. There's the power, the water, the beer cellar to sort. I can't just drop everything and go now!'

'Our instructions are to round up everyone, Jack, regardless of the circumstances. Look, get everything secured here and make your way down to the quay. There are buses leaving from there too. But take an umbrella or cover yourself well. There's black ash falling with the rain and God knows what's in it.'

Jack watched as the hotel guests, together with other neighbours in the road were ushered quickly onto the waiting bus by the police officers. Their yellow, hi-vis raincoats speckled with black dots despite the unrelenting rain. He made his way around the hotel, checking locks, shutting off gas appliances but leaving vital electric equipment like fridges and freezers plugged in. He made a quick inventory of what he might need: his phone had no signal but he should have his charger; he may be running a hotel but he was still a journalist at heart. Something had happened at Thorphead, he was sure, and he was on the spot, so laptop and notebook. All this, along with his personal effects was in the bungalow 50 metres along the road. He would have to call in at home on his way down to Holmbeach Quay.

The hotel phone started ringing. Mobile reception was out but the landline was still working. 'Answerphone,' thought Jack. Better record a message to say the hotel is closed. People are bound to be calling to find out what's happening. But he'd have to deal with the incoming call before he could reprogramme the phone. As he picked up the handset he heard a familiar voice.

'Jack, is that you?' His mother calling from the Lake

District where she and Dad had escaped for a well-earned break. 'Are you alright? We've just seen the news on the tele. They are saying the power station has blown up and everyone is being evacuated.'

Jack explained the instructions they had received and that the guests and staff had already been taken off to Riverbridge by the police.

'Then why are you still there? They say there are worries about nuclear fallout. Don't worry about the hotel, son. It's just bricks and mortar but you have to get away, now.'

'Don't worry, Mum. I have done all the safety checks now and I need to stop by the house on the way down to the Quay. There are buses leaving from there and the police know I am on the way.'

Jack explained about the mobile reception and promised he would call his parents at their holiday cottage with news whenever he could. After several promises to be careful and assurances he would leave, he finally managed to allay his mother's concerns to the point where she was happy to end the call ('How can I get away quickly Mum, if I am still on the phone to you!')

But despite his mother's concerns, something did not sit right. He went back into the lounge and turned the TV back on. Since the instruction to evacuate, all attention had been focused on the guests and the staff and he hadn't had time to check on the latest news. There was rolling coverage on all channels and so far, only one outside broadcast – the local BBC station had a crew and reporter at Riverbridge Leisure Centre, but no closer. From the announcements and the scrolling ticker along the bottom of the screen, Jack was quickly up to speed with the news that his mother must have seen. But his instinct was not to flee. He thought back to his time with the WATER campaign, Michel Bernadetti's construction reports and John Forster's papers on the nuclear waste legacy and high dependence on water. At no point did any of them ever discuss a nuclear accident and its consequences. The news reports were all linking the explosion to Storm Hilda and so-called experts, along with the TV weatherman were all talking about radioactive particles being carried eastwards across the country. But Holmbeach was to the south and west of Thorpehead. The explosion was probably the cause of the black rain, which the police officers had been out in, but did it also mean the town was at less risk? There was no mobile phone coverage from the time of the explosion. OK, perhaps not surprising. But surely that would be temporary? The landline was still working, electricity and water were still on, even the satellite TV. Holmbeach was in the process of being evacuated. Soon, there would be no one in the town. There surely was a story to be told and despite everything that had happened to him in his twice-curtailed career, Jack Makepiece was a journalist.

He had no idea how long the current situation would last. If the all clear came in a couple of days then there would probably only be scope for one article, everything would be back to normal and his staying behind was no problem. But if this was as serious as his mother seemed to think, then this needed to be chronicled from within, regardless of any risks to his wellbeing. For now, he was living in a hotel. The fridges, even the bar was well stocked. So he was decided. He would base himself at the Boar's Head for the immediate future and try to observe events from within the exclusion zone they had started talking about on the TV. For the time being he would lie low, literally, in case the police or anyone else came back looking for him. He would wait for evening and then retrieve all he needed from home. Then he would start to tell the world what it is really like to live next door to a nuclear power station.

✳✳✳✳✳

News 24.com

12.25 pm: Update

Panic in Bristol following evacuation message

There are scenes of chaos and panic across Bristol after residents received instructions to prepare for evacuation using the Government's Emergency Alert text service. Traffic is gridlocked around the city and there have been reports of violence and looting from shops.

This follows the explosion at Thorpehead Nuclear Power Station some 80km away earlier this morning (see 10.20 am and 11.40 am). The reactor core is understood to have suffered meltdown, releasing a radioactive cloud into the atmosphere which is being carried on the gale force winds of Storm Hilda.

The text message was released via the Emergency Alerts service at 10.40 am advising residents to return home and prepare to be evacuated. People have been told to pack clothes and any medication to last a week and to wait for further instructions.

Within minutes, it appears that offices emptied, schools and shops closed as people heeded the message and headed for home. The consequence was a rush hour the likes of which Bristol has never seen before. To make matters worse, Bristol Transit issued the instruction for all bus drivers to return to their depot and then go home, leaving many with no option other than to walk. There have been multiple incidents of cars colliding on roads where drivers have lost patience with crawling traffic and, as yet unconfirmed reports suggest that emergency services have been ordered not to respond to any road traffic incidents but remain on stand-by to assist with any evacuation procedures.

And there has been criticism of the Government's much-heralded but little-used Emergency Alert service. One reader contacted News24.com to say: "The whole thing is just chaos. I work in an open-plan office. Some people's phones started ringing with the message and others (sic) didn't. People started freaking out when they read the message and others were going nuts because they didn't know what was happening. And every few seconds, more people were getting the alerts then trying to contact their kids at school but not getting through. In the end, the bosses just told us to shut down our computers and go home. Then we found there were no buses and it is going to take me at least two hours to walk home in the rain. I'm really scared. My nan is in a care home, what's going to happen to her?"

Elsewhere, there have been reports of retailers being overwhelmed by mass shoplifting. While trying to close their shops, they have had to deal with customers helping themselves to goods, including tinned food, alcohol and vapes, before leaving without paying.

News24.com has asked the police and Bristol Metropolitan Council for a comment. More to follow …..

15 - Four hours later

Cabinet Office Briefing Room, Whitehall

The Cabinet Office Briefing Room looked remarkably different to the way it had just a few hours earlier. Where members of the secretariat dotted around the edges of the room had been quietly going about their business in the alcoves, each work station was now a hive of activity with one person seated at a computer, another on the phone and usually a third ferrying messages around the room. The bank of screens was fully animated. Charts and maps on some, the faces of military or emergency services staff on others, sound muted but clearly in conversation with civil contingencies. New bodies had joined the previous committee members around the boardroom table as the next meeting of COBRA was about to be convened. Field Marshal Leighton Parks was accompanied by Rear Admiral Martin Jepson, his deputy chief of defence staff. Also in full uniform, sat at the far end of the table was the Commissioner of the Metropolitan Police, the highest ranking police officer in the country. Chief Scientific Officer, Professor Derek Beaumont was flanked by members of SAGE, the Scientific Advisory Group for Emergencies and other spaces around the table were taken by members of the Local Government Association, Fire Services and National Health Service – the category one responders in respect of civil emergencies. The TV monitor at the end of the boardroom table was active, although currently all it displayed was an empty chair. Gold Commander Oliver Merton was about to join the meeting from Exeter.

Gordon Strathyre and Archie Wilks entered Briefing Room 1 accompanied by Home Secretary Nadia Yadav. She took up her position on the opposite side of the table, facing the Prime Minister and his cabinet secretary.

'As you are now aware, the 2015 Civil Emergencies Act has now been invoked. I spoke to His Majesty earlier and he expressed great concern over the potential damage following this morning's incident. Not least, I should add, because one of his private estates potentially lies in the path of any radioactive cloud. Be that as it may, the Civil Emergencies Act provides additional powers for the Government to use in the event of a large-scale emergency. So, before we consider any such action can I ask you, Mark for a status update?'

All eyes turned towards the end of the table and Mark Brooks. As the Director of Civil Contingencies prepared to describe the current position, Chief Constable Merton took up his seat on screen.

'I stated earlier that the three priorities are the fire, public safety around Thorpehead and danger of radioactive fallout. Starting with the fire in the reactor, it continues to burn and we are still unable to get fire crews close enough for any amount of time to have any noticeable effect. Tackling the blaze from above is still not yet an option due to the weather. However, in discussions I have had with fire service chiefs, sending helicopters with either water or to dump sand may not be the most effective course of action.'

'Why not,' asked the Prime Minister.

'First,' said Mark, looking for reassurance from the fire service representatives across the room, 'we have to consider the safety of the crews. Not only are we exposing them to radiation but with so many particles being sucked up with the steam, there is the danger of ingestion into the engines or contact with the rotors. They used helicopters to drop boron at Chernobyl, but there was a school of thought to suggest this destabilised the remaining reactor structure and the rotor blades whipped up more radioactive particles into the atmosphere.'

Strathyre was starting to get irritated. 'So we just let it burn and spew out God knows what into the atmosphere?'

'There is no effective intervention open to us at this moment in time. Even if you were to order me to deploy helicopters, Prime Minister, they remain grounded due to the weather. Bicarel's central control office has given us the last recorded temperature before the core blew, which was almost three thousand degrees. The fire crews at the site are measuring not just the radiation levels but air temperature and it does seem that the fire could be burning itself out, albeit only slowly at this stage. If there is any good news at this point it does look as if Professor Beaumont's hypothesis of China Syndrome may have been averted. And if we can allow for the fire to burn out by itself it will mean we can concentrate more resources on the immediate consequences of the fire – by which I mean the safety of the public and plans for evacuation.'

'Well, on that piece of "good news" perhaps we can move on to evacuation.' It was hard to tell whether Strathyre's tone was intentionally sardonic.

The Civil Contingencies Director started to give the Prime Minister his response, maintaining a cool and unemotive tone as if this were the next item on the agenda at a local council meeting.

'As to ensuring the safety of the general public, we have to consider three aspects: the health and wellbeing of those living closest to the explosion, the evacuation of larger population areas sitting along the projected path of the radiation cloud and the creation of a longer-term exclusion zone.' Before that last phrase had time to sink in, particularly among the politicians sitting around the table, Mark Brooks quickly sought to bring the Gold Commander into the conversation.

'Oliver, can you bring us up to speed with events?'

In an instant, the various monitors on the far wall of Briefing Room 1 were replaced by one image of Chief Constable Merton's head and shoulders. The clearer definition highlighted the five o'clock shadow and puffiness around his eyes that had not been apparent during his previous appearance on the Zoom call.

'Despite losing all mobile phone masts, presumably in the explosion, we have almost completed the physical evacuation of Holmbeach and Burford. This has been achieved through local radio and TV messages, loud hailer announcements and my force travelling door to door. Residents are currently being housed at the Riverbridge Sports Centre and other sites between there and Exeter. I see this as a temporary measure until plans for the larger-scale evacuation are confirmed. We have so far accounted for just over eight thousand people which is still below the actual population. This may be due to administrative delays in counting and recording and it may also mean that a significant number of residents have ignored the instructions and staying put in their own homes.

'At Thorpehead itself, all but twenty staff have been accounted for. Those missing are presumed dead. Anyone working close to the reactor building would simply have been vaporised. The control building has collapsed in on itself but we cannot get close enough to it to even consider search and rescue. Of the casualties from the administration building, six have undergone surgery and are not considered to have life-threatening injuries. Some have started to show initial symptoms of radiation exposure such as sore throats, red eyes and dizziness, but Riverbridge General Hospital only has one dosimeter. They have only just begun testing patients for radiation and have so far only taken rudimentary precautions such as removing clothes and shaving the heads of those who needed surgery. They have prescribed potassium iodine tablets to everyone who was treated from Thorpehead but only have limited supplies, which have now been exhausted. The hospital chief executive told me that an emergency disaster drill was supposed to have taken place before the power station opened but was postponed due to budget constraints.'

'Did you know about this, Nadia?' Strathyre fixed the Home Secretary with an icy glare.

'I will have to check, Prime Minister. I am unsure whether the hospital drill would have been my department or within the Department of Health remit.'

Mark Brooks intervened before the Prime Minister had time to respond. 'Civil Contingencies were actually planning a multi-agency drill at Thorpehead just over two years ago, Home Secretary. But the project was actually deferred on the instructions of the Ministry for Energy which at the time had sole responsibility for the power station project.'

'But that's not all,' the voice returned over the speaker and Oliver Merton's face filled the giant screen. 'My officers have spent the last three hours in the area without any form of protection. We have very few Geiger counters or dosimeters at our disposal and I am concerned I am putting them at undue risk. Then there is the evacuation itself. Many people drove themselves to the reception centre in Riverbridge but we also used a fleet of buses which made multiple journeys. My team at Riverbridge do have radiation meters and the readings they have just got from one of those buses are over 70 roentgens. We are going to have to isolate and probably dispose of the vehicles somehow.'

'Someone tell me this isn't happening,' the Prime Minister murmured.

'I'm afraid it doesn't stop there,' Mark replied, still sanguine as if this sort of thing happened to him every day.

'Chief Constable, please be assured we are addressing the issue of protective gear, radiation meters and iodine tablets as we speak. We have resources from elsewhere in the country on their way and more supplies ordered from abroad.'

'That's good to hear, Mark but we are stretched to the limit here already. We are going to need more personnel as well as equipment if the evacuation is anything more than temporary.'

'Well, that does lead us right into what is the far more pressing issue. The establishment of an exclusion zone and the full-scale evacuation of all residents living within it.' Returning to the laptop in front of him on the edge of the boardroom table, the Civil Contingencies Director reduced the face of Gold Commander Merton back to the TV monitor and returned the array of charts and maps to the giant screen on the wall. 'I said at the earlier meeting that the Met Office has been tracking and plotting the wind speed and direction by the minute. The winds are abating and the rain is likely to stop over the next two to three hours. But the fire in the reactor continues to burn, and will do so for some time. But the Met Office has been able to plot the course of the radioactive steam cloud, or fallout zone which Thorpehead has been emitting.'

Not everyone around the table was at the earlier COBRA meeting, but there was a similar gasp as Mark brought up the weather map and the red band swept across it in almost an identical path from the Bristol Channel to the Deben Estuary. 'Given the strength of the wind, the meteorologists now believe that wider dissipation of steam and particles to the north and south is unlikely, and so they have narrowed the width of the band down to a maximum of fifteen kilometres. But within that area it is likely that radioactive material will have fallen to the ground with the rain. We are monitoring air quality along the course of the red band on the screen and while at present the risk diminishes the further east you travel, the continuing weather conditions and the fact that the fire is still burning, will alter that. For now, we have to consider a ten-mile-wide exclusion zone from west to east across England and implement the immediate evacuation of an area which includes Bristol and Swindon.'

'Do we really have to evacuate everyone and all at once?' The Prime Minister now sounding more anxious than annoyed.

'We are already picking up readings of 80 roentgen in Bristol. The human body starts to show significant signs of radiation sickness at around 100 roentgen, so yes, Prime

Minister, we cannot delay. We have already used the Emergency Alerts text messaging service to advise people to return home and prepare for evacuation. The Civil Contingencies Secretariat is currently liaising with local authorities as Category One responders on how and where to accommodate large numbers of evacuees. Obviously the exclusion zone poses one major challenge. People below it can only be evacuated southwards or northwards. We must avoid people crossing the zone. Fortuitously, as the tourist season has yet to start in earnest, our local authority colleagues are looking at holiday accommodation in the first instance as well as reviving the family host network which worked well a few years ago following the Russian invasion of Ukraine. With Devon and Cornwall on one side of the exclusion zone and South and West Wales on the other, there is significant capacity within the holiday rental sector. My staff are still working on the precise numbers and I expect to be able to brief you more fully, Prime Minister in the next hour or so.'

'And just how are we going to enforce a ten-mile-wide exclusion zone the breadth of the country?' Home Secretary Nadia Yadav.

'Assuming we can evacuate the population without any resistance there are of course going to be complications.' Mark Woods brought up another chart on the screen. 'A straight line on a map is not so on the ground, as you can probably imagine. It will cut through properties, cross rivers, railway lines, et cetera. If we were to enclose it entirely we are talking of more than two hundred and fifty miles on each side, allowing for kinks in the line. That's a lot of fence and, according to our reckoning, almost three hundred thousand posts. We are looking at where we can source that much material but there is also the question of who is going to erect it and how long it will take?'

'We have no choice but to use the armed forces,' responded the Home Secretary.

Field Marshal Leighton Parks had so far been sitting through the briefing in silence. He sat upright and cleared his throat.

'Thank you, Home Secretary. I was wondering when we would get a mention. The Rear Admiral and I have already been discussing this and while I am sure we have excellent engineers to erect a five-hundred-mile fence, the Civil Contingencies Director's report concerns us in many other ways. First, we still do not know if the incident is terror-related. We have heard that the police locally are already stretched and we are already getting reports of chaos on the streets of Bristol. The two of us are of the opinion that while the military will be expected to provide logistical support to the Civil Contingencies Directorate, we should be prepared for a greater threat of panic and civil disobedience. Your department, Mister Brooks will no doubt be providing us with a clearer picture on numbers but we must factor in security.'

MI5 Deputy Director Bridgette McAndrew spoke up. 'We have continued to investigate but neither my Director nor our friends across the river in MI6 have found any indication that terror is a motive. From the last data available from the Bicarel central control office, there appears to have been a sudden failure in the cooling operation leading up to the explosion, although I am not a scientist, so cannot comment further. But we have no evidence that points to any form of outside impact on the reactor.'

'Well, at least we may be able to stand down some units

from other power facilities in the country,' said the Field Marshal. 'But can I just remind you, Prime Minister, and everyone else in this room, that the military does not have unlimited resources. We have been forced to scale back numbers in recent years but still have to maintain commitments, both to our overseas territories and to NATO. Please do not expect to say "send in the troops" as the fallback response to the many challenges that now lie ahead.'

'I also think we have only just scratched the surface regarding the ongoing health risks,' Chief Scientific Officer Professor Derek Beaumont jumped in, taking advantage of the pause while the committee considered the Field Marshal's chilling advice. 'If the experience of Chernobyl tells us anything, it is that there are both short and long-term consequences of radiation poisoning. While the number of casualties directly as a result of the blast may be relatively low, symptoms of contamination through ingestion take longer to present but cause irreversible damage to the internal organs. Then, as we know, there are the longer-term problems of gamma radiation which affect the thyroid gland, particularly in children. We will need to consider regular testing of the white blood cell count for those who have been exposed to any significant degree.'

'Your concerns are well-founded and noted, Professor,' replied the Prime Minister. 'We will proceed with the evacuation process as recommended by the Civil Contingencies Director and Mark, can you update me further in an hour?' At that point, his Cabinet Secretary pushed a scrap of paper along the desk to him. He quickly read the message and started to rise to his feet. 'Given the trajectory of the radioactive cloud, I have a duty to warn the governments of France, Belgium and the Netherlands what might be heading their way, even if it is just precautionary. Once the evacuation of Bristol is ready to go, I will have to address the nation. Archie and I will start to prepare for that and Mark, one hour please in my office.'

'Just one last thing before you close the meeting, Prime Minister.' The Home Secretary had one more question for the Civil Contingencies Director. 'So Mark, once we have created this fallout zone which cuts the country in two, how long will the people have to stay away?'

'That really depends on how much radioactive material has fallen with the rain. Almost everything, buildings and vehicles will be contaminated and nothing grown in the fields will be able to go to market.'

'But are we talking weeks, months or even years?'

'Certainly years, possibly hundreds of years.'

Outside 10 Downing Street

The camera crews were in place. Journalists were packed tightly behind the crush barriers erected in a U-shape facing the door of Number 10. Behind them, photographers were perched precariously on step ladders, all waiting for an announcement from the Prime Minister that the calling note had said would begin 20 minutes ago. Finally, the door opened and Gordon Strathyre stepped out and up to the lectern amid a flurry of flashlights and lens clicks.

'Good afternoon. At just after nine-thirty this morning there was an explosion at the Thorpehead nuclear power station on the Bristol Channel. I regret to announce that there have been a number of fatalities and some staff remain unaccounted for. The injured are being treated for their injuries at Riverbridge General Hospital although most are not considered to be serious. I offer my sincere condolences to the families of

those affected.

'The cause of the explosion is as yet unclear and, along with the security services, we are continuing our investigations. A fire has been burning in the core of the nuclear reactor and while tackling the blaze has been made more difficult due to the severe weather conditions in the Bristol Channel, the emergency services are confident that the situation is now almost under control.

'However, the blast has resulted in the release of radioactive elements into the atmosphere which have been carried in an easterly direction thanks to Storm Hilda. As an immediate precaution, people living in the vicinity of Thorpehead were evacuated safely this morning. We do not as yet know to what extent radioactive material has escaped from the reactor or how much is being carried with the wind but the Met Office has predicted the likely path of any possible contamination. There is a further threat to health where any of that radiation falls to ground with the heavy rain that has persisted throughout the morning.

'This morning, I informed His Majesty the King that the Government is invoking the 2015 Civil Emergencies Act which will allow it to react more efficiently to any ongoing threats caused by this incident. As a further precaution, I have used my powers under the act to order the full-scale evacuation of Bristol and people living between the city and Swindon are also being put on stand-by for possible evacuation. Furthermore, until the situation becomes clearer, the M4 motorway between Cardiff and Reading is being closed to all traffic and rail services between London, Bristol and South Wales suspended.

'As you can appreciate, these are drastic measures which are going to have a significant impact on many people's lives. My message to everyone, regardless of where you live is therefore the following: For the next twenty-four hours, you must stay at home; offices, leisure and retail outlets are to close; do not attempt to travel, even if you live far from the affected area. All rail and local bus services will be suspended for twenty-four hours as of nine o'clock this evening. Military reservists are being

called up and medical staff are being prepared for possible mobilisation. Until we know the full extent of the impact from Thorpehead, we need to keep all emergency and infrastructure resources available to react to the situation where and when they are needed.

'For those of you living in or near to the affected area, we are using the Government Emergency Test Alert service as well as the local media to keep you informed with developments. I, and my ministers will continue to make regular broadcast announcements as the situation develops and you will also be able to keep up to date using the HMGov.uk website.

In closing for now, I would like to stress these two important facts: these measures are still precautionary at this stage but they are serious. You may feel that if you live far from Thorpehead then why should you bother? This is a critical incident which could potentially affect us all. We all therefore have a duty to do what's best for our country, so please heed the instructions I have just outlined this afternoon. Thank you'

The Prime Minister turned and headed towards the door of Number 10. From behind the barriers came a barrage of unanswered questions from the press corps.

'Is this another Chernobyl, Prime Minister?'

'Is this a terrorist attack?'

'How will you protect us from nuclear fallout, Prime Minister?'

'Where does this leave our nuclear energy policy?'

'Were the critics of Thorpehead right all along, Prime Minister?'

Inside 10 Downing Street

Gordon Strathyre was seated behind his desk. Facing him in a semi-circle were his Cabinet Secretary and close adviser Archie Wilkes, Home Secretary Nadia Yadav and Civil

Contingencies Director Mark Brooks. Field Marshal Leighton Parks was sitting on the sofa on the other side of the room, drinking his coffee and studying a report.

Following the Prime Minister's address to the nation, the group was assembled in Number 10 to consider Mark Brooks's initial report on the plan to evacuate almost half-a-million people from the Greater Bristol area.

'Well, we have the systems in place with a network of reception centres both to the south of Bristol as well as in Gloucestershire and South Wales,' Mark began. 'We are using motorway service areas, sports grounds and retail parks – all places which can accommodate a large number of vehicles. They will have to be checked for radiation but in all likelihood, the majority of cars will have to be left there and the residents transferred onwards to longer-term accommodation in Devon, Cornwall or the Gower Peninsula by bus. We will need to set up more reception centres as the situation develops and the capacity of accommodation continues to be fluid. That's the theory, but I have concerns going forward.'

'Such as?' asked Strathyre.

'Principally that the system becomes overwhelmed. Evacuation instructions have been issued in Bristol and we are already seeing signs of panic and traffic chaos. There are reports of accidents and emergency services are unable to reach the scene as the roads are gridlocked. Meanwhile, further east, around Swindon, people are simply leaving and not waiting for further instructions. Again, we are seeing traffic chaos and getting reports of crime and looting. If you can excuse me, Prime Minister I really need to get back to the Cabinet Office to liaise with Gold Command in Exeter.'

'Yes, Mark, off you go. Thanks for the report and you'll

obviously keep us up to date.'

Once Mark Brooks had left the room the Prime Minister muttered, as much to himself as the others left behind. 'What a total clusterfuck. How the hell are we going to contain this?'

'I fear this is only the beginning, Gordon,' Home Secretary Yadav opined. 'And if you don't mind me saying, I thought you weren't entirely honest in your speech outside earlier.'

'In what way, for fuck sake?'

'Well, the security services have ruled out terrorism but you chose to let the public believe it may have been a factor. Then, you also tried to reassure people that the evacuation was just a precaution when we already know it is far worse than that.'

'Archie here felt that not ruling terrorism would make people take the matter seriously but at the same time, we should not have been creating panic.'

'Well from what Mark has just told us, that seems to have worked a treat, Archie!' Nadia Yadav's eyes bore into the Prime Minister's adviser sitting to her right. This was not the first time the two had clashed. Young and ambitious herself, the Home Secretary had become increasingly frustrated by what she saw as the Prime Minister deferring the bigger decisions in government to his close adviser, an unelected, and frankly deeply mistrusted member of the inner circle. Mistrusted by all except Gordon Strathyre that is.

Before Archie Wilkes could unleash one of his usually barbed and, in Nadia's case, misogynistic responses, the Prime Minister's internal phone rang.

'The Minister for Energy is here, Prime Minister.'

'Send him in.'

Roland Smith entered the office and was shown to the seat recently vacated by Mark Brooks.

'So Roly, we don't have a lot of time as you can imagine. I've just got a couple of questions for you,' Strathyre began in a business-like manner.

'How the fuck does a nuclear power station, your department has been telling anyone and everyone is the start of this country's pathway toward energy security, suddenly blow up after twelve months? Oh, and while we are at it, looks likely to leave a trail of radioactivity from one fucking side of England to the other, effectively cutting the nation in two!'

Roland's jaw dropped as he sat there motionless for a few seconds. It was as if he was back in the headmaster's study at his boarding school.

'Prime Minister, as far as we can see, the incident at Thorpehead was an accident, put down to a freak set of circumstances that could not have been foreseen. We have been talking to Bicarel's control centre in Milton Keynes and it seems the reactor's cooling system was compromised following seismic activity in the Bristol Channel which caused the water intake pipes to collapse. The tremor also combined with a high tide and gale force winds to overwhelm the sea defences which temporarily knocked out the power, and with it the ability to release pressure which had built up in the reactor.'

'Are you really telling me that those were events which couldn't have been foreseen? Your department had full authority over the planning procedure for Christ's sake.'

'Of course we analysed all the emergency modelling which the company had carried out. Our experts told us that the safety measures were more than adequate and an event such as this was so unlikely as to be unimaginable.'

'Well, guess what Roly, it looks the unimaginable has just been imagined.'

Nadia Yadav turned to her left and half opened the file which had been sitting on the desk.

'We learnt this morning, Roly that an emergency response drill planned for Thorpehead before it opened was cancelled on your orders. A problem with funding. Is that correct?'

Roland Smith again did not reply for a moment. 'That is correct, Home Secretary, but the reason was not financial. Everything was in place and set to be green-lighted, but if you remember we had a lot of opposition locally at the time. The campaign group there had got a lot of traction and the story had gone national. We thought we had more or less got control of the situation at the time but I had major concerns that staging a rehearsal for how to deal with an emergency might just re-awaken negative publicity. So I ordered the Cabinet Office to complete a desk top survey instead.'

'My God, this just gets worse and worse!' The Prime Minister now held his hands to his face.

'And there is one other thing,' Nadia said. 'In the light of everything that has happened since this morning, this isn't at the top of my agenda just at the moment. But I think ultimately that you may have some questions to answer about your relationship with the owners of Bicarel.'

'I was at Oxford at the same time as Baliyashvili and Ellrington but I have had virtually nothing to do with them since. We had a reunion a couple of years ago and I did attend the stock market launch of Bicarel – at the invitation of the member for Holmbeach and West Tyneford. James Whiteligh-Howse was also at Oxford at the same time. It's all in the ministerial diary. You surely can't be thinking this terrible tragedy is the result of some old boys' network? The selection process was conducted with all due process and at arms-length from my role as minister.'

'Like I said, Roly. It's not for now, but it is something you will need to be ready to answer if the opposition or the press get a whiff of it.'

'I think that will do for now, Nadia,' The Prime Minister had visibly composed himself once more. 'I'll let you get back to the department, Roly but just remember one thing.' Gordon Strathyre may like to portray himself as everybody's friend but he would not have made it to the top of his party without a ruthless streak which usually lay deeper below the surface.

'The buck stops with me as the PM. There's nothing I can do about that. But if it transpires that this fucking mess is not an unforeseen tragic accident but the result of someone cosying up to his mates instead of doing their job, I will not be the one falling on his sword. Do I may myself clear Roly?'

'Perfectly, Prime Minister.'

With that, the Minister for Energy left the room, followed a few minutes later by the Home Secretary. Field Marshal Parks was still sitting quietly on the sofa although he had long since stopped reading his report following Roland Smith's entry into the Prime Minister's office. Strathyre and Wilkes moved across from the desk and joined Parks, sitting in the armchairs opposite which made up the break-out area on either side of the fireplace.

'Drink, Leighton?' Gordon asked, reaching for the cut

glass decanter set on a silver tray on the coffee table beside him.

'Bit early for me, Prime Minister.'

'It is for me too, but today is different.'

'So what is it you wanted to discuss with me alone, Prime Minister? Or can I already guess?'

'It looks like you were right to be concerned about civil disorder. We don't know how big this thing is yet but all the signs are that the country is facing a crisis much worse than the miners' strike or even the Blitz. The Civil Emergencies Act gives me the power to introduce laws quickly and without reference to the Privy Council or those stupid bastards in the House, but Archie is concerned that we may face resistance from the public if we try to enforce some of the more unpopular measures.'

'Like what exactly, Prime Minister?'

The Cabinet Secretary took up the narrative. 'The Civil Contingencies Director didn't mention it but I am sure he realises. We have raised the issue of securing the exclusion zone, but if it reaches right across the country, Westminster will be one side of it and governing the largest part of the British Isles on the other. Imports through the port of Dover will get no further than London and the whole supply chain will need to be reconfigured. There are going to be shortages of fuel and food in the North, much of which will be otherwise unaffected by events at Thorpehead.'

'We are going to need the military, not just to look after the exclusion zone but to enforce government policy going forward,' Strathyre added.

'I'm ahead of you, Prime Minister, as I think you may already have realised. But as I said at COBRA, we don't have the resources to do everything and be everywhere at once.'

'What Archie and I are saying is that resources are no longer an issue, Leighton. I am fully aware of the struggles you have faced with the Secretary of Defence in the last few years over budgets and manpower. As of today, you have an open cheque book. Whatever you need, just tell Archie and you will have it.'

'That's all very well, but the one resource that my new budget won't be able to provide is the one I will actually need, people. Even if we reactivated our recruitment programmes, it will take years before we will have the trained soldiers we need. Unless you are considering conscription?'

Strathyre and Wilkes looked at each other. 'It's funny you should say that, Field Marshal,' the Cabinet Secretary responded. 'The Prime Minister and I weren't exactly using that word, but it is clear we will need more bodies and quickly. The evacuation of the exclusion zone will mean that a lot of people will no longer be able to do their jobs, either because businesses are closed or they are living several miles away. We certainly can't afford to furlough them all like we did during the pandemic, so some form of civil duty force may well be an answer.'

'Civil defence militia could certainly be deployed more if we don't have to give them full military training and I expect there will be a large number of roles within such a force that would not require military training,' the Field Marshal responded thoughtfully.

'That's what the Prime Minister and I thought. There's going to be a lot of administration work around the evacuation which will be too much for the local councils to handle while all the category one and two response agencies are going to need extra hands. Then there's the fallout zone itself.'

'And crucially,' added the Prime Minister. 'It will free your combat-ready forces to deal with civil unrest.'

'Are we talking about martial law as well?'

'Call it that if you want, Leighton. The fact of the matter is that difficult decisions will need to be taken and implemented quickly. Regardless of COBRA or Parliament, the three people making and enforcing those decisions are sitting around this table.'

'Perhaps I will have that drink, Prime Minister.'

16 - Twelve hours later

News 24.com

9.20 pm: Evacuation and mass shutdown following nuclear explosion

The mass evacuation of Bristol and cities across the breadth of England has begun after the Prime Minister ordered a total shutdown of the nation for 24 hours.

Prime Minister Gordon Strathyre addressed the nation earlier this afternoon in the wake of an explosion which destroyed the reactor at the recently opened Thorpehead nuclear power station on the Bristol Channel. Radioactive particles released from the reactor have, and continue to be carried across the country by storm force winds and then falling as rain. People living along a path between Thorpehead and Bristol and as far as Swindon have now been told by the Government to leave their homes and report to reception centres being set up on either side of the affected area. Residents in Buckinghamshire and as far east as Harlow and Chelmsford in Essex have also been warned to prepare for evacuation. Arrangements are being made to house displaced populations in holiday accommodation in the far South West, South Coast and West Wales. No specifics have been given as to how long they will need to stay in temporary accommodation. Instructions issued via the Government Emergency Alert text messaging service advised packing for a week but experts are already saying that if radioactive material is falling as rain, the land could remain contaminated for several years.

The Cabinet Office, which houses the Government's Civil Contingencies Department, issued the following statement: "Following the Prime Minister's address to the nation in which he ordered everyone to remain at home for 24 hours, arrangements for the mass evacuation of residents in the areas of Bristol and Swindon have been put in place. The situation following the explosion at Thorpehead nuclear power station continues to develop and the Civil Contingencies department is monitoring the position and coordinating the response on an evolving basis. The Prime Minister's call for businesses, schools and transport services to close was for two reasons: the first was the as yet unknown effect on the road and rail network of the potentially hazardous material being carried in the atmosphere from Thorpehead; the second, and the reason why the instruction to stay at home applied to the whole nation, was to hold emergency services and other responders such as transport and utility companies on stand-by, ready to be deployed where necessary. Working with local councils throughout the country, we are currently coordinating efforts to rehouse members of the public in areas away from the towns and cities currently at risk. In the first instance, they are being asked to report to reception areas around the affected zone, from where they will be transported onward to more permanent accommodation. This operation is being supervised by the military and the police. The full scale of this operation has yet to be determined while we continue to monitor the progress and carry out regular tests for radiation along a predicted path across central England. The Government wishes to thank both the emergency responders for their immediate work and the public for its understanding of what, for many hundreds of thousands, is a worrying situation. COBRA remains sitting and we will be issuing further updates throughout the day."

Rail services were due to stop at 9 pm this evening, at which point the entire length of the M4 motorway between Swansea and Hammersmith in London was also closed. Barriers were positioned across the entrances at every junction along the 300km route while police vehicles patrolled the motorway itself. Our reporters in the South West also tell us there was a similar police presence along the M5 between Exeter and Bristol. The motorway is expected to be a major evacuation route for the Bristol area. We have also been receiving reports of major troop movements in the area as reception centres are set up for the evacuees. One reader called us to say soldiers and police officers arrived at Somerset Services on the M5, forcing stragglers to get in their cars and leave. As they drove off they noticed soldiers climbing out of troop carriers wearing hazmat suits and carrying guns.

People living closest to the Thorpehead nuclear power station have already spent the day in temporary shelters in the Riverbridge. The port of Holmbeach and nearby village of Burford are deserted and it is assumed that those people evacuated will now join the larger ranks from Bristol and Swindon that the Government is planning to send further south and west into Devon and Cornwall.

Emergency services are still to confirm casualty figures from the explosion at the power station but News24.com understands that as many as 20 workers are still unaccounted for. A number of casualties remain at Riverbridge General Hospital.

Holmbeach

It was dark outside now. Mum and Dad had not come home at lunchtime like the note had said. Shelley had used the house phone to call her parents' mobiles. Neither of them answered. Her own mobile had no service, and neither did Evan's, which meant he was suffering TikTok withdrawal symptoms by now. She had tried calling the Thorpehead Power Station switchboard but all she heard was the continuous 'number unobtainable' signal. There was food in the fridge but all Evan wanted was more Cocoa Krisp and, in the absence of TikTok to keep him entertained, he had commandeered the TV, plugged in his games console and played Minecraft with his headphones on for the whole of the afternoon. Meanwhile, the rain continued to lash the windows, depositing a grey, oily sludge which further restricted the daylight coming into the house. She didn't know whether Evan was annoyed at his parents' late return or simply bored. Either way, he clearly didn't want to have anything to do with his sister. With no mobile service, Shelley couldn't seek any solace or distraction with her school friends on Chat Teen and there was no way she was going out to see them, even if her mum had been at home. So the afternoon had been spent mostly listening to music and reading magazines in her room, interspersed with regular and repeatedly failed attempts to call her parents' place of work.

Evan had finally given up on Minecraft because he was hungry. A fact he decided to share with his sister at maximum volume from the bottom of the stairs. Shelley was back in the kitchen, microwaving baked beans and about to toast some bread to go with it. She picked up her mother's note again and re-read it. She was definitely planning to come home with Dad. Even if she had been asked to stay on, Dad would have come home as normal. In fact, he would be getting ready about now to head back for his next shift. Something wasn't right and she had to call the police. Was it an emergency, though meriting a 999 call? A teenager and sibling home alone? She found the number for Riverbridge Police Station in the booklet beside the house phone. It rang, and rang and rang before cutting off after a couple of minutes.

Just then she heard a vehicle noise outside. They were

home, finally. Or was it them? This was a much lower but louder engine noise than Mum's Ford Focus. This was much larger. Shelley went to the lounge window and pulled back the full-length velvet curtain. It was a covered army lorry, parked on the opposite side of the road outside Mrs Fulton's house. But the men who emerged from the back of the lorry didn't look like soldiers. They were almost rectangular in shape, like Evan's Lego characters. They wore reflective yellow suits that looked as if they were inflated. Shelley could not see their heads or necks, just a rectangular hood with what looked like a screen for a face. Two of the Lego men were now walking down the drive on either side of Mrs Fulton and helping her to climb aboard. Then, the family living next door also appeared from their front door, hurrying against the wind and rain, one of them carrying a small suitcase and similarly being ushered up into the lorry. The curtain was suddenly snapped shut from behind her. Evan had been watching too.

'What's going on, Shel? Who are those strange blokes and where are they taking Mrs Fulton?'

'I have no idea, Ev. Should I go and find out?'

'No way. I'm scared, Shel. They're taking everybody away. Do you think they're aliens, come to get us?'

'Don't be silly, Ev. It looks like everyone in the street is going willingly, whatever is happening. I'll get my coat and go and find out.'

'No, don't leave me alone, Shel.' Evan drew the curtain aside, just wide enough to peer through, then jumped back, hissing. 'They're coming over here, Shel, quick hide. Turn out the lights and don't make a sound.' He flicked off the lights and pulled his sister down behind the settee. A shadow, thrown up by torchlight, then appeared to fill the frosted glass of the front door. The doorbell rang, followed by a firm knock on the glass.

'Hello, anyone at home. We are evacuating your street. Make sure you have your ID and any medication you require for the next 24 hours. Hello. Anybody at home?' Shelley went to move towards the door but Evan grabbed her around the waist and hauled her back to the floor.

'It's a trick, Shel. Stay still and don't say anything.'

There was more knocking and the bell rang, more urgently this time. After a couple of minutes, they heard the footsteps recede down the drive. Neither of them moved. Finally, after another 10 minutes, they heard the lorry's engine rev up once more. It was leaving the street.

It was still raining but it seemed to Jack that the wind was easing when he finally decided to retrieve his things from home. He'd spent the afternoon in one of the front-facing bedrooms at the hotel from where he could both keep an eye on the road outside and keep up to date with events on the small TV fitted in every room. The police had not come back. In fact nobody had come by, either on foot or in a vehicle. He'd taken time during his vigil to reflect more on his decision to stay behind in Holmbeach. Having no mobile signal would limit his ability to contact media outlets – and then there was the slight problem that his reputation probably still preceded him in newsrooms at the national dailies. And in any event, once he began filing from within the exclusion zone, everyone would know and the game would be up in any event. No, this project would have to be a retrospective record, an account of what life was like living next to an exploded nuclear reactor. He'd need good pictures too if he was planning to get close to Thorpehead so the camera was added to his list of effects to bring back from home.

Although the last person he had seen today was the friendly policeman, Jack still took no chances and left the Boar's Head via the rear kitchen. The wind hit him as he reached the front of the building which stood facing the Atlantic. He was used to the howl of the wind and the background noise of waves crashing against the foot of the cliffs, but even without traffic, there was another sound. It wasn't a roar but more than a hum. Although his parents' home was only a short distance down the road, he decided to turn right instead and walk up to the headland. From here he could take in the wide sweep of Tyneford Bay and at its far end, the Thorpehead nuclear reactor. During the day, its vast domed roof was unmistakable. It was dark now but Jack knew exactly what he was looking at. Despite the wind, despite the rain, the bay was illuminated by a giant roman candle spewing streams of bright red and orange flame upwards and then inland at an almost 90-degree angle. He took out his iPhone and ran a short video, conscious of the fact that the wind noise would probably dominate the footage, pitch black except for the blazing reactor. Maybe he could play with a few of the filters once he had retrieved his laptop from home. But once he had everything set up back at the Boar's Head, his report would start tomorrow morning at this very same spot.

17 - One day later

M5 motorway, Somerset

The light was fading as they finally approached the service station slip road. Like several thousand other Bristol residents, they had received the latest emergency alert from the Government by text that morning. It told them to head for one of the many reception centres which had been set up, in their case, a service station on the M5 from where they would be transferred to longer-term but temporary accommodation. They had been told what to bring – ID, medication, phone, charger, clothes for a week – and also what not to bring. This included perishable foods, large household items and pets. Incredibly, faced with the risk of potential radioactive contamination, the great British public seemed far more concerned about being separated from their dogs, cats and goldfish. The tabloid press was having a field day over this outrage and social media was in meltdown. One conspiracy theorist TV pundit had claimed exclusively that he had read all sixty pages of the Government's own 'Evacuation and Shelter Guidance' document issued a decade earlier which actually contained a whole chapter specifically relating to the evacuation of pets and animals. It needed a Government spokesperson to highlight that the first sentence in that particular section started with the words, 'only in the most extreme circumstances is it realistic to expect evacuees to leave their pets behind', and a full-scale evacuation of Bristol and a wave of towns and cities to the east was indeed extreme.

So here they were, the Boulton family from south Bristol, making tortuous progress west in their Peugeot 3008. Dad Jeremy at the wheel with his teacher wife Fiona beside him. In the rear were children Esme, eight years old, her three-year-old brother Harvey, and Smart the dog. Mostly Fox terrier but with a bit of something else, the Boultons couldn't be sure as he had been acquired from an animal rescue centre last year. From that point on, the Boulton family had three children not two and while Esme loved her little brother dearly, her best pal ever was Smart. So it was little use Fiona trying to explain the importance of messages from the Government or evacuation and shelter guidance procedures to an eight-year-old. Seizing on the underlying messages that she had heard on the TV programmes that this 'precautionary' evacuation was only going to be 'temporary' Esme could not see how having a small, short-haired dog along would make any difference. She would take full care of him. After almost half an hour of arguments, screaming and tears, Jeremy, anxious to actually get moving, finally sided with his daughter over his wife.

By the time they joined the single lane queue on the approach to the slip road they had been driving for almost six hours, having not succeeded once in reaching top gear. On a normal day they could have made the journey in around 45 minutes. The worst part had been from their house to joining the motorway itself. The gridlock started at the end of their own street. Jeremy had tried a couple of the rat runs he had used a few times when rush hour traffic had built up, but not surprisingly, so had everyone else. In the end it was simply a case of joining the rest of the traffic which was in any event heading in the same direction. At they passed petrol station where Jeremy had fortunately filled the tank only a couple of days earlier, there was a chain across the entrance and a hand-written notice hanging from it announcing there was no more fuel. The lights in the kiosk were off but the door was open, obviously forced, and three young men were calmly walking out. Two were carrying trays of cider and lager cans while the third had a large black bin liner which was clearly bulging. Making no attempt to disguise their appearance, the three left the garage on foot, heading in the opposite direction to almost everyone else. As they reached the sign hanging from the chain, the one holding the black bag took out a marker pen and wrote 'No cigs' just below the message about fuel.

It was worse when they reached the high street. Every retail outlet had been closed since the Prime Minister's TV address but the shops that lined the precinct were open to the elements. Windows had been smashed, doors were hanging open and even those with shutters had been forced. Some people were still entering and leaving with armfuls of foodstuffs from the supermarket, drugs from the pharmacy, even clothes and TV screens. And these people were clearly the latecomers. As Fiona looked through the car window almost every shop along the high street that she could see inside simply had bare shelves.

Acute Radiation Syndrome

Briefing note

Prepared by the Scientific Advisory Group for Emergencies

Executive summary

- *Acute radiation syndrome (ARS), also known as radiation sickness or radiation poisoning, is a collection of health effects that are caused by being exposed to high amounts of ionising radiation in a short period of time. The severity depends on the type of radiation exposure and length of exposure. Even the slightest exposure, without any initial reaction, can have destructive effects with rays and particles of alpha, beta and gamma radiation snapping strands of DNA, causing exposed cells to die.*

- *Early symptoms are usually nausea and vomiting together with reddening of the skin. The danger is that these symptoms can pass within one to two days and the patient enters a deceptive latency period. Depending on the severity of the initial exposure, this latency period can last for days or even weeks before the development of additional symptoms from which recovery is often not possible.*

- *Initial analysis of the explosion at Thorpehead Nuclear Power Station indicates the presence of both alpha and beta contamination as well as high levels of gamma radiation in the form of Iodine 131.*

- *People living closest to Thorpehead and first responders in particular will have suffered both alpha and beta contamination. Depending on the level of exposure, initial symptoms would present after between one and six hours. These include sore eyes and throat, dizziness, nausea and vomiting.*

- Clothes should be removed and destroyed. Heads and facial hair shaved and lengthy showering is recommended. Potassium iodine tablets are to be taken.

- The most severe exposure can cause death within 24 hours but in more healthy victims, recovery from the effects of alpha radiation is common.

- Beta radiation contamination is more serious and symptoms take longer to present (between one week and one month, depending on the degree of contamination). Beta radiation leads to the loss of white blood cells. External symptoms include hair loss, skin discolouration and ulcers on the limbs and torso which do not heal. This is often followed by loss of appetite, vomiting and abdominal pain.

- Gamma radiation does far more damage internally. Concentrating on the thyroid gland, it causes irreversible changes to DNA and organ failure. Mortality follows within days.

- Gamma radiation also has longer-term effects. Even subjected to lower levels of contamination, the case of Chernobyl highlights a continuing growth in cases of childhood leukaemia and other cancers decades after the explosion in 1986.

- Early casualty reports following the explosion are light, although it has to be noted that there are still more than twenty people missing, presumed dead. These are all members of staff employed at Thorpehead and working closest to the reactor.

- It has to be expected that emergency first responders will start to present with initial symptoms within the coming days, if not hours.

*   *We continue to monitor the course of the radioactive cloud emanating from the reactor at Thorpehead and analysing particles which have been falling with the rain. It is highly likely that members of the public living under the path of the radioactive fallout will have been contaminated, albeit to a lesser extent, prior to their evacuation. It is vital however, that this evacuation process continues at pace so that citizens living further away from Thorpehead do not suffer a similar fate.*

*   *There will be fatalities, even if numbers cannot yet be estimated. Based on the medical information received so far on patients being treated at Riverbridge General Hospital, we anticipate the first mortalities will occur within a week.*

*   *And the means of disposal of bodies is another urgent matter. Those victims of the higher levels of radiation poisoning will require burial in zinc coffins and in designated areas only.*

Cabinet Office Briefing Room

'Right, this meeting of COBRA is now officially in session.' Strathyre looked around the room. There were no faces at the table that he didn't already know or recognise. The only change was opposite him where Field Marshal Leighton Parks was now seated alongside Nadia Yadav, the Home Secretary. In the alcoves behind the briefing room table, more of the people sitting at desks and monitoring laptops were in military uniform.

'Mark, can we have an update on the last twenty-four hours?'

The Civil Contingencies Director tapped a couple of keys on his own laptop which instantly woke the giant screen behind him into a Battenberg of charts and live camera footage.

'Thank you, Prime Minister. If I can start with the fire.' His mouse hovered over the image in the top left of the display, clicking on it to occupy the full screen. 'The weather has improved and we have been able to get helicopters close to Thorpehead. This was filmed just over one hour ago and it's the first time we have been able to look into the reactor core. Clearly, it is still burning and releasing particles into the atmosphere but the Fire Service have examined the footage and believes the decision to let the fire burn itself was the correct one.'

'How much longer will that take?' asked the Prime Minister.

'Too early to say, Prime Minister. But as you can see from where the helicopter was filming upwind, it is still not safe to get much closer to the reactor. We are hoping to be able to launch drones tomorrow and they should be able to give us a better idea. It won't be immediately, though. The temperature was almost three-thousand degrees when the reactor blew. The better news is that with the winds dropping, the dispersal of radiation may not be as widespread as it has been. The forecast is promising too, with no strong wind or change of direction over the next three days. That's not to say it's the end of the problem but it does mean we can concentrate our efforts on the more pressing areas.'

'Which are?'

Mark Brooks drew a deep breath. 'Evacuation initially, but then the prospect of a nation split in two by an exclusion zone. As you are all aware, evacuation of an area from the Bristol Channel to Swindon has been underway since last night and people living in Buckinghamshire to Essex have been put on notice to depart. I'll ask Gold Command to give us an update on the first part of that. Chief Constable Merton?'

Attention switched to the separate TV screen positioned immediately behind Mark Brooks' seat. The police chief, now wearing his tactical top rather than uniform shirt and epaulettes, was once more attending the meeting by Zoom from Exeter.

'Thank you, Mark, Prime Minister, ministers. Mass evacuation commenced last evening. The system appears to be working so far, although paradoxically, the traffic chaos in some areas may well have actually regulated the flow of evacuees arriving at the reception centres. Those centres are almost entirely manned by military personnel. It's still too early to have accurate figures but I am receiving reports that the number of evacuees being processed is lower than expected. It is evident that a number of people living in the affected areas have simply left in the last twenty-four hours, most likely to stay with friends or relatives in other parts of the country. The alternative scenario is that they are choosing to stay put. I'm not sure at this stage that I have the manpower to go checking door-to-door or whether I can put more personnel at risk of contamination.'

'I agree, Gold Commander,' Field Marshal Parks responded. 'We will be able to carry out drone surveillance from tomorrow morning, although it is of course a massive area to patrol. I certainly don't want to see patrols rounding up stragglers in every neighbourhood, and I am not sure what sanction we can impose at this stage for those who ignore the order to evacuate.'

The Home Secretary stared across at the Prime Minister. 'I am sure there is an offence of ignoring your evacuation order under the new powers you have invoked, Prime Minister, although I am not sure my department has been notified of exactly what that crime might be. But I am assuming the idea of arresting offenders and bringing them before a magistrate is not high on your to-do list at the moment?'

'I'm struggling to decide whether that is an expression of genuine concern for the law or an attempt at sarcasm because you think you've been missed out of the loop, Nadia.' Strathyre's voice was beginning to rise in anger. 'Whichever it is, you are right. It's not the most important issue right now.'

Field Marshal Parks jumped in to diffuse the moment. 'I think it is clear, Gold Commander. We will do all we can to ensure anyone still in the exclusion zone does heed the importance of the evacuation notice and is aware of the risk to their health if they stay. There is only so much we can do and I certainly do not want any military or police personnel being put to any greater risk than they are already.'

'Thank you, Field Marshal. Can I also ask you about the large number of military personnel who have arrived at Gold Command in the last couple of hours? They are telling me that they are here to provide tactical and logistical support but I am unsure of the chain of command right now.'

'Chief Constable. You are Gold Commander and I am thankful to you for everything you have done in the last twenty-four hours,' Prime Minister Gordon Strathyre responded. 'The Field Marshal and I have been discussing this and we feel that as the situation develops from the fire and evacuation, Gold Command will require assistance in other areas of expertise. But please be assured, you are Gold Commander and it is you that COBRA is relying on to help frame the committee's decisions. Now, the Field Marshal has just referred to acute radiation sickness or ARS, can I assume everyone has read the Chief Scientific Officer's briefing note on the effects of radiation sickness?' the Prime Minister's voice had now regained its normal level of control. A rustling of paper and affirmative murmuring around the table. 'So, Derek, what is the current situation?'

Derek Beaumont gathered his papers in front of him. 'Can I start by explaining to those of you who have managed to read the whole report rather than the summary about the terms of measurement we have used. Roentgen is the unit used to record levels of radiation in the atmosphere while levels of contamination absorbed by the body are expressed in the report in Grays or Sieverts. But, as the executive summary makes clear, there are two variables which we cannot quantify fully at this stage without more data – the amount of radiation that people have been exposed to and for how long. Using previous nuclear accidents as a basis, there is an understandable assertion that the contamination risk diminishes the further away you are from the scene of the explosion.

'But at Thorpehead we have the further complication that radioactive particles have been carried further by the strong winds as well as falling with the rain. As yet we have not been able to get close enough to the reactor to take actual measurements, but we are now testing the first evacuees as well as the emergency services personnel who were first to respond. I have to say, Gold Commander, if they have not already been withdrawn from duty, they must be immediately. It is more than likely they will have suffered from alpha and beta radiation at the very least.'

'Are you saying that police and fire officers will die?' the

Home Secretary came in.

'There are going to be fatalities as a consequence of radiation contamination. We cannot pretend otherwise. My feeling is that if the majority of the local population was indoors at the time and remained there until they were evacuated, then their risk is not significant. But the emergency services that responded to the fire and have been organising the evacuation have had far greater exposure. It's more than likely that many will start to display some of the symptoms described in the report from now on. That's why we want them removed from action and treated as soon as possible.'

'We do have five police and fire crew in hospital at the moment, Professor,' Chief Constable Merton's voice was heard before his face appeared on the screen. 'They have been vomiting and complaining of headaches.'

'As I thought. I fear there will be more Chief Constable, and not just at Thorpehead. You will need to ensure that any forces working in or close to the exclusion zone are not only protected but also limited in the amount of time they are there.'

'Do you have an estimation of likely fatalities yet?' the Prime Minister asked.

'Far too early to say, Prime Minister. But given the trajectory of the radiation cloud, I would say this is just the beginning. Hundreds of deaths certainly, but I haven't ruled out thousands. And then we have the further question of what to do with the bodies.'

'I think now might be a good time to consider the other major issue.' Mark Brooks took advantage of the momentary silence in the room to wrestle back the agenda. Enlarging one of the screens to display a map of England. 'The precise boundaries of the exclusion zone have now been determined.' Just as on the previous day when a click of his mouse superimposed a red band across the map charting the predicted path of the radiation cloud, today a series of blue dots appeared in a generally similar pattern. 'Work has already begun to erect post and wire fences on the parts already evacuated and REME tell us that they will continue to move eastwards over the coming days as more areas are emptied. As was mentioned yesterday, we will soon have created our own version of the Berlin Wall from one coast of England to the other. This has significant consequences for the transport infrastructure. Apart from removing key sections of the motorway and rail networks, it effectively ends any form of north-south travel. This is going to affect everything from food to fuel supplies, not to mention people currently working on one side of the exclusion zone and living on the other. University terms are due to end next week, potentially trapping thousands of students who are prevented from going home.'

A silence fell around Briefing Room 1 as the Civil Contingencies Director continued his briefing. 'We currently import almost fifty per cent of our food, and the vast majority of that comes in via Dover and the south coast ferry ports or the cargo terminal at Heathrow Airport which is currently closed. None of that produce will be able to travel beyond the exclusion zone. In the short term we also have to consider that there may be more than two million extra people living in that area due to the evacuation, but the major supermarkets have warned us that they would run out of supplies in the rest of the country within three to four days. For fuel, it's the reverse position. With only one refinery located south of the exclusion zone, we are going to have to hope at this stage that it will be sufficient to meet demand. But the priority for our department is revising shipping movements and diverting food imports to ports such as Immingham, Hull, Swansea and Liverpool.'

Nadia Yadav looked away from the screen displays towards Mark Brooks. 'It seems with every issue you start to address, another unforeseen circumstance is uncovered. Would that be fair to say, Mark?'

'It certainly looks that way at the moment. Even with the evacuation so far today, we are discovering most of the vehicles from the Bristol area are contaminated. We've no plan as yet for what to do with them other than leave them in isolation at the reception areas.'

The Home Secretary then turned towards the Prime Minister. 'Normally, I would be asking whether we should be making a statement in the House, but the Cabinet Office has already advised me of a problem there too. It looks like we have got Members here who can't get back to their constituencies and others there who will be unable to come back to Westminster. I am worried about how the Government will be able to function at a time when the country needs us most, Prime Minister.'

'I wouldn't worry too much about Westminster Nadia. I am going to see the King shortly to request the prorogation of Parliament. The Civil Emergencies Act gives me the power to take the necessary decisions in the current circumstances and given what Mark has just been saying, it's clear that the situation remains dynamic. Scrutiny can come later. Thank you, Mark, thank you, Gold Commander, that's all for now. COBRA will reconvene shortly. Field Marshal? With me please.'

With that, the Prime Minister left Briefing Room 1, closely followed by Field Marshal Leighton Parks.

M5 motorway, Somerset

The sign still read 'Welcome to Somerset Services' but it soon became clear this was no ordinary welcome. As they came around the bend from the slip road the Boulton family was met by two hazmat-suited officers, one holding a SIG MCV carbine. They didn't know whether these were police or military, and behind their visors, they weren't even sure whether they were men or women. Jeremy halted the Peugeot as instructed and wound down his window at the signal from the armed officer. At the same time, the other officer walked to the rear of the car and started scanning the bodywork with a Geiger counter. Fearing that Smart would react at the sight of two strange figures in suits and hoods, Esme pulled the blanket over the dog which was nestled asleep on her lap.

'Good evening, sir,' the armed police woman said. Taking the signal from her colleague who had now reached the front bumper of the car, 'Kindly park your vehicle in lane 26 up ahead. Then take everything you need with you and enter the service station building opposite. Leave your car keys in the ignition but take any other keys for your house et cetera with you. Once you have been registered inside, you will leave from the other side of the building and be taken to your allocated accommodation by bus.'

'What about my car? Why do you want my keys?'

'Your vehicle is showing high levels of radiation contamination, sir. You will not be permitted to take it any further than here.'

Jeremy was starting to panic. 'But I need my car. If it's

contaminated like you say, then what about us?'

'You will all be tested once you're inside and we'll have the details of your car. But for now, it's not as important as getting you to safety. Please do as I have told you and quickly.' From the manner of her voice, not to mention the SIG slung loosely over her shoulder, Jeremy knew this was no petty jobsworth but someone used to being listened to. He drove towards the marked lane while Fiona gathered up the passports and other personal items they had with them inside the car. Esme picked up her rucksack and opened it. There was nothing inside it other than the rug Smart usually slept on at home and a couple of doggy treats. Gently, she lowered the dog into the rucksack, shushing him as she loosely closed the flap.

They went through the entrance to the service station and immediately joined one of the lines which zig-zagged through what used to be the self-service cafeteria. If Esme thought this was like queuing at airport security before going on holiday, any similarity disappeared when they reached the control point to be met by a line of hazmat-suited soldiers with hand-held Geiger counters. Most of the people being scanned were moving on towards a line of desks Esme could see at the far end of the room, but sometimes one person was being led off in a different direction and taken behind a screened-off area. And further on, she could see other people re-emerging into the main rooms wearing one-piece coveralls and with shaven heads. When the Boultons reached the front of the queue they split into two groups. Jeremy took Harvey and Fiona moved forward to the adjacent station with Esme (and Smart).

'Don't be afraid,' one of the soldiers said to Esme. 'We are just going to check your radiation levels before you go on to register. You will all be given potassium iodine tablets to take as a precaution.'

'What's with the head shaving and the overalls?' asked Fiona.

'Some people have been exposed to more radiation than we would like so that's just a precaution. Better safe than sorry,' the female soldier said as she passed the Geiger counter up and over Fiona's head. 'But you're fine, Madam. Now let's check on your daughter.' As she scanned from Esme's feet up to her head the dosimeter was only recording background levels, but as she brought it down across her back and the rucksack, the clicking immediately became faster and louder. 'I'm sorry Miss, I'm going to need your backpack.' With that, she lowered the strap off Esme's shoulder. The soldier felt the weight shift as she held the bag, just as a little snout and two brown eyes appeared from under the flap. Esme let out a wail as three more hazmat-clad soldiers appeared out of nowhere, one of them holding a SIG. One held the backpack while another removed Smart and held him at arm's length. Without a word, the three soldiers about turned and left the building through a side door.

'You were specifically told not to bring pets,' the woman officer turned towards Fiona, her initial friendly tone, now quite official. 'I realise your daughter may be upset but you saw for yourself what happened with the Geiger counter. Animals are more likely to have radioactive contamination on their fur, which is why we can't let them go any further. Don't worry, you are not the first to try to bring their pet with them.'

Fiona was struggling to hear what the soldier was saying while attempting to console and control her daughter's anguished screams. But Smart was gone. 'What's going to happen to our dog now?'

'Not for me to say. You'll have to give the details at the registration desk and they will be able to explain the next steps.'

Jeremy was now waiting for them, with Harvey in his arms, also in tears. He hadn't witnessed everything but had seen Smart being taken away by soldiers in strange suits and holding guns. And now his big sister was bawling inconsolably. Jeremy looked at Fiona without saying a word. 'I told you so' was easy enough with just the eyes.

'Come on, we need to get registered and find out where on earth we are going to stay tonight.'

'Oh, what a surprise! Another dog for us to look after!' Lieutenant O'Farrell was just finishing a phone call as the three soldiers brought Smart into the makeshift kennels in a tent alongside the service station building. It had been erected as a storage area for hazmat suits and protective gear that the soldiers would need, but had rapidly been commandeered as a kennel once the evacuees started arriving, ignoring instructions to leave their pets behind. Although the lieutenant was part of the Royal Army Veterinary Corps, he had been dispatched to the Somerset Services as a regular soldier and part of the evacuation force.

Once it became apparent he was a qualified vet he was charged with finding a solution to this unintended consequence of the Government's evacuation order. Smart was just the latest addition to the day's tally which currently stood at over fifty dogs, cats, rabbits and hamsters, not to mention a cockatoo. With no prior provision for animals, the current holding arrangements included makeshift restraints, empty cardboard boxes and even wire wheeled crates more often used for deliveries from the lorries to the various retail outlets in the service area. The dogs were barking incessantly, the cats and rabbits were escaping and the whole place stank of animal excrement.

Lieutenant O'Farrell called to the team that had just delivered Smart as well as the other soldiers who were busy trying to round up cats wearing their Hazmat suits and avoid stepping in shit.

'I've just got off the phone with command. It's as we assumed. Most of the animals are already contaminated, there is no question of being able to treat or look after them and they cannot just be left to roam wild. They have to be destroyed. Our only concern must be the safe evacuation of the public. Now that may not come as a surprise to any of you. The only downside from my position as a vet is that we have no pentobarbital and I am the only person qualified to administer it if we did.' O'Farrell glanced at the SIG Carbines which had been propped against the wall by the soldiers while they attended to pets. 'There is only one quick and effective way of dealing with the problem. I am still awaiting instructions about disposal as most, if not all of them have been showing higher levels of contamination. But for now, you have a job to do. All I ask is that you show some respect for the families who have had to leave these animals behind. This is not a turkey shoot but we cannot let any animal escape and run wild. You are soldiers and I expect you to act professionally. Let's get to it.'

By the time the Boultons had completed the registration procedure, Esme and Harvey had at least stopped crying. Now a harsh reality had started to sink in. Jeremy had received assurances that his car would be safe but that it would continue to be monitored for radiation levels. The only answer to questions about Smart was that they should not have brought him in the first place. They had been allocated a two-bedroom holiday apartment in a resort in the far west of Cornwall, almost at Land's End. Ironically, they had been considering a family holiday there, possibly next year, but these were most definitely not the conditions in which they considered they would be making their first visit. As the waiting coach began to fill with other families heading for the same location, there was none of the building anticipation which might normally be associated with such a departure. Instead, bewildered children and terrified parents sat in silence as the realisation of events over the last 24 hours became increasingly apparent. Nobody spoke as the coach rolled forward and headed towards the M5 motorway. The only sound came from the giant marquee which had been built alongside the service station. Dogs were not just barking but howling. Then came a regular dull popping nose, a short series of single shots being fired. Before long, the noise of the dogs abated completely.

News 24.com
10.35 pm: Update
Chaotic scenes as evacuation gets underway

There have been scenes of panic and chaos as the mass evacuation of Bristol and Swindon gets underway with traffic gridlock and reports of widespread looting.

Having been ordered to prepare for evacuation yesterday, residents of Bristol and Swindon have received further emergency alert texts giving details of their nearest reception centre to report for onward evacuation. A number of centres, manned by military personnel have been set up overnight in places from the M5 motorway services to Cotswolds Airfield and Didcot railway station. The move has sparked panic in city centres and caused traffic gridlock in several areas. The situation has not been helped by some people ignoring the initial message to await further instructions and deciding to take matters into their own hands by leaving immediately. There have been incidents with long queues at petrol stations which have subsequently run out, leading some motorists to become violent. A number who did manage to fill their tanks then simply drove off without paying. Many retail stores which were forced to close yesterday following the Prime Minister's address to the nation, have been broken into and looted.

Residents have been told to bring identification, clothes and any medical supplies for a week and given details of their reception centre. Buses and coaches have been seen gathering at some of these centres, suggesting people will be taken onwards to their allocated accommodation. Local councils in tourist resorts in Devon and Cornwall have issued notices to hotel and caravan park owners, in effect commandeering their accommodation to house evacuees. An appeal has gone out to individual home owners who can take in guests, similar to the scheme which ran a few years ago to take in refugees from Eastern Europe displaced by the Russian invasion.

18 - Two days later

News 24.com

9.45am: Exclusion zone after Thorpehead blast?

News24.com understands an exclusion zone is being established from the Bristol Channel to the Deben Estuary in Essex due to radioactive contamination from the Thorpehead power station explosion.

Mass evacuation of people living west of Bristol and as far as Swindon started yesterday (see yesterday 10.35pm) with other towns and cities put on stand-by. Now it looks as if the Government is set to evacuate everyone living along a 15km wide corridor along that route. This will include large parts of the Home Counties and Essex towns including Harlow and Chelmsford. The M4 motorway remains closed, although large lengths of it would now fall within the proposed exclusion zone. Military vehicles have been seen in several locations including the Royal Electrical and Mechanical Engineers (REME) with diggers and heavy equipment.

A Government spokesperson declined to comment on the speculation when asked, but told News24.com that a COBRA meeting was currently taking place and that there would be a ministerial announcement later this afternoon.

Inside 10 Downing Street

Archie Wilkes was pouring the coffee. On the sofa opposite sat Field Marshal Leighton Parks. Prime Minister Gordon Strathyre sat in the velvet upholstered wingback armchair between the two of them.

'You decided not to chair this morning's COBRA then Prime Minister?'

'No, I have handed that to our very capable and extremely ambitious Home Secretary. Dear Nadia has her eyes firmly on my position, or at least she did before this shit show happened. I suspect she would rather be sniping from the side lines and waiting for me to fail, so it won't hurt for the great British public to see her at the centre of the Government's decision making right now. She'll be briefing me later in time for my TV address this evening although I am not sure anything that comes up in COBRA this morning will change what I need to say.'

'Yes, likewise. The Rear Admiral is there for me and we'll be having lunch later. No doubt you've seen the update from the Civil Contingencies Director about the exclusion zone. I'm staggered we managed to secure so many posts in such quick time but it looks as if the whole of the exclusion zone will be marked out today. The fencing itself is another matter and REME say they are a few days behind which means we are having to patrol much of the remaining perimeter manually. Given the Chief Scientific Officer's instruction to limit the time my men actually spend in the at-risk areas I have to say I am, to all intents and purposes, out of troops. We have some returning from overseas postings and the Rear Admiral has recalled an aircraft carrier from a NATO exercise in the North Sea but I can only see the demands on my forces increasing over the coming days and weeks. I think it is time to implement your plan to press-gang civilians.'

'We're ahead of you Leighton. Archie has been working on this since we talked yesterday and I am minded to make it the focus of my address this evening. By the end of tomorrow we will have hundreds of thousands of people in limbo, living in temporary holiday accommodation and unable to work. They could quickly become restless if we are unable to give them any positive news about their future, and between the three of us, we know that's unlikely to be happening anytime soon. We can turn this back on the displaced to answer the nation's call in a time of critical emergency. To do their patriotic duty and mobilise in support of our emergency services.'

'Steady on Prime Minister. We don't want it to sound too Soviet. We're not going to war.'

'It's interesting you say Soviet, Field Marshal,' Archie Wilkes looked up. 'After Chernobyl, that's precisely what the Soviet Union did with the local population. They called them liquidators and as many as six-hundred-thousand were called up to assist with anything from firefighting and civil defence to driving lorries and buses. They were treated as heroes and even awarded medals. We don't have go that far but being paid to help the Government's response rather than sitting on your hands at a Butlin's holiday camp is a valid call for us to make. But of course, it can't be optional.'

'Well we could start by calling forward everyone who is currently unable to carry out their normal employment because of the evacuation. Then we could expand this to anyone of working age that isn't sick or has care responsibilities. There are bound to be several who already have occupational skills that we need. And presumably we already have the registration details of all those who have been evacuated.'

'Yes and no, Leighton,' said Strathyre. 'The Civil Contingencies Director will no doubt be giving COBRA the current figures and yes, we do already have details of hundreds of thousands of people evacuated. The process is still ongoing and there is a natural delay in processing so much data. But, and this brings me to second point we have to discuss this morning Leighton, there appear to be significant gaps.'

'Gaps?'

'Yes, the figures aren't adding up. The number registered from the Bristol area, which was the first to be evacuated, is nowhere near the electoral roll let alone the likely population. There are three probable explanations: we know many simply fled to stay with relatives or friends in other parts of the country, but we don't know exactly how many; given the high volume and speed of the operation, we cannot rule out data failings; and that leaves the third one, which is the one that concerns me.'

'And that is?'

'There are still people left behind in the exclusion zone. That may be by accident or intentional but the longer they are there, the more they are at risk from radiation. Finding and removing them to safety will use even more of your already stretched resources Leighton as well as putting them at greater risk of harm as well.'

'But we can't let it be seen to be OK to stay behind either,' Wilkes added. 'At the moment there is still a perception that the further east the radioactive cloud has spread, the less the risk. Mark Brooks and Professor

Beaumont both say that is not the case but we are afraid that there might be more resistance to evacuation today in the Home Counties and Essex.'

'You did mention this previously and I said we would start flying drones over the evacuated areas once the weather conditions allowed. But as I also said, the full exclusion zone covers almost half-a-million square miles. Even if the drones find people, we don't have too many options available. Chances are they will have moved on and hidden elsewhere if they spotted a drone and will be long gone by the time we could get troops there. Can I ask, is the infrastructure still functioning in the first areas of the exclusion zone – electricity, water, telephones?'

The Prime Minister's cabinet secretary scrolled on his iPad. 'Civil Contingencies told us the gas supply was halted as a safety measure but other than some damage to masts et cetera in the immediate area around Thorpehead, all other services are still functioning as well as they can be.'

'Then can I suggest that we continue to urge those left behind to leave using broadcast media. I am sure anyone still in the exclusion zone will be following the news while they still have access to a television or radio, but then, after a few more days, we turn off the water and electricity.'

There was a brief silence in the room before the Prime Minister spoke. 'If you think that will drive them out, then why not do it sooner?'

'You're not following, Prime Minister. By that time, anyone still living in the exclusion zone will have been exposed to radiation for a week. If they are still alive then they will most likely be very sick and require medical attention. According to that SAGE briefing document, the chances are that even then it will be too late. Putting it bluntly

Prime Minister, if they don't heed our call to be saved, why should we still have to feel responsible for them?'

'You mean just turn off the lights and leave them to die?'

'As things stand, they are far more likely to die than those who have heeded the call to leave and those are the people we should prioritise. And that brings me to another issue which the Professor raised at yesterday's COBRA. He is correct. There are going to be deaths regardless of what measures we are taking to prevent them. And you don't simply bury a body that's contaminated with radiation. I have been reading some of Professor Beaumont's analysis of the radioactive particles that have been recovered from the Thorpehead area and even cars in Bristol. While Iodine 131 and Xenon 135 cease to be dangerous pretty quickly, they have been finding a lot of Cesium 137 and even Plutonium 239 in the samples. According to the Chief Scientific Officer, these have half-lives, basically when they cease to contaminate, of several years. Or in the case of Plutonium 239, thousands of years. You may not want the public to know this yet, Prime Minister, but the people evacuated from the exclusion zone over the last 48 hours will never be going home. Everything there - cars, buildings, humans – will remain contaminated for anything up to twenty-thousand years. So not only must we leave everything where it is, I think we will need to consider the exclusion zone as the place to dispose of contaminated bodies.'

Holmbeach

It was daylight when Shelley and Evan woke. They'd fallen asleep on the lounge floor, still huddled behind the settee. She had tried to get up during the night but Evan had dragged her back and clung tightly to her. He had never done that before. In fact, Shelley couldn't remember if she had ever received a gesture of affection from her annoying little brat of a brother. She gently stroked his hair. 'Ev, wake up. It's morning.'

Evan stirred, sitting up and wiping his eyes until he suddenly remembered where they were and what had happened. He shot up and crossed the room to open a tiny gap in the curtains. 'Looks like they've gone, Shel. I can't see anyone around. Where's Mum and Dad? Why aren't they home yet?'

Shelley checked her phone. Still no signal. Calling Thorpehead using the landline brought the same result as the previous day, a high, continuous beep meaning number unobtainable.

'There must be some problem at work, especially if the telephone isn't working. They may have sent a message but my phone still has no signal. Only one thing for it. We'll go to Thorpehead and ask to see them. Who knows, maybe I'll get a signal on my phone somewhere other than here.'

'Good idea Shel, let's get going.'

'First things first. Mum may not be here at the moment but that doesn't change the routine. Shower, teeth and breakfast. What do you think she'll say if we go looking like we've slept on the lounge floor all night?'

Thirty minutes later they were both wearing fresh clothes, Shelley having eaten her usual breakfast and Evan having had dried Cocoa Krisp, he finished the last of the milk last night. She'd charged her mobile even though there was still no signal and stuffed some biscuits and a soft drink into a backpack. It was only a short bus ride to Thorpehead but she knew her brother would complain he was hungry. There was no rain and the wind had dropped when they left the house but something was different as they walked to the bus stop. It was quiet. Not Sunday morning sort of quiet, really quiet. There was nobody out walking their dogs in the street and no cars. They'd seen the strange men taking their neighbours away the night before but the longer they walked, they still saw nobody. Shelley checked the timetable on the bus stop. The Thorpehead bus was due in ten minutes. Ten minutes came and went, then another ten, and another.

'I don't get it Ev, Something's not right. We haven't seen the bus and we haven't even seen another car since we've been waiting. And there's still no signal on my phone.'

'Why don't we walk then. It's not that far is it? If the bus comes we can flag it down or someone might give us a lift.'

'It will probably take an hour to walk. I know the way. You sure you're ok with that?'

'No problem Sis, let's get moving. But could I have a drink and something to eat first?'

Jack had slept surprisingly well in the front bedroom he had used as his lookout post the previous day. He had never actually slept in the Boar's Head since returning from London but could now appreciate what so many of the guests used to say about the comfortable mattresses. Having gathered up all he needed from his house last night he had treated himself to a sirloin steak in the hotel kitchen, washed down with what turned out to be a whole bottle of Malbec. They had ordered in extra supplies for the walking group's stay so it would only be going to waste. He had caught up on the news coverage, Thorpehead being virtually the only story, before he must have fallen asleep with the TV still on. After breakfast this morning he uploaded last night's footage from his phone to the laptop and started to prepare for his day out reporting. He'd decided that video reports should complement his written coverage but was still unsure about how best to distribute his news. Along with his laptop, binoculars and camera, Jack also picked up the old computer that Michel used to use during the WATER campaign a couple of years ago. It still had all the log in details for the social media accounts and he wasn't really sure they had been properly closed down. After Michel disappeared and John Forster fled to Spain, all that side of the campaign was simply discontinued. So if he wanted an immediate audience for his findings Jack was sure he could access a massive TikTok audience. He still had no mobile phone coverage but could access the Internet. Scrolling back through his emails he also found the encrypted Proton account he had used to liaise with Michel in France via Elodie. He made a mental note make contact with her. Like Jack, she was convinced Michel's sudden disappearance had something to do with the Thorpehead campaign and he felt she would probably still be interested in what had just happened. Perhaps he could send his reports to her in the first instance for security.

It was shortly after 9 am when Jack set out from the Boar's Head. The rain had cleared and the wind had dropped but there was still that low rumble in the background. Before heading down into Holmbeach, his first stop was the headland to see the scene of the devastation in daylight. Although it was now clear in his mind what must have happened at Thorpehead, nothing prepared him for the sight that greeted him as he looked over Tyneford Bay.

The plume of orange flame was still rising up from where the reactor building had once stood. But what he hadn't been able to see last night was the accompanying grey and black cloud of smoke on either side of the blaze which was rising and then being carried away in an easterly direction on the wind. It was also a case of what Jack didn't see. The dome topped reactor building had become a familiar landmark over the last two years, but so also had what he'd assumed was the control centre, a box like structure about two-thirds the height which stood alongside. Now, there was nothing. The whole area around the burning reactor core had been razed. Further towards the main entrance to the site, the three-storey administration block was still standing, but only just. The steel framework was buckled in places, melted possibly, but the concrete and glass which used to make up the building's exterior was missing. The leeward side of the building was more recognisable, albeit without a single window intact and with remnants of venetian blinds flapping in the wind. The reactor fire was burning but there were no fire crews. In fact, there didn't appear to be any movement at all. Jack trained the binoculars towards the main entrance gate and only then did he find a human presence. A hundred or so metres further up the road he spotted a military lorry pulling up in front of a temporary barrier, patrolled by armed guards wearing full hazmat suits. More troops emerged from the back of the lorry, obviously relieving the original sentries, but first they began to hose down their colleagues from the portable pumps they were now holding. After a few minutes, the departing soldiers climbed aboard before the lorry which turned in a wide arc in front of the barrier and headed back the way it had arrived.

Jack took out his iPhone and started filming in a panoramic sweep from the sea to the reactor and finally the sentries standing guard beyond the power station gates when he heard the low thud of helicopter rotors approaching. He threw himself to the ground and rolled quickly into a clump of bramble bushes. Now lying prone in the undergrowth he kept his phone focussed on the power station as the noise of the helicopter engine drew closer. It must have flown directly over him before finally he could see the military helicopter hovering above the bay. Jack's first thought was it might have been attempting to combat the fire from above like with forest fires but now he could see that this wasn't one of those Chinook heavy lift copters but something more like a Wildcat. It continued to hover over Tyneford Bay, upwind of Thorpehead for a few minutes before it banked to the west and headed off. Jack waited until he could no longer hear the rotor blades before extracting himself from the bushes. With only a couple of scratches and some thorns embedded in his jeans, he dusted himself off and headed for Holmbeach town centre and the quay to continue his research.

Shelley's estimate of an hour's walk proved to be way off. Needless to say, the bus hadn't caught them up and nobody had stopped to give them a lift. After almost two hours of Evan moaning and complaining he was hungry, or thirsty, or tired she finally saw the sign up ahead for the Thorpehead access road. For the last half an hour of the journey, they had become aware of a cloud of black smoke blowing across the horizon.

'Not much further Ev. We'll soon be able to see Mum and Dad.'

She recognised this road. Her parents had brought them here when they first arrived to show where Daddy was going to work. Dad pointed out a derelict cottage, Coombe Farm, and told them the story of an old man who used to live there and tried to stop them building the power station. It was just as Shelley had remembered it. Wide with smooth tarmac (the tyres used to make a different sound on the road when the car turned off the old coast road) and bordered with dry stone walls, so common in this part of the world. But, just as it had been since they left the house this morning, there was nobody around. There were always people coming and going at the power station but there was no traffic at all today. They were probably halfway along the access road when the silence was broken by the sound of a vehicle approaching.

'Typical,' Shelley shouted in frustration. 'We're almost there when our first chance of a lift turns up!'

But Evan wasn't answering. He had heard the approaching engine noise and had frozen. Then, he grabbed his sister's arm and pulled her to the side of the road. There was a five-bar gate leading to a field and Evan put his right foot on the second rung and literally threw himself over the top.

'Quick Shel. It sounds like the lorry from last night. Get over.'

Shelley didn't stop to argue but joined her brother in a slightly more graceful fashion. She had no sooner joined Evan, now crouched behind the wall than the distinctive diesel engine roar was upon them. The lorry rolled passed on the road and Evan dared to poke his head around the edge of the stone parapet, just catching a glimpse of its rear. He was right, it was a military vehicle, and underneath the canvas awning sat four more figures dressed in bright yellow suits and hoods. Neither brother nor sister moved.

'It's them Shel. They're looking for us!'

'Don't be silly Evan. Why would they be looking for us? I can't understand why there is no one else around. And there's a fire. Something's definitely not right.'

With that, the engine noise grew louder. The lorry was coming back. Shelley and Evan instinctively threw themselves flat behind the dry-stone wall as the lorry approached, seemingly going faster than on its first journey. But it drove right by without even slowing. Once the siblings were happy it was safe to emerge, they left the field by simply opening and closing the unlocked gate and continued along the road towards Thorpehead. The smoke cloud was thicker now but was high in the sky and blowing across them.

'We're almost there Ev. When we reach that bend up ahead it's all downhill to the power station.'

But when they reached the left-hand bend, everything suddenly became clear. Thorpehead was no longer there. Up ahead, there were more soldiers in yellow suits standing guard, the remains of an office building stood as if someone had dropped a bomb on it and the reactor building where Shelley and Evan's parents worked was the centre of a giant fireball which was spewing smoke up into the atmosphere. Neither of them had noticed earlier but around them on the tops of the dry-stone walls and the hedgerows, were flakes of grey dust and ash.

'What's happened Shel? Where are Mum and Dad?'

As a teenager, Shelley was no stranger to hysteria. Not be allowed to stay out with her friends as late as she would like, being told what she could or couldn't wear or having to stay in and look after her brother. Anything which didn't agree with her own view on how to lead her life would bring on a temper fit and tears. But faced with the realisation that her parents had met an unimaginable fate and that she and Evan were literally alone in a disaster area, Shelley was remarkably in control.

'Look Evan, that fire is where Mum and Dad worked. There's obviously been an explosion and that's why the soldiers are all in special suits. We aren't going to find them Ev, and we can't stay here. We're not safe.'

'We can't go home Shel, we're not safe there either. What are we going to do without Mum and Dad?'

'I don't know Ev, but I promise I'll look after you. I'll have to work something out but for now we must get as far away from here as possible.'

Shelley and Evan began the long walk back towards Holmbeach with no clear plan other than to get as far away from Thorpehead as possible. They had heard the distant whirr of a helicopter's rotor blades but when they looked up, all they could see in the sky was the grey plume of smoke and ash being carried like an approaching storm cloud. As they drew level with Coombe Farm they could see that it was no longer habitable, just four crumbling walls and a slate roof sagging in the middle. Evan was complaining he was hungry but they both agreed there would be nothing in the farmhouse which merited the risk of breaking in or the roof collapsing. At the main road, instead of returning the way had come, they decided to take the coast road south towards Holmbeach town centre. Hopefully they would find someone there who could help.

It was now the middle of the afternoon and Evan was desperate for food and something to drink. It didn't seem the realisation had sunk in that he had lost both his parents. Either that or his constant whining about being hungry or thirsty was his own way of blocking out that realisation. They were no longer directly beneath the smoke cloud and they hadn't seen any more lorries with soldiers in yellow suits as they made their way along the narrow lane with high hedgerows on either side. After another hour they arrived at a gate with the sign for Hillcrest Farm. They could see the cottage some fifty metres or so along the drive with a rusty Landrover parked outside. A faint trace of smoke was rising from the chimney.

'Looks like there's someone home. Let's go and see,' said Shelley.

'Hopefully they've got something to eat,' her brother replied.

There was no answer when they knocked at the kitchen door but trying the latch, Shelley found it was unlocked.

'Hello,' she called on entering.

There was no answer. The kitchen was as traditional as you could find with a flagstone floor, dark oak dressers with rows of plates, bowls and pots hanging on hooks. There were no electrical gadgets such as a microwave, kettle or air fryer, just a large black enamel Aga range and an open fireplace taking up most of the far wall. A wood fire was smouldering in the fireplace and at the table in the centre of the room there was a single chair. On the table itself stood a teapot and a half-drunk cup of tea beside it.

'There's somebody here,' Shelley said, calling out 'Hello' once more.

'Great, let's see what there is to eat,' said Evan, making for one of the cupboards.

'No, Evan. That's not polite. Let's find who lives here first and explain what's happened to Mum and Dad.'

There was still no sound or movement in the cottage.

'Perhaps they're in the barn. Let's go and have a look,' Shelley said, making for the door and the large outbuilding on the other side of the courtyard. The large double doors were closed but was Shelley approached the wooden latch there was a loud crack and a shower of splinters exploded from the barn door. Before she and Evan could work out what had happened, another shot rang out from behind them and a bullet ricocheted off the cobbles a metre or so to their right.

'Bugger off, get out of here and leave me alone,' came a shout from the direction of the farmhouse. As they turned around, all they could see was the barrel of a rifle protruding from a gable window on the first floor.

'Please, we need help. Our parents have died in the explosion,' Shelley cried. For the first time today, her emotions were catching up with her.

'I don't want anyone here. Leave me alone and get away,' came an elderly male voice, quickly followed by another shot, this time into the air above Shelley and Evan's heads.

The two, didn't wait to try and reason. Whoever lived here was clearly not looking for company and certainly wasn't likely to offer any explanation for what was going on, nor any food or drink. They quickly ran back to the road leading towards Holmbeach town centre and didn't stop until they were well out of range from the farmhouse.

'Why did he shoot at us, Shel?' Evan asked his sister when they had regained their breath enough to talk.

'I don't know, Ev,' she gasped in return. 'We're not safe out here. Let's keep going to Holmbeach. Hopefully we'll find a better welcome there.'

'And something to eat. My tummy thinks my throat has been cut.'

News 24.com

10.15pm: Mass evacuation, nuclear fallout and military call-up as the full extent of Thorpehead explosion becomes apparent.

A radioactive exclusion zone will cut England in two and 'volunteers' are to be called up to help the military and emergency services deal with the consequences of the explosion two days ago at the Thorpehead nuclear power station on the Bristol Channel.

Earlier this evening, Prime Minister Gordon Strathyre gave his second television address to the nation, providing more information about the incident and its devastating consequences. In his statement, he confirmed that a catastrophic failure in the cooling system caused a build-up of pressure inside the Thorpehead reactor and subsequent explosion. The fire is still burning and radioactive particles continue to be released into the atmosphere, carried on the strong winds of Storm Hilda, across the country in an east-north-easterly direction. These have also been falling with the rain, risking further contamination along a corridor approximately 15km wide and stretching as far as the Essex coast.

As News24.com reported yesterday, evacuation has already commenced in the Bristol area and as far as Swindon. Other locations were put on stand-by and the Prime Minister has now confirmed that the mass evacuation of residents living along the full length of the perceived exclusion zone will now commence. It is understood that the total number of people affected could exceed two million. Soldiers, mainly from the Royal Electrical and Mechanical Engineer (REME) Corps have been at many locations along the course of the exclusion zone preparing or installing fencing.

This evening Prime Minister Strathyre said he wanted to be honest with the people about the risks they faced: "Every decision we have taken so far has been precautionary. The situation continues to evolve and we are constantly updating our understanding of the consequences. But I have to tell you that we now know many areas have received radioactive contamination from the rain that has fallen since the explosion at Thorpehead. There is a serious risk to health for anyone living along the path we have plotted using wind direction and speed. We are still analysing particles to ascertain the exact composition of the radiation being released from the reactor, which continues to burn.

"There is no easy way to say this but for many people, a return to a normal life in their current home will not be possible any time soon. For others, living further away, you must heed any instructions you receive to evacuate. Sitting tight and hoping for the best is not an option."

The Prime Minister also said that the Government's Civil Contingencies Department was continuing to liaise with local authorities and issuing instructions to residents via its Emergency Alert text messaging system. The large majority of people evacuated so far are being housed in tourist resorts in the South West and in Wales. But an appeal has now gone out nationwide for home owners with spare accommodation to come forward in the similar way to the recent Ukrainian refugee crisis. The Prime Minister also announced the creation of a civil defence force, drawn initially from among those displaced, to provide manpower support for the military and emergency services.

"You will not be surprised when I tell you that our fire, police and ambulance services on the spot have worked tirelessly over the last 48 hours, ably supported by our military. It is clear that this is going to be a much longer-term operation than anything we have encountered since the Second World War. So I am also announcing that work has started to create a civilian support force which will be able to provide much needed assistance to those front line workers. Initially we will be looking to those displaced evacuees to help us. Most will be unable to continue with their normal occupations because of the evacuation and many may well already possess skills which will be vital to our response work. But we will also be appealing to the wider public in the rest of the nation to volunteer their support. I will be announcing more details about *recruitment in the next 24 hours."*

Meanwhile, transport has been affected across the country due to the exclusion zone. Motorways remain closed in several areas and rail services suspended. Lorries arriving at the port of Dover with destinations north of London are being held on the M2 motorway in a reverse of the established stacking system which is often imposed when there is disruption on ferry or tunnel services. Supermarkets have also reported problems with deliveries, particularly to stores in the South and South West and it can only be assumed the situation will deteriorate with the extension of the exclusion zone.

✳✳✳✳✳

The Clarion newspaper (Hollingsworth Media)

PRIME MINISTER LEVELS WITH PUBLIC ON THORPEHEAD

Prime Minister Gordon Strathyre has called on residents to do their patriotic duty as Britain faces its greatest challenge since World War Two.

Following the accident at the Thorpehead nuclear power station two days ago the Prime Minister gave his second televised address to the nation last night, evoking the spirit of the great wartime leader Winston Churchill and urging citizens to join a volunteer support force which will provide assistance for the hard-pressed emergency services and military.

The Prime Minister was frank and honest in his appraisal of the situation following the blast, confirming that a temporary exclusion zone had been established right across the country from the Bristol Channel to the Wash due to concerns over radioactive fallout. He stressed that the measures being put in place were purely precautionary at this stage while the situation was still being evaluated but he pulled no punches when it came to the potential longer-term effects. He told viewers: "There is no easy way to say this but for many people, a return to a normal life in their current home will not be possible any time soon. For others, living further away, you must heed any instructions you receive to evacuate. Sitting tight and hoping for the best is not an option."

There is still no confirmation of the cause of the explosion at the revolutionary nuclear power plant which opened just over a year ago but the Clarion understands that terrorism has not yet been ruled out. The populations of Bristol and Swindon have already been successfully evacuated for their own safety and residents are being housed in holiday accommodation in the West Country and Wales. Gordon Strathyre last night confirmed that people living further east along the course of the fallout cloud are similarly being prepared for evacuation and he asked families who responded to the recent Ukraine crisis by opening their homes to refugees, to come forward and do the same for the new wave of evacuees.

The closure of large stretches of the M4 motorway between London and Wales as well as the suspension of rail services has had some knock-on effects, stranding some passengers and disrupting supplies to shops and supermarkets. The Prime Minister said that some further disruption was inevitable but expected the situation to return to normal once the civilan support force was up and running.

Holmbeach

Jack had spent a busy evening writing up his observations from the day. The Faustian scenes of Thorpehead burning out of control and the eerie silence of Holmbeach town centre where shops, businesses and homes all looked as if their occupants had just stepped out for five minutes and would return at any moment. He'd captured a lot of film on his iPhone, which still had no signal, and was able to upload and edit it on his laptop. With the broadband still working at the hotel he'd also made contact with Elodie in France.

There was so much they needed to say to each other, about the disappearance of Michel, the dirty tricks which scuppered the WATER campaign and more importantly, what was happening in Holmbeach right now. He would send her his first report in the morning, and at the same time, would set about posting reels on social media. He had also been following the latest news online and on TV. It wasn't just Holmbeach which had been evacuated in the aftermath of the explosion, but seemingly a whole swathe of the country. An exclusion zone was about to split the country in two. News of government by emergency powers as well as the military call-up of volunteers or conscripts rang alarm bells for Jack Makepiece the journalist. In other circumstances, events like that would be precursors to government control of the media. Other than ensuring someone else, Elodie, would have copies of his work, he still had to be clear how and where he published those stories. Perhaps TikTok would have to wait.

As far as he could tell, he was alone in the exclusion zone and that would quickly become apparent when his reports were published. A government using emergency powers and sensitive to media interpretation may well decide to do something about it once they found out. One item in the local TV news, which hadn't made it to the nationals as yet was news that the daughters of local MP James Whitleigh-Howse were among the first casualties being treated following the blast at Thorpehead. One report said they had shown initial symptoms of radiation poisoning but had later been discharged. Jack thought it strange there was no mention of the MP himself, nor the Energy Minister Roland Smith, two of the main protagonists in the original project to bring the nuclear power station to Holmbeach in the first place. There was plenty to think about and much to do tomorrow. But for now, after a full day and another empty bottle of Malbec, Jack decided it was time to enjoy once more the comfort of the Boar's Head's temperature-regulating and adjustable tension mattresses.

It was evening before Shelley and Evan finally walked onto the quayside in Holmbeach. Spooked by their experience back at Hillcrest Farm, they had given any other isolated properties a wide berth and stuck to the main road in the hope that somebody other than soldiers might stop to help. But having seen nobody by the time they reached Holmbeach town centre, neither of them was particularly surprised to find it deserted. There were cars parked in the main car park and side streets but no signs of life. Most of the shops were locked closed and the supermarket was shuttered, much to Evan's dismay. Their spirits were raised when they noticed a light shining in one of the shop windows. When they reached the door, it was unlocked too. But there was no one at home. What made things worse was that it was a book shop. Nothing to eat or drink there, just books to read. Shelley imagined that the owners must simply have left in a rush, presumably when the yellow-suited soldiers turned up, and simply forgot to close up properly.

'This is useless Shel, there's nobody here. We're going to have to break in somewhere if we want anything to eat.'

'And how are we going to do that. Didn't you notice the shutters on the supermarket? The police station is at the end of the quay. If there's anyone here, that's where they're most likely to be. Come on, let's have a look.'

But they knew, almost a hundred metres before they got there that the idea was just as pointless. The blue police sign was still illuminated but behind it, there was not one light on in the building. Shelley tried the door just in case, but it was locked and the reception area was in darkness. A notice on the front door gave an out-of-hours number to call if the station was unmanned, but her phone still had no signal and she supposed that the notice was a standard instruction and nothing to do with what they had seen earlier at Thorpehead. The light was fading as she stood on the quay, wondering what to do next.

'There's a light up there,' Evan said, pointing up to the headland and the Boar's Head hotel. 'Come on, Shel, let's check it out. There might be someone staying at the hotel, and they're bound to have some food up there.'

Despite having been walking all day, their pace quickened as they climbed the hill out of Holmbeach towards the landmark hotel, using Jack's bedroom window as their guiding light. Then suddenly it disappeared.

'The light's gone out Shel,' Evan's voice a mix between deflation and panic.

'Don't worry, Ev. If the light has gone out, someone must have switched it off. There's got to be someone there.'

Jack switched off the TV and extinguished the bedroom light using the bedside controls and turned over. Having read and watched the reports about the evacuation and exclusion zone, he had satisfied himself he was alone and there was no longer any need to hide. He preferred sleeping with the curtains open and being woken by the dawn light. There was little need to activate the alarm system at night either, as there would be no unwelcome visitors. No visitors at all in fact. Despite everything he had experienced in the day and all that was going through his mind, the Malbec had done the trick and as soon as his head hit the pillow he sensed the dreamy wooziness that preceded sleep.

When they arrived at the front door, the Boar's Head was in darkness. If their spirits had deflated, Shelley and Evan's mood soon changed when they pushed on the front door to find it unlocked. There was a traditional brass call bell sitting on the reception desk and Evan delighted in thumping his flattened hand down onto the ringer. As the ding faded away, they found they were still alone in an unlit reception area. Shelley called out, enquiring whether anyone was at home. Still nothing. Evan thumped the bell repeatedly but nobody came and they remained in darkness. Evan then noticed a reading lamp sitting on the lower shelf on the receptionist's side. He stepped around the unit and switched it on, finally giving the pair a low-light view of their surroundings. The lamp was probably used by the night porter as a row of room keys lay immediately behind it. But there was no night porter and only one of the cubbyholes did not have a key. For the first time today, Evan was the more confident of the pair. Events seemed to be catching up with his sister and Shelley had been quiet and uncertain since they had arrived at the hotel.

'Look Shel, whether or not there is anyone here, we are in a hotel. All these keys mean there are rooms free so we have somewhere to sleep. But first, there's a restaurant just behind, which means they've got a kitchen, which means food. I'm starving. Let's find ourselves something to eat and then get some sleep. We can sort everything out in the morning.'

'But we can't afford to stay at a hotel!'

'Come on Sis, keep with the script. There's no one around. If there is someone staying here, then apart from that farmer who shot at us, they'll be the first person we have seen today.' With that, Evan made his way to the kitchen where he quickly found the light switch and the fridge.

Deep sleep usually occurred quickly for Jack so he was surprised to note the time on the LED bedside clock when he opened his eyes again. He had only been asleep for a few minutes. Had something disturbed him or was that part of a dream? He turned over but could not settle again. Were there noises coming from somewhere else in the building? He lay still for a few moments. He had become accustomed to the absolute still of an empty Boar's Head over the last 24 hours. There had always been comings and goings during his time here but he had strangely become accustomed to the absolute tranquillity very quickly. Now there were definitely sounds of movement, possibly even faint voices in conversation.

He got out of bed, for some reason pulling on his jeans, and quietly opened his bedroom door. Creeping barefoot along the corridor to the top of the stairs he became aware of the soft glow of light which was bathing the reception area below. He couldn't be sure whether or not he had locked the front door when he got back to the hotel earlier. He had dispensed with the need to sneak in and out through the rear entrance but he knew he had not been anywhere near the reception desk. Moving quietly down the stairs he could definitely hear voices, young voices, coming from the illuminated kitchen. Passing the reception desk, he leaned over and retrieved a hammer from the second drawer where they always kept bits of maintenance equipment and moved on to the kitchen. Looking through the porthole window he could see the chestnut coloured hair on the back of someone's head. One of the full-length fridge doors was open on the other side of the work surface. Jack kicked at the spring door and burst into the kitchen.

'What the hell do you think you're doing!' he screamed, the hammer raised above his head.

'Please no,' Evan cried. Behind the door, a milk bottle smashed on the floor as Shelley emerged and screamed. Everybody froze for a split second before Evan ran into his sister's arms and the siblings both burst into tears. Jack lowered his arm and placed the hammer on the preparation table as he stared at the two youngsters, not even teenagers, holding each other so tightly they could break, both sobbing uncontrollably.

For the next hour, once Jack had managed to convince them they were in no danger, Shelley and Evan told their story of the strange men in yellow suits and hoods that had come looking for them in the night, how they had gone looking for their parents at Thorpehead and seen the wreckage and how they'd been shot at by the farmer. Jack filled in the gaps with what he'd learned from the news reports. The men in suits who had come to their house were part of the evacuation team taking anyone living within the potential fallout area to safety. Shelley had already worked it out, but it made Jack's job no easier to have to conclude that if their parents had been working that close to the reactor at the time of the explosion, their fate would have been sealed. Shelley insisted on clearing up the mess she had made when she dropped the milk bottle on the floor and Jack offered to make them some food. Neither of them felt like sirloin steak and Jack's other culinary skills ran to scrambled eggs. Shelley accepted gratefully while Evan asked if they had any Cocoa Krisp at this hotel. Jack opened another bottle of Malbec, keeping them company as they devoured their first meal of the day.

'We've got the most comfortable beds in the whole of the West upstairs. You must be shattered. Once you've finished your food we'll get you settled for the night. Tomorrow we can decide what we're going to do next.' Jack chose the twin room right next to his own and Shelley and Evan were soon in bed and fast asleep. Not so Jack. From the heavy-eyed satisfaction following a productive day just a couple of hours ago, he was wide awake and buzzing. Taking the opened bottle of wine back upstairs with him, he opened his laptop and began writing the postscript to his report for Elodie.

19 - Four days later

News 24.com
08.35am: Parliament prorogued

Parliament will be prorogued today and Prime Minister Gordon Strathyre will make decisions using powers under the Civil Contingencies Act.

The Cabinet Office has announced that Prime Minister Gordon Strathyre had another audience with His Majesty the King yesterday (the second in less than 48 hours) to seek the prorogation of Parliament. An announcement will be made in the House of Lords this morning, bringing the current session of Parliament to a close. Prorogation brings all Parliamentary business to an end, including any bills currently in the legislative process. Ironically, this includes the Government's controversial Nuclear Power and Future Strategy Bill which was due for its final reading next month, ushering in a new wave of small nuclear reactors similar to the one at Thorpehead. A spokesperson told News24.com that the decision to suspend the work of Westminster was to allow the Government to concentrate its efforts on the response to the nuclear explosion on the Bristol Channel. They also said that the functioning of Parliament was going to be potentially compromised with MPs unable to combine their constituency work with attendance at Westminster due to the exclusion zone. It is known that some members of Parliament are stranded at Westminster, unable to travel back to their constituencies and vice versa. The exclusion zone itself includes over 40 constituencies, many of which have been entirely evacuated.

Unlike dissolution, prorogation of Parliament means that MPs retain their position, as do government ministers and civil servants. Prime Minister Strathyre's first visit to the King was to invoke powers under the 2015 Civil Emergencies Act and it is understood that all government decisions taken until Parliament reconvenes will be taken using those powers.

Opposition leader Robin Llewellyn has expressed his anger at the announcement. Speaking late last night when informed of the Prime Minister's visit to the King, he said: "The Opposition naturally stands with the Government following this terrible event and expresses its deepest sympathy to the families of those who have lost their lives. Several of our constituencies have seen mass evacuation of residents already and we stand ready to help those people in any way that we can. But we are concerned that the Prime Minister is now in a position to act unilaterally without being held to account, not by the Privy Council nor the House. This is surely the time to form a government of unity, embracing knowledge and experience from all parties. I am concerned that a small number of Government ministers, some of whom do not have the best of track records, will be making decisions in private which cannot even be scrutinised."

The Clarion newspaper (Hollingsworth Media)

OPPOSITION LEADER'S SOUR GRAPES OVER PROROGATION

Opposition leader Robin Llewellyn has thrown his toys out of the pram following the Prime Minister's announcement that Parliament will be prorogued.

Gordon Strathyre yesterday went to see His Majesty the King to announce that the current session of Parliament will end and all key decisions relating to the Thorpehead nuclear power accident will be taken by the Prime Minister and Cabinet under emergency powers contained within the 2015 Civil Emergencies Act, invoked earlier this week. Prorogation means that Government business is still carried out by ministers but the Houses of Parliament will no longer sit. The move, according to the Government, is aimed at focusing all efforts on the response to the Thorpehead situation, but it is also understood that the creation of the temporary exclusion zone has impacted day-to-day operations at Westminster. Some MPs have had to leave their constituencies while others are stranded in London.

But that hasn't prevented the opposition leader from trying to throw the Government off course as it tries to deal with an unprecedented situation, worse even than the Nazi blitz of the Second World War. Mr Llewellyn reacted to the prorogation announcement by claiming he should have a seat at the cabinet table himself in a government of unity. The last time this country did have such a government was during the Second World War when Conservative, Labour and Liberal party members worked together under the leadership of Winston Churchill. While current Prime Minister Gordon Strathyre has been likened to the wartime leader, that is where the similarities end as far as the Opposition Party is concerned. Robin Llewellyn has been a vocal critic of this Government's Nuclear Power and Future Strategy Bill which aims to secure Britain's energy security, and earlier this year his party voted against its first reading in the House. But it seems Mr Llewellyn is not happy that the Prime Minister will be able to take decisions without the Opposition leader being able to scrutinise, or should that be criticise them. Yesterday he said: "I am concerned that a small number of Government ministers, some of whom do not have the best track records, will be making decisions in private which cannot even be scrutinised. This is surely the time to form a government of unity, embracing knowledge and experience from all parties."

Riverbridge

Martin Walsh wasn't sure how long he had been at Riverbridge Hospital. He'd been on a ward with the rest of the crew but now he was alone in a separate room. Their fire engine had been the first on the scene at Thorpehead after the reactor blew and he'd quickly ordered them to turn back once he saw the Geiger counter readings and realised what had just happened. Later in the day, some of the team were complaining of sore throats and dizziness and he noticed the blotches on the back of his hands for the first time. They had all been sent straight to A&E at Riverbridge, where the only treatment was iodine tablets and hours spent in the showers. The rest of the crew were discharged the next day but Martin had been kept in, "under observation", while they carried out further tests. A consultant said something about white blood cells. He had received one blood transfusion, maybe two, but the days seemed to be merging into each other.

When he slept he had nightmares, perhaps not surprising considering what he had witnessed. But when he woke, he had no idea how long he had been out. Was it the next morning or just a few minutes? Nurses seemed to come and go; they took blood samples. They brought food but he wasn't hungry. The ulcers in his mouth – he couldn't remember having ulcers before – meant he couldn't actually chew anything solid and when they tried to give him clear soup, he had just brought it back up. He hadn't looked at his face in a mirror but the doctors were concerned about his complexion. The red blotches had disappeared but he could see his hands were now a grey, wax-like colour. What was happening? Where were his crew and what's the situation at Thorpehead?

'I've never encountered it personally but all the test results are consistent with the classic symptoms.' Doctor Sanjeev Gupta was the consultant haematologist attached to Riverbridge Hospital. Sitting at his desk, he was in the middle of a Zoom call with Gold Commander, Chief Constable Oliver Merton. This was not the first time the two had been in conversation over the last 48 hours.

'The fire crew were the first on the scene and nobody has been as close to the reactor as they were. Most were discharged the next day but the commander, Martin Walsh was giving us more cause for concern. His white blood cell count had fallen off a cliff and blood transfusions weren't making much difference to his overall condition. Normally, I would be considering a bone marrow transplant but we don't have the facilities here. The nearest hospital would normally be Bristol so that's a non-starter, but frankly, I fear it may already be too late to do anything. Commander Walsh looks to have had much greater exposure to the radiation than the rest of his crew; his skin complexion is changing, his mouth is full of ulcers and he can't keep any food down. I'm concerned for the rest of the crew, too. Their rapid recovery may well signal a period of latency which appears common. It doesn't mean they have fully recovered and may well develop similar symptoms to their boss, albeit at a slower pace. They are not the only ones we have been treating for initial signs of radiation exposure, though. More people are arriving at A&E presenting similar symptoms.'

'What are the radiation levels like within the hospital. I trust you are still monitoring?'

'Commander Walsh has been isolated and we are taking precautions with the staff who are looking after him. The readings are higher in his room but not dangerous for short-term exposure. I'm concerned that the emergency department may be at risk if, as I suspect, we start to see more cases. It will compromise the functioning of the rest of the hospital.'

'I'm in constant dialogue with Civil Contingencies about whether Riverbridge is a safe evacuation point or if it is too close to the exclusion zone. We may have to consider a further evacuation of the town. Do you have a plan in place, Doctor?'

'All elective surgery was cancelled when the critical emergency was declared. We have discharged most of the non-urgent cases and transferred others to Taunton, primarily to have capacity to treat casualties from Thorpehead. But what we would do with the ARS cases, assuming there will be more, I don't have an answer right now.'

Martin Walsh could hear screaming. The room was bathed in bright pink. The cries for help were coming closer. He tried to sit up but couldn't. He was held down by chains attached to his bed which criss-crossed his chest and legs. Suddenly, through the wall facing him, a figure emerged, dressed in the familiar yellow Tyvek suit of his watch at Thorpehead. Then another figure followed through the wall, which otherwise remained intact. The cries of "Help me, Martin" became louder and louder as the hooded creatures got closer to his bed. He tried to lift his head but couldn't move. In a moment, the bed was surrounded by bodies in protective suits. In a synchronised move, each figure leaned forward over the bed to look down on Martin. He was frozen, unable to move his head or his body but his eyes were drawn to their face visors. Who were these people? His crew? Did they not survive? They were all in A&E together with Martin just the other day, surely? But he didn't recognise the faces because he couldn't see any features. Behind each visor was a wall of red blood, cascading from top to bottom as if sprayed from a hose. He tried to scream but no sound came out of his mouth.

'It's all right, Martin. You've been having a bad dream,' said the first nurse. 'Let's try to make you a little more comfortable. She raised the back of the bed so that Martin could sit up, but as she gently held the back of his head she noticed some hairs attached to the fingers of her protective gloves. There was hair on the pillow too, where Martin's head had been. The second nurse, clearly more senior, had noticed too.

'Lesions, hair loss, hallucination,' she said to her colleague, her raised eyebrows not visible behind her visor, but she had said all that was necessary.

As they raised the fireman into the sitting position his blanket slipped down, exposing his bare arms. Black blisters, similar to those already on his lips, now covered his forearms. They were raw and unlike the burns he and the rest of the crew had presented with on arrival, these didn't look as if they were showing any signs of receding. Lifting the covers back further, they found more blisters on his legs, even larger than those on his arms but more than that, the patient had soiled himself. As he had been unable to keep anything down over the last 24 hours, this may have been a surprise to the two medics but they immediately knew that the bloody diarrhoea that was staining the sheet was not the natural consequence of a patient losing control of their bowels.

They had been warned that the final stage of gamma radiation contamination following the three that the senior nurse had mentioned moments earlier, was the disintegration of the internal organs and the bloody mess they were observing was the remnants of Martin Walsh's intestines. Moments later, and without ever responding to the nurses, he slipped into a coma from which there would be no recovery.

20 - Eight days later

News 24.com
07.30 am: Concerns for 'missing' evacuees

With a full-scale evacuation underway in towns and cities across central England, there are concerns that many people are missing or possibly left behind in the exclusion zone.

Bristol and Swindon are the two major population centres to have been evacuated following the explosion at the Thorpehead nuclear power station but concerns have already been raised about the numbers not adding up. Local authorities and the Cabinet Office's Civil Contingencies Department have been coordinating the evacuation of more than half-a-million residents into temporary accommodation, predominantly in tourist resorts in the south-west of the country. But News24.com understands that the number evacuated is well below the actual population in some cases. It is known that many people simply left to stay with family in other parts of the country in the immediate aftermath of the incident and therefore have not featured in the count. But the real concern is that others, either intentionally or by omission, have been left behind. News24.com has asked the Cabinet to comment, but was told it was too early to draw any conclusions due to the vast amount of data which is still being processed from multiple locations around Bristol. Drone footage which has appeared on social media shows several areas of suburban Bristol deserted, however, with no visible signs of life.

It also appears that no sooner have evacuees been settled into their new accommodation than some families have already been split, with one parent immediately drafted into the Government's new civil defence force. Prime Minister Gordon Strathyre announced the creation of the civil defence force to assist the military in its response to the Thorpehead crisis during a televised speech earlier this week.

As we also reported previously, Parliament has risen following the announcement of prorogation. The work of the Government will now be carried out by the Prime Minister and his cabinet while COBRA continues to meet on a daily basis. MPs who were able to return to their constituencies have done so although as many as 40 of those have been, or are in the process of being evacuated, dispersing constituents far and wide.

Cornwall

'What I am saying is that when they had to abandon their homes and their lives at a moment's notice following the dreadful event at Thorpehead, Cornwall welcomed them with open arms. We have fed them and given them shelter in response to an emergency. But we also need to know how long the situation will last. Cornwall is now full and that puts a significant strain on our infrastructure, but so far the Government can't, or won't tell us whether this is a short or longer-term situation or how we are going to be compensated for our generosity.'

Miles Chenoweth was taking part in a radio phone-in programme on Riviera FM from his study at his 18th-century farmhouse overlooking the Helford Estuary. Since the arrival of the first evacuees from Bristol, the MP for Cantarrock had been much in demand with both the local and national media. Born Miles Pasco Chenoweth on Easter Sunday thirty-eight years ago on the family farm on the Lizard Peninsula, he was seen as Cornish through and through, particularly by those living outside the county. Others were less convinced. Perhaps it was the public-school accent he had acquired prior to a degree in engineering at Cambridge University. The next decade was spent in Africa on various mining projects, some said rare earths, others diamonds, although Chenoweth himself was always very evasive when asked specifically.

Meanwhile, back in his beloved Cornwall, his parents followed the path taken by many land-owning farmers in that part of the world, gradually withdrawing from agriculture in favour of the new cash cow, tourism. Having transformed their own dairy farm into one of the most successful holiday parks in the county, they had embarked on a steady process of acquisition over the following years and today had a broad portfolio of caravan parks and leisure complexes on both of Cornwall's extensive coastlines. When Miles returned from Africa to join the family firm, he also found time to invest in some speculative mining ventures, from re-opening an old tin mine to exploiting the county's known lithium deposits. Some ventures were spectacular failures while others were still being described as potential gold mines. Nobody really knew how much money had been invested or where it had actually come from. When efforts to attract government funding failed, one particular project was rescued by mystery investors via front companies based offshore.

But five years ago, Miles Pasco Chenoweth was elected to represent the constituency of Cantarrock on behalf of the Teylu Kenerweck Party. To call it a party was a bit of an exaggeration. He was effectively an independent candidate fighting an election where the only certainty was that the incumbent stood no chance. A member of the governing party at Westminster which was widely expected to be expelled from power by a landslide, the people of Cantarrock, like much of the country, had been expected to vote for anyone but the sitting MP. But independents never do well at General Elections so Chenoweth rediscovered his 'Cornishness' and started to campaign on a Cornwall first agenda. The party name meant Cornish Family but this was not a political party in any normal sense of the word. There were no elected officials or policy committees. Teylu Kenerwek was registered as a limited company at Companies House with one director and shareholder, Miles Chenoweth, and two other paid employees. The election was a shoo-in. His campaign manifesto was simply about standing up for Cornwall and the Cornish. Left behind by the "ruling elite" and always at the back of the queue when it came to government funding, Chenoweth put himself up as the person who would be a constant thorn in the side of the new government, making sure that Cornwall received the attention it deserved. Since then, he had become something of a media darling; the BBC for one, could not broadcast a story about a policy decision on Wales or Scotland without including the reaction from Cornwall via its only Member of Parliament.

In the county itself, Chenoweth had attained celebrity status, speaking at events, opening fairs and dropping in to pubs unannounced and engaging the locals in both witty banter and more serious issues which were affecting them. These "spontaneous" dialogues usually found their way onto social media as did reels of raucous renditions of The Song of the Western Men, better known simply as Trelawny, led of course by the MP from the Cornish Family Party. During that time, Chenoweth also appeared to have acquired a faint Cornish burr which came to the fore particularly when there were microphones present. Some within the county were sceptical, especially people who had known Chenoweth in his early days or had had the misfortune to deal with him over his irregular business ventures. At Westminster he was viewed with either bemusement or mild irritation, but as a single independent in a Parliament with a large government majority, he was not considered any kind of threat. But to those Western Men, the family of Cornwall, Chenoweth said what many people thought. He may have been a populist, but he was Cornwall's populist.

'You say Cornwall is full, Mister Chenoweth. Well, isn't that what you want? It's not even summer and you've been on this programme before complaining about empty beds.' The Riviera FM presenter counted herself among the sceptics as far as Chenoweth was concerned and the two of them had clashed during previous appearances on her show.

'Yes we're full, but not with tourists spending money in our shops and restaurants. These are refugees, anxious to know what's going to happen to their lives. They're not taking the kids to the theme park or even buying ice creams on the beach. But they are using our health and welfare services which, as you know, are already seriously underfunded compared to the rest of the country. I want to ask our Prime Minister what he is doing about it but guess what? He's gone and shut down Parliament so I can't even ask a question in the House.'

'That must be the first time I have heard you complain about not being able to get to Westminster, Mr Chenoweth. Your attendance record isn't that impressive is it? What with your business trips abroad and promotional work for the tourist board.'

'Oh that's just typical of you, Jenny. You know it really saddens me that you, and Riviera FM, a Cornish company, are always looking for an excuse to have a go at me when all I am trying to do is my best for the people of Cantarrock and of Cornwall more widely. Instead of continually sniping at me for putting the people of Cornwall first, why aren't you out doing real journalism and reporting on the refugees with radiation sickness who risk contaminating us locals?'

'We are not aware of any cases of radiation sickness, Mr Chenoweth. Do you have any evidence for that accusation?'

'I haven't seen it myself yet, but my office is hearing from people who have seen families at the Brea Holiday Park where children have blistered skin and vomiting. They're worried they may become infected too.'

'I must say, Mr Chenoweth, even coming from you, that's pushing things a bit. Second or third-party testimony about a child being sick? You seriously think that equates to Acute Radiation Syndrome, which is not contagious in any event. It can't be spread from person to person!'

'All I am saying is what my constituents are telling me. They are concerned that people coming from an area contaminated with radiation are now living here amongst them. Of course, I wouldn't expect a radical station like Riviera FM to be interested in that when it's much easier just to criticise the only person who seems to want to help. Goodbye Jenny.'

A long continuous beep sounded before the presenter cut in.

'Well it looks like MP Miles Chenoweth has a more pressing engagement to get to. We'll play some more music now which will take us to the top of the hour and the news and weather.'

*****

Social media
Teylu Kenerwek chat page

@Miles Chenoweth MP

Don't know if you heard my interview with Jenny Briggs on Riviera FM this morning. Usual loony lefties. I'm worried about the impact all these refugees will have on our area and all she wants to do is talk about my attendance in Westminster – even though Parliament is no longer sitting.

@BuccasBill

Someone send that bitch on a one-way trip to Thorpehead!!!

@RedRough

Listened to the show. Well said Pasco. Refugees are eating our food and using our water and what do we get? Radiation sickness.

@Miles Chenoweth MP

I don't know if it's true but reports of children with nausea and blisters are a worrying development. We have enough to concern us as it is without that.

@Liz Helby

Radiation sickness is not contagious.

@RedRough

If they are carrying radiation on clothes, hair or even baggage and someone else touches that, they can pick it up too!

@Miles Chenoweth MP

People are saying there may be more cases of nausea and sickness among the refugees. I don't know but there are so many refugees spread around the county, it may be true.

@BewtyChuff

RedRough. Eating our food alright but I heard the shops are running out cos deliveries can't get thru.

@BuccasBill

Perhaps they should all die from radiation then. Won't have to share our food then!

@Liz Helby

Are you serious?

@BuccasBill

Got a better suggestion?

@Miles Chenoweth MP

I have tried to raise the problem of food supply with HM Gov, but you've guessed it – no response. Perhaps they are making sure that the liberal elites around London are taken care of before turning their attention to little old Cornwall – which just happens to be bearing the brunt of the Gov's evacuation plan at the moment.

@Liz Helby

That's not fair Miles. People from the exclusion zone have been sent to several other places too – South Coast, Wales, Norfolk .. We're all in this together.

@BewtyChuff

And no doubt they will all get food supplies before us in Cornwall.

@Miles Chenoweth MP

I must say I am concerned. The population has doubled in

Cornwall overnight. If we can't guarantee food supplies and there is a further complication with radiation sickness then there will be serious consequences. I think we saw this morning that the media aren't bothered about it but if this Gov does not sit up and take notice then I fear for public order in Cornwall.

21 - Nine days later

News 24.com
8:30 am: Millions displaced, transport chaos, food shortages and conscription – just a week after nuclear power station explosion

More than two million people are living in temporary accommodation and the country's transport infrastructure is in chaos because of a radioactive no-go area which has effectively cut England in two.

It's just over a week since the dramatic explosion at the Thorpehead nuclear power station but already, life has changed forever for millions of United Kingdom residents. A 15km wide exclusion zone has now been established right across England from the Bristol Channel to the Deben Estuary on the North Sea coast. Everyone living beneath the radioactive path has been moved for their own safety and more than two-and-a-half million people are currently living in temporary accommodation. Many are in holiday homes in tourist resorts while others have been taken in by friends and relatives or volunteer families. There is no official word yet as to how long the exclusion zone will remain in operation but some experts have warned that many families may never return to their homes. Professor Michael Steinberg, Head of Centre for Nuclear Engineering at Imperial College, London told News24.com that much will depend on the composition of the radioactive cloud which was blown across the country on the back of Storm Hilda. "Some of the particles which are most likely to have been dispersed, like Xenon 135 for instance, will cease to be dangerous after a matter of hours and will have quickly dissipated in the atmosphere. But if there are others, such as Strontium 90 or Cesium 137, then we are counting in decades. Just look at Chernobyl. The exclusion zone is far smaller there but it's already been 40 years and there is no chance of life returning to normal within my lifetime."

Meanwhile, the radioactive exclusion zone has brought Britain's transport infrastructure crashing down. East-west road and rail connections are all but non-existent with large sections of the M4 motorway and Great Western Railway line falling within the no-go area. Vital north-south trunk routes such as the M1 and M5 have effectively been cut in two while the M25 London Orbital is only open south of the River Thames.

London Heathrow and Bristol airports are both closed and other airports are suffering major disruption to services as airlines are forced to divert planes away from flight paths which include the exclusion zone. Food deliveries to shops and supermarkets on both sides of the zone have been affected and the Department for Transport has been working with cross-channel ferry operators and freight shipping lines to divert services to alternative ports around the coast. The backlog of lorries held in a 'reverse stack' operation on the M2 motorway in Kent is beginning to ease although the decision to temporarily suspend ferry crossings from Calais is still causing tailbacks on the other side of the Channel. The mass evacuation has also had knock-on effects for industry with several companies reporting staff shortages. This is particularly acute in the capital where large areas of the commuter belt have been evacuated. Workers unable to get to their jobs are unlikely to be sitting idly for long however. One of Prime Minister Gordon Strathyre's first decisions under the new powers granted to him by the 2015 Civil Emergencies Act, was to call up displaced workers into his new Civil Defence Force. News24.com has been told that the process started immediately after his most recent TV address to the nation and men and women are already securing the exclusion zone in some locations. Others, with relevant skills such as IT or with heavy goods vehicle licences, have been attached to military units or the emergency services. When we asked the Government for more details regarding the call-ups, a Cabinet Office spokesperson told News24.com: "At this relatively early stage in the country's response to the dreadful incident at Thorpehead, the Government is still assessing its resource needs in liaison with the emergency services and the military. It was clear from the very start of the evacuation process that many people would be unable to continue with their regular work but still possessed many of the skills we would require as part of our response. It makes perfect sense."

11.47 am: First Thorpehead victims named

The Department for Energy has released the names of twenty victims, missing and presumed dead, after the reactor at Thorpehead nuclear power station exploded last week.

All the fatalities were employees of Bicarel, the company contracted by the Government to build and operate the first small modular reactor in the country. They are all understood to have been on duty, working close to the reactor building or in the adjacent control centre which was devastated by the blast. The full list of names can be viewed here.

At least thirty people were admitted to nearby Riverbridge General Hospital following the explosion, including fire crews and emergency staff who were first on the scene. Most were treated for superficial burns and possible radiation exposure; however there has been one fatality. Watch commander Martin Walsh has been named as the first confirmed death from acute radiation sickness.

2.24 pm: EU restarts iodine supplies to Britain

The European Union is currently holding a summit to consider the impact of the Thorpehead explosion on member states.

The Prime Ministers of France, Belgium and the Netherlands voiced continuing concerns over the radioactive cloud which was carried across England from the Bristol Channel to the Essex coast by Storm Hilda. Residents in coastal areas there were put on alert immediately after the explosion, but fears of an evacuation similar to large parts of central England receded in the following days as weather conditions improved. The situation continues to be monitored and local authorities in West Flanders and Zeeland are warning residents to remain vigilant.

The pharmaceutical company Medoteek BV has now resumed supply of iodine tablets to the United Kingdom, having initially withheld stocks for use in the Netherlands, the Dutch Health Minister Jan Breskens informed the meeting in Brussels this morning.

Ministers are also discussing the ongoing situation at the Calais and Dunkerque ferryports where lorries are backed up following the temporary suspension of services to and from Dover. Hauliers in France have been lobbying ministers for help with several cargoes of perishable goods stuck in the log jam and uncertainty over whether drivers would be able to complete deliveries to destinations on the other side of the exclusion zone. There is a further concern over European lorry drivers currently in the United Kingdom and unable to return home. The French Government is working in tandem with its British counterparts and the ferry companies to divert sailings from Calais to other ports but the closest usable alternative, Immingham, is a 12-hour sailing (opposed to 90 minutes to Dover).

3.30 pm: Cornwall is full and evacuees risk spreading radiation, says local MP

Miles Chenoweth, the Teylu Kenerweck MP for Cantarrock has said the county is full to breaking point and people evacuated following the Thorpehead power station explosion risk contaminating the people who have taken them in.

During an extraordinary exchange with local radio station Riviera FM,

Chenoweth continually referred to the evacuees being housed temporarily in holiday accommodation as "refugees" and berated the radio station for pursuing a personal vendetta against him rather than reporting on locals becoming exposed to radiation sickness by the recent arrivals. When asked to provide evidence for his claims, the MP abruptly ended the phone-in.

Chenoweth was elected an MP at the last General Election, representing the Cantarrock constituency in West Cornwall on behalf of his self-styled Teylu Kernewek (Cornish Family) Party. It is not a party in the usual sense of the word but a limited company set up and owned by Chenoweth himself. At the time of his election he vowed to stand up for the people of Cornwall against the "ruling elite" at Westminster, but has more often made headlines with his business and commercial interests outside of Parliament.

Social media
Teylu Kenerwek chat page

@BewtyChuff
It's started. Just been to the supermarket. No milk, no bread and people panic buying. Manager says they haven't had a delivery since Monday and doesn't know when the next one is due.

@RedRough
Well that's odd. Just went past the Atlantic Holiday studios. Full of refugees and 2 home delivery vans outside. So we are running out of food and they are getting theirs delivered!

@Jimmy the Bell
My cousin in Plymouth says the lorries are still coming off the ferry from France loaded with goods. Where's all that going then?

@Miles Chenoweth MP

No doubt heading for London to make sure they can still get fresh vegetables and seafood for their dinner parties. Don't worry, I'm sure we'll get some scraps from their tables! Seriously though, I am chasing the Cabinet Office 24/7 to get assurances on sustained food deliveries.

@Liz Helby

It doesn't help if people start hoarding. We're in the middle of a major crisis and we all need to work together and share.

@RedRough

Get real sister. Spose you're another blowin as well. They get all the food and we get all the refugees to look after, all glowing with radiation.

@Liz Helby

I can't believe what I am reading. No, not a blowin. Born and bred here. Only difference is I was paying attention at school when the ruling elite were handing out educations.

@BuccasBill

Sounds to me like you still need some proper Cornish inside you. Take care on your way home sister cos that could be happening sooner than you think!

@Jimmy the Bell

Miles Chenoweth. Chase as many ministers as you want but I don't see the lorries stopping by in Cornwall on their way to London. Think it's time we did something about it ourselves.

@BewtyChuff

Who iz up for a bit of Dick Turpin outside the dock gates. Stand and deliver for the people of Cornwall! Save all those food miles driving it to London just to send it back here. Let's cut out the middle men and start feeding ourselves. Anyone else up for it? DM me.

@Miles Chenoweth MP

As an MP I have to advise officially against any direct action which breaks the law. As a proud member of the Cornish family, I can only empathise.

Trethewy, West Cornwall

There was no mistaking Chy-an-Gov for anything other than holiday flats. Trethewy Beach began at the narrow, humpback bridge that carried the coast road over the river. Calling it a river might be a bit of a stretch, particularly at low tide when its gentle flow becomes absorbed into the golden sands and peters out long before reaching the sea. At that point it was difficult to even see the Atlantic breakers from the bridge, just the occasional white lines across a blue-green horizon. But when the tide came in, those waves came crashing down, just metres from the bridge, re-energising the river and creating currents which passed under the bridge and further upstream. Other than the temporary car park, only accessible at low tide, there was nothing else to spoil the natural idyll of Trethewy – apart from the ugly, rectangular box standing three storeys high that was Chy-an Gov.

The usual reaction of anyone confronting Chy-an-Gov for the first time was, 'how did anyone get planning permission to build that here?' The unimaginative design belonged to an era, four or five decades ago when architectural aesthetics played no part in the planning process. A time, in fact when planning decisions depended on who you knew or how large the brown envelope. The building belonged in the worst of the worst inner-city housing estates, but from the inside looking out, Chy-an-Gov was everything a beach lover or a surfer could wish for as a holiday destination. You might have to put up with the failings of cheap-built 1970s accommodation that stood in the face of the Atlantic roar but it was a small price to pay for enjoying the elements at close quarters. An outside staircase to the side of the building led to two floors of basic holiday apartments. Each had a bedroom, bathroom, kitchenette and lounge with a bed-settee. They were accessed by way of an exterior veranda on the leeward side, allowing the front-facing rooms to enjoy spectacular sea views – even if the Atlantic breeze would howl through the ill-fitting panoramic windows. The ground floor was given over to under-cover car parking as well as storage space for surfboards, kayaks and waste bins. Built many years before the 2005 Fire Safety Act, there had been some retrofitting of alarms and fire-resistant front doors, but modern-day requirements such as sprinklers or safety cladding were simply not a practical option for such a building. There was a grey area too over what regulations applied to what was usually classed as seasonal accommodation due to its relatively short letting period each summer. Today, Chy-an-Gov was not welcoming surfers or wild swimmers, but full of shocked and confused families who had been forced to abandon their homes and possessions in Bristol just a week ago.

Fiona Boulton had not had a good day. She hadn't had a good day since they arrived at Chy-an-Gov. With no car, they had all been stuck there with the other evacuees. A bus had been laid on once a day to take them to the shops or the council offices, but the staff there had very little new information about what was happening next and the tiny fridge and microwave oven that made up the kitchenette meant that shopping for food was a restricted activity. If the weather was fine, Esme and Harvey spent a lot of time on the beach, but it had been raining today so they were stuck in their tiny flat with nothing but terrestrial TV. To cap it all, Jeremy had been 'press ganged' – that was how it looked to Fiona – to become part of the new Civil Defence Force only a day after they arrived from Bristol. She'd been able to speak to him only twice since then as he was stationed at an army barracks in Wiltshire and patrolling the exterior of the exclusion zone most of the day or night. If getting through to Jeremy was difficult, so too was the helpline number she, and presumably every other person evacuated from the exclusion zone, had been given. Endless hours listening to holding music while the charge on her mobile dwindled and when she did manage to get through, it was just like the staff at the council offices. No word on how long they would be stuck in the Gerry-built hovel on a deserted beach at the ass end of nowhere, no chance of retrieving their car from the motorway service station and not even any record of their dog Smart. How was she even going to try and explain that to Esme?

She and Jeremy were not really drinkers. If there was any wine back at their home in Bristol it was seldom opened unless they had guests. But with yesterday's home delivery order from the supermarket Fiona had included a bottle of Pinot Grigio. She remembered one of the teachers at school singing its praises and she decided there should be something at the flat to 'celebrate' the first time that Jeremy came back from Wiltshire. But the trouble was, neither of them had any idea when that would be, and the bottle was already half empty following a run-in last night with an emotional, and increasingly hormonal teenage daughter about when and how they would get Smart back. Today had been grey and wet outside and dank and cold inside the poky flat. The kids were in the bedroom, doing god knows what and the TV only seemed to have more depressing news updates following Thorpehead or depressing documentaries about Chernobyl and Fukushima. As what was left of the little daylight began to fade, Fiona decided that the best she could hope for today was to see off the remainder of the wine and raise a toast to tomorrow, ushering in some good news for a change.

Holmbeach

Life had quickly settled into a routine for Jack, Shelley and Evan. They had all slept soundly that first night after the siblings had first walked into the Boar's Head. There was still plenty of food in the well-stocked kitchen and the teenage Shelley had proved to be a far better cook than her adult host. Even Evan had been tempted away from his standard diet of Cocoa Krisp and was becoming a fan of steak and chips. But when Jack wanted to go out and snap some more pictures, all three of them had to go. Despite the relative security of the hotel, Evan could not contemplate staying there alone, even with his sister present. The siblings still froze at the sound of helicopter rotor blades approaching, even though the aircraft never seemed to hover but were always on their way somewhere else.

Part of the daily routine was always to check what was happening at Thorpehead from their vantage point on the opposite side of Tyneford Bay. There was never any activity other than the changing of the guard at the site entrance but it was clear that the fire was slowly burning itself out. Shelley and Evan remained remarkably stoic, returning each day to observe the site where their parents had succumbed to the explosion. Jack had continued to follow the unfolding events surrounding Thorpehead both online and by watching the rolling news coverage. A couple of days earlier, the first official list of fatalities had been published and it included the names of Geoffrey and Abigail Marsden. Jack had had the unenviable task of confirming to the children what by this time, they already knew and, once again, he was surprised how little emotion they had shown. They had also discussed what to do next about reuniting them with any remaining family. Shelley had said that her father's parents had both died a long time ago. So had Abigail's mother, Granny Josephine. Gramps Edward was in a care home in Cumbria, suffering from dementia. There was an aunt, Geoffrey's sister and Shelley and Evan's two cousins lived in Swindon, but she didn't know the address or phone number. With Jack's help they had managed to track them down online and found a telephone number but it just rang out. No doubt, like several thousand other residents living under the path of the radiation cloud, they had been evacuated and there would be no way of tracing them until Shelley and Evan made themselves known to the Civil Defence Force. But Shelley and Evan had both reacted violently to this idea, for now preferring the comfort and safety of the Boar's Head and Jack.

So, after another day of information gathering around the deserted streets of Holmbeach, Jack was sat at his computer teaching Shelley how journalists prepared and filed their stories as they prepared the latest instalment of his 'life inside the exclusion zone' diary to forward to Elodie. Shelley had taken a genuine interest in what Jack was doing, media being one of her favourite subjects at school, and she was proving remarkably adept at editing and formatting the video clips. Evan meanwhile, was in his element with a games console and a choice of flat screen TVs without parents or a bossy sister telling him when to stop.

Trethewy, West Cornwall

She sat with both hands around the neck of the bottle, wedged between her thighs on the front seat of the car. Normally she would be high on adrenaline, along with some other synthetic stimulant at this time of night, as Mervyn threw the Imprezza around the bends of the deserted coast road. But this evening Mervyn was driving as if he had just spotted a police car in his rearview mirror. The Imprezza strained as if unused to travelling at a sedate 30mph, even slower around the steeper corners, so as not to spill the precious cargo being transported by the front seat passenger. Jenna had let Mervyn have both barrels verbally as they left the pub car park with the familiar wheel spin tearing up the gravel, but he was quickly reminded of the risks by the smell, as much as his girlfriend's invective.

It had been a quick and seamless progression from a normal conversation around the table in the pub to Mervyn driving with unusual care along the coast road with his girlfriend sitting beside him, clutching a home-made Molotov cocktail. Two more goons were sat in the back of the car, including the one who started the whole thing off. Jimbo. The sort of guy who could start an argument in an empty room, he had the type of voice that when he opened his mouth, everybody else in the pub was privy to whatever he was saying. It started with goon number two, Eric. He was busy scrolling through his social media posts while the others were talking about something or other that he wasn't too interested in.

'Listen to this,' he said, reading out a message someone

had posted about their child playing with 'one of those refugees' in the park this morning and now complaining of a sore throat and she's sure, what looks like a red blotch on her arm. When Jimbo reacted, the whole pub was brought into the debate. Others had heard stories about refugees receiving priority treatment at the health centre; that hostels were receiving bumper food orders while the shops were running out; the amusement park had laid off staff and announced it was closing because of the lack of tourists; parents were keeping their children home from school for fear they would have to mix with incomers; someone's next-door neighbour had been diagnosed with radiation sickness after working with the new arrivals. One couple in the bar who had tried to inject a sense of realism into the debate, suggesting all these stories were just hearsay with no supporting evidence, were branded 'lefty liberals' and pointedly asked to leave by the landlady. This was clearly a hotbed of support for local MP Miles Chenoweth and everything he had said, including referring to the evacuees as refugees, was both correct and fully justifiable.

Things moved on even quicker when Jimbo had suggested the locals should do something to let these refugees know they are no longer welcome. They should be sent a message that it was time to move on elsewhere. They may have had to leave everything behind but the people who actually lived here had their own problems too. Before they knew it, someone had Googled Molotovs and was proudly displaying a video of how to make an impromptu incendiary device. With a bottle from the landlady, a piece of rag from another customer still in his painter's overalls and just short of 500ml of petrol from the can Mervyn always carried in the boot of the car (with a thirsty Subaru and few petrol stations open at night in this corner of the world, it was always good to have enough fuel to get him home), here they were, heading for Trethewy Beach to send the 'refugees' at Chy-an-Gov a warning.

Mervyn put the car into neutral as they crested the humpback bridge and freewheeled into the Chy-an-Gov car park. Jenna wound down the window with her left hand and raised the bottle in her right.

'What you doing?' her boyfriend said.

'I'm going to throw it like in the video.'

You've got to light the bleddy thing first!'

'Light it? I ain't got a lighter!'

A hand reached over between the two front seats. Eric lit his Zippo under the rag. 'Now throw the fucking thing and let's get out of here.'

Jenna hurled the bottle as hard as she could. It smashed on the ground just in front of two wheelie bins. She covered her eyes with her hands but there was no explosion, just a whoosh as the bottle smashed on the ground and a flash of flame rising no more than a couple of feet in the air.

'Is that it?' she called, almost in disappointment.

'Never mind that, we're out of here,' Mervyn snapped, slamming the Imprezza into drive and making one of his trademark exits. In the rearview mirror he could see the flames still burning in the darkness until they were across the bridge and on their way home.

What Mervyn couldn't see was the closest wheelie bin starting to melt in the flames. As the bin started to lose its shape under the heat, globules of molten plastic dropped into the flames, providing fresh fuel to the fire. In a matter of seconds, the contents of the waste bin ignited, causing mini eruptions and spreading the flames to the neighbouring bin. Before Melvyn, Jenna, Eric and Jimbo were a mile from Trethewy Beach a fire had caught hold in the under eaves of Chy-an-Gov. Fire rises naturally, but in an enclosed area it becomes trapped when it hits the ceiling and then travels horizontally. From one corner of the building, the flames made their way along the supporting steel beams of the garage to the opposite side and the exterior staircase. At that point, the fire was able to rise, fanned by the evening breeze coming off the Atlantic Ocean.

Esme was woken by the throaty roar of an engine accelerating away somewhere outside. She turned to Harvey who was still sleeping untroubled on the other twin bed. The sound was receding as the car was obviously heading away, but even though she turned over, she couldn't settle. Before long she knew something else was wrong. There was an acrid smell of burning plastic and the back of her throat was dry. She jumped out of bed and ran across the room to open a window. The smell was getting stronger and, despite the dark, Esme saw the first plumes of smoke rising. The now familiar sound of the ocean was joined by a crackling which seemed to be getting louder. She ran back to her brother's bed.

'Harvey, wake up. Something's wrong, we have to get Mum.'

Harvey sat up, his eyes blinking as Esme pulled him by the arm towards the bedroom door. Fiona was lying asleep on the settee in the foetal position, the empty bottle of Pinot Grigio and a half-full glass on the coffee table. She slowly came to life from the children's shaking and sat up, still taking time to realise where she was.

'Mum, there's smoke. Something's burning.'

By now, Fiona could smell burning, her eyes began to

sting and the air seemed like it was being sucked from the room. It was getting harder to breathe and Esme and Harvey started to cough.

'There's a fire somewhere. We need to get out. Leave everything and just come with me now,' she said, trying to remain calm and authoritative like she was with her class at school.

The fire had spread horizontally across the whole width of the service area and now, like a pot on a gas ring, the flames were licking up the side walls of Chy-an-Gov. The crackling sound had turned into a whoosh as more oxygen was sucked into the fire. Small explosions could still be heard as items in the waste bins and Calor gas canisters ignited. With the ground floor now completely enveloped in flame, the first and second floors quickly became obliterated behind a thick, black blanket of smoke.

If the holiday apartments had properly maintained smoke detectors, they would have been activated long before the Boulton family had worked out for themselves what was happening. But for now, all Fiona had to worry about was getting herself and the children safely out of the flat and down the steps to safety. With an arm around each of their shoulders, she ushered Esme and Harvey towards the front door. She'd seen fire safety videos where the advice was to touch a door to feel for any heat before deciding whether it was safe to open it. Fiona pushed her hand flat against the inside of the door. It wasn't a particularly heavy door to begin with and she could safely touch it. But it was on the seaward side of the building that the blaze was making more progress and the flames had by now almost reached the level of the bedroom window Esme had opened only moments earlier. As Fiona opened the front door, the back draught sucked a ball of flame through the bedroom and lounge to the front landing of the building as if there had been an explosion. With no further obstacles to hinder the fire's progress, all four sides of Chy-an-Gov were now ablaze. Its other occupants, who became alerted to the situation only a matter of moments after the Boulton family, awoke to find themselves choking in acrid smoke with their only effective escape route enveloped in flames.

22 - Ten days later

News 24.com
6:30 am: Thirty dead in Cornish fire hell

Thirty people died, more than half of them children, after a fire swept through a holiday apartment last night which was being used to house evacuees from the Bristol area.

The fire is believed to have started just before midnight at the Chy-an-Gov holiday flats on Trethewy Beach. By the time emergency services arrived at the isolated location, the three-storey building was already engulfed by flames and there were no survivors. Twelve adults and 18 children were recorded to have been sleeping there, according to the local council. The accommodation had been allocated to family groups although it is understood that most units had only a single parent, the other already on duty with the Civil Defence Force. The cause of the blaze has not yet been determined but already there are concerns about the speed with which the fire spread. A Fire Service spokesperson told News24.com: "We are still actively involved in damping down and securing the building. When it is safe we will commence recovery of the victims and investigation of the cause. The 999 call came from a passing motorist. Trethewy Beach is very isolated with no neighbouring residences. We are concerned that the blaze must have spread so quickly that nobody in the building was able to call for help."

11:20 am: Update

Arson suspected at Cornish hostel blaze

Fire services have found evidence to suggest the tragic fire at Trethewy in Cornwall last night (see 6:30 am) was started deliberately.

Twelve adults and 18 children died in the blaze at the Chy-an-Gov holiday flats at the Cornish resort, all of them understood to be families forced to leave their homes in the Bristol area following the Thorpehead nuclear disaster. Now, the fire brigade says they have found evidence of an accelerant being used at the seat of the fire, in a corner of the ground-floor service area.

Superintendent Jacob Matteson from Cornwall Police has issued the following statement: "This incident is now being treated as arson. We are appealing for anyone who was in the area last night or may know anything about this appalling activity to come forward. There are no words to express our anger and disgust. The victims all had to leave their homes and everyday lives behind in the wake of the nuclear disaster. One member of each family at the Chy-an-Gov apartments was already doing his or her duty in the Civil Defence Force, helping with the response to the events at Thorpehead. Now, one of my officers is going to have to try to explain to them what happened here last night. I am sick to my stomach and cannot begin to imagine what was going through the mind of the person or persons responsible for starting this fire."

A Government spokesperson told News24.com: "We wish to express our deepest sympathy to all those affected by the dreadful news from Cornwall this morning. Rest assured, we will leave no stone unturned to discover the events leading up to the fire at Trethewy and, if a crime has been committed, to apprehend the culprits. These are difficult times for government services as well as the people whose lives have been disrupted by the accident at Thorpehead nuclear power station. We ask for everyone's patience and understanding as we continue to respond to the consequences."

2:24 pm: Ferry services suspended after lorry hijacks

The Government has ordered the closure of Plymouth Ferryport following what it describes as a 'targeted' attack on lorries arriving from France last night.

Having cleared customs at the port, the trucks were halted as they left and subjected to further inspection by groups of unidentified operatives wearing hi-vis jackets and masks. While some were allowed to continue their journey, as many as six were boarded and forced to leave in a different direction. Two have so far re-emerged, their drivers unharmed but without their cargo. A police helicopter has been deployed in the search for the other missing vehicles. A Devon Police spokesperson told News24.com: "This appears to have been an organised and targeted operation involving a large number of people outside Plymouth docks last night. They seemed to have had a clear idea of what goods they wanted to hijack. We have heard from one driver who was let through the blockade because his cargo was industrial machinery and not food. We know the situation is difficult with food deliveries to shops but taking the law into your own hands is not the answer. Highway robbery may have ended in the 19th century but this is still theft. Police resources may well be stretched at the moment due to unprecedented events, but we will not tolerate criminal acts carried out by mobs and we will use the full force of the law to deal with these culprits."

The driver of one of the freed lorries told the BBC that he had been treated courteously by his hijackers and three men had joined him in the cab and directed him to an industrial estate in Cornwall. He was originally bound for Spitalfields Market in London with a cargo of fruit, potatoes and green vegetables, but his rig had been emptied within minutes of arriving. Two masked men then accompanied him as far as a layby on the A38 near Exeter before returning his phone to him and sending him on his way.

The management at Plymouth Ferryport have issued the following statement: "On the orders of His Majesty's Government, Plymouth Ferryport is now closed to commercial shipping. This follows an incident last night in which lorries recently arrived on the ferry from France were blocked by crowds on exiting the port. All faced further inspection of their goods and some were boarded and forced to depart to destinations unknown and against their will. The Ministry of Transport is now liaising with the shipping companies on the diversion of services to other ports and we are currently unable to say when Plymouth Ferryport will be operational once more."

The radiation exclusion zone following the Thorpehead explosion has already impacted ferry services in and out of Dover with arriving lorries being stacked on the M2 in Kent. Several services from Calais and Dunkerque have subsequently been diverted to other ports on the east coast, leading to long delays and disruption. But until now, ferries to south coast ports at Plymouth and Portsmouth have continued as before, albeit restricted to freight services only. Last night's events in Plymouth have come amid growing concerns over food shortages in Devon and Cornwall as supermarket deliveries are progressively disrupted by the exclusion zone.

Only this week, outspoken MP Miles Chenoweth accused the Government of ignoring Cornwall as it deals with the repercussions of Thorpehead. After some inflammatory messages on social media, the independent representative for Cantarrock for the so-called Cornish Family (Teylu Kernewek) Party took part in a heated debate on the BBC's flagship News Review programme. He told the programme's anchor Ed Jacobson: "We were happy to help out in the light of the tragic events at Thorpehead but now we are full. Holidaymakers go home after a couple of weeks but these refugees are putting extra strain on our health and education services, they are eating our food and using our water. And what do we get from this Government? Nothing. No extra funding, not even extra food supplies. Quite the opposite, in fact. Every day, lorry loads of food arrive at Plymouth docks and then head straight up to London so the liberal elites don't run out of their artichokes or edamame beans (whatever they are!) How many of those lorries then come back to Cornwall with the basic foods our now doubled population needs? Well, clearly nowhere near enough. I have constituents calling my office in tears because there is no baby food in the shops. I tell you, the people of Cornwall feel they have done their bit in this emergency but are getting no thanks for it. If the Government can't sort this out, don't be surprised if Trelawny's Men start doing it themselves."

Holmbeach

Jack closed his laptop having just read the latest posts on the *News24.com* website. Food shortages, lawlessness and now, women and children dead in an arson attack. With the power still on at the hotel, although they had had to revert to bottled gas, and broadband connected, he had managed to keep abreast of developments following the explosion at Thorpehead. But now it seemed the social fabric was breaking down. The shocking news from Cornwall and the lorry hijackings were dominating the headlines but some of the newspaper websites were also carrying stories of similar unrest in parts of the north and even Scotland.

Holmbeach seemed like an oasis in the desert. The town lay a few miles due south of Thorpehead and was sheltered by a headland from the wide expanse of Tyneford Bay and the power station at its farthest extreme. Jack had seen the destruction there with his own eyes and read the reports of pandemonium in the towns and cities which lay beneath the path of the radiation being blown eastwards across the country. Even Riverbridge, which lay a few miles along the estuary had ultimately been declared too close to provide a safe haven and had been evacuated. But in Holmbeach, it felt like everyone in the town had gone to a football match and would be back any minute. Some, but by no means all of the abandoned vehicles were coated with a layer of greyish black dust, but the strong winds had presumably dispersed any debris from the more exposed parts of the town.

The daily journal had just been emailed to Elodie and she had been responding, updating Jack on the situation as it was being reported in France along with how it was impacting life over there. There was no risk of contamination as far south as Normandy but there were problems with supply lines and farmers angry at not being able to export their produce. The lorry drivers were threatening to go on strike unless they were given guarantees for their safety when delivering to the United Kingdom, along with a hefty bonus payment for taking the risk. But the biggest news in France was that the Government was about to cancel its contract with Bicarel and was seriously considering its whole approach to nuclear energy in future.

With today's report filed and having caught up on the news, the new routine dictated that Jack, Shelley and Evan would gather in the hotel kitchen for dinner. As he came down the stairs holding his laptop he could hear the other two were already there and talking in what seemed to Jack as an adult way. For fourteen and ten-year-old siblings, the usual bickering which had been apparent even when they first arrived at the Boar's Head, had been replaced by a far more pragmatic and mutually appreciative tone. But the conversation stopped abruptly the moment the lights went out, plunging the ground floor of the hotel into darkness.

'Don't worry. Probably just a fuse tripped,' Jack called out as he went behind the reception desk to retrieve a torch from the drawer and then opened up the fuse cupboard. But the fuse had not tripped. All the switches were in the up position. Jack went into the lounge bar but neither the lights nor the TV were working. The internal phone line was dead, too. He opened his laptop and walked back into the kitchen where the blue light of the screen highlighted the frozen, silent figures of Shelley and Evan.

'What's happening, Jack?' Shelley's voice had the same anxious timbre as on that first night when they arrived at the hotel.

'I don't know Shelley. It wasn't the fuse. We may have lost power. I'm just going to check the Internet.'

But when Jack tried to connect to his browser it soon became apparent there was no broadband either.

'I guess it's only to be expected. After what's happened at Thorpehead, it's a wonder we have had power for so long. There are some torches at reception and we've still got bottled gas. I think we should have the last of those steaks tonight but tomorrow we will have to think seriously about what to do next.'

'Can't we just stay here? I like it here,' a hint of panic rising in Evan's voice.

'But Evan, if we have no electricity that means no computer, email or TV. The fridges and freezer won't be working either which means our food supplies won't last long.' Even in the pale light, Jack could see the realisation dawning by the changed expression on Evan's face. Shelley, meanwhile was still sitting frozen and not saying a word.

They ate their last meal of steak and chips in silence. When they had finished, Shelley gathered up the plates as was her habit and went to the sink to rinse them. When she turned on the tap, the water ran lamely for a few moments and then gurgled and stopped.

'Brilliant. We've no water either,' were Shelley's first words since the lights had gone off.

'That settles it,' said Jack. 'It's time to get back to the real world – if that's what you can call it. We'll have to make ourselves known to the authorities and make sure you two are taken care of properly.'

'Don't leave us, please,' cried Shelley, now desperation in her voice. 'We only feel safe with you, Jack.'

Jack didn't know what to do. He'd not spoken to his parents. He didn't want them to know he was still at the Boar's Head. He had no idea what would happen to the orphaned Shelley and Evan, whose only remaining family had probably been evacuated. There was no way they'd be allowed to stay together. From what he'd read already, as a young, single man he would no doubt be 'volunteered' into the civil defence force rather than look after two young children. He tried his best to reassure Evan and Shelley that they would stay together, whatever happened, but that they should all get some rest before setting out in the morning. But Jack knew that he had a lot of thinking to do and that none of them would get much sleep until the sun came up in the morning.

10 Downing Street

The three were at their now familiar positions around the coffee table inside the Prime Minister's office. Field Marshal Leighton Parkes and Archie Wilkes on the sofas facing each other and Gordon Strathyre in his armchair.

'What the hell is going on in the Wild West, Leighton? Hostels firebombed, lorries hijacked. It was you who first raised the question of civil unrest so how come it caught you unawares?'

'With respect, Prime Minister, that's hardly very fair. We did indeed have security concerns over food imports coming off the ferries in lorries and we had a unit on its way to Plymouth for that very reason. I'm afraid we had no intelligence to suggest evacuee accommodation was under any threat, other than your MP making wild accusations. But we have diverted the Plymouth unit to Cornwall as a show of strength and ordered the ferryport to cease operations until we have the situation under control.'

'He's not MY MP, Leighton. He's a so-called independent, but you are right, he is generally considered to be a charlatan who showboats simply to gain attention. S.I.S. surely don't suspect he's behind the attack?'

'He said a few crass things on local radio.' Archie Wilkes cut in. 'But there's no evidence that points to anything more than that at the moment, and as Leighton said, there was no chat to suggest anything like that was going to happen.'

'Thirty deaths though,' the Prime Minister blew through his teeth. 'The press are having a field day. It's bad enough already. Did you see the latest rant on *News24.com*? Millions displaced, food shortages, transport chaos … Just negative and critical, as if it was a Government decision to blow up a nuclear power station in the first place.'

'I've already spoken to Sir Ian, Prime Minister. *The Clarion* is running a leader tomorrow that spins the *News24.com* comment in a totally different direction and heralds the efforts we are making in unimaginable circumstances.'

'It's not enough, Archie. If *News24.com* gets its teeth into the arson attack and the lorry hijackings we could see civil disorder spread across the country. It's not enough just to publish our side of the story after *News24.com* has hit the headlines. You said yourself that traffic to their site has rocketed this last week.'

'It's true recent visits to their sire have jumped out of all proportion. We did think this was in part the continuing shift away from print, especially with newspapers having delivery problems just now. But I have just been given more data this morning which confirms their page views and engagement time have both seen sharp rises over the last week.'

'Which means?' asked the Field Marshal, clearly in unfamiliar territory.

'It means, Leighton, that more people are paying attention to what fucking *News24.com* is saying,' the Prime Minister said icily. 'We are going to have to do something about that, Archie before we lose control of the narrative.'

West Cornwall

'Pull yourself together, maid,' Mervyn said, sitting across the pub table from an inconsolable Jenna.

'Thirty dead, Merv, eighteen of them children. We were only supposed to frighten them!'

'And keep your bleddy voice down,' he hissed.

Mervyn moved around the table and sat down close to Jenna. Last night they had been buzzing. Mervyn drove around the bends in the coast road like a man possessed while the other three let out screams and whoops. They dropped

Jimbo and Eric back at the pub which was closed to the public but always open to locals who knew about the habitual back bar lock-ins. Then the couple drove to their favourite spot at the end of a quiet lane where they had frantic sex on the back seat of the Impreza. But Jenna had woken up this morning to the news on Riviera FM of the suspected arson and deaths at Chy-an-Gov. She'd called Mervyn in a panic but he'd shut her up, saying not to talk on the phone and he'd come and pick her up. Now, here they were in their usual corner of an otherwise empty pub. Empty except for Eric and Jimbo who had come to join them, each with their first, or maybe second pint of the day. Mervyn took Jenna's hands in his.

'Look. There were no witnesses. Nobody saw us and nobody in the pub is going to say anything without implicating themselves. Those people shouldn't have been here in the first place. There's not enough food to go around as it is with this fucking delivery business without having to give it away to outsiders. Perhaps now the authorities will do something about it. It happened Jenna, but that's history now. Best we just don't talk about it ever again.'

'But I will still think about it. I'm not sure I will ever be able to think of anything else,' Jenna said through her sobs.

'They would have died anyway, so what's the problem?' Eric said, not looking up from his phone.

'What are you talking about, pisshead?'

'Them was all infected with radiation. That's what old Pasco Chenoweth was saying. At least now we won't catch it off 'em.'

'Radiation isn't an infectious disease you idiot, it's …'

Even Mervyn was dumbfounded by this latest pearl of

wisdom but stopped short of trying to explain when he saw that Eric had not even lifted his head from his mobile when he had spoken.

'New phone, Eric?'

'Yeah, my brother got it for me. Gave it to me this morning and I'm still trying to set it up with my old data.'

'Looks like the latest iPhone. That's a bit of a step up from your old thing. You come into some money then?'

'Probably one of them hijacked lorries knowing your brother.' Jenna momentarily seemed to be back in the real world.

'Nah, they only took lorries carrying food. The phone is brand new, still in its box an' all. It come from a phone shop up in Riverbridge.'

'But that's near Thorpehead. In the exclusion zone.'

'Yep, the people have all gone, the town's empty but the shops are all full.'

'So how does your brother get through all the security up there?'

'Security my ass,' Eric snorted. 'Me brother says there's hardly anyone guarding the place. It's such a big area, they can't be everywhere at once. They've been up there twice already and not seen a single patrol. Just straight in and out along the same road. Last night they picked up phones, TVs and sound systems. Brother has just been selling it in the car park outside. That's why I'm here so early. He says he's going back tonight to stock up on food, and I'm going with him. If you need any groceries, then just give me a list!'

Just then they heard a low rumbling noise coming from outside. As the volume increased, the pub customers looked out of the bar window to see a convoy of military lorries pulling into the car park. Soldiers, some of them armed, jumped down from the leading two trucks to await the rest of the convoy which included a low-loader carrying portable toilets and another with a CAT wheel loader and forklift. There was further hissing of air brakes as more lorries arrived and troops began to unload elements of marquee-style temporary accommodation.

'What the hell's happening out there?' Mervyn called across to the landlady behind the bar.

'They didn't waste any time,' she answered. 'It's the army. Come down to keep law and order following that business at Trethewy. I only got the call an hour ago to say they've commandeered the car park. Emergency laws an'all that. Looks more like a military invasion.'

Mervyn looked across at Jenna. Her face was white.

'Remember what I said, Jenna. Not a word to anyone.

'Eric, better tell your bro to be careful where he tries to offload them phones!'

23 - Twelve days later

Cabinet Office Briefing Room, Whitehall

'Well, can I start by welcoming the Prime Minister to this meeting of COBRA. We all realise he has been very busy these last couple of weeks proroguing Parliament and building a private army, but let's not lose track of the fact that this committee has met every day since he last graced us with his presence.'

'Thank you, Home Secretary, for setting the tone of this meeting so perfectly,' Gordon Strathyre responded as he took his seat in Cabinet Office Briefing Room One, flanked by his Cabinet Secretary Archie Wilkes and Field Marshal Leighton Parkes. Nadia Yadav's icy stare remained fixed on the Prime Minister, now sitting directly across the conference table from her.

'The fact remains, Prime Minister, that we have been receiving daily briefings from Civil Contingencies, SAGE and Gold Command only to get back to our departments and learn of decisions that have been taken unilaterally by you and your two wingmen here using "emergency powers,"' said the Home Secretary, using finger quotes.

The Prime Minister employed his customary tactic when riled, mentally counting to three before answering. 'Look Nadia, I know that in normal times you would use occasions like this for self-promotion, but these are not normal times. They are not even unusual times. This country faces an existential crisis like nothing before in its history. I'm sorry to sound as if I am the only grown-up in the room but I am having to deal at the same time with the actual consequences of this nuclear disaster as well as the longer-term effects. Be assured that I do read the COBRA briefings daily but am also involved in other discussions that for several reasons, must take place between as few people as possible.'

'Those would presumably include the exact number of deaths so far from Acute Radiation Syndrome?' the Home Secretary fired back. 'We don't seem to have a precise figure yet to share with the public but I know that's one of the points the Civil Contingencies Director wants to cover in his update. If it's OK with our grown-up in the room, perhaps we can ask Mark to take over?'

Mark Brooks was at his usual position at the top corner of the table, sitting in front of his laptop. The bank of monitors behind him was idle, simply displaying the Cabinet Office logo on a white background. 'Thank you, Home Secretary, Prime Minister. Perhaps I can start with the fatalities? Until this morning, I have been receiving regular updates from Gold Command who has been liaising with hospitals across the region. It does appear that, much as the SAGE briefing document had predicted, cases of ARS have spiked around ten days after the explosion at Thorpehead. This corresponds to the period of latency following initial symptoms, many of which were treated at hospital emergency departments and patients discharged. It is now clear from the numbers, that in several cases the initial signs of sore throat or lethargy were either not reported or not considered serious enough for treatment. It is the hospitals mainly in areas where evacuees from Bristol and Swindon were being housed, which have felt the brunt and many were simply overwhelmed by so many admissions at the same time. The fatality rate among ARS admissions is 100%. The hospitals are hopeful that the latency period is accurate and that the admissions have therefore peaked, but now there is a second problem: what to do with the bodies. Protocol requires zinc coffins and burial in clay but we are talking about huge numbers.'

'Does the Gold Commander have an accurate figure?' the Home Secretary asked.

'Well, that's the thing. Yesterday, Chief Constable Merton told me the number of fatalities was possibly in excess of thirty thousand.' There was an audible gasp from all around the table, except seemingly, the Prime Minister, Field Marshal and Archie Wilkes. 'He was due to let me know a precise figure this morning and what arrangements are currently in place for dealing with the bodies, but he called this morning to tell me he was being replaced. The Colonel in charge of the military platoon based at Gold Command has now been ordered to coordinate the removal of the bodies.'

All eyes turned once again to the centre of the table and the Prime Minister. 'That's correct, Mark. The Field Marshal and I discussed this yesterday. The Gold Commander has done an excellent job in unprecedented circumstances over the last couple of weeks and we are extremely appreciative. I will be telling him so personally once this meeting has concluded. But the Field Marshal fears that with the recent, dreadful situation of the fire in Cornwall together with the spate of lorry hijackings in Devon, the Chief Constable has a lot on his plate down there. We always feared civil unrest would be a potential issue; indeed, I believe it was you who first raised this, Mark? We think it is now time to separate the immediate effects of the Thorpehead disaster from the day-to-day policing matters. While the military and Civil Defence Force will deal with the former, we will be releasing the Chief Constable to concentrate on the latter.'

'And just what will the military be doing with 30,000 radioactive bodies?' The Home Secretary tried not to sound as if she was enjoying the question.

'First, Nadia. We haven't had that figure confirmed but thank you for asking, as it highlights the very reason why the decision-making is being restricted to a closed group. There are a lot of figures and potential scenarios which have to be discussed in the utmost secrecy. We need to keep the pubic re-assured and not panic them unnecessarily. I'm warning you all, if the figure that has just been mentioned leaks out from this room before we are able to confirm it, then whoever is responsible will be signalling the end of their careers.'

'So, we should deliberately mislead the public, Prime Minister?' Nadia was actually enjoying this.

'We have to manage what we say and when, Nadia. We must demonstrate we are in control of the situation and not do anything to further worry the public. The last thing we need at the moment is a cabinet minister briefing one of his or her pet journalists and more wild speculation breaking out in the press. The country is split in two, hundreds of thousands are displaced, food supplies are struggling and the incidents in Devon and Cornwall show just how potentially incendiary things are at the moment. Even with the Civil

Defence Force, police and military are stretched. I'm sure as Home Secretary, Nadia, the last thing you want to be dealing with is riots in towns and cities across the country.'

'Well, while we are still honoured with your presence, Prime Minister, perhaps I can ask the Civil Contingencies Director to give us an update on the situation? Mark, if you please.'

Mark Brooks tapped on his laptop, bringing the bank of screens behind him to life. 'Thank you, Home Secretary. If I can start with food deliveries, the Road Hauliers Association are telling us that every supermarket and retailer has had to recreate their logistics networks on the basis of north and south of the exclusion zone. That's been further complicated by the disruption to food imports which are now arriving through different ports. But the new systems are now settling in and shops on both sides of the EZ are now receiving regular deliveries. Images of empty shelves should become a thing of the past. In his last report, the Gold Commander advised me that there have been isolated incidents of public unrest but these have been largely contained. There have also been reports of looting taking place within the EZ but he felt these would cease as more food was available in shops. This data is twenty-four hours out of date however as the Gold Commander is no longer in post.'

'Yes, thank you for reminding me, Mark,' the Prime Minister interrupted. 'I think I need to speak to the Chief Constable now before I'm distracted any further. The Field Marshal and I have other matters to discuss as well, so ladies and gentlemen, if you will excuse me …' With that Gordon Strathyre closed his file, got up and left the room, closely followed by Field Marshal Parkes and Archie Wilkes.

No. 10 Downing Street

Back in the Prime Minister's office, the three sat around the meeting table with their coffee. 'Things were getting a bit tetchy at COBRA this morning, Prime Minister, if you don't mind me saying,' the Field Marshal reflected.

'Even now, that bitch still has one eye on her own future. It's one reason why I have been keeping her at arm's length from our conversations. The other is I wouldn't trust her with some of the information we have.'

'She has a point over the fatalities though, Prime Minister,' Archie Wilkes reacted. 'There are a lot of bereaved families who will want to know what has happened to their loved ones.'

'And the thirty-thousand figure looks like it's pretty accurate too, according to my colonel,' added Parkes.

'For now, I think all the relatives can be told is that we have removed the bodies to a secure site while we assess the radiation situation. On no account can we let people know the sheer scale of that operation.'

'Nor what's actually happening to the bodies,' his Cabinet Secretary coolly replied.

'I'm not being paranoid but we really have to keep a lid on things and remain in control of the narrative. The last thing we need is some nosy journalist looking to make a name for themselves with a big exposé. I know we have most of the media that matters on our side and they will continue to help us push out the message that there is hope, but we don't have them all. News24.com are increasingly assuming the role of speaking truth to authority and we can't ignore their reach has grown exponentially since all this shit happened.'

'You know the drill by now, Prime Minister,' Archie Wilkes came in. 'If there are any negative stories, we deny, deny again and then we put out our alternative version, or what Kellyanne Conway said about President Trump's inauguration, "alternative facts." When enough of our supporting media repeat them enough times, people only remember the headlines.'

'That's all well and good, Archie but have you read the investigators' initial report on Thorpehead? They've only got the control centre data to work with at the moment; no one has been able to get close enough to the site for a detailed inspection, but from the readings prior to the explosion, the indications point to a design fault. Bicarel have some serious questions to answer but my problem is that fucking twat of an Energy Minister. How did nobody pick up on Roly Smith's links to those guys? My predecessors had enough problems with cronyism and "jobs for the boys." If the media get a sniff of that, it won't matter how many Fleet Street editors we have in our pocket, we won't be able to control it. We're going to have to do something about the Right Honourable Roland Smith.'

'I'm happy with the volume of positive news we can push out through the Hollingsworth papers, it will drown out any questions News24.com might be asking,' Archie Wilkes said reassuringly. 'And if they persist, we've still got one or two cards we can play to make them toe our line.'

'And leave Roland Smith to me, Prime Minister,' Field Marshal Parkes said without looking up from the report he was reading. 'I think I know what to do.'

Holmbeach

As soon as it was daylight, Jack, Shelley and Evan began to pack what they thought they would need for the next part of the journey, or more precisely, the next stage of their lives. After chronicling the events of the last 10 days Jack was sure to take his laptop, camera and chargers. Hopefully, he would soon be in a place which had mobile phone coverage and be able to make contact with his parents who were presumably stranded somewhere in the North. He made sure to empty all the cash from the hotel safe. Shelley and Evan had turned up at the Boar's Head with nothing more than the clothes they stood in and their mobile phones. They had been able to supplement their wardrobes, primarily with Boar's Head logoed polo shirts and kitchen overalls which were baggy on Shelley and ridiculously large on Evan. They would be taken into care, at least until their aunt from Swindon could be located, if that was even possible. But after that, who could say what their future would look like?

With the speed of the initial evacuation from Holmbeach, the Boar's Head car park was still full of cars belonging to the walking group. Some had left their keys at reception when they arrived and Jack had already been able to check which had the most fuel left in the tank, settling on a modern Ford Puma with automatic transmission. The three of them set off in silence, as if it were the last day of a holiday that nobody had wanted to end. Shelley and Evan both sat in the back of the car and Jack threw his camera and his iPhone on the front seat beside him. From the news reports he had read, he knew that reception centres had been set up along the M5 motorway heading south from Bristol but figured these had probably now processed everybody fleeing the city. So he followed the road to Taunton, convinced that they would shortly have their first encounter with the authorities when they left the exclusion zone. Sure enough, they had only been on the road for a few minutes when they heard a high-pitched buzzing. Jack didn't notice it at first but then in the rear view mirror he spotted the drone for the first time. A moment later, it was hovering above the road in front of them before rising higher and disappearing over the Exmoor horizon.

'That's it, they know we're coming,' Jack said into the mirror. 'We can't be far from a control point.'

And then they saw it as they came over the brow on the next bend. A line of post and wire fencing, some three metres high stretched out across the moorland and on the road up ahead, a security post and raisable barrier. But the barrier was down and behind it stood three military personnel in hazmat suits, with their Heckler and Kochs trained on the approaching vehicle. Behind the barrier, an old Bedford truck with canvas canopy was parked and Jack could see more, similarly dressed soldiers sitting in the rear. Before Shelley or Evan had even had the chance to ask what was happening, they heard the first shots above them. The three armed soldiers had clearly fired warning shots into the air. Jack didn't need any warning. Instinctively, he hit the brakes and pulled the steering wheel hard to the right. The Puma's tail spun as the car slowed, almost completing a three-hundred-and-sixty-degree turn a hundred metres or so in front of the control post. At the very point the car was about to reach a halt, Jack took his foot off the brake pedal and stamped down on the accelerator and sped off the way he had just driven as he heard more shots, and this time they were not just warnings.

Back at the barrier, the Lance Corporal spoke into his

Falcon Radio. He confirmed that the vehicle picked up on the drone surveillance had approached Checkpoint 20 on the B3645 road and warning shots had been fired. The vehicle had exercised an emergency turn and was headed back into the Exclusion Zone. When he asked whether his patrol was to pursue the vehicle, he was instructed that the new orders were to contain anyone still in the EZ and not to let them pass.

'What's happening, Jack?' Shelley was screaming. 'Why are they shooting at us?'

'I told you they were after us, Shel. They're going to kill us.' Evan was balling.

'I really don't know what's going on,' Jack said, trying to portray an air of calm while inside his heart was thumping so hard he was sure they could probably hear it. 'First things first. Let's get away from here and make sure they're not following us.'

Heading back towards Holmbeach, Jack suddenly swung right onto the Riverbridge road. There was a picnic site about a mile further on where people used to go to enjoy the views of the river estuary and Jack knew it also had a clear view back along the road they had just travelled. He pulled in and positioned the car so he could look back along the road. There was no lorry following, and no sign of any drones in the air.

'Looks like we're safe,' he said to his terrified back-seat passengers. 'They were clearly trying to prevent us from getting through the checkpoint. Almost as if they were trying to frighten us off.'

'So are we going back to the hotel then?' Evan asked hopefully.

'There's no point, Evan,' Jack tried to reason. 'There's no power and no water, and it doesn't look as if they'll be sending any rescue teams in based on what we've just seen at the checkpoint.'

Jack was trying to process what had just happened and what it could mean. Perhaps they weren't the only people left in the Exclusion Zone? There had been messages on the TV in the days immediately after the explosion, urging people to leave but nothing about enforcing the boundary to keep them in. But the more immediate problem was what to do next. At the exit of the picnic area the road signs pointed left to Holmbeach and Taunton and right towards Riverbridge. Jack knew that Riverbridge was the first place that people had been taken after the explosion and that the hospital had treated the first Thorpehead casualties. The decision to ultimately evacuate had only been taken a few days ago. Perhaps they might still have power and water, and maybe even mobile phone coverage. There almost certainly would not be anyone trying to shoot at them.

Jack pressed the start button and edged the Puma towards the car park exit.

'Okay, listen up you two. Here's the plan.'

Cornwall/Devon boundary

Eric was sitting in the middle of the bench seat of the Ford Transit Custom. His brother Davey was to his left while Jago, a friend of Davey's, was driving. Eric knew him vaguely but his brother was more of a friend. It was Jago's van and he had driven steadily, not having spoken a word since they left Cantarrock.

'How you getting on with your new phone then Eric?' Davey asked.

'Yeah great. Took a while to transfer all the data but it does so much more than my old'n.'

'Top of the range it is. Only the best for my little bro!' Davey said proudly. 'Mind you, don't get thinking you'm getting special treatment. We got a whole load of them from that phone shop and half of West Cornwall will have one by the time I've shifted them all. Sold six down the pub this afternoon.'

'So what's the score then tonight?' Eric asked his brother.

'Simple. I've got a mate who volunteered for that civil defence force thing. Well, he didn't volunteer. They said they would stop his benefits if he didn't join up. So he's up near Taunton in the command centre. They've built this bloody exclusion zone with barbed wire an'al but there are so many roads crossing it, they just don't 'ev enough troops to guard them. So he tells me where the patrols are going to be and we goes in on one of the other roads. We just lift the barrier and put it down again afterwards. Even't seen a soldier yet. So, tonight we'em going into Riverbridge. The patrol is over near the coast. Riverbridge was functioning normally until just a few days ago so we reckons there must be a lot of food still there. Jago here says there's a famous butchers' shop in the town centre. Reckon we can liquidate the cold store and everybody down 'ome can ev a good Sunday roast this weekend – for the right price of course.'

'And there's no danger of being caught?'

'Well there ain't no bugger left in Riverbridge and Jago's mate says they only have one patrol on tonight. E's on duty himself so he can call if anything changes.'

'So we're only going for food tonight?'

'Mainly, yes. But if you see anything else you fancy along

the way, just help yourself.'

'Aren't you afraid about radiation an'all that?'

'Na, bruv' Look, we're in and out in no time. Jago and I ev been up loads of times already and no one's dead or even glowing in the dark yet.'

Riverbridge

Jack had been to Riverbridge more times than he cared to remember but even in the early hours of a Sunday morning, he had never seen the town this deserted. Just like in Holmbeach just a few days earlier, it looked like everyone had simply stepped out for a few minutes. Some shops were shuttered but the houses didn't look as if their owners had locked them up in anticipation of a long absence. The traffic lights were not working but Jack still drove with caution at the first couple of junctions before it dawned on him that there would be nothing coming the other way. There might not have been tumbleweed rolling down the main street but the sight of stray dogs and cats was one sign that Riverbridge was not simply sleeping but had been abandoned. He drove once around the town centre just to satisfy himself that they were indeed alone. There were no signs of life at the police station or the fire station next door and all the indications were that the power was off here too.

'I'm not sure it's going to be much better here than at the hotel,' Jack said, looking up into the rearview mirror at his back-seat passengers. 'Let's look for somewhere to shelter for tonight while I work on a plan B.'

'What's our plan B, Jack?'

'Still working on that at the moment. Perhaps some food will help me think more clearly.'

They were now on their second tour of the town centre and a place Jack knew well. On one side of the street, Kitto's Fine Foods and Poultry, one of the main suppliers to the Boar's Head. Opposite stood a detached, stone-built manor house, which served as both a surgery and family home for the local GP whom Jack had known vaguely. The traditional granite frontage gave way to an extensive home for the doctor's wife and two children. Jack immediately thought that, in addition to a probably well-stocked larder, they would probably also find clothing for Shelley and Evan who were probably about the same age as the children who used to live there. He stopped the car, remembering the times he had stopped outside Kitto's to pick up some emergency supplies for the hotel, only to find a ticket on the windscreen when he came back out. But once again, he did a double-take, realising there would be no traffic warden lurking around the corner or even any traffic.

The house looked as if it was alarmed but Jack reasoned that with the power off, the system probably wasn't activated. But rather than risk cutting himself by smashing a window, the three of them walked around the path to the rear of the house. To their amazement, when Evan tried the handle of the conservatory door, it was unlocked. The half-finished bowls of cereal and full coffee cups on the kitchen table suggested that the house had been vacated with little or no notice. As Jack had hoped, there were tins of food in the cupboard which, although consumed cold, provided a supplement to the diet of dry Cocoa Krisp that Evan had already begun to feast on. And upstairs, the GP's children had indeed left a wide selection of clothes and underwear the correct size for him and his sister.

With no other 'plan B' beyond checking out other

potential crossing points out of the exclusion zone, the three decided on an early night before heading back out of Riverbridge at first light. But no sooner had Jack's head hit the pillow, he heard the noises coming from outside. First there was the sound of a vehicle, then voices from across the road, followed by banging and crashing. By the time Jack got out of bed, Shelley and Evan were already in his room.

'Did you hear that, Jack? There are people across the road. Evan saw them and they're not soldiers like before,' said Shelley, excitedly.

Jack drew back the curtain in the bay window. Through the darkness he could see torch lights flickering in the shop window of Kitto's Fine Food and Poultry opposite. There were definitely people there and, by the noise they were making, they didn't seem to be bothered about who knew.

'Come on, let's go and see,' Jack said, pulling on his shoes and picking up the torch he had found earlier in the kitchen.

The three of them left the GP's house via the front door and crossed the road towards the butcher's shop. They immediately saw the Transit van parked in the alleyway with its rear doors open and made their way towards it. As they drew level with the rear entrance to the shop, a figure appeared out of the darkness carrying half a dozen boxes which he then proceeded to stack in the van. Inside, they could hear another two male voices.

Eric, Davey and Jago were busy sorting through the stock. Davey had smashed his way into the deep freeze with his crowbar. Although the power must have been off for around 48 hours at least, the room had remained sealed and he reckoned a good number of carcasses would still be fresh enough to eat as long as they got them back to Cornwall and sold them the next day. He and Jago were busy sorting the best ones – beef and lamb would fetch the best prices, but they'd leave the 'posh' stuff like venison and pheasant as they would need quick sales. Meanwhile, Eric was loading the tins of pate and game soup into the van. As Jack went to follow him back into the shop, he knocked into an empty can of cooking oil that was stacked outside the rear door, sending it rattling down the alley. Suddenly, the voices inside stopped.

'Hello,' called Jack. 'Don't worry, we're not armed. We just want some help.'

No answer. With Shelley and Evan close behind, Jack shone his torch towards the back door and stepped forward.

'We've been left behind in the evacuation and we're trying to get out, but we had a problem at the control point this afternoon….'

As Jack turned the corner into the store room he was struck full in the face by a catering-sized tin of potted pork terrine. His legs immediately buckled and he hit the floor and lay motionless, his nose a mass of blood and sinew.

'What the fuck …,' Davey cried, shining the torch on Eric, still holding the offending can. 'Where did he come from? Better get this stuff in the van and be out of here, just in case. Better drop that tin, though bro. No one's going to buy it with all that blood on it.'

But Davey's torchlight had also picked up something else.

The terror-stricken figure of Shelley who had been standing right behind Jack as they entered the store room.

'Well, lookie here. Our friend had a bit of crumpet with'e. Well now darlin', your boyfriend ain't going to be much use to ye now, is he? Certainly won't be able to give'e what thee needs right now, will he?'

The torchlight blinded Shelley. She wanted to scream,

she wanted to run, but once again, she was frozen and speechless.

She couldn't see the man with the funny accent leering but she sensed his mood change.

'Grab 'old of 'er, Jago.'

'What you doin', Davey?' Eric shouted, having thrown the tin away.

'Time to show 'er what a real Cornishman is like,' Davey said as he undid his belt.

Shelley smelled the body odour and rancid breath as two strong arms gripped her and dragged her to the ground. Inside, she was screaming as Jago had her shoulders pinned to the ground, but no sound came from her mouth. Then the polo shirt she had only recently liberated from the Doctor's daughter's wardrobe was ripped open from the front and the similarly acquired shorts pulled down. In Jago's torchlight she could see the silhouette of Davey and felt his rough hands forcing her legs apart. And then, all of a sudden, the figure froze. She heard the breath hiss out of his mouth as he dropped on top of her.

'Get off my sister, you bastard.' Evan stood screaming at the now motionless body which lay with a 20-centimetre meat cleaver embedded between its shoulder blades.

Shelley now found her strength and her voice, managing to squeeze out from underneath Davey's prone body just in time to see Evan with a torch in one hand and reaching for another meat cleaver hanging on the wall. But Jago was already out of the door and heading for the van as her brother turned his attention towards Eric, whose turn it now was to remain frozen and speechless.

'No Evan, that's enough,' she cried.

'Davey. My brother. You've killed my brother,' Eric was saying, still rooted to the spot. Whether shock or fear, he didn't express any emotion, just repeated the words as if processing the information.

'Jesus, what happened?' Jack struggled to his feet, blood streaming from his nose and mouth, he surveyed the scene as he tried to remember what had happened after he first walked into Kitto's. He saw Shelley, her polo shirt ripped and trying to get back into her shorts; her brother, a meat cleaver in his hand facing Eric and a body lying face down on the floor with another butcher's implement in its back.

It only took a second to join the dots. 'We've got to get out of here now,' he said to Shelley and Evan. 'Who are you? Where have you come from?' he turned to Eric. Whether it was Jack's voice or the sound of the van starting up outside, Eric immediately woke from his torpor. 'Me too, I'm gone,' said Eric as he stumbled in the half-light towards the back door.

'No wait. Can't you help us? We're trying to get out but the road is closed and the soldiers were shooting at us,' Jack pleaded.

'Nothing to do with me but Davey's dead and we've got to go. If you want to get out, take the Hillingdon road. There are no patrols there tonight.' With that, Eric was gone. They heard the van doors close and the squeal of tyres as it drove off up Riverbridge High Street.

The three of them returned across the road to the GP's house and went straight to the surgery. Shelley found some cotton wool and Evan fetched bottled water from the kitchen. Together, they were able to clean up the mess around Jack's nose and mouth, which wasn't looking quite as bad as it had when he first came around at the butchers. His whole head was pounding but the painkillers they had found in the surgery cabinet were starting to have an effect.

'What actually happened back there?' he asked.

'They were attacking my sister. I had to do something,' Evan's voice was breaking as he spoke.

'They were going to rape me, Jack. Evan saved me.'

'She's right, Evan,' said Jack, trying to reassure Shelley's brother. 'You did the right thing. You're not in any trouble but if what that bloke was saying about the patrols is right, we should get out of here now. I know the Hillingdon road, it won't take us long and there's plenty enough petrol in the car.'

They each went to gather up their few belongings and Shelley managed to find a pair of jogging pants and a hoodie to fit from her new wardrobe. They took the rest of the bottled water and some remaining tins of food in case of emergencies and made for the front door.

'Oh, wait a minute,' Shelley said as they reached the surgery door. 'It won't hurt to take some more painkillers and petroleum jelly for that face of yours, Jack. No one is likely to miss them.'

'Good idea, Sis,' said Evan. 'And can you look for something for me? I've had a bit of a sore throat all day and,' rolling up his sleeve, 'I've got these blisters on my arm.'

24 - Thirteen days later

Devon/ Somerset boundary

The advice they had been given about the patrols was correct. Although Jack's eye was starting to close over from the bruising, he managed to drive at a steady pace along the Hillingdon road. When they reached the control post, there were no guards, just as Eric had said. Even the barrier was raised, presumably the looters in the van hadn't bothered to lower it again after their own flight. Jack thought for a moment and decided to get out of the car and bring the barrier back down once they had driven through so as not to arouse any suspicion if a patrol did ultimately turn up. He had no other idea of what to do next other than to put some distance between themselves and the exclusion zone and to get some rest. Despite the painkillers, his head was pounding, his nose throbbing and his right eye gradually closing over. Once through Hillingdon itself Jack wondered whether to head west or east. Assuming that his attackers back in Riverbridge were Cornwall-bound, he instinctively chose east, heading across Wiltshire in the general direction of Salisbury.

After an hour they reached the A303 and pulled into the

first rest area they came across on the dual carriageway. It was clearly a truck stop, but with no trucks. The lights were off in the transport café and Jack chose a parking spot in the far corner of the car park. Maybe they would be able to get some cooked food in the morning and decide on a course of action from then on. But for now, all Jack wanted was to close his one open eye and sleep. Evan was already fast asleep but Shelley had spent the whole journey staring out of the window in complete silence. As Jack reclined his seat as far as he could without disturbing Evan, Shelley snapped back to reality, offering to apply some more petroleum jelly to Jack's nose, but he declined, suggesting they waited until first light. No sooner had he settled than Jack heard a phonic ping, followed by another, then another. Looking to the side, his iPhone display was illuminated. They had mobile phone coverage. They were back in the real world, or what was left of it.

The next morning, things were starting to look brighter. Awoken by the hiss of air brakes, they found the rest area alive with lorries, vans and cars coming and going. Apart from their encounter with the looters in Riverbridge these were the first real people Jack, Shelley and Evan had seen in almost two weeks. And none of them was wearing protective suits or holding a rifle. The toilet and shower blocks were operating, the cafe was open and it had Wi-Fi. The only difference was a notice explaining the ATM was not working which the waitress later explained was due to the stampede to withdraw cash immediately following the Thorpehead incident. Card payments were still fine and Jack had the wad of cash from the Boar's Head safe in any event.

So after cleaning themselves up a little, some more treatment for Jack's face and a few more painkillers, they were all ready for a cooked breakfast and a chance to catch up on their phone messages. Jack managed to contact his parents. As he imagined, they were still marooned in the Lake District and were being treated as evacuees in temporary accommodation. Jack was evasive about his own circumstances, blaming the lack of mobile phone coverage and a lost charger for his radio silence. Avoiding any mention of his decision to stay behind when he should have been evacuated or his subsequent adoption of orphaned siblings, he told his parents he was on his way to stay with friends south of London with the prospect of some work in the media. For Shelley and Evan, they quickly confirmed their assumption that there were no messages from their parents and apart from the odd text from a school friend, Shelley caught up on the events of the last few days via TikTok while Evan played games. But he soon tired of that and seemed rather listless. While Jack and Shelley had dived into their full Englishes, Evan had hardly touched his. Shelley and Jack helped themselves to his sausages while he went to take a bowl of Cocoa Krisp from the cereal buffet, from which he subsequently only nibbled at the odd one.

'What's wrong, Ev?' his sister asked. 'It's not like you to be off your Cocoa Krisp.'

'I'm not really hungry, and anyway, my mouth hurts when I try to swallow. See.' With that, he opened his mouth. Shelley immediately saw the angry red swelling around his gums.

'My God, Ev! Why didn't you say?' she cried.

'I told you I wasn't feeling well last night. And these things on my arms are getting worse.'

Then, he rolled up his sleeve. What last night under torchlight had looked like burn blisters, were now deep red sores, which to Jack, appeared the colour of the well-hung meat he sometimes ordered from Kittos. There was something about Evan's complexion too that seemed to have changed over the last 24 hours. Shelley reached for the bag which contained the emergency medicines they had liberated from the GP's surgery in Riverbridge.

'Let me put some jelly on those sores Ev, they don't look very nice at all.'

'I don't think that's going to help much, Shelley,' Jack interrupted. In his mind, he had worked out what the symptoms meant. 'I think we need to get him to A&E and let a real doctor look at him.'

Jack settled the bill with the waitress. When he asked her how far they were from the nearest hospital emergency department, she naturally assumed it was because of his face, but confirmed that Salisbury General was only half an hour further along the A303.

Salisbury

When they arrived at the hospital, there was much more activity than normal, even for a busy Accident and Emergency department. A line of stationary ambulances filled one lane of the approach road, most with their rear doors open and paramedics engaged in triage. Police and military uniforms blended with medical scrubs as personnel hurried in all directions. Jack dropped Shelley and Evan right outside the entrance to A&E, telling them to show the nurses Evan's arms. He would join them once he'd parked the car.

If finding somewhere to park at Salisbury General was difficult in normal times, these were clearly not normal times. As Jack toured the hospital grounds he found large areas of the car parks sealed off. Many had been commandeered by military and police vehicles while a number of temporary marquees had been erected in others. A police officer stepped out three cars in front of Jack, halting the traffic to let a large covered military lorry emerge from one of the marquees. It left the car park with a police escort vehicle in front and another falling in behind. Eventually, he gave up looking for a car park and left the hospital grounds in search of a space in the neighbouring streets.

It was more than half an hour before he had walked back into the A&E department. As he approached the reception desk he heard Shelley's voice.

'Jack, please, help me!'

He looked across the waiting room to see Shelley with a nurse on one arm and a female police constable on the other, both trying to usher her through a set of double doors leading to the wards. 'They've taken Evan and won't let me see him. They're trying to take me somewhere else but they won't say where!'

Jack leapt over the tape barrier and ran towards Shelley.

'Stay where you are, Sir,' the policewoman said, moving her free arm towards her belt and her hand hovering over what Jack assumed to be a spray canister. 'There's nothing to be concerned about. Evan is in good hands and we need to check that Shelley is OK.'

'So why does it need the police to do that?' Jack shot back. 'You're clearly taking her against her will.'

'If you sign in at reception, Sir, someone will be able to explain what's happening.'

Shelley was becoming hysterical now. 'Don't let them take me, Jack, they'll put me in care.'

But she was helpless to resist as the nurse and the police

officer led her forcefully through the doors which sealed shut behind them. Jack stood there feeling helpless with no choice but to do what the police officer had said and returned to the reception desk. Jack's attempts to find out what had happened in between dropping Evan and Shelley at the door of A&E and parking the car, fell at the first hurdle. A frazzled-looking man in his forties sat behind the glass screen giving the impression of being busy on his keyboard. A half-raise of the eyebrows towards Jack was presumably his cue to speak.

'I dropped two young children off here a few minutes ago and it seems they have both been admitted. Can you tell me where they are, please?'

'Patients' name?'

Jack was lucky he could remember Shelley and Evan's surname from the time they spent at the Boar's Head searching the Thorpehead casualty list.

'And are you their father?'

'No, I'm a friend.'

'You're not a relative then.'

'No, like I just said, I'm their friend.'

'If you're not a relative I am unable to supply any patient information.'

'But their parents are dead and we think their aunt has been evacuated from Swindon. Right now, I'm the only family they have.'

'If you're not a relative I am unable to supply any patient information.'

Jack was starting to lose his composure. 'Look, I know this may go against all your working principles but a couple of weeks ago, a nuclear power station blew up, you may have heard about it? Well, their mum and dad were working there at the time and since then those two kids have had to endure such hardship that I won't bore with the details, and I have been the only adult in their lives. Just now, the girl has been dragged away from casualty with the police in attendance. I know this must be really inconvenient for you, but I would be most grateful if you could just remove yourself from your bureaucratic straightjacket and let me know where they are and what is happening to them.'

'There is no need for you to adopt that attitude towards me,' the receptionist responded in the same tone as he had used throughout the conversation so far. 'You have been told twice that I can only give information to relatives, and you are not a relative. Please stand aside now if you don't want me to ask security to do it for you.' Jack then heard the click of the intercom being switched off and the receptionist returned his regard to the computer and started typing once more. He remained frozen to the spot. Dumfounded by the lack of empathy and frustrated by the attitude which seemed oblivious to the momentous events of the last couple of weeks, even though the hospital itself was clearly dealing with the consequences. He felt a hand on his shoulder and turned around to see a young woman in her late twenties dressed in mid-green scrubs.

'Hello sir, my name is Claudia and I'm a junior doctor in the emergency department. That's a nasty mess on your face. Do you want to come with me? You can tell me about the door you walked into while I clean you up. You may need an X-ray on that nose, too.'

Jack took a moment to realise what the doctor had said.

'No, that's fine. I'm trying to find out what happened to two young children I brought in earlier. I can look after myself once I've found out what's going on.'

But Doctor Claudia was insistent and there was something in the conspiratorial movement of her eyes that made Jack take notice. He followed the young doctor into the emergency department but she led him past the line of occupied treatment cubicles into her small side office. Closing the door behind Jack she began to assemble gauze, cotton wool and antiseptic.

'I will treat your face Jack, but I need to speak to you out of earshot of the consultant. I heard you at reception and unfortunately that horrible old man was right about relatives only. But I was here when Evan and Shelley arrived and she asked me to look out for you. I'm afraid there is no easy way to say this but things are not looking good. Evan is presenting advanced symptoms of Acute Radiation Syndrome. It looks like he has been contaminated by gamma radiation which is attacking his internal organs. Shelley is not showing any signs at present, but while Evan is in the isolation ward, she is being kept in for observation.'

'I did fear it was something to do with radiation when I saw his blisters,' said Jack. 'So will he be OK now you're treating him on the ward?'

Claudia hesitated. 'I'm afraid he's not being treated, Jack. Unfortunately, by the time the external symptoms are apparent it is too late to do anything about the internal damage. They are keeping him in isolation and just trying to make him as comfortable as possible.'

Jack was silent. 'How long has he got?'

'Days, a week at most. Believe me Jack, we have seen a lot of these cases in the last few days. They are all the same. Once the blisters show, the organ damage is well underway.'

'And Shelley?'

'At the moment, she seems unaffected and she is being given potassium iodine. The problem is that patients often show initial symptoms and then appear to improve. It's only a few days later that the problems really begin.'

'But how come they are not both showing the same signs? And what about me?'

'It really depends on the level of contamination and what type of radiation. Some people are fitter or healthier than others and the body reacts in different ways. From what Shelley told me, she and her brother went quite close to the power station before they met you, so that could be one reason. I'll get you some potassium iodine tablets once I've had a look at your nose though, just to be safe.'

There was another brief pause before Claudia continued. 'I'm afraid the other problem for Shelley is that once she's finished here, whenever that is, she will be taken into care. Matron had no choice but to notify the authorities once we had their admission details. That's why the police were with her earlier.'

Jack was struggling to process all the information. Evan was going to die and even if Shelley didn't, she would have lost her parents and her brother within a matter of days. Was this his fault? Should he have insisted on getting them away from Holmbeach as soon as he found them, rather than rope them in for his selfish adventure to chronicle the days following the Thorpehead disaster for a newspaper story that he couldn't even be sure of getting published?

'Can I see them?' he asked.

'Evan, not a chance. He's in the isolation ward and irradiated. Even the staff are limited in the amount of time they can spend in the ward, and that's wearing protective gear. I'll check up on Shelley shortly and see what I can do. No promises though.'

'You're being very honest and helpful,' Jack replied. 'But why did you say you wanted to talk to me about this in secret?'

Claudia moved to the door to check there was nobody out in the corridor then closed it again. 'It's not just circumventing hospital protocol over relatives, Jack. There's so much more going on and we're being forced to keep quiet. Shelley told me you were a journalist and had been taking pictures and writing stories about Thorpehead after the explosion. You see, Evan's case is not a one-off. The reason I know so much about the symptoms and outcomes of radiation sickness is that we have been dealing with hundreds of cases in the last few days.'

'Hundreds?'

'Yes, literally hundreds of deaths. Horrible, slow and painful deaths. And we're not alone. We've been told not to talk about it with anyone outside the hospital but sometimes we have to talk to colleagues at other hospitals. We've been running short on specialist equipment and medication and when we talk to other sites like Exeter or Southampton, it's clear they are in the same position. We were warned to expect deaths from ARS within ten days of potential contamination and last week, right on cue, we were overwhelmed with a raft of cases. They were all evacuees from Swindon being lodged at a holiday village in the New Forest. Protocol requires any victims of radiation contamination should be removed in zinc coffins. But guess what? We don't have any zinc coffins! Over forty-eight hours, we had so many fatalities that the army had to come and erect a temporary mortuary in the car park. And then we discovered that as soon as the bodies were delivered to the temporary facility, they were being taken away in lorries. Nobody has any idea where, or those who do are saying nothing. We have been told that the removal of victims is a military matter, requests for burial information from families are to be passed directly on to them and under the emergency legislation, anyone at the hospital who talks about it risks imprisonment.'

'So why are you telling me if you're risking your job and your freedom?'

'Something isn't right Jack. We're all running on fumes here. These last couple of weeks have put everyone under incredible strain, but bereaved families still have a right to know what's happened to their loved ones and that their remains are being treated with dignity and respect. You're a journalist Jack. Someone needs to find out what's going on and the public has a right to know.' With that, the office door opened.

'Everything alright in here, Claudia?' the staff nurse asked.

'Yes, all fine. This is the chap who brought in the two ARS kids earlier. He needed his own injuries looking at and all the cubicles were full. We've almost finished here now so you can leave the door open.'

Jack walked out of the Salisbury General A&E Department in a daze. He was armed with a fresh supply of painkillers and Claudia's number on his phone. She had promised to keep him updated on any events using his Proton email account. But all he could think about was the teenage girl and her kid brother who had been the only source of normality in his life amidst the crazy events of the last couple of weeks. Now, young Evan was facing a slow and painful death alone while Shelley was about to lose her only known remaining relative. Jack would have no hope of even keeping track of her once she disappeared into the care system. It had quickly become apparent there was no chance of getting to see her while she was under observation at the hospital and although Claudia had promised to keep tabs on her progress, she was not confident Jack would be able to visit.

He had no idea what he was going to do next with his own life but for now, Jack was certain of only two things: he wasn't leaving Salisbury until he knew more about Evan and Shelley's wellbeing and he needed to put the events of the last 24 hours on record. As he made his way out of the hospital grounds towards the side street where he had left the car, Jack walked past the giant marquee in the main car park that he had seen earlier. With what Claudia had told him about the temporary morgue and the convoy he had witnessed pulling away when he had first arrived, it was safe to assume the covered lorry he had seen was taking away contaminated bodies. Two armed policemen stood at the entrance to the marquee so as Jack passed on the opposite side of the road, he took out his phone and held it to his ear as if he was in conversation. But he was talking to no one and the phone was set to video camera. By turning his head as he spoke, he was confident he had picked up the full sweep of the marquee and its guarded entrance for his latest film report to send to Elodie.

Although it was only mid-afternoon, Jack was already exhausted. The escape from Riverbridge and the previous night spent in the car was starting to take its toll. Returning to the car, he decided to find a hotel where he could unwind, physically and mentally, while spending some time on his laptop to update his Thorpehead diary. He soon found himself on the A36, which took him around the edge of the city and an anonymous roadside hotel with a restaurant attached, with free Wi-Fi in every room. Jack checked in for two nights with the possibility of staying longer. The receptionist seemed unfazed, telling him the hotel was never more than half full these days. While hotel beds and holiday lets elsewhere were being snapped up by the Government to house evacuees, places like Salisbury were apparently deemed too close to the exclusion zone and found themselves in a sort of stasis.

As Jack took his key and headed for his room he picked up a copy of the local free newspaper from the dispenser at the reception desk. *The South Wiltshire Gazette* was, he assumed, the Salisbury equivalent of *The Moorsman* and indeed, he soon discovered that it too was part of Sir Ian Davison's Hollingsworth Media group. Since the power went down back at the Boar's Head, it had been harder to keep up with the news reports regarding Thorpehead so before going online to the nationals, Jack decided to start with the local news. But flicking through the pages of *The South Wiltshire Gazette* he could find nothing about the high death toll or the military presence at Salisbury General. In fact, he found no stories at all that related to the Thorpehead explosion or the evacuation of thousands of residents from the exclusion zone that extended as far as a few miles up the road from Salisbury. There were articles about planning applications, picture stories about ribbon cuttings and village fetes, and the format mirrored most editions of *The Moorsman* before the explosion. It was almost as if Thorpehead hadn't happened at all. Jack threw the local rag aside and fired up his laptop to start reading through the national newspapers and websites. Remembering how graphic and detailed some of the reporting was in the hours and days following the power station's destruction, he was surprised how little time it took to get up to date with the news. The evacuation itself dominated the early headlines but was largely viewed as a triumph of logistics. There had been some subsequent resentment among locals, particularly in Devon and Cornwall but the intervention of the new Civil Defence Force appeared to have rapidly restored order. As to be expected, the largely pro-government publications were trumpeting the decisive actions of Prime Minister Gordon Strathyre in response to the crisis. The more extreme titles were championing the efforts of the military and emergency services as well as the stoic patriotism of the British public, in Churchillian terms. But more generally, it appeared to Jack that many publications were treating Thorpehead as past news, like a major rail disaster or a fire in a tower block. Life was moving on and there were other stories to put on the front page.

Having caught up on the red tops and the Hollingsworth Media titles, Jack was interested to compare their coverage to *News24.com*. As the only major news outlet not in the control of a billionaire, usually non-domiciled proprietor, the rolling news website had always prided itself on its independence. It combined factual reporting with holding decision makers to account. Governments of every persuasion had learnt to treat *News24.com* with respect. The website had effectively replaced the BBC as the trusted source of news and its respect in media circles was now grudgingly shared by those in power. Scrolling back through the news reports to the first post, just an hour after the

Thorpehead explosion, Jack certainly found a lot more detail. Casualty numbers, chaotic scenes around the evacuation, prorogation of Parliament, disruption to the food supply chain, the appalling events at Trethewy Beach in Cornwall, lawlessness and looting – something he had first-hand experience of. And yet there was something missing. *News24.com* had a reputation for speaking truth to authority and its opinion pieces were legendary. Historically, the editors of *News24.com* had been credited with the resignation of one Prime Minister and a clutch of senior politicians as a consequence of revelations they had published on the site. As far as Jack could tell, *News 24.com*'s more recent coverage of Thorpehead was high on fact but somehow lacking in comment. With the country effectively being run by the Prime Minister and the head of the military, surely a media organisation which prides itself on truth and accountability would be in full swing? It was a question for tomorrow, though. Realising he hadn't eaten all day, Jack went down to the reception and retrieved a sandwich and a bottle of Coke from the vending machine before returning to his room to update his journal for the last 48 hours and sending the latest update to Elodie. But by bringing the story up to date, it of course had ended at the hospital with Evan and Shelley. Up to that point, he had convinced himself he would be ready for bed once his story was complete, but when it came to lying down in the bed, Jack was wide awake, his thoughts only on what was happening at Salisbury General.

It was gone midnight but Shelley couldn't sleep. The main light was off but her room was bathed in the blue half-light of the equipment monitors around her bed. She had her phone but was restricted in her ability to use it by the sensor clipped to her index finger. At hourly intervals, a nurse dressed in protective clothing would come in to check the readings and leave her food and drink or make her take more of those horrible potassium iodine tablets. She was under observation but felt fine. No one would tell her where or how Evan was, and nobody even knew who Jack was. Although the nurse had not long left, the door opened again. Claudia. Thank God, a friendly face.

'Hi Shelley. I haven't got long. Put these on and I'm going to take you to see Evan.' Claudia held out a protective gown and gloves while removing the clip from Shelley's finger and pausing the machine. Before Shelley could express her relief, Claudia's tone lost its usual familiarity and resembled that of the observation nurses who had been coming in each hour.

'There's no easy way to say this Shelley, but Evan is dying. He has advanced radiation sickness which is affecting his internal organs. He must have been exposed to extreme radiation while you were in Holmbeach and I am afraid the doctors can do nothing for him. He's being kept as comfortable as possible but he will most likely pass into a coma before long. He's not supposed to have any visitors because he is still radioactive but I want him to be able to see you while he still can. Please, don't say anything. Just come with me as quietly as possible.' She then she guided Shelley out of the room and into a wheelchair, heading for the isolation ward. When they arrived on the top floor, the nurse on duty in the anteroom gave Claudia a knowing nod, picked up a file and left. As she passed, she whispered 'Three minutes, maximum exposure limit.'

Shelley had not said a word during the short journey up from the observation ward and although her mouth opened when she saw Evan, no words came out. He was lying, partly propped up in his bed and attached to a drip. His head of curly hair had gone – fallen out or shaved, she could not be sure. But he had no eyebrows either and his skin was a brownish black. But he smiled when he saw his sister. 'What do you look like, Sis? All dressed up in that garb just to come and see me. You look just like all the other nurses, except you're in a wheelchair!'

'I'm fine Ev,' she said, standing up and moving closer to the bed. She was about to ask how he was feeling, but immediately thought better of it.

'How's the food? Have they managed to find you any Cocoa Krisp?' she said, trying to sound light-hearted.

'Not really hungry, to be honest. Tired and sleeping a lot. Mum and Dad have just been in. You must have just missed them.'

'Sorry, Ev. What do you mean?'

'Yeah, they've just been in to see me. Said sorry but they got stuck at work. But they're coming back tomorrow to take us home.'

'But Ev, Mum and Dad are …..' Shelley felt Claudia's hand on her shoulder.

'He's hallucinating,' she whispered. 'It's quite common.'

'And guess what, Sis?' Evan's voice was becoming weaker. 'They've bought us a puppy. A Golden Retriever, like we always wanted. They say I can name it when we get home. I think I'm going to call it ….' Evan's voice was fading and his eyes began to close.

'Ev? What's happening?' Shelley turned to Claudia. 'He's not dead?'

The regular beep continued to sound as waves appeared across the monitor beside Evan's bed.

'He may be slipping into a coma, Shelley. I'm sorry,

there's is nothing else we can do. I think we should leave him in peace now.' Claudia gently guided Shelley back into the wheelchair and pushed her out of the room. Outside, the nurse had returned to her station and Claudia mouthed a quiet 'thank you' to her as they passed the desk. Back in the observation room, Claudia removed the protective gear and reconnected Shelley to her own monitor.

'I'm really sorry about Evan, Shelley. I wanted you to see him before it was too late but I'm afraid you won't be able to see him again. You shouldn't have to be going through this on your own, but believe me, Evan is not the only case like this that I have seen recently. Hundreds of people are suffering from the same thing. If it's any consolation, it looks like you are going to be fine, and Jack is staying in a hotel just around the corner. All being well, he should be able to come and see you tomorrow.'

Back in the isolation ward on the top floor, the rhythm of beeps accompanied the regular wave movement across the monitor next to Evan's bed. And then it didn't. The beep became constant, and the waves a flat line.

25 - Fourteen days later

Hampstead Heath, London

Although he had lived in London almost all of his life, Archie Wilkes had never seen the City of London as it was this morning. It wasn't yet seven in the morning, Hampstead Heath was deserted and while the sun was just rising, he shivered as he sat on a bench on Parliament Hill. The sky was clear and a faint blue but immediately below his vantage point, a candyfloss cloud still enveloped the capital with the Shard, as well as the tops of the Gherkin, the Cheesegrater and Walkie-Talkie buildings the only reference points he had to convince him where he was. He knew that as the sun continued its ascent over the Docklands, the mist would soon dissipate and leave nothing behind but condensation on windows and windscreens, unlike the cloud which enveloped much of the country just a few weeks earlier.

'One really does have to be the early bird to catch the Prime Minister's chief advisor on his own, then.' Field Marshal Leighton Parkes was standing behind him. Whether it was his military training or the fact that Archie had been lost in his thoughts, he wasn't sure. The Chief of Defence Staff had seemingly appeared out of nowhere and was wearing a light coloured raincoat over a pair of beige cargo trousers and a violet crew neck sweater. It was the first time Archie had seen him in civvies and he wasn't sure whether it was because of the time of day or the covert nature of the meeting.

'I'm glad you could manage to slip away from your lord and master for a short time, even if it means having to heave myself across to this side of London first thing in the morning. Shall we go for a walk? Still a bit nippy to be sitting on a park bench,' the Field Marshal continued.

'PM is having a family breakfast so I've got a later start today. Wants to spend some time with the kids before they're whisked off to the country estate in Scotland. Despite all the travel restrictions, it looks like he's been able to arrange a special flight for the family so they can sit out this mess in the relative safety of the Highlands.' Archie got up and fell into step with Leighton Parkes.

'I'm glad we've been able to meet, Archie. I wanted to have a conversation outside of Number Ten or the Cabinet Office, and you'll soon understand why. You see, I have only really been in close contact with the PM and yourself in the last couple of weeks but I get the distinct impression that Gordon tends to do what you tell him rather than the other way around.'

'I am his special advisor, Leighton. Although I would prefer the word "suggest" rather than "tell".'

'Quite. But perhaps what I mean is that rather than receiving your good counsel, the Prime Minister, certainly before this dreadful explosion, was more of a mouthpiece for the views of Archie Wilkes, and even now, his actions in response to this tragedy are not necessarily his own ideas?'

'In what way?'

'Oh, let's say the immediate decision to invoke the Civil Emergencies Act, prorogation of Parliament, limited information shared with the Cabinet, controlling the media. How am I doing? Don't get me wrong, I'm not opposed to any of those decisions. They just don't seem to chime with the character of the Gordon Strathyre I have known for the last few years.' Archie let the comment sink in, biding his time before deciding what next to say.

'I hope you're not suggesting that I'm acting without the PM's consent?'

'Absolutely not, Archie. It's just that when I compare what I have known to be Gordon's views on matters of state with your own, and you should know that I have read the security service vetting on you prior to your appointment, I can't help thinking the Prime Minister's ship at the moment is being steered from the engine room rather than the bridge.'

'Where are you going with all this, Leighton?'

'That will become apparent soon enough. But first, I just want to know, or rather confirm what I think I already know about the real Archie Wilkes.' It was time for the Prime Minister's right-hand man to lay his cards on the table.

'Well, if you've been talking to our friends in the security service then you will already know I have very clear views that governments should be allowed to govern and not be constrained by neo-liberal views within the civil service. The current system favours self-preservation and regardless of what government is in power, civil servants manage to pull the wool over the eyes of what in many cases are inexperienced, even stupid ministers. Nothing is ever achieved, the government falls at the next election and they start all over again with a new cohort of ideological dullards. And when they finally decide they have had enough, it's a handsome pension, a gong from the Palace or even a knighthood to take into retirement. The system has sold the country short for decades. Now nobody wants to take a decision which might upset one part of society or the other and so our governance, and our judiciary, I have to add, do all they can to remain within cosy guidelines that don't rock the boat. Well, I do believe that boat needs to rock, if only to tip out the ballast. I realised that if I wanted to change things, and the only way I could do that was from the inside.'

'Working for one of those "very inexperienced, even stupid ministers"?'

'I think you know yourself, Leighton that Gordon Strathyre didn't seize the opportunity to become PM in order to serve the nation but to serve Gordon Strathyre. The leadership contest was an opportunity I wasn't expecting so soon but I couldn't turn it down. So yes, all of the lobbying, all those speeches, they were all my own words, spoken by an actor - probably Gordon's only real talent. Give him a speech and he'll deliver it precisely the way it needs to be, but don't expect him to stop and reflect on exactly what it is that he's saying.'

'So, the perfect mouthpiece for the policies of Archie Wilkes, in fact?' the Field Marshal's tone was mocking.

'Give him a little credit, Leighton. He's not entirely stupid, but he's no ideas man either. You know him well enough. If he can see himself saying something that will hold the attention of the House or the wider public, then he's sold on the idea. That's all become a lot more difficult since Thorpehead, so now the challenge is to keep as many outside influences as possible at arm's length.'

'Well then,' said the Field Marshal. 'Let me tell you where I stand at the moment. It won't surprise you to learn that as someone whose whole life has been in the military, discipline has always been key. In my professional role, I have observed our military capability diminished over the years through one government cutback after another, while I detect increased security threats from almost everywhere else in the world. And at home, law and order has either broken down or the system completely turned on its head. We arrest people for saying the wrong things but are prevented from dealing with the true perpetrators of crime because of the human rights lobby.

'I won't bore with the sermon but basically, I am off the pastures new. Or at least I was until two weeks ago. My time at Chief of Defence staff is still theoretically up at the end of this year, at which point I am due to take up a consultancy role for a major petrostate in the Gulf. The Sheikh wants to beef up both international and domestic security and is prepared to throw serious money at the project. Before the unfortunate events at Thorpehead I was about to announce my retirement in order to oversee this new development in the Gulf. Precisely when or how that will take place is now in some doubt, but His Highness is clearly following events. I have been keeping him in the loop as far as I can without breaching security protocols, but yesterday, he contacted me with a proposal that I thought you would want to know about.'

Salisbury

It had taken Jack a long time to fall asleep. Each time he closed his eyes, images of Evan filled his mind. Cheeky with an air of childhood innocence despite what he had witnessed over the last weeks, and yet instinctively decisive. He had saved his sister from being raped and, in so doing, almost certainly saved Jack's life. Now, each time that Jack turned over, the digital alarm on the bedside table had merely advanced by a minute or two. Finally, and with dawn appearing through the thin bedroom curtains, fatigue finally won and he slept until mid-morning.

As was now becoming routine, he switched on the kettle to make a cup of coffee from the hospitality tray and settled in front of the laptop to catch up on events since last night. Once more, Jack began to feel that much of the media had moved on from Thorpehead. There were stories about the King opening a new cargo port on Tyneside, workers at a distribution warehouse in Birmingham were striking for improved pay and conditions, tensions were rising in the South China Sea where the Americans and the Chinese were building up their naval presence. No updates about the devastating explosion in Jack's home town, the millions of people displaced, and nothing concerning events he had seen and experienced himself over the last few days. The only relevant story this morning was, thankfully from *News24.com*, but even that was more of a speculative article about the future of the United Kingdom based on reports coming out of Northern Ireland and Scotland. Nationalist members in Stormont were openly calling for reunification of the island while Holyrood was due to debate whether independence could be declared unilaterally following Prime Minister Gordon Strathyre's refusal to sanction a further referendum on the issue. But even that article was more concerned with the political ramifications, and while Jack could clearly comprehend the circumstances under which the Northern Irish and Scottish administrations should seek a better future than in a post-Thorpehead Britain, the word 'Thorpehead' or any reference to the consequences was missing from the article. One thing that did stand out from the article was the byline. Zac Benenson. With a name like that there could only be one Zac Benenson in the national media. Zac was part of the same graduate intake just a few years earlier and while Jack would join financial investigations, he remembered that Zac was assigned to shadow the paper's Westminster correspondent. How their careers had followed different paths. For Jack, redundancy from a country weekly, Zac, 'Political Editor' at News24.com.

He picked up his phone and was about to call Zac but thought better of it. He knew from the *News24.com* website that they had an encrypted system for potential whistleblowers to send messages, so opened up his Proton account and started composing an email instead. He didn't want to antagonise Zac by criticising the lack of controversy in his article, particularly as he would have been sure to remember the whole story surrounding the name of Jack Makepiece. But he needed to attract his attention and interest in the wider story Jack had to tell. So he managed to encapsulate the events of the last three weeks and his previous involvement with the WATER campaign into half a dozen short sentences. He then attached an image of Thorpehead taken in the days immediately after the explosion and his rather shaky footage of the temporary morgue at Salisbury General and pressed send. He didn't have to wait long for a response.

'Jesus Jack, nice to hear from you too! Are you still in Salisbury?' Jack replied *'yes'*.

'Rose Café. Opposite station entrance. 1500.'

That was it. No other reaction to his message or attachments.

Just a rendezvous as if this were some sort of spy novel.

Jack's head had been swimming since he left the hospital. Claudia had warned him about Evan but that hadn't made facing the reality of his death any easier. Now Shelley. What did the future hold for her, and could things have been otherwise if he had made a different choice back in Holmbeach? Claudia had tried to reassure him that the damage had already been done before Shelley and Evan had come into his life, and from her own experience of the last few days, they were far from the only children suffering the consequences of the Thorpehead nuclear explosion. And what of Claudia herself? She clearly shared Jack's view that something needed to be done but he got the impression she was not just interested in Jack because he was a journalist. Did he imagine it or was the eye contact as she spoke and the gentle touches on his arm simply down to her Latin heritage?

He tried to process all these contrasting thoughts as he wandered with no real purpose around the back streets of Salisbury, making him late by the time he remembered his clandestine rendezvous at the Rose Café. It was only five past three by the time he walked through the door, but the café was surprisingly busy for the time of day with more than half the tables occupied. There was no sign of Zac. Jack wondered whether to order a coffee and wait but the smell of burnt bacon was already in his throat and the smeech stinging his eyes. He decided to leave and wait across the road in case Zac was also delayed, but as he was about to close the door behind him a hand held it back.

'It's Jack, isn't it?'

'Who's asking?'

'Don't worry, Jack. I'm Martin Eddings, Editor at *News24.com*. Why don't we go for a walk and we can talk more easily?'

He was tall, probably just short of two metres, wearing jeans and an indigo canvas jacket over a pink, open-neck shirt. The newspaper industry had changed a lot in recent years and Jack knew the name already, but there was absolutely nothing about Martin Eddings' appearance to suggest he was a hardened Fleet Street hack. He fell into step with his companion who clearly knew where he was going as they walked along Fisherton Street. As they crossed the river in front of the King's Head, Jack got his first sight of the cathedral. His mind returned to the story of the two Russian GRU agents who were sent to the town to eliminate the former spy Sergei Skripal and their claim to be simple tourists, attracted by the 'world famous one-hundred-and twenty-three metre spire'. But he had questions, the first of which was 'where's Zac?' Seemingly reading his mind, Martin ended the potted history of Salisbury he had been giving as they walked.

'I expect you're surprised to see me and not Zac,' he turned to Jack

'I was wondering why the news editor of the most respected media outlets was on a day trip to Salisbury and not in the newsroom holding this government to account,' Jack answered, not attempting to disguise any of the sarcasm.

'You think we're going easy on the Government?'

'I think you could do with growing some balls.'

'Let's go down here, it will end up at the cathedral,' the editor replied evenly. As they turned towards the High Street Gate. Eddings continued to talk but looking straight ahead, not at Jack.

'The reason Zac isn't here is because he's under surveillance. First, his phone calls but now he's being followed whenever he leaves the office. I'm officially on sick leave, but as you can see, I'm perfectly fine. The *News24.com* trustees were given an ultimatum after we started asking awkward questions about the awarding of the Thorpehead contract. *News24.com* is not funded like the BBC or owned by a wealthy business tycoon, so financially we are still vulnerable in certain conditions.'

'So who's doing this? MI5, Bicarel, the Government?'

'Since Strathyre invoked the Civil Emergencies Act, it's hard to tell the difference anymore. It's a pretty draconian act in many respects and it gives the Government extraordinary powers in several areas. But with Parliament prorogued, there is nobody even to challenge the Prime Minister and the military is acting increasingly like his private police force.'

'But surely, aren't those precisely the circumstances in which a media outlet like *News24.com* should come to the fore?'

Martin gave a short laugh. 'Let me explain how it works, Jack. It's a classic "ignore, deny and attack" strategy. At the beginning, it was simple stonewalling. If we asked for a comment on a story we were writing, we would get the usual "we'll get back to you", and of course, no one did. If we went ahead and published the story, including the catch-all "we asked the government to comment" tag, the Government would simply deny the claim and accuse us of sensationalism. Then, an alternative version of our story would be released through their tame publications and championed by the likes of Hollingsworth Media. Because of the media storm generated by so much press coverage, the good old Beeb would then feel obliged to report it and thus amplify the story. In some ways, that's no different to the way the government has always reacted to criticism from *News24.com*, whether economic or foreign policy, but then things began to change.'

'In what way?'

'I'm sure it's because the public were tending to believe *News24.com* was more accurately portraying the situation following the explosion than the Government accounts being peddled by the likes of Hollingsworth Media. But the Government suddenly switched from reactive to proactive. First, it was the withdrawal of government department advertising revenue – not a killer but a sizeable chunk of money nonetheless. That was followed by corporate advertising from some of the multinationals, coincidentally owned by high-profile supporters of this government. Then it really became really sinister. The Prime Minister's office began demanding that our reporters reveal the sources of their stories, claiming the Civil Emergencies Act gave them the powers to do so. When two of our journalists refused, they were both arrested. The first one was bailed to appear at some future court hearing, but the other one was refused bail and is being held on remand. His family haven't even been told where he is and no one has heard from him since. Our lawyers say there is no provision in the Act that allows the Government to arrest journalists for refusing to reveal their sources, but there is no word as to when the trials will take place nor even what the precise charges are. If Parliament was sitting, it would be up in arms, but of course, it isn't.'

The two were now sitting on a bench in front of West Walk, looking directly across at the magnificent cathedral facade. Jack had questions to ask but sensed that the *News24.com* editor hadn't finished yet.

'It's the real reason I am on sick leave. After our first two staffers were arrested, I decided to dare them to come after me by putting my name to an article on the background to the Thorpehead contract award. You'll be pleased to know, Jack that my sources were not whistleblowers but the old WATER campaign websites that you were involved with, if I'm not wrong? Don't worry, I refused to reveal my sources when the government demanded, but rather than arrest a high-profile news editor, my removal from the front line was one of a raft of concessions the trustees were forced to accept. If they hadn't done so, I have no doubt that there would no longer be a *News24.com* today. But it does mean that any article that even mentions Thorpehead or the consequences actually has to pass through the censors at Number Ten and Zac's surveillance isn't so much to find out what he's doing but to remind us of the threat.'

Jack had so much to ask but could only come out with one word.

'Why?'

'It's far more than just controlling the media,' Martin continued. 'I mean yes, of course they would like the public to think that life is returning to normal, or as close to normal as it is ever going to be. Certainly, the good news stories they are pumping out through the Hollingsworth papers and websites fit that narrative, but there's more to it.'

'They don't want the cause of the explosion landing on their doorstep?' Jack cut in. 'Michel had genuine concerns about the design from his experience in Normandy and they came down heavy on John Forster once he started to suggest links between Bicarel and the Minister, not to mention our esteemed local MP, who seems to have gone very quiet, by the way.'

'I don't know if you were aware, but Whitleigh-Howse lost his wife and children in the aftermath and yes, he's stepping back from politics for the time being.' Martin used finger quotes to accompany the words "stepping back".

'Sure, nobody wants to be caught holding the baby when the time comes to investigating Thorpehead but I think it is far more fundamental than that. Strathyre simply does not want us to know the full extent of the fallout from Thorpehead, and I don't just mean radiation. Nobody knows how many people have died or how long we are going to have to suffer a nuclear exclusion zone splitting England in two. Or rather, some people know, but by controlling the media, shutting down Parliament and using the military to impose martial law, the Prime Minister and his weasel special advisor are the only ones who know the full picture.'

'But that's just not possible.' Jack was flabbergasted. 'This is the United Kingdom, not some Third World banana republic. We're still a democracy when all is said and done.'

'Fine words, Jack. You may not have been out of the loop for very long but things happen quickly in politics, as you well know. Strathyre has simply taken control. Parliament can't stop him, the media is gagged and even the judiciary can't challenge him so long as he has the military to enforce his will. I've already told you two of our staff have been arrested under emergency powers, but it's far more serious than that. And this is what I really need to talk to you about.'

'The message and attachments you sent to Zac were very helpful.' Martin continued. 'They confirmed some of the other information we have been receiving over the last couple of weeks. You see Jack, despite what you think of

News24.com just now, we haven't simply rolled over to do the Government's bidding. We do intend to hold Strathyre to account before the British public, but not until we have all the ammunition we need to withstand the obvious pushback. I'm assuming from your message that you have a lot more information. Is it safe?'

'Yes,' Jack replied. 'I have a third party in France who receives a copy of everything I have written and filmed and would know what to do with it in the event of anything happening to me.'

'That's good to know. Particularly in view of what I am about to tell you. You see, we have been receiving a lot of information from inside the exclusion zone thanks to an activist group. They are well-resourced and make regular expeditions behind enemy lines to chronicle events about which the general public is being told nothing. They're not crackpots, far from it. I suppose you have heard of Mike Danvers?'

'The environment guy? Yes, of course. He was a firm supporter of our campaign against Thorpehead. He raised our profile enormously.'

'Well, it won't surprise you to learn that he continued the fight against Thorpehead even after you guys were shut down, And it won't surprise you either that by doing so, he managed to ostracise himself from most of the mainstream media. TV documentary series were suddenly cancelled and News24.com was the only outlet still publishing articles he wrote by the time of the explosion. There have been no "I told you so" articles since, as even we are banned from publishing them, but he is using his wealth to fund the activists. Ostensibly, he is providing emergency accommodation in the grounds of his estate for people evacuated from the exclusion zone, only each of these 'evacuees' has an ulterior motive for being there. What's more, one of them is an embedded journalist from *News24.com*. They make regular sorties into the zone and record their findings. Danvers is working closely with us to collate and secure the footage until the time is right.'

'And you want my material to complement your findings?' asked Jack.

'More than that, Jack. We'd like you to join the group at Mike Danvers' place and conduct your own research for us.'

'Sounds intriguing, but won't I be getting in the way of your own journo?'

'Well no,' Martin hesitated. 'Last week, they heard a rumour about mass burial sites being prepared inside the zone. You see now why your footage from the hospital was so interesting? Anyway, the exclusion zone is so large, it's impossible to guard it all and our guys have come to know all about the patrols by now. But when they went in last time, security was far heavier around the supposed burial site, far more than anything they had encountered before. The short story is that they were spotted and challenged, only the soldiers weren't asking questions. They simply opened fire. Most of the group got out safely but two were killed. One was our man.'

'And you'd like me to take his place. Why, because I don't work for *News24.com* I would be deniable if something happened to me?'

'It's not like that at all Jack, and you would certainly be one of the *News24.com* staff if you decide to go in. But this is about far more than just a media scoop. Gordon Strathyre is potentially doing greater damage to this country than

Thorpehead has already. If it is ever going to return to being a democracy, it will be thanks to the likes of Mike Danvers and *News24.com*. I just think you could play a significant role in that movement, Jack.'

Jack sat silently and started to shiver. Whether it was the drop in temperature or Martin Eddings' words, he wasn't sure.

'Look, I know this is a lot for you to take in Jack, and I can't promise to keep you safe. Only you can make the decision. I'll understand if you say no, and we'll still be grateful for whatever information you send us.'

He pressed a folded piece of paper into Jack's hand. 'If you decide to go through with it, just make contact with these guys. Good luck, Jack.' And with that, Martin Eddings stood up from the bench and disappeared, mingling with a crowd of tourists coming out of the cathedral. Jack needed time to digest all that Martin Eddings had just told him, so continued his walk. He did have first-hand experience of the rich and powerful trying to shut down negative press coverage, and it was not just his own untimely departure from Fleet Street at the hands of a wealthy businessman and his expensive lawyers.

Since leaving *The Moorsman* he became increasingly suspicious that the "management restructures" that led to his redundancy and Barney's early retirement were not unconnected with the paper's growing interest in Bicarel and the contract to build Thorpehead. But both of those cases involved big business, not government. Was the Government, or rather the Prime Minister now really controlling the media? As he walked along High Street he started to piece together his own experiences over the last few weeks. He had seen the damage at Thorpehead with his own eyes, but could he remember any similar images in the news coverage since? Had he read any reports of looting inside the exclusion zone? They were real enough. Then there was the army shooting at Evan, Shelley and him as they tried to reach safety. Finally, Claudia's account of events at Salisbury General and the temporary morgue in the car park. Everything fitted Martin Eddings' narrative, and the man himself, despite the outward confidence of someone in his position, was clearly paranoid about security.

The light was beginning to fade as he retraced his steps through Castle Street towards Churchill Way and his hotel. At one point he found himself outside the Zizzi restaurant and then the Maltings shopping centre. He instantly recognised the scenes which he had seen so frequently during the TV coverage of the Skripal poisonings. He remembered how the city had effectively been closed down by the incident and the effect it must have had on the locals. Now, it was no longer the centre of Salisbury that was a no-go area but following Thorpehead, it was a whole swathe of the country. The folded note that Martin had given him was still in his hand, inside his jacket pocket. He took it out and read the details once more. When he was back at the hotel he would send the email to Mike Danvers.

There was no one at the reception desk when he finally reached the hotel. Jack wasn't feeling particularly hungry but decided to get another sandwich and a drink from the vending machine before going up to his room. As the bottle of Coke dropped into the tray, he heard a familiar voice.

'Jack?'

He looked around and saw Shelley, with Claudia at her side.

26 - Fifteen days later

Salisbury

When Jack woke up his first thoughts were of last night. Did it really happen or was it a dream? Rolling onto his right side, he immediately knew it was the former when he saw the form of a body under the duvet on the opposite bed. And if he still needed convincing, there was movement under the covers as a young female form emerged.

'Morning, Jack.' It was Shelley. Wearing just her pants and a crop top, yet totally uninhibited as she headed for the en-suite. Jack rolled back and lay staring at the ceiling as he replayed the events of last night and how he had ended up sharing his hotel room with a fourteen-year-old girl. Fortunately, there was no one on duty in reception when they had finally returned. Attractive as Shelley was, there was no way of hiding her adolescence and alongside a man of Jack's age, it would have been easy to draw entirely the wrong conclusion.

Jack had been ready to retire to his room with his sandwich and contact Mike Danvers, but when confronted with Claudia and Shelley they decided to head for the pizza restaurant on the far side of the hotel car park so that they could talk more easily. Shelley explained that the ward matron had come to see her earlier in the day, accompanied by a woman from Wiltshire Council Social Services Department. Shelley's white blood cell count had remained consistent, and with no other symptoms of internal organ damage, they were happy that she was showing no signs of the Acute Radiation Syndrome that had claimed her brother. The consultant was most likely to discharge her the next morning into the care of social services while the search continued for Shelley's aunt from Swindon. The woman from the council explained that in the meantime, she would be cared for at a specialist home that had just been established somewhere near Warminster to look after children who had been orphaned in the wake of Thorpehead. As was increasingly becoming the case, Shelley said nothing, only giving a cursory nod to the matron when repeatedly asked if she had understood. It was not until Claudia dropped by on a break to see how Shelley was that the dam burst. Sobbing uncontrollably, she repeated what the matron and woman from social services had said and became increasingly hysterical, claiming she would take her own life rather than be taken into care. Claudia tried to calm her and dismissed one of the nurses who came to see what all the fuss was about, saying she was best placed to deal with the situation. Holding Shelley in her arms and stroking her hair, the convulsions eased and her breathing gradually returned to normal. After a couple of minutes, she lifted her head from Claudia's shoulder and simply said 'I need Jack.'

So they made a plan for Shelley to discharge herself. Claudia told her to wait until the time her shift ended then get dressed, pack her things and simply walk out of the main entrance and head for the petrol station at the end of the road. Claudia, meanwhile would leave via the Emergency Department, thus ensuring there was no CCTV footage of the two of them together. It was right to take precautions but Claudia was convinced no one would actually notice or care. A minor absconding from hospital supervision would normally be a major security issue but in the current state of chaos, the matter would probably be supplanted in no time by something far more pressing. She had heard that there were literally thousands of people still unaccounted for following the mass evacuation. When they were safely out of range of the hospital security cameras the two met up and walked on towards Jack's hotel.

Once they were settled at the restaurant the mood lightened considerably. Having refused food all day at the hospital, Shelley was ravenous and scoffed the sandwich Jack had bought from the vending machine before they had even ordered their pizzas. Claudia had clearly had yet another stressful shift – still more radiation victims arriving in A&E and departing to the temporary morgue – and was de-stressing by matching Jack glass for glass on the red wine. The decision for a second bottle wasn't even debated. Shelley was more animated than Jack had seen her since the early days when the three of them were lying low at the Boar's Head back in Holmbeach and at one stage, even tried to help herself to some wine before her elders intervened. Jack suddenly realised that the last time he had done something as normal as having a meal in a restaurant with friends was well before that fateful day at Thorpehead. And what of Claudia? He still couldn't work out whether the eye contact and all the nudges were her natural behaviour or something more. It may have been the wine that was relaxing her but he felt sure she was sitting closer to him as the evening progressed and those little touches on the arm were lingering longer. It could well have been a fun evening out if it wasn't for the conversation the three of them were having. Jack brought them up to date with his meeting earlier in the day with the News24.com editor and of joining Mike Danvers and his activists.

'That sounds great,' Shelley said. 'So we're off in the morning then?'

'There's no "we", Shelley,' Jack replied calmly. 'It's dangerous. The guy I'm replacing was killed by the army. I couldn't live with myself if something happened to you while you're in my care.'

A pin prick had just deflated the atmosphere around the table. Shelley sat quietly. Jack couldn't look at her but could feel Claudia's chestnut eyes were drilling into him. Then, and not for the first time in Jack's experience, Shelley managed to surprise him with a maturity well beyond her tender years.

Rather than behave like a teenager who had just been told she couldn't go to the party, she reached out and took Jack's face in both hands. Turning him so she could look right into his eyes, she said. 'You will never know how important it is for me right now to know there is someone who cares about me and wants to keep me safe. In normal times Jack, I would understand what you are saying. But these are not normal times and things are never going to go back to the way they were. None of us knows what's even going to happen tomorrow. Who's to say I won't still get what Evan had? Who's to say we won't all get shot by soldiers? The truth is, all I have to live for at the moment is the present, and that present is with you two. If it all ends tomorrow or the next day, I don't really care as long as I am with you when it happens. So you don't have to look after me or take care of me, just be with me. And the only other thing I can add is ..' Shelley let go of Jack's cheeks, picked up his wine glass and took a large gulp of red. 'Cheers!'

Jack sat motionless for a few seconds and turned towards Claudia in search of some kind of support. But the mood was broken as her solemn face dissolved into fits of laughter.

'Well, Mr Journalist? Got nothing to say? This time I think Shelley has stolen all the best words!'

Shelley was laughing now as well, and finally Jack joined them. 'Just promise me one thing. No more drinking. If I have to live with a know-it-all teenager, I'd rather a sober one.'

By the time they had finished their pizzas, Claudia was starting to yawn. It had been a long day and with the best part of a bottle of wine inside her, it would only be a few hours until her next shift was due to start. As they walked back across the car park towards the hotel Claudia slipped her arm through Jack's. A moment later he felt Shelley doing the same thing on his other side, but when they arrived at the hotel entrance she announced she was tired and going straight to bed. She and Claudia locked in a long hug while Shelley continued to thank her for all she had done. Her eyes were moist as she broke off the embrace and headed through the door, leaving Jack and Claudia outside in the dark. 'The same goes for me,' said Jack. 'I'm not sure what would have happened to either of us if it wasn't for you.'

'Don't thank me, Jack. Just make sure to get your story out there. We're all counting on you.' She moved closer to Jack and he bent to kiss her on both cheeks the way he knew Italians did. But she turned her face square on to his and kissed him full on the lips. Jack found the soft warmth of her tongue, tinged with the scent of red wine and cigarettes. Not a combination he usually liked but tonight he was not complaining. It was as if he had touched a crumple button inside her mouth as, all at once, her body seemed to fold into his, her hips pressing hard against his crotch and his unmissable arousal. Seconds seemed like minutes until they broke for air. 'Come with us tomorrow,' Jack whispered.

'I can't, Jack. It's not that I don't want to or am afraid, I'm just needed here. Even if I can't help most of the patients coming in, as a doctor I have to try. And I can't let my team down by going AWOL. We're all flat out as it is.' She kissed him again.

'I have a job to do here, Jack. And so do you. But make sure you come back safely.' As she broke off, she gently lowered her hand and brushed his groin area. 'It's clear we have unfinished business!'

And with that, Claudia turned and head down, walked quickly back in the direction of the town centre. Jack took a few moments to process what had just happened and how he would be able to deal with it in the light of the journey he was just about to embark upon. He turned and walked through the hotel entrance only to find Shelley still standing there with a smile on her face, the likes of which he had never witnessed before.

Salisbury/Hampshire

Shelley emerged from the bathroom and slipped on a pair of shorts. It seemed to Jack that last night and the prospect of an adventure with Mike Danvers had somehow energised her. She certainly had no qualms about walking around in front of Jack in her underwear and she hardly stopped talking as she packed up her bag. Jack was less certain of himself and slid discreetly from under the duvet and into the bathroom to shower and shave. He had used the contact details given to him by Martin Eddings last night when they returned to the room and while Shelley had been in the bathroom, Jack had checked his emails to find that Mike Danvers himself had replied a little under half an hour later. Within twenty minutes they were both packed and armed with directions to reach Mike Danvers' country residence in Hampshire. As Jack had pre-paid his stay on check-in, he was nevertheless relieved at not having to present himself at reception with a female minor who wasn't with him when he arrived. He keyed the coordinates into his phone and the journey south-westwards took less than an hour.

There had been no address or postcode with the instructions, just the grid reference and the reason soon became clear to Jack. The last town they had passed through was Stockbridge, about twenty minutes ago and religiously following the verbal instructions from the phone app had taken them down increasingly narrow lanes. Just as Apple Maps declared they had reached their destination, the road widened and Jack and Shelley found themselves facing the gated entrance to a country estate.

The road only extended a further ten metres at most before it met two gatehouses built in Purbeck stone situated about fifteen metres apart. Wrought iron railings connected them to the centrepiece of the entrance, two Doric pillars, also in Purbeck stone supporting a double iron gate at a similar height to the railings. Jack reckoned from the style of the gatehouses that they were probably Georgian but he could see immediately that the ironwork was contemporary - well, at least the cameras which hung from the railings, not to mention the antennae on one of the gatehouses, were definitely post-Jane Austen. As they approached slowly, the gates began to open just as a man in his thirties emerged from the gatehouse and directed them to park just inside.

'Jack Makepiece?' he enquired as the car came to a halt. 'If you and your passenger could just step out of the car and follow me to the office. Mr Danvers is expecting you but we just need to do some checks first. Jack and Shelley followed the man as a second person, wearing the same colour polo shirt emerged holding a Geiger counter. 'Don't be alarmed, it's just a precaution. We do the same for anyone who has recently been inside the exclusion zone. As his colleague passed the wand over Jack, he noticed more people emerging from the opposite gatehouse, this time in protective suits and carrying portable pressure pumps who then started to spray the Ford Puma. Shelley froze. The last time she had seen people dressed like that was at Thorpehead when she and Evan had gone looking for their parents. But she snapped out of it when she heard the security man speak.

'You're all good to go. I've told Mr Danvers you are here, although he had assumed you would be alone. He said to go straight up to the house and you can talk there. Just follow the drive for about half a mile, then you won't be able to miss it.'

Jack and Shelley drove on in silence. Was this really the home of Mike Danvers, soap actor, game show host and environmental campaigner? So far it was more like a Bond movie. The scene became even more bizarre as they rounded a right-hand bend on the drive and an encampment of caravans, old buses and converted horse transporters came into view in the fields below. It reminded Jack of Marjorie, secretary to John Forster's WATER campaign to stop

Thorpehead. She gave the appearance of someone who had led an uneventful life until one evening in the pub, she began to tell her story of a life on the road with 'new age travellers' in the 1980s, living in converted buses like the ones he was passing, and her arrest in the infamous Battle of the Beanfields near Stonehenge. Jack had had to look it up afterwards and had been shocked at the levels of police violence. He assumed that these campers were the evacuees among whom Martin Eddings' journalist had been embedded, but as he drove on he soon became aware that these were far from the new age travellers of Marjorie's vintage. There were no weather-beaten complexions or straggly hair. Everyone looked like they went to work in an office. Most were clean-shaven and wearing polo shirts similar to the guys at the gatehouse. And when he looked closer, Jack also noticed the power cables, satellite dishes and antennae on many of the caravan roofs. In front of a horse box closest to the drive, one couple was sitting either side of a table supporting a cafetiere. One was engrossed in their laptop while the other was scrolling on their phone. These new-age travellers had broadband and Wi-Fi. The driveway continued past a small wooded copse before straightening out once again.

Now, directly ahead they could see the house, a Georgian mansion with a stone staircase leading up to the entrance. There were two panelled windows on either side and five more across the first floor. Smaller windows lined the ground floor/basement level area beneath the staircase, presumably where the servants once lived. As they pulled up on the gravel path, the front door opened and out stepped Mike Danvers. Wearing a formal shirt over a pair of denim shorts and Burberry sliders on his bare feet, he bore little resemblance to the TV version of Mike Danvers that Jack was vaguely familiar with. His face was thinner than Jack could remember and in letting his hair grow longer, he was also displaying tell-tale streaks of grey.

'Welcome, Jack, I'm glad you decided to come,' he said as he walked down the four steps towards the car. 'But I didn't realise you were bringing company. Who is this young lady?' Jack briefly explained Shelley's story and it soon became clear that bringing her along was not going to present a problem.

'Well, Shelley, I am sure you have quite a story to tell too. Come inside, the two of you. You'll be staying in the house with me and my team. I expect you noticed our campsite on the way in, but we can offer you just a few more creature comforts here. We'll have some refreshments then I'll give you the tour and explain what we are doing here.' He led them through the entrance hall and into the dining room where a spread of coffee, juice and pastries awaited. Neither Shelley nor Jack had had breakfast that morning so did not hold back. Danvers poured himself a coffee and sat down with them at the end of the long, mahogany table.

'Quite a place you have here,' Jack said through a mouthful of croissant.

'The fruits of my labours,' he replied, spreading his arms wide. 'There was a time when the soap was at its peak that the TV companies were just throwing money at me. I'd never really had any vices or expensive habits. People used to laugh at me because I still drove my old VW Golf – it's still out front as it happens. But I was never one for flash sports cars or fancy watches. All I ever wanted was my own place in the country, a farm where I could grow my own stuff. This place came up about 10 years ago. It was a bit of a rundown dump.

The old boy had no family to inherit so he'd let it go to pieces in the years before his death. I only finished restoring this house last year, but from the day I bought the farm I set about turning it into a pesticide-free haven for crops and wildlife. It's remarkable how quickly nature can restore itself if given the chance. All the farms around here used chemical fertilisers and pesticides for years and it had taken its toll, both on the quality of the soil and the river because of the run-off. Initially, I just left the fields as they were and didn't attempt to grow anything. Within twelve months I could already see the growth in wild flowers and pollinators. It wasn't long before a complete ecosystem had been established here with bird species and fish in the river that had not been seen around here in decades. Some of the neighbouring farms still use chemicals, but not as much and we are now regularly enjoying bumper harvests of wheat and even oats.

'Is this oat milk on my cereal?' Shelley spoke for the first time since arriving.

'Well spotted, Shelley. Rather fortuitous as it happened. Dairy production has been severely impacted since the explosion, particularly by the restrictions on grazing in much of the country. As you saw, I have rather a lot of mouths to feed at the moment so producing our own oat milk has been a godsend.'

'What is the story with the camp?' Jack asked.

'The official line is they are evacuees from the exclusion zone. Many of them really are. They are in receipt of the state aid paid to evacuees and I am being paid for accommodating them. But there are many more living in those well-appointed caravans and buses. Some lost their jobs because the company they worked for no longer existed and others simply decided they wanted to join the cause.'

'And what's that cause?'

'Well, it's pretty much an extension of what you guys started with Thorpehead. You tried to prevent the power station from opening by highlighting all that can go wrong with nuclear energy. Now, we want those in authority to come clean about the full extent of the damage and be honest with the British public over how they got into this mess.'

'I suspect that even if you succeed with the first part, getting the Government to admit they were to blame isn't going to happen.'

'You may be right, Jack. But our first aim is to unmask what they have so far been covering up. Once we do that, the public will work out for themselves who or what was to blame. But more importantly, they need to know the full extent of the damage Thorpehead has caused, like Bristol being uninhabitable for hundreds of years. Only then can we start to grasp the reality of our future. At the moment, Starthyre and his army are hell-bent on pumping out good news stories and shutting down dissent, increasingly forcefully as I am sure you are now aware.'

'Yes, Martin Eddings told me about the journalist who was killed. He wanted me to be sure of all the facts before I made the decision to come here in his place.'

'He was a nice guy. Everyone liked him and it's not as if he was doing anything more dangerous than the others. He was just in the wrong place at the wrong time. But those soldiers shooting at us? They weren't warning shots. They were meant to kill.'

'What exactly have you been doing here then? Shelley

had been sitting quietly and listening until her intervention.

'Like I said earlier, it all began really with the campaign that Jack and his newspaper were involved with to stop the power station. Until then, as an environmentalist I saw nuclear as one of the clean alternatives to fossil fuels and paid no attention to the potential consequences. The WATER campaign really opened my eyes.'

'And I remember at the time, it was your support that helped raise our profile. People began to take the threat seriously,' Jack added.

'I couldn't understand at first why it all stopped so suddenly. I heard that you were made redundant from the paper, but I had been due to meet John Forster and then simply received a message that the campaign group had disbanded and John was nowhere to be found. What must have happened only became clearer a few months later due to my own circumstances. There may not have been a WATER campaign group any longer, but I carried on investigating the main concerns about the amount of water these new reactors needed to function and the ongoing issue of what to do with the radioactive waste. It was clear by that time that Thorpehead would be going ahead regardless, so I directed my arguments against the Government and its decision to continue development of similar sites around the country. I soon began to appreciate what happens if you try to take on this Government.'

'Did you have as much support as we had at WATER?' Jack asked.

'Oh yes, probably more. We had action groups set up in all the areas the Government had confirmed for new reactors and were bombarding the local MPs – all Government party constituencies by the way – and whereas opposition to

Thorpehead was largely local, we really were beginning to build a consensus nationally. That's when the problems started.'

'What happened?' said Shelley.

'It was subtle at first. The BBC pulled the plug on the next series of my nature watch programmes, even though we had already begun filming. The official reason for public consumption was budget cuts but the producer told me it was because I had become a figure of controversy with the anti-nuclear campaigning and the Beeb feared for its impartiality. But then we found that none of the commercial TV channels were interested in picking up the series. Normally, a show with the sort of viewing figures we were getting would have created a bidding war. Soon, my agent was discovering that nobody was interested in hiring Mike Danvers for any acting roles, let alone environmental programmes.'

'You were cancelled then?' Jack concluded.

'And not just on TV. My regular newspaper and magazine columns all began to dry up until only *News24.com* was left. Then, as Martin probably told you, even they were forced to drop me. But it didn't stop there. The Hollingsworth Media rags started running stories about my finances and that I was supposedly hiding large sums of money offshore to avoid paying tax. It was total bollocks of course but as you well know Jack, if enough of the media report it, for many people it becomes fact. But then things really became sinister. I had a call one day with an invitation to meet Sir Ian Davison, Chairman of Hollingsworth Media. Naively, I hoped this might have been an olive branch, the beginning of my rehabilitation as a columnist. When I arrived at his office there was another guy there who simply introduced himself as 'Archie.' I discovered later that that was Archie Wilkes, the PM's cabinet secretary. Anyway, Davison had a folder sitting on his desk and he started removing selected sheets from it and laying them in front of me. Witness statements and drafts of newspaper articles accusing me of improper and illegal relationships with underage girls. He said there were even photos but he wasn't going to show them to me just yet.'

'It's not true, is it?' Shelley's mood had clearly changed.

'Believe me, Shelley, Jack, it was all total fiction, but the threat was implicit. Unless I pulled back from my campaign to stop the nuclear power stations, they would start to release these stories through their various papers.'

'Well, if it was all made up, why didn't you just tell them no?' replied Shelley.

'Jack will know how these things work, Shelley. It's not important that the stories were a pack of lies but the fact that they have been published which would do the damage. Hollingsworth is a massive organisation with highly paid lawyers. Even if I were to win a court case it would be years later, and the accusations would have been around for all that time and my name forever linked to those stories. It was either desist or face a ruined reputation along with a career.'

'So what did you do then?' Jack asked.

'I did counter with the threat of libel but couldn't do anything more as they had yet to publish the accusations. I stepped back initially, but then Thorpehead blew up and I guess both the Government and Hollingsworth Media have more to concern them than my campaign.'

'I still don't see how we have gone from there to sitting here drinking your coffee.' Jack was looking around the magnificent dining room as uniformed staff were busy clearing away the dishes.

'The immediate reaction from many people around the country was "Mike Danvers was right." But naturally you won't have read that in any newspaper or seen it on TV. But our social media went wild after the incident. "What are you going to do, Mike?" "We want to help you," all that sort of thing. Then, The Government was looking for places to accommodate people being evacuated from Bristol and Swindon so I contacted the local council and offered the farm as a temporary campsite. The council paid for sanitation and power to the field and even helped source the mobile homes. And they have been paying rent to me for the units ever since. But, as you already know, not everyone is an evacuee. So many people wanted to help bring this Government to book for what happened that they have come anyway. Some genuinely didn't have a job to go to because their employment was located within the exclusion zone, but others just wanted to join the cause and turned up with a caravan in tow. We've got an incredible mix of skills here now, from scientists to IT engineers, lawyers and accountants. We have two missions: gathering as much information as we can from within the exclusion zone and reviewing the actions of this Government from the legality of the martial law it has imposed right back to the original decision-making process of awarding the Thorpehead contract. Our aim is ultimately to defrock Gordon Strathyre and his so-called Government and present the British public with an honest view of the country as it really is. Only then can we address the more important question of what to do for the future. But that's enough of my moralising. As Martin probably told you Jack, our primary task is collecting information until we are ready to use it. If you have finished your coffee, I'll show you around our little operation.'

Mike Danvers led Shelley and Jack back outside where, parked next to his trusty VW Golf stood a shiny new Pangea 4x4 electric buggy.

'Jump in, I'll show you around the site first and then we'll come back and see the nerve centre.' The buggy glided swiftly away and down the grass bank towards the mobile village and as they got closer, it became apparent that this was far more than some new age traveller camp. To Jack, it looked more like one of the holiday villages at Tyneford Bay, particularly when Danvers steered the buggy towards the amenity area and its sanitary block. The grouping of prefabricated buildings also housed a supermarket and even a bar.

'Life needs to go on as normal,' Danvers said. 'Most of these people are doing important work but they also have partners and families. It's important that when they are not working, they can still enjoy their downtime. We even have entertainment and quiz nights at the pub.' Travelling on through the ranks of caravans and mobile homes they arrived in front of a large milking shed, although it was clear that it had not seen a cow for some time. On the tarmacked apron in front of the shed stood more Pangea buggies, a couple of Land Rovers and a Mercedes Sprinter van. 'This is our stores depot. Worked out just fine as things happened.'

He pulled up outside the double barn doors and motioned Jack and Shelley to follow them inside. 'I got rid of the dairy herd a few years earlier. Keeping cows just didn't sit comfortably with my other views on the environment. How could I run a chemical-free farm and have cows producing half of our methane emissions? The shed itself was sturdy enough, so it was easy to convert.' Inside was a hive of activity and the warehouse was split into two distinct halves. To the left, it resembled a cash-and-carry with forklift trucks buzzing between alleys of racking and shifting pallet loads of foodstuffs and household products. To the right, men and women, all wearing the now familiar black polo shirts, sat at benches, working on electrical components. Jack could recognise drones, cameras and night vision goggles on some of the benches while behind them, large boxes marked Tyvek were stacked against the far wall. Protective equipment, surely?

'Impressive, eh?' Mike Danvers said, waving his arms.

'We have almost three hundred people living here now and they all need feeding and watering.' Then, turning in the opposite direction. 'And this is where the magic happens? Everything we need for our sorties into the exclusion zone to capture and record what's there. Obviously, the attrition rate is very high because of the radiation so we are constantly having to set up new equipment.'

'This must cost a fortune,' Jack said, looking around the warehouse. 'Are you paying for all this yourself?' Mike's face creased as he looked at Jack and Shelley. 'That's the delicious irony in all this. Yes, my money got things started here but the ongoing costs are all being paid by Gordon Strathyre. The Government is just throwing money at me for looking after these "evacuees." The system is totally chaotic as you can probably imagine. They don't even know for sure how many people have been displaced and there's nobody to check where the money goes. I wouldn't say I was cheating the system but if I did want to make a fast buck right now, I can't imagine anyone would be any the wiser. But that's not the whole of the story. Wait 'til you see what's next.' With that, he led them back outside and into the buggy.

When they arrived back at the house, Danvers drove to the rear and parked in front of the low steps leading down to the basement, presumably once the servants' entrance. Just as with the milking shed, all was not as it might have seemed from outside. Entering through an airlock system they then walked along a glass-walled corridor. On one side, more black polo-wearing workers were sat behind computers in rows, just like a financial business or call centre. On the other side were smaller offices, some occupied by one or two people, others empty and clearly set up as meeting rooms.

'What's everyone doing here?' It was Shelley asking this time.

'In the main room, most of them are analysing press and social media coverage while the guys on this side of the room are mainly doing more of the background stuff. Looking for clues as to the cause of the explosion and digging into the original contract award. You'd be surprised at the level of expertise we have here. Not just lawyers and accountants but real top-drawer guys and girls. Experts in their fields. The only skill we don't have is journalism, until now that is,' giving Jack a smile. As they continued along the corridor, one or two people stopped Danvers as he passed with a question or confirmation of an upcoming meeting before they finally arrived at a secure door at the far end. Mike punched in the code and ushered his two guests in. The room was low-lit and dominated by a large screen occupying most of the far wall. In front of it, a row of desks, each with an operator sitting behind a laptop and a joystick. An aerial view of the Hampshire landscape was moving on the screen and Jack and Shelley quickly noticed the house and estate coming into view.

'The ops room,' Mike said. 'They're testing drones for tomorrow's mission.' Behind them was another smoked-glass wall through which they could see more screens and equipment. 'Let me show you the edit suite,' their host said as he opened the door. A solitary woman sat behind a video edit console, raised her head as they entered. Although Jack's background was solely print media, he had been inside enough TV studios to know that the equipment here was both new and high-end. 'This is Gemma, our VT expert. Gemma meet Shelley and Jack, our new reporter.'

'Hi Shelley, hi Jack.'

'I want Gemma to show you some of the footage we have from earlier trips we have made into the exclusion zone, but I'm thinking that perhaps Shelley, you shouldn't be seeing this. It's not been edited and some of it is pretty hard to take.' Jack was not surprised by what came next.

'Look, Mister Danvers,' Shelley began calmly. 'I know I'm only fourteen and still a girl but in the last few weeks I have seen the place where my parents were killed, have lived on the run with my brother, who then died. Someone tried to rape me, soldiers have tried to shoot me and I had to flee social services because they wanted to put me into care. I do know things are pretty shit right now and they'll never be the same as before. But I was a child before. I'm not now and really would like it if people didn't treat me like one.'

'She's got you there, boss!' Gemma looked up at Shelley with a smirk.

'Understood, Shelley. I'm sorry for misjudging you.' Mike shrugged and nodded to Gemma. 'But I warn you, even I find some of this footage difficult, and I've already seen it a few times.'

Gemma began tapping on her keyboard and the footage she had been working on disappeared, replaced by a screen, blank except for a moving time stamp. Mike explained that the expeditions into the exclusion zone primarily monitored radiation levels, the results of which then dictated where they went and how long they stayed. To penetrate any further, they were reliant on drones but sometimes even those had a limited lifespan. Once they had completed filming they had to ditch the drones as they were too contaminated to bring back to base and use again. As the screen flickered, Mike explained that they were about to watch drone footage shot in the eastern suburbs of Bristol just under a week earlier. It began with an aerial view above rows of terraced houses running off both sides of a major road. It could have been a still photograph as nothing was moving. The camera zoomed in as the drone descended to roof level and began flying along one of the avenues. Closer to the ground now, the picture definition was clearer and it was possible to see movement. A cat shot out from a doorway and took shelter under a parked car, presumably spooked by the sound of the drone overhead. Moving along the street they could see more abandoned cars. Many of the front doors were half open and some houses had their front windows smashed. 'That wasn't caused by the explosion, surely?' Shelley asked.

'Looters most likely,' said Mike. The drone continued into the next avenue and the camera zoomed in on more movement. A group of feral dogs were busy gnawing at something lying on the pavement. The carcass of a dead animal, perhaps? Disturbed by the drone whirring overhead, they broke off from their carrion and Jack and Shelley could see on the screen that there were rags left behind as well. Rags or clothes? As the drone got closer it soon became clear that the shape was human, or at least the remains of a human.

'Gross,' said Shelley.

'There are more of them,' Mike replied as the drone continued along the street, recording footage of more skeletal remains in varying states of decay. 'We can only assume these are people who either got left behind or chose to do so. They were probably able to go about their daily lives until such time as the radiation build-up just broke down their DNA and they died where they were. It wouldn't surprise me if there were several more dead inside their houses. But that's not all. Gemma, do you want to fast forward?' Gemma nodded and the footage sped into a blur until she hit the space bar on her keypad. The drone was now flying over a residential park. The children's play area and the boating lake, now deserted. But where there should have been a vast expanse of green, there was, what looked at first sight, as a ploughed field. On closer examination though, there were no rows of ploughed furrows, just a mound of overturned earth over an area the size of a football pitch. And as the camera zoomed in, arms and legs were clearly visible protruding from the earth, probably a result of animal scavenging.

'Is that what I think it is?' Jack could hardly speak while Shelley was numb.

'Yep, looks like they've just dug a shallow grave and dumped the bodies.' Mike Danvers' voice was on the point of breaking. 'As if it was some wartime genocide, except these people weren't at war.' At that point the picture started to break up and the screen filled with static snow before turning black.

'That's it. We lost the drone after that. Our guys reckon

the radiation levels must have been so much higher there because the stupid bastards didn't even think that digging up radioactive soil might cause even more contamination.' It was the first time since Jack and Shelley met Mike Danvers that they had seen him anything other than his cool and calm on-screen self.

'Still, one good thing has come out of it. Our techies have found a way to attach Geiger counters to our drones so we can take measurements from a distance instead of risking our people. The military must have learnt from this as well because in fly-overs we have done since, it looks like they are preparing more disposal sites in less highly contaminated areas and they are not digging trenches.'

'What, they're just dumping bodies in the open?' said Shelley, incredulous.

'That's what we're trying to find out. It's what the patrol was doing when they started shooting and we lost our journalist. And it's what tomorrow's mission will try to confirm. But that's enough for now. Shelley, Jack, we've prepared rooms for you upstairs. I suggest we go back now, get freshened up and you can meet the rest of the team at the pub tonight. I think it's quiz night as well.'

27 - Sixteen days later

Hampshire/Swindon

Jack was back in the old milking shed which Danvers had taken him and Shelley to the previous day as part of his tour. Only today, he was zipping up his Tyvek suit alongside his most recent acquaintances, all of whom had been at the pub quiz the night before. Doug, an expert on all things Arsenal Football Club, was already sitting behind the wheel of a very new and expensive-looking Land Rover Discovery. Charli and her partner Alina, despite their age, had proved to be the font of all knowledge whenever a music question had come up, demonstrating encyclopaedic recall of bands and songs right back to the seventies. The tattoos and body piercings were no longer visible under their protective suits and both were busy assembling equipment. Charli had a Canon V1 camera in her hands while Alina was taking background radiation readings on a Geiger counter. The Discovery tailgate was down where the last member of the team, Andriy was busy loading the drone. While his command of English was excellent, the nuanced questions in the pub quiz had largely passed him by and his contribution last night had been to fetch more drinks for his team mates when they needed refreshment and for himself in between those moments. There was clearly no breathalyser requirement to pilot a drone.

Jack had expressed surprise last night when they told him the mission would take place during daylight but Doug had explained that security around the exclusion zone was stretched due to its sheer size, and the military had tended to prioritise their resources into nighttime patrols. This was on the assumption that looters were more likely to work in the dark, but the irony was that they could travel undetected in broad daylight and, Charli was quick to point out, it was better for filming too. With all the equipment stored, Doug gave the signal and they headed out from the Danvers estate towards Swindon.

They drove north-eastwards through Pewsey and crossed the River Kennet into Marlborough. Jack knew the town from his short tenure in London but as they turned in front of the red brick buildings of Marlborough College, he was surprised to see the town centre deserted. Normally, cars would be parked along the whole length of the High Street on the central reserve while the independent shops, tea rooms and fancy restaurants linked to celebrity chefs were thronged with visitors. But today, the pubs and restaurants were closed and the shops shuttered. Doug explained that although Marlborough lay outside the exclusion zone, it was close enough and so nobody came to visit any longer. Many residents had left as a precaution if they had somewhere else to go and even the famous boarding school had sent its students home. It was only a few miles further along the A346 that they encountered the exclusion zone. The wall of post and wire fencing was just as Jack had seen before at Hillingdon, broken only by a control booth and double gate, as high as the fence which straddled the main road. As predicted, the guard hut was unmanned but the gates were secured by a chain and padlock.

'See how clueless they are, Jack?' Doug exhaled, almost in sympathy. 'They go to all that trouble to secure the entrance, but just watch this.' With that, Doug put the Discovery into four-wheel drive and mounted the kerb before edging the vehicle down a grass bank and onto what looked to be a bridal path and farm track no more than three metres below. Doug edged the Discovery along the tractor tracks for about a hundred metres and under a bridge which must at one point have carried a railway line. Emerging on the other side, the path bordered fields of untended wheat for a few hundred metres more, whereupon Doug threw the Discovery hard to the left and returned onto a metalled road. Jack soon saw a road sign that confirmed they were back on the A346 heading towards Swindon. 'Welcome to the exclusion zone,' Doug said.

Jack heard a clicking noise coming from the seat behind him and half turned to see Alina checking her Geiger counter.

'Don't worry, Jack. Radiation levels no problem yet. But make sure you don't touch anything on ground when we stop,' she reassured him. They drove on and passed through the gate of what was once a water park. Sailing dinghies lined the shore of a vast lake of still, blue water, probably an old gravel pit. Alongside stood a deserted adventure playground with a crazy golf course. Doug pulled into the customer car park and parked in front of the boarded-up café. Charli was the first one out and quickly started filming the scene of abandoned leisure facilities. Jack felt obliged to follow, taking still shots on his iPhone. Andriy was at the rear of the Discovery, preparing to launch the drone.

'How long have we got?' Jack asked.

'We're fine for at least 30 minutes,' Alina answered. 'As long as you don't touch anything or kick up any dirt from the ground.' The silence was broken by the high-pitched whirl of the drone lifting into the air. Andriy was now holding the joystick between his thumb and index finger while monitoring the camera output from an open laptop now perched on the tailgate. It didn't take long for him to say something. 'Come and look guys,' he was nodding at the computer screen. 'Just behind those trees.' Jack, Charli and Doug stood around the rear of the vehicle. As Andriy brought the drone lower, the monitor filled with a tangled mass of what looked like bodies. It took Jack a moment to realise that's precisely what it was. Featureless and grey-skinned cadavers, some with hair, others without. Jack remembered the archive footage he had seen on TV after the concentration camps were liberated during World War Two and the apocalyptic scenes from Srebrenica during the Balkans crisis, except those bodies were largely emaciated and in rags. But what they were looking at here was far different. Some appeared to be wearing hospital gowns, others were fully clothed and dressed for a trip to the shops, or even a visit to a water park.

'We were right then,' said Doug, breaking the eerie silence in which the group had been watching. Only Alina remained inside the Discovery, headphones on and her eyes fixed on the Geiger counter, as if she knew what the others were looking at and did not want to see. 'Seems like they learnt their lesson from trying to dig up the soil last time. Now they're just dumping the bodies in the open. Jack and Charli, you need to get closer to film this. Andriy, take the drone higher and try to see if there are any more dumping grounds nearby.'

Charli made for the trees with Jack in tow. As they approached the copse, they could see the tyre marks left by the trucks which must have brought the bodies. 'Looks like this was quite an operation, Jack. This is much bigger than just the hospital in Salisbury.' Moving closer, they were soon confronted by the smell of rotting flesh although given the size of the burial mound, Jack was surprised it was not stronger. 'Irradiation Jack,' Charli said, seemingly reading his mind. 'It would slow the decay and hopefully deter feral wildlife. Probably the only dignity those poor bastards have left.'

The path opened out onto the field whereupon Charli and Jack were confronted with the full horror of the site confronting them. Bodies were piled, two and sometimes three deep across an area around twenty metres deep and five or six wide. Tyre marks suggested that lorries must have arrived on each side of the mound and simply tipped their loads as if at a waste landfill site. Charli was right, there was precious little evidence of rats or foxes as yet, the bodies must only have recently been deposited here, but their flesh was wax-like and monochrome. Jack could see extended arms which still bore watches or rings on the fingers but as he approached in the vain hope of trying to find any identifying items, Charli pulled him back. 'Not too close, Jack. Let's just film as much as we can.' She was keeping a close eye on the time, having received very clear and precise instructions on how long she had from Alina. 'You stay here, I'm just going to video shoot all the way round the outside.' And then, Charli was gone.

Jack could hear the distant whirr of Andriy's drone and

could see it flying over the rest of the water park, but he thought he heard another noise, lower in pitch but becoming louder. Then he heard the single crack and looked up to see a small flash and plume of black smoke where Andriy's drone had last been. Suddenly, Charli came running back. 'Time to be going, Jack,' she called as he ran by. Jack followed her back through the wood and when they emerged into the car park, the Discovery was packed and loaded with its engine running. Doug moved off the moment Jack and Charli were on board, trying to avoid kicking up any stones with his acceleration. 'We've been spotted,' he calmly declared. 'Army drone. Big bastard. Took out Andriy's drone but we still got a lot of footage.'

'Will they be shooting at us too?' Jack's voice was shaky.

'Nah, should be OK. They usually only carry single shots. Saw them in Ukraine. Used them to take out Russian spy drones.'

'You were in Ukraine?'

'Yeah, long story. Later. But I'm more than just a Gooner, you know. No idea where the drone came from but I'm guessing if they're patrolling remotely, there are no troops close by. Can't take any chances though.' And with that, the Discovery left the pathway and climbed the grass bank back up to the A346. As Doug had surmised, the guard post was still unattended and he put his foot down and headed for Marlborough.

When they arrived back at the grand entrance to the Danvers estate, the procedure was much as Jack and Shelley had encountered just a couple of days earlier. As the double gates swung open, a small group of hazmat-clad figures emerged from one of the gatehouses carrying hand pumps.

Doug, Charli, Alina, Andriy and Jack all got out of the Discovery and started to remove their own suits as the others set about hosing down the vehicle. A final sweep with a Geiger counter and the group were back inside the car and heading towards the house, drawing up on the gravel driveway. Charli and Jack got out and headed for the edit suite where Gemma was already waiting to download the film from the camera and Jack's iPhone.

'We received all the footage before the drone was lost. Pretty grim, eh,' Gemma said, removing the memory card from the Canon. 'I assume your close-ups are even worse?'

'Not something I've ever seen before, nor want to again, to be honest,' Charli replied. Jack opened AirDrop on his phone and began transferring his own images.

'From the aerial shots it was hard to tell but we reckoned there must have been close on two hundred bodies there.' Charli and Jack both froze. Despite having been so close to the scene, neither of them had actually stopped to consider the scale of what they had just witnessed in simple numeric terms.

'I'm going to have to shut myself away somewhere quiet and get my head around what I have just seen before I can even think about putting it into words. But I had better check in on Shelley first. Have you seen her around?'

'She's up in the woods I think, Jack,' said Gemma. 'She's been helping out with the crèche and they've taken a group of the kids off to collect berries. Don't worry about her, Jack. She seems fine and the kids seem to love her.'

Jack went upstairs to his room to start writing his piece. Mike Danvers may have said they were still in the information-gathering phase but surely they now had proof of the mass dumping of dead bodies? True, there was no evidence of the military actually depositing the bodies at the water park, but these were clearly not like the other corpses they had seen in the earlier footage where people who had remained inside the exclusion zone and ultimately succumbed. But two hundred bodies dumped like household waste at the tip. This was organised and inside a zone protected by the military. The public would not need any persuading of the link when they saw these images. Danvers had to go public with this material, and if he didn't, Elodie certainly wouldn't sit on it when she received her copy. Jack took one final scroll through the images on his phone, opened his laptop and began trying to create the words to accompany the horror of what he had just witnessed – as if any words were necessary.

He heard the sound of the rotors first. The tranquillity of the Hampshire countryside was disturbed by a low-frequency, repetitive thud which was rapidly increasing in volume. Jack went to the window to see if he could spot the approaching helicopter. What was Danvers up to now, he thought to himself. The noise level was rising but Jack couldn't work out which direction it was coming from until he saw the flash on the horizon, followed a millisecond later by the sound of an explosion which shook the windows. The sound of rotor blades was right above him now and he looked up to see the undercarriage of what must have been an Apache attack helicopter as it banked and flew low towards the field and the mobile home encampment. As it disappeared behind the trees, the sound of rapid cannon fire could be heard. A cloud of thick black smoke was now rising in the distance. The door burst open and there was Doug, the Arsenal-loving, Ukraine veteran, driver.

'They've taken out the depot, Jack. Seventy-millimetre rockets. We're under attack. Get your stuff, we've got to get you out of here.' Jack shut his laptop, threw it into his messenger bag and followed Doug downstairs. Outside, the Apache had left a trail of devastation in the encampment as caravans burned, augmented by explosions from propane gas cylinders. Bodies were strewn across the grass while others tended to the injured as the Apache prepared for a second sweep of the site. The sound of more rotor blades filled the air, this time slower and louder. Two Chinooks appeared over the horizon and as they came in to land on the adjacent field, armed soldiers discharged from both, making for the manor house.

Meanwhile at the entrance to the Danvers estate, three Bulldog armoured personnel carriers approached the Doric pillars. The first simply drove right through the double iron gate without slowing. As the unarmed security team ran out of the gatehouse to see what was happening they were mown down by the 7.6-millimetre machine guns of the following two Bulldogs. The convoy then made its way along the drive towards the house, two further lorries following, loaded with armed troops.

Jack and Doug reached the basement to find a surprisingly calm atmosphere in the operations centre. The people he had first seen the other day, sitting behind computer screens were largely doing the same thing, if perhaps the conversation was a little more animated than previously. Gemma emerged from the edit suite holding a plug-in hard drive in her hand. 'Take this, Jack. It's the back up of everything we've filmed since we've been here. They've just broken down the gate so they've got support for the helicopter troops as well. We're trying to live stream from

393

some of the cameras but we've lost the signal from a lot of them already and no doubt they'll be knocking out the broadband as soon as they can. You've got to get out with the evidence, Jack. You know where to go, Doug?'

'Sure thing. Follow me, Jack.' With that, he led Jack through a door at the far end of the operations room into what must have been the old kitchen and food store, emerging on the far side of the house where another four-wheel-drive Pangea was parked. The two jumped in and Doug set off across a field to an area of woodland fifty metres further ahead. 'We should have cover from the helos now,' Doug said as they entered the woods. 'I can only take you so far in this, then you'll be on your own. I'll point you in the right direction but the wood runs right down to the river and from there it's only about five clicks to Birchingham. It's a totally different world from here. You wouldn't even think there's been a nuclear explosion.'

'What about you, Doug?'

'I'm heading back. They'll need everyone they can get at the house.' Then Jack suddenly remembered Shelley. 'Wait, I've got to come back with you. I have to find Shelley.' Doug stiffened. 'Jack, this is serious shit. We don't even know where she is and those soldiers aren't taking any prisoners. You didn't see what that Apache did to the camp. We've all got a job to do Jack, and yours is to make sure the world sees what's been happening here. Wherever Shelley is, she's with us and we'll look after her the best we can. But right now, I'm needed back there and you are needed out there,' Doug said as he pointed along a narrow footpath. 'Stay on the track, when you reach the bottom of the valley, keep the river on your right and you'll be in Birchingham before you know it. Good luck, mate.' With that, Doug was back in the Pangea and gone.

Mike Danvers had been in his kitchen at the time the first Apache had swept over the estate. Shelley and the crèche supervisor had brought him some of the fruit left over from their successful berry picking expedition with the children, and the three of them were carrying out the precautionary washing, even though the chances of radiation contamination were pretty low. It was the explosion followed by the cannon fire over the mobile home village which brought them out to the front door just as the advance party of troops from the Chinooks arrived at the house.

'What the fuck is going on? This is private property. You people have no right to be here. Get off my land immediately.' But Mike Danvers knew exactly what was going on. If you poked the bear enough, it would become angry and the little filming expedition to the water park had not surprisingly provoked this reaction. But other than the noise, Mike Danvers was not aware at this point of the scale of that reaction, what had already happened at his depot, what was actually happening at the mobile village, nor what was about to happen at his very own home.

Trusting that someone in his team, or indeed the CCTV cameras on the front of the house would be filming this exchange, he began to express his outrage more loudly, gesticulating with his arms. A short staccato burst of machine gun fire then sprayed the elevated front porch from left to right, sending shards of concrete ricocheting into the air and causing the three people standing before the door to fall backwards and lifeless to the ground. Meanwhile, the sound of stun grenades echoed from the basement, followed by more machine gun fire and the shattering of plate glass. By the time the motorised convoy of Bulldogs and troop carriers arrived from the main entrance, it had been joined by a fleet of empty, canvas-topped lorries. The clean-up operation had quickly swung into motion.

28 - Seventeen days later

10 Downing Street

'I imagine you want to start today's meeting with an update on events in Hampshire?' Field Marshal Leighton Parkes announced in his fall-back formal tone as he placed his coffee cup back on the table.

'I think that would be a good idea, Leighton,' the Prime Minister said from his armchair. 'Particularly as I had no prior knowledge of the raid and that a one-time popular TV personality appears to have been killed.' Ignoring the barb, the Field Marshal took a short breath and continued.

'You were indeed aware, Prime Minister, that we had suffered incursions into parts of the exclusion zone we had designated for the disposal of radioactive bodies.'

'Radioactive bodies? That's a bit cold.' Archie Wilkes looked up from the other side of the table. 'Can't we be a little more empathetic? Victims, casualties, deceased?'

'Call them what you like, Archie. There are thousands of them and my men have been given the job of dealing with the problem. Radioactive bodies are precisely what they are. But I digress. You will remember that a patrol was forced to fire on one group of intruders last week. Yesterday, drone surveillance picked up another group which had penetrated the security perimeter at our most recent site at the Swindon water park. They were filming on the ground and with a drone. They managed to leave the zone in a Landrover before we could send in any troops but we were able to track them by drone back to the country estate of Mr Danvers. Once they were out of their protective suits we were able to run facial recognition on all four of the occupants. Three were already known to us as activists including one who was ex-military. The fourth was a journalist, a Jack Makepiece. Interestingly, the intelligence service has come up with a link to Thorpehead. He was the local reporter down there and involved in the campaign to try to prevent the power station being built. He's been a bit quiet recently so they're currently looking into his movements to see how he ended up on the Danvers estate. But that's just the start of the story. It seems Danvers had quite an operation and a small army of followers. We are in no doubt now that the former nation's TV favourite has been behind much, if not all the anti-government rhetoric which has been circulating, as well as the source of the online photos and videos the intelligence services keep having to intercept. Our men have found highly technical media and communications equipment on the site.'

'But what actually happened to Danvers?' the Prime Minister asked with not a little irritation in his voice.

'Shot, resisting arrest, according to the Commanding Officer. Mr Danvers and two colleagues were standing at the entrance of the house, warning the troops not to advance any further. When they saw him raise his arm they believed he was preparing to fire and took the necessary action.'

'And was Danvers armed?'

'It would appear not. None of the three were.'

'Were there any arms at all found on the site?' Archie Wilkes added.

'A couple of small pistols, found in the belongings of the former soldier.'

'That's helpful then,' Archie replied, picking up his iPad.

'We can at least say arms were found on the site.

'And am I right?' the Prime Minister added. 'There were no survivors at all. Not even children?'

'Well interestingly, the only person not accounted for is our journalist, Mister Makepiece.' As he spoke, the Field Marshal's phone pinged. He glanced down at it for a moment before continuing. 'He definitely was not among the casualties and I have just had a message from intelligence. They are trawling through CCTV to see if they can find him since. It's difficult because there aren't many cameras in that part of the world. But they've managed to find where he was prior to that. It seems he's been in Salisbury with a young girl who's been identified among the dead, and a junior doctor working at the hospital. They'll let us know when they've caught up with her.'

The Clarion newspaper (Hollingsworth Media)

TV PERSONALITY KILLED IN RAID ON TERRORIST CAMP

Mike Danvers, former TV star and environmentalist was killed yesterday when military forces stormed a terrorist training camp at his country estate in Hampshire.

Working on intelligence, a coordinated attack by ground and air forces was launched on the rambling estate close to Birchingham. It is understood that as many as two hundred people were living on the estate under the guise of evacuees while in fact engaging in subversive activities and paramilitary training. There were no survivors although it is believed that some may have escaped and are being actively pursued.

Arms were found during a search of the farm, along with drones, technical surveillance equipment and radiation protection suits. Mike Danvers himself was shot on the steps of his manor house while attempting to fire on approaching troops.

A military spokesperson told The Clarion: "Yesterday at 15.45, a raid was carried out on the estate of Mr Michael Danvers near Birchingham in Hampshire. Forces were deployed using Apache and Chinook helicopters, supported by troops in armoured personnel carriers. The targeted location was believed to be operating as a terrorist training facility. A number of casualties were reported during the operation, mostly fatal. There were no military casualties. A subsequent search of the site uncovered a number of drones, surveillance equipment and small arms."

The Government has refused to confirm how long Mike Danvers' operation had been under surveillance or whether there is any terrorist link to the explosion last month at the Thorpehead nuclear power station on the Bristol Channel. Although an enquiry has already been launched into the cause, it has yet to be confirmed whether it was accidental or the result of exterior forces.

Mike Danvers was a high-profile objector to the power station and a vocal critic of the Government's future nuclear strategy. The one-time TV soap opera star and presenter had dropped out of the public spotlight in recent years and was believed to be busy on his organic farm in Hampshire. Now, it appears that he was also being paid by the Government for providing temporary shelter to people evacuated from the radiation exclusion zone, except that those people were being trained in subversive and terrorist techniques. A Government statement last night stated: "Earlier today, our armed forces mounted a pre-emptive strike on a terrorist training camp located on the estate of former TV star, Mike

Danvers. A large number of participants at the camp in Hampshire were killed, including Mr Danvers, who, it seems, was resisting the armed forces. A subsequent search of the site revealed a highly resourced armoury of technical equipment and guns, and we now believe it to be the source of a number of recent incursions into the exclusion zone as well as hacking attacks which our security forces have been attempting to combat. It is too early to say whether there is any link between the activities at this camp and the dreadful incident at Thorpehead nuclear power station, but nothing has been ruled out at this stage.

"It is sad to see someone who was considered a national treasure through his TV and environmental work resort to such activities, especially at a time when this Government has more than enough problems to be dealing with. It is perhaps even more disappointing that the funding for his activity appears to have come from the Government itself, which was compensating Mr Danvers for providing temporary shelter for people forced to leave their homes following the power station explosion, or so we thought at the time."

Turn to page 9 for a profile of Mike Danvers' career.

29 - Eighteen days later

News 24.com

6.30 am: Mike Danvers among several killed by Government forces

TV personality and environmentalist Mike Danvers was killed yesterday by Government forces during a raid on his Hampshire estate.

The estate, close to Birchingham came under attack from a helicopter gunship before troops stormed the grounds. Initial footage of the attack from security cameras was streamed live on social media and Danvers' own website before the sites were taken down.

After leaving his role as a TV presenter, Mike Danvers became an outspoken critic of the Government's nuclear energy policy and his campaign group had been questioning events surrounding the explosion at the Thorpehead power station last year. He ran a monitoring operation from his Hampshire estate which had obtained film evidence of the bodies of victims from radiation sickness being dumped at locations within the exclusion zone. Around three hundred volunteers, including children, were known to be living on the estate before the attack and it is not known whether any have survived. News24.com can now confirm that one of its own journalists, Rashid Bhati, had been living among the volunteers but was killed in a separate incident involving the security forces just last week.

Residents of Birchingham report hearing helicopters in the area yesterday afternoon followed by the sound of explosions in the distance. A Government source has claimed the attack was a counter terrorism measure and that arms were found during a subsequent search of the estate, but failed to provide any more details. We are also waiting for confirmation of the number of casualties or fatalities.

Update (replaces article of 6.30 am)
7.30 am: TV personality killed in raid on terrorist camp

Mike Danvers, former TV star and environmentalist was killed yesterday when military forces stormed a terrorist training camp at his country estate in Hampshire.

Working on intelligence, a coordinated attack by ground and air forces was successfully launched on the rambling estate close to Birchingham. It is understood that as many as two hundred people were living on the estate under the guise of evacuees while in fact engaging in subversive activities and paramilitary training. There were no survivors although it is believed that some may have escaped and are being actively pursued.

Arms were found during a search of the farm, along with drones, technical surveillance equipment and radiation protection suits. Mike Danvers himself was shot on the steps of his manor house while attempting to fire on approaching troops.

A military spokesperson told News24.com: "Yesterday at 15.45, a raid was carried out on the estate of Mr Michael Danvers near Birchingham in Hampshire. Forces were deployed using Apache and Chinook helicopters, supported by troops in armoured personnel carriers. The targeted location was believed to be operating as a terrorist training facility. A number of casualties were reported during the operation, mostly fatal. There were no military casualties. A subsequent search of the site uncovered several drones, surveillance equipment and small arms."

A Government statement last night read: "Earlier today, our armed forces mounted a pre-emptive strike on a terrorist training camp located on the estate of former TV star, Mike Danvers. A large number of participants at the camp in Hampshire were killed, including Mr Danvers, who it seems, was resisting the arrest. A subsequent search of the site revealed a highly resourced armoury of technical equipment and guns, and we now believe the group was responsible for a number of recent incursions into the exclusion zone as well as hacking attacks which our security forces have been attempting to combat. It is too early to say whether there is any link between the activities at this camp and the dreadful incident at Thorpehead nuclear power station, but nothing has been ruled out at this stage."

30 - Nineteen days later

The Clarion newspaper (Hollingsworth Media)

NEWS WEBSITE CLOSES SUDDENLY

The popular news website News24.com closed suddenly yesterday without any prior warning.

A landing page on the site simply announces that the organisation has ceased operating and none of the archived articles can be accessed. The doors are locked at its London headquarters and there are no signs of life.

Eighty people are known to have worked there with many reporters and correspondents based externally. Editor Martin Eddings, who had overseen the website's rapid growth over the last five years, has been on sick leave for the last month but when the Clarion attempted to contact him at his home, neighbours said he had left suddenly the previous day.

News24.com was owned by a charitable trust and accounts filed at Companies House show the business was not in any financial difficulty. But for all media organisations, trading conditions have become more challenging in recent years and the situation has been exacerbated by disruption following the Thorpehead power station incident.

Media experts have concluded that while News24.com was claiming increased traffic to its website, advertising revenues may not have been keeping up with spiralling costs.

In response to the loss of News24.com, The Clarion has launched its own 24-hour news coverage to complement the more in-depth reporting of its daily print edition. You can keep up to date at www.clarionnews24.com or download the app.

10 Downing Street

'So that's it then, no more *News24.com?*' Prime Minister Gordon Strathyre was sitting behind his desk with the morning papers spread out in front of him.

'Yes,' Archie Wilkes replied. 'It's not like they hadn't been warned. It appears Martin Eddings finally couldn't button it up inside and authorised release of the story. He probably wrote it himself. The trustees claimed they knew nothing about it and that he overrode our monitoring protocols, but that changes nothing. They did take the story down as soon as we told them and it was replaced with our own article but I felt we couldn't take the risk of having a loose cannon out there any longer. The staff are all going to be compensated and some have been offered jobs with Hollingsworth, as long as they all sign non-disclosures. Looks like Eddings has done a runner though. Guess he knew we would be coming for him once he published the story.'

'And what about Danvers and his estate?'

'Leighton tells me all evidence has been safely removed. There's nothing left there but the shell of the manor house.'

'And by all evidence, you mean bodies as well?'

'Collateral damage, Prime Minister. And yes, there's no trace left. Looks like we'll be saving a few quid too. The council told me how much they were paying in furlough and to Danvers himself for accommodating the terrorists.'

'That's what we're calling them is it?'

'Doesn't hurt to keep the terrorism narrative going, even if we know the real cause. With emergency powers still in place, it does rather make some of our decisions easier to swallow.'

31 - Twenty days later

Hampstead Heath, London

It was less than a week since Archie Wilkes had sat at this vantage point on Parliament Hill and marvelled at the spectacle of the City of London bathed in early morning mist. He couldn't see it today either because of the low cloud and steady rain which was falling and merging the horizon into a damp sea of grey. He was walking alongside Field Marshal Leighton Parkes, who was sheltering them both under the large golf umbrella he was holding.

'The Sheikh's plan hasn't cropped up anywhere in the COBRA meeting notes, so do I assume, Archie that it has been discussed with the PM on a need-to-know basis?'

'You can indeed, Leighton. Although it does look like we will have to announce His Highness's Reconstruction Fund sooner than we might have wished, if only to keep the Treasury in line. You won't be surprised to know that the country's finances are in a bit of a mess, to put it mildly.'

'You can be sure the Sheikh is already aware of that, but how much longer do you think it will be before the Government has to declare a crisis?'

'I'm surprised we haven't done so already,' Archie said, turning towards the Field Marshal. 'It's not just the extra costs of the evacuation, furlough and welfare payments, not to mention your rapidly growing Civil Defence Force, Leighton. We're effectively maxed out on borrowing. We can't issue any more bonds without the price collapsing completely and we effectively have zero GDP. Even collecting tax revenue that is due is proving problematic. HMRC is physically fragmented by the exclusion zone and there are very few businesses which haven't been affected in some way or other. If they haven't lost staff because of the evacuation, many businesses have simply been mothballed. The Chancellor really is looking for loose change down the back of the settee at the moment.'

'And how does the Prime Minister view the Sheikh's Reconstruction Fund proposal?'

'To be honest, Leighton, he hasn't looked beyond the money that would be coming in. He's like a beggar being offered a five-pound note. He's not even stopped to consider the consequences or what assets might be passing to the Gulf longer term.'

'But there's surely going to be pushback from the Cabinet once they learn all the details?'

'Trust me Leighton, the PM is not even aware there are limitations on his emergency powers granted under the Civil Emergencies legislation and while the House is not sitting, scrutiny is minimal, thank goodness.'

'Will it be a problem for us, going forward?' slight hesitation in the Field Marshal's voice.

'I can't think of the last time the Prime Minister ever read a briefing paper from the first to the last page. As you said last week, he finds it easier to rely on his advisors, or currently, his advisor. I think the Reconstruction Fund will be presented as just that. And it will come into being precisely because of the emergency powers the Government currently relies on. How else do you think your army has been able to grow exponentially or your proposal to suspend judicial process in favour of military courts was implemented?'

'Indeed,' Parkes replied before a short pause. 'And I assume there will be no further questions about our recent "counter-terrorism" measures with Mr Danvers?'

'I'm not expecting any resistance, especially as we seem to be getting on so well with the Home Secretary now. The PM seems to have moved on, and he's obviously more than happy about News24.com's demise. He did mention one thing this morning, though. We're still not sure whether our Energy Minister will stay on track. Awfully honourable is our Roly and I'm concerned he might suffer an attack of conscience further down the road.'

'You can tell Gordon not to worry. I did say I had a plan for Roland Jones, and I still do.'

Riviera FM website

Local MP's links to hostel fire

Tune in to Jenny Briggs tomorrow as she reveals who actually owns the Chy-an-Gov holiday flats at Trethewy Beach where, last month a fire killed 30 people.

The Health and Safety Executive (HSE) said last week it had major concerns about whether smoke detectors were working at the holiday apartments, which were housing families evacuated following the explosion at the Thorpehead nuclear power station. There were no survivors and the three-storey building was completely destroyed in the blaze. A separate criminal investigation is underway by Cornwall Police after it was confirmed that the cause of the fire was arson.

Investigators at the HSE want to interview the owners of Chy-an-Gov but have encountered difficulties in tracking them down. So at Riviera FM we did some of our own digging and have come up with an answer which lies worryingly close to home. On tomorrow's show, Jenny will describe how a complicated chain of ownership through shell companies and offshore tax havens actually leads to the Helford Estuary and the front door of none other than the Cantarrock MP, Miles Chenoweth.

Land Registry records show the holiday flats are owned by a company called Chy-an-Gov Ltd, which was first registered at Companies House in 1993. The directors at that time were our MP's parents, Jacob and Belinda Chenoweth. But in 2015 the shares were transferred to an Isle of Man registered company called Douglas Futures. With the help of our colleagues at Manxman Radio, we found that the registered address for Douglas Futures is just a brass plate office and mailing facility. The trail then leads through companies in Luxembourg to Belize, a well-used tax haven with a reputation for secrecy.

Jenny's programme will highlight the separate strands of her investigation which lead to Miles Chenoweth. In 2015, the year the ownership of Chy-an-Gov was transferred out of the family, Miles Chenoweth returned to Cornwall from overseas to work with his parents. Eighteen months later, his ill-fated project to re-open the Boscarrow tin mine was spearheaded by a company with an almost identical ownership structure to Chy-an-Gove Ltd. until it collapsed with multi-million-pound debts. Riviera FM also looked at other holiday properties which the Chenoweth family were known to have purchased or developed in the 1980s and 1990s. Like Chy-an-Gov, the Atlantic Holiday Studios and Brea Holiday Park are each owned by a dedicated limited company. And just like Chy-an-Gov, in 2015 shares were transferred to Isle of Man registered companies with links back to secretive Belize.

The Cantarrock MP has been very vocal recently, claiming on Riviera FM and other media outlets that Cornwall is full and struggling under the strain of providing temporary homes for people evacuated following Thorpehead. But Jenny will highlight one person who is definitely not struggling – yes, our MP Miles Chenoweth. She has seen documents from the local council which detail the rental payments being made to all the holiday rental establishments currently housing evacuees. Chy-an-Gov Ltd was receiving £11,400 a week before the tragic fire. That works out at £950 per unit. It is still early season in rental terms, and last summer, when Chy-an-Gov was available to book on the open market, the highest charge (for late July and August) was £750 per week.

The council only holds full fire safety certification for last year, but Chy-an-Gov has been closed to the public all winter and local building companies were known to have been contacted earlier in the year about possible remedial works before the season began. What the HSE currently wants to establish is whether new smoke alarms were installed. A representative interviewed by Jenny in the programme raises concerns about the speed with which the fire started and the fact that nobody in the building seemed to have been aware until it was too late.

These are questions Riviera FM has tried to ask our MP but as yet he has not responded to any of our approaches. We'd really welcome Mr Chenoweth to take part in tomorrow's programme, whether in person or by issuing a statement. You can find out if he does by tuning in at 10 am. We'll also be discussing the sudden closure of News24.com and asking whether this signals an end to impartial news reporting.

Prime Minister's residence, 11 Downing Street

Gordon Strathyre woke up in the bedroom of his flat above the Chancellor of the Exchequer's official residence. It was much more than a simple flat as the living quarters extended over two floors, and with four bedrooms, it was much more spacious than his supposed official residence in the eaves of Number 10. Since the time of Tony Blair, it was quite common for Prime Ministers with families to swap flats with the Chancellor and while Strathyre's two children were still only young, they had no real need of all four bedrooms. But No.11 was bigger and more comfortable and he was PM. So the Chancellor just had to put up with it and move, with his larger family into the flat next door.

As he turned over, the indent in the pillow confirmed to him that someone else had slept here last night, but the bed was empty. With that, the bedroom door was nudged open and there stood Alice, stark naked and holding a cup of coffee in each hand.

'For goodness' sake, Ali. This may be the private residence but that doesn't mean secretaries and house staff can't let themselves in. It's really not a good look, bumping into someone dressed like that.'

'Oh relax, Gordie. There's nobody else here and I only went to the kitchen next door,' replied Alice Singleton, Policy Adviser at the Party Central Office and long-time 'squeeze' of the Prime Minister. While it was an open secret that Gordon Strathyre struggled to keep his penis inside his pants, his wayward practices had been curtailed, at least in public, since his elevation to high public office. But it had always been different with Alice. Work had thrown them together and, since masterminded the landslide victory at the General Election, their relationship reached a new level. Strathyre's long-suffering wife, Marjorie, had been well aware of his regular dalliances but couldn't dismiss the situation with Alice so easily from her mind. Now, whenever Gordon said he had a strategy meeting at Party HQ, she knew not to wait up.

'I must say, I'm honoured to be sleeping at Number Ten.'

She handed the Prime Minister a coffee. 'This is a first. I assume Marjorie and the kids are in Scotland?'

'Yes, that's right, and quite honestly, I can't see them coming back here any time soon. Marjorie said it's almost as if nothing has happened there. No food shortages and the kids have settled straight into school. What would they have to look forward to back here?'

'Whoa, that's a bit deep from the man who uses every media opportunity to tell the nation that things are getting better with every day,' Alice said as she placed her cup on the table and slipped back into bed.

'It seems I'm saying whatever my advisor "advises" me to say at the moment. I can only hope I'm not still around by the time people start waking up to the reality of the situation and ask for an explanation.'

'I'm sorry, Gordie. Just what are you saying here?'

'It's not what I signed up for, Ali. When the leadership came up, I thought Why not? A few years as PM, recognition on a world stage, an address book full of A-List contacts and then retire to a life as an international statesman. But, not only am I saddled with this unholy mess that's guaranteed to have no happy ending, there's a chance the original contract to build the bloody power station was awarded via the old boy network. The very thing I promised to stamp out once I became leader.'

Alice took a sip of her coffee before replacing the cup on the bedside table. 'I thought Archie said we were in control of the media narrative and it is agreed Party policy to push out constant good news stories, partly to drown out issues like the cause of the explosion?'

Gordon Strathyre sat up and reached for his coffee. 'Oh

Archie and his new best friend the Field Marshal are certainly taking control of the media, along with anything else they don't like the look of. But sooner or later, there will have to be an inquiry and we can pump out as many positive stories as we like. But if the public don't actually feel things are getting better, we are just wasting our time.'

'So that's it? You're throwing in the towel at the time the country needs you most?'

'Oh Ali, there's no need for the drama with me. I'm not going to do anything rash but I do see a point, not far off, where I could step back with grace and hand the rebuilding of the country over to someone with the drive and ambition to see it through. To be honest, the way Archie Wilkes is driving the agenda at the moment would not be so concerning if it weren't for the fact he clearly has the support of the military. I'm not sure I want to be around when the full extent of our restructuring deal with the Arabs becomes apparent but I think that's some time away at the moment.'

'And do you think there is someone ready to step in who has the "drive and ambition?"'

'Oh, don't worry about that. The lovely Nadia seems to be well in with Archie and the Field Marshal already. The days when they fought like cat and dog are long gone.'

'Well, that's a shame,' Alice said thoughtfully. 'To think the first time I've fucked the Prime Minister at Number Ten, and it might be the last.' Strathyre put down his coffee and took hold of Alice's hands. 'Don't worry, I'm not going anywhere in a hurry. Whatever those bastards want, I'll go on my terms and when I think the time is right. And as my wife is unlikely to be coming back to London, you can take as much time as you like.' With that he guided Alice's hands down towards his crotch.

32 - Twenty-two days later

Knightsbridge, London

Roland Smith sat at the large oak desk which dominated the study in his coach house. With no wife or family, this was both his principal residence and his London pied-a-terre just a short drive or comfortable walk from Whitehall. He'd bought it with the legacy from his parents and hardly had to do anything to it as the previous owner had carried out an expensive conversion. The former stable was now a bright, open plan kitchen diner and lounge while the open staircase led up to three well-appointed bedrooms, the smallest of which had been commandeered as the minister's office. Not that he needed a room where he could shut himself away from the rest of the house, as there was seldom anyone else here. The second bedroom was only used on the rare occasion that friends or distant relatives came to visit, and in the master bedroom only one side of the bed ever seemed to see any use. The mews cottage was situated between Hyde Park and Brompton Road so he had every possible distraction from work on the doorstep, but it was work that mattered most to Roland Smith, Minister for Energy.

But today, and in fact for the last few days, there was very little work despite, or perhaps because of what had happened at Thorpehead. The ministerial red box sat open on the desk but there was little of any consequence in it. Most of the papers his department was handling currently were classified as 'secret' and did not leave the Ministry and he was aware that of late, many of these were being dealt with directly by his Permanent Secretary Sir William Potts. In fact, since he had had his ears chewed off by the PM and the Home Secretary, Roly had the distinct impression that he had been sidelined. Was he being lined up to be the scapegoat or was it because of his links to Mark Ellrington and Viktor Baliyashvili from Bicarel? He genuinely didn't have any contact with either of them prior to his appointment as Minister and the decision to award the Thorpehead contract. And then there was his old friend James Whitleigh-Howse. What must be going through his mind after losing the lovely Charlotte and their two little girls in the aftermath of the explosion? Surely, he didn't hold Roland Smith responsible?

His reverie was disturbed by the doorbell ringing. Roland sat up and looked out of the window into the mews but his sight line did not reach the front door. He assumed it must be someone he knew, otherwise his close protection officer would have intercepted any stranger before they reached the door. As he walked down the stairs he could see a large, dark form filling the transom above the door. He soon discovered that large form to be a thick set man standing almost two metres tall with short cropped fair hair. Military or ex-military, Roland recognised the type from his childhood spent following his father around the world.

'Who are you, and where's my security officer?'

'Don't worry, Roly. We're just here for a chat. We've sent

your CPO's off for a coffee.' With that, a second man appeared behind the speaker. Not as physically dominating but military nevertheless.

'Can we come in then?' number one heavy said as he advanced across the threshold. In an almost seamless movement, the two men entered the cottage, closing the door behind and taking an arm each, lifted Roland off the ground and marched him back upstairs to his study.

'Who are you? Army, S.I.S?' he shouted while being forcibly lowered into the chair behind his desk.

'Now, Roly you don't get to ask any questions in this little conversation. Suffice it to say, we're just doing a job here. Carrying out orders so to speak. So, first up, have you got a pen and a piece of paper.'

'Here we are,' number two heavy said lifting a pad and Roland's Mont Blanc pen from the edge of the desk.

'OK, next thing Roly. You are to write the following on this sheet of paper. Ready? "I am so sorry." Then just sign your name underneath. That's it. Simples.'

'What do you mean? I'm doing no such thing.' Number two heavy walked around the desk and crouching, spun Roland's chair around so he was almost face to face. Roland could smell whisky on his breath as he spoke. 'My friend here has already told you that this is a one-way conversation. You simply do as we say, no questions and no tantrums. That way, you don't get hurt. Now write the fucking message and we can be away and leave you in peace.'

That was it then, Roland decided. They were indeed setting him as the fall guy for Thorpehead. These two goons certainly weren't going to leave before they got what they wanted, or rather had been ordered to get and the political career of Roland Smith, MP and Government Minister was most probably over in any event. The only question was who had given the order? Scheming Yadav, the Home Secretary or had this come from the top? Strathyre had made it clear he wasn't going to be left holding the baby. Roly wanted to ask, but his visitors had made it quite clear already that there would be no questions.

'Alright, alright,' he sighed. 'I'll write your note but then I want you out of my house.' He scribbled the text and signed his name.

'No worries, Roly. Well done. We didn't want to get nasty with you as you seem like a nice bloke. A bit tense though, if you don't mind me saying. You really should try to relax more. What do you use to destress? Alcohol? Or perhaps something a little stronger?'

'Don't be ridiculous. I'm a Minister in His Majesty's Government.'

Before he could say another word, number two heavy had hold of his left arm and was busy pulling up his shirt sleeve.

'Nah, mate,' number one shouted. 'Other arm. Didn't you just notice him writing his note? He's left-handed.' He then pulled out a syringe from a case in his breast pocket as his colleague released Roland's left arm from his tight grip and rolled up his right sleeve. Meanwhile, his left arm was being held tightly behind his back and no matter how hard Roly struggled, his attacker was so strong he could not move. He felt the prick in his forearm and then the sensation of the brown liquid entering his vein. They had obviously done this before. Before long, Roly's resistance weakened as his breathing became shallow. His eyes were becoming heavy and he sensed he was beginning to float. The two intruders were becoming fuzzy silhouettes moving and saying words that he couldn't here. Roland Smith, MP and Minister in His Majesty's government then closed his eyes for the last time.

The Clarion **newspaper** (Hollingsworth Media)

SHOCK AND SADNESS AT MINISTER'S SUDDEN DEATH

The Government has been rocked by the news that Energy Minister Roland Smith was found dead at his home last night.

He was found at his Knightsbridge house by his security officer who became concerned when the Minister failed to answer his phone. Police have so far refused to comment on speculation that Mr Smith may have taken his own life but colleagues have remarked that the Minister had been under considerable stress since the accident at the Thorpehead nuclear power station last month. As Minister for Energy he was responsible for agreeing the deal with the multi-national firm Bicarel to construct and operate the power station which only opened last year.

The son of an army colonel, Roland Smith was educated at Winchester College before going to Oxford where he gained a First in Philosophy, Politics and Economics. From there he joined a policy think tank and spent three years working at the Party Central Office before becoming the MP for Harlesden West. During his time at Westminster, he was Parliamentary Private Secretary to the Minister of Defence before becoming a Junior Minister at the Department for Transport. His major promotion through the ranks occurred six years ago when he was chosen to head up the new Ministry for Energy with the specific brief to secure the nation's future energy security. He piloted the Nuclear Energy and Future Strategy Bill, promoting a new generation of small modular nuclear reactors which would reduce the reliance on imported fossil fuels. The Bill was due to have its final reading in Parliament next month.

Last night a party spokesperson told The Clarion: "Roly, was a dedicated politician and trusted friend to many of us. We are still trying to come to terms with the news that he is no longer with us. He lived to serve his country in the best way he could and for almost two decades he has done that through tireless work for the party and latterly, in key positions within the Government. Despite the terrible events of the last few weeks, he maintained his commitment to his ministerial role and discharged his duties with the utmost dignity. Roly had no immediate family as such but he will be mourned by a large number of his friends

33 - Four months later

West Cornwall

Mervyn, Jenna and Eric stood outside the pub. Only a few weeks earlier, they would have been comfortably ensconced inside, but today they stood in a line of locals which stretched around the car park, under the watchful eye of armed soldiers. For the last three weeks, this had become the Tuesday ritual, queuing for basic rations of food and household supplies. The pub had closed because it simply ran out of beer once the weekly dray deliveries stopped and it didn't take long for the local supermarkets to follow the same fate. In truth, going to the pub hadn't been as much fun since the military had moved in and set up camp in the car park. Jenna, still burdened with guilt over her involvement in the Trethewey fire, simply refused to go, fearing irrationally that someone would ask questions.

But despite initial assurances that food supplies would continue to reach West Cornwall despite the problems of the exclusion zone, the reality was soon the opposite. Ports like Southampton and Dover had seen almost all their shipping diverted to Immingham and Liverpool, while the vigilante action of some locals had resulted in the closure of

Plymouth's ferryport following the lorry hijackings. And while some basic necessities were finding their way to the far west of the country, the population was still swollen by large numbers of evacuees. The military had already been forced to intervene when frustration boiled over at some supermarkets and so now, the safest and most efficient way to distribute basic foodstuffs was almost a return to wartime rationing. Residents had to present themselves, along with identity, at designated distribution points throughout the county on a specified day of the week. And for Mervyn, Jenna and Eric, it was today.

'Just think, Eric. Your brother Davey could have made a killing if he was still selling his knocked-off meat,' Mervyn said. 'Have you heard from him lately?'

'Na, nothing. By which I can only imagine he's enjoying himself.' Eric hadn't said a word about that night in Riverbridge when Davey had been killed while attempting to rape a teenage girl. He had simply told his parents that his brother had stayed behind in Riverbridge, determined to make it out of the exclusion zone on the north side and pursue a new life in Ireland or Scotland. Once back in Cornwall, Davey offloaded the meat they had stolen and then sold the van, so wouldn't be available for any further black-market expeditions.

'Pity though,' Mervyn said thoughtfully. 'Nice bit of steak would be perfect just now and you can be sure there will be nothing like that when the army here starts dishing out our rations. Seems old Pasco Chenoweth was right. All the food goes to them posh gits up London way and we get the scraps. But where is our MP? I thought he'd be up in arms over all this.'

'No one's seen him since that business on Riviera FM,'

Eric said. 'Seems all the time he was banging on about the elites, he was one of them himself. Taking all the Government money for those holiday lets full of the refugees he didn't want here! Someone said he'd' done a runner back to Africa.'

'Ah, well he ain't getting rent any more for Trethewy Beach, that's one thing,' Mervyn joked.

'That's not funny, Merv,' Jenna cried. 'How can you even joke about something like that?'

'OK Jen, take it easy. Sorry, yes it was a bit insensitive. But it happened and now you just have to move on.' Mervyn noticed that there was activity at the front of the queue and Civil Defence Force workers were starting to hand out this week's provisions. 'Look out, we're on the move,' he said. 'Wonder what delights await us this week. What do you think, chicken or pork?'

'I'm surprised you can even make stupid jokes about that either.' Jenna was becoming emotional. 'I think all of this is just our punishment. God knows, life wasn't going to be very good after that explosion, but if queueing up for food rations is going to be our life going forward, I'm not sure I want to be a part of it.'

'Steady on, Jen,' Mervyn said, putting his arm over her shoulder. 'I'm only trying to lighten the load. Do you think I'm happy about living under an autocratic military dictatorship?'

'I heard that,' said a soldier standing port-arms and supervising the advancing queue. 'We're only here to keep you Janners safe from yourselves so you don't go around hijacking lorries or burning down buildings.'

'We're not janners, you stupid Pongo,' Jenna screamed at the soldier. 'Janners are Plymouth and they certainly ain't

Cornish.'

The people on either side of the queue all began to laugh. The soldier straightened. 'Listen, luv, why don't you just keep moving along, and if you are a good girl, maybe my colleagues there will give you something to eat. They've probably got some sanitary towels as well, as clearly you're in need of them right now.'

Before Jenna could react, Mervyn shoved the soldier backwards. 'I don't care who you are, but you don't talk to anyone like that. Not my girlfriend, not any woman. Got it?'

The soldier immediately swung his rifle from his chest and pointed it at Mervyn. 'Listen, Cornish big man. We've all got a job to do here, but you seem to be forgetting something. You're the ones who go around burning people's homes and playing Robin Hood with food lorries. We're the ones with the guns who've been sent to keep you rabble in order.'

Within seconds, the mood in the pub car park changed. Others who had witnessed the exchange left the line and approached the soldier. The distribution of food and supplies came to a halt as both military and civilians diverted their attention towards the altercation. The group advanced on the soldier.

'Keep your distance, I'm armed. Stand back.'

The crowd grew bigger and kept moving towards him.

'Stay where you are or I will be forced to shoot!'

There was a shot. Jenna fell to the ground as if her legs had been cut from under her. A warning shot in the air would usually be enough to disperse a crowd, according to military training, but that wasn't a warning shot and these were Trelawny's men - and one of them had just been shot. The crowd ran, but not away. As they advanced on the lone soldier, the lieutenant standing at the distribution table could see clearly what was happening and immediately took to his radio.

'Code red. Officer in danger. Clear armed response.'

The shots rang out and the pub car park soon emptied. Those who hadn't fled lay where they fell, many just feet from the frozen soldier, whose only shot fired had been the one Jenna had received through her chest. Her bleeding body now lay on the Cornish cobbles between that of Mervyn, Jago, surrounded by the bodies of Trelawny's men and women.

34 - Six months later

Deal, Kent

The text message simply mentioned Deal Castle and the time. Jack Makepiece stood in the shadow of the outer walls, looking at the English Channel. The weather had been benign today with clear skies and just a gentle breeze. A perfect day for sailing, or in Jack's case, hopefully a boat ride to the relative safety of France. The light was fading and the day trippers had gone home, leaving just the occasional dog walker on the shingle beach. He thought of the irony. Deal Castle, looking like a giant stone wedding cake with its tiers of circular turrets, built by Henry VIII to repel invaders from France. It was now the preferred rendezvous point for the gangs, seemingly doing big business helping people escape to France. Less than a year ago, anyone could make that journey on a ferry from along the coast in Dover for just a few pounds. Today, with only emergency goods allowed in on ferries and nobody allowed out, the journey to Calais in a rigid inflatable was costing several hundred times more. Jake was an hour ahead of the appointed time and the instructions had been clear about not hanging around and attracting attention, so he decided to take a stroll up to the pier and back to kill time.

The last weeks had passed in something of a blur. After being sent on his way by Doug back on Mike Danvers' estate, it was a couple of days before he was able to grasp the full extent of what had happened during the attack, and the obvious conclusion that Shelley had perished along with all the others. He'd read the news reports and the ludicrous claims of terrorism, even News24.com was saying so. At first, he wondered whether this was what Mark Eddings had been warning about, that the Government was controlling the news flow. But when, only a day later it looked like the *News24.com* site had been taken down, he had his answer.

By that time, he had made his way back to Salisbury and found Claudia once more. She agreed to shelter him in her rooms close to the hospital and despite the continued military presence, Jack felt safer hiding in plain sight rather than checking into a hotel where his details might show up on a system. Claudia was distraught at the thought that Shelley had been killed during the raid, but otherwise she was exactly the same towards Jack as she had been the last time they were together. The matter of their 'unfinished business' was resolved quickly, rather too quickly in Jack's case. He couldn't even remember the last time he had had sex, so shouldn't have been surprised. But Claudia was kind and reassuring, telling him it didn't matter and would be better the next time. And it was, early the next morning before she left for her shift at the hospital.

Jack spent most of the day on Claudia's couch, sorting through the material on the plug-in drive that Donna had given him just as the attack on the Danvers house was starting. He'd managed to forward a lot of the film to Elodie but there was so much evidence that the team had gathered, it was taking him a long time to review it. When Doug suddenly appeared in shot or he heard Charli's voice in the background, Jack had to stop, being transported back immediately to the sound of combat helicopters, explosions and his own escape through the woods.

It was dark when he woke, still stretched out on Claudia's sofa with his laptop and the plug-in drive resting on his stomach. He looked at the time. Claudia should have been back hours earlier. He checked his phone but there were no messages. It was not unusual for her to work additional hours or even extra shifts given the current situation at the hospital, but surely she would have let him know? When he called Claudia's number it went straight to voicemail, which was not surprising if she was still working. Jack decided he needed some air and as it was dark outside, he wouldn't be risking much to walk over to the hospital emergency department to wait for her. When he reached the reception desk, he recognised the same 'jobsworth' who was on duty the day he had arrived with Shelley and Evan. The man didn't look up, and probably wouldn't have recognised him in any event, but his reaction changed the minute Jack asked if Claudia was still at work.

'Just take a seat and somebody will be out to see you,' came the reply through the speaker on the glass partition. Jack sat down in the waiting area and it was only a matter of moments before a short woman in her forties, wearing a navy-blue uniform with red piping on her collar, was standing in front of him.

'I understand you are asking about Claudia,' the matron said. 'Do you mind telling me who you might be?'

'I'm just a friend who's staying with her at the moment. I've come to walk her home.'

'Are you Jack, the boyfriend?' Jack was immediately speechless. Was it the shock that the matron knew his name or that she used the word 'boyfriend'?

'It's just Claudia asked me to let her boyfriend know. She was quite insistent.'

'Well yes, that's me, I suppose. What's happened? Where is Claudia?'

'It's all a bit of a shock to be honest, Jack. She had only been working for an hour this morning when three men marched into the department demanding to see her. They each had Security Services ID and said they needed to speak to her about her visa status. I thought it was odd that MI5 would be checking on visas but as soon as she arrived in my office they arrested her on suspicion of terrorist activity, handcuffed her and marched her away. I've been trying to find out what's happened to her since but with no luck. I've rung the police and the immigration services but nobody knows anything. The hospital chief executive is trying to get to the bottom of it but he's not had any luck so far. Do you know anything, Jack?'

'I'm afraid I have no more idea than you, Matron.' Jack spoke before really being able to process the news. But he thought he did know. They'd already been able to link him back to Salisbury and the hospital. 'Well, if she's not here, I had better go back to her rooms. Maybe there is something which might help there. I'll make a few enquiries myself, but to be honest, we hadn't been together very long. Perhaps I didn't know her as well as I thought.'

Jack promised to keep the matron updated and made as quick an exit as he could without arousing suspicion. It was only a short walk back to the staff hostel but he needed to make some decisions quickly. Could he help Claudia? If she was being held by the Security Services it was because they were looking for Jack, not her. She had done nothing wrong so surely no harm would come to her. They would have to let her go. The priority was to get himself and the evidence on the plug-in drive as far away as possible. As he turned the corner, the first thing he noticed was two black Range Rovers parked half on the pavement in front of the hostel entrance. Jack ducked into a doorway on the opposite side of the close from where he could see more clearly. Both vehicles had a driver sitting behind the wheel and a third man, tall with close-shaved hair, stood on the pavement smoking a cigarette. With that, the hostel door opened and two more men in dark suits emerged carrying cardboard document boxes. They were followed close behind by a fourth man with a black bin liner in one hand and a laptop computer in the other. Jack's laptop! Without a word spoken between any of the visitors, the document boxes were loaded into the rear of one Range Rover and the two men climbed in. The man carrying the bag and laptop got into the back of the first vehicle, the sentry stubbed out his cigarette and got into the front passenger seat, and both vehicles quietly drove off.

So that was it. They knew where Claudia lived, and probably where Jack had been staying and they had his laptop. That meant they must have had the plug-in drive too. But if they thought he was coming back, why had they all left? Or had they? He only saw them leave. Jack had no idea how many had arrived. Maybe there was someone waiting inside? Should he wait until the coast was clear or flee now? He tried to slow down the multiple thoughts and scenarios playing through his mind. Deep breaths, clear your mind, start again. How did they make the link between him and Claudia in the first place? Facial recognition, no doubt from when the drone buzzed their sortie into the exclusion zone. There were enough CCTV cameras around Salisbury that they would surely have picked him up during the days he spent there the previous week. Perhaps they were following Martin Eddings at the same time. It would have explained his own rather odd behaviour. CCTV would no doubt have picked up his encounters with Claudia at the hospital, the restaurant and probably outside the hotel. But did they know he was back in Salisbury? Probably not. Most likely, they came to turn over Claudia's flat looking for evidence of Jack. But now they had found more, much more than they had probably expected. The moment those goons got back to base, they would know for sure. If nobody was waiting for Jack at Claudia's, there soon would be. His only option was to turn and run.

Ganirvan, Kyrgmanistan

Mark Ellrington hugged the waiting Viktor Baliyashvili in the arrivals hall at Ganirvan International Airport. It had been a comfortable flight from Frankfurt, where he was now settled. Although most of his business interests were still rooted in the United Kingdom, the City of London was losing its lustre. Brexit had set the wheels in motion towards London losing its crown as the financial centre of Europe, but since the explosion at Thorpehead had also created a physical barrier to reaching the City, the real money was rapidly transferring to other centres like Paris and Frankfurt. While Mark had always enjoyed Paris, he found doing business there was noticeably harder if you didn't speak the language. Despite all the archetypal clichés about German bureaucracy, Frankfurt was far more diverse and welcoming to foreigners while English was accepted as the language of business. The bonus came when he moved into his Westend apartment and discovered all the parks and greenery, culture and fine dining that was on hand, just a short walk from his new office. But here he was, back in Kyrgmanistan for the first time since, he couldn't remember when exactly, certainly well before Thorpehead. And it wasn't a social visit either. He'd received a short message from Viktor telling him to get there as soon as he could as his uncle, the President required their presence.

'So, my old commie mate. How's it going? We're off to the palace to see the big man then?'

'Yes, but not palace,' Viktor replied. He seemed tense when they had embraced and he didn't appear the usual fun-loving bear that Mark had known for over twenty years. He might have been mistaken but it didn't seem like Viktor had been drinking either. Perhaps that explained the cool reception. 'President is at his mountain retreat, but he's sending helicopter. Come.' Mark followed Viktor outside the terminal building where a uniformed chauffeur was standing beside a waiting white Maybach with the door held open. The car drove them around the perimeter to a discreet, single-storey VIP lounge on the opposite side of the airport from the main terminal building. They were ushered in to a deserted open-plan lounge looking out onto the runway and as Mark sank into the soft, leather sofa, a hostess appeared at his side holding a silver tray and flute of champagne. Viktor sat in the chair opposite him with a glass of orange juice in his hand.

'Tell me that's a fucking Screwdriver, Vik. You haven't jumped on the wagon for fuck sake.'

'No, too much to drink last night, that's all.'

'When's that ever fucking stopped you?'

'Well, I want a clear head when we meet uncle. He's not happy about Bicarel.'

'In what way exactly? Thorpehead was an accident at worst. And they've still not officially ruled out terrorism. My source says the Ministry report will point to an unforeseen combination of weather factors creating the fallout problems.'

'You still have a source in the Ministry after Roly?'

'Yeah, that was fucking awful. Lovely bloke Roly, but he always took things too personally.'

'But he's dead, Mark. And it wasn't his fault.'

'Don't worry about that, Vik. I'll explain it all to your uncle. I'm confident Bicarel will be cleared in the enquiry.' Mark said, coolly draining his glass and holding it up to signal he wanted another.

'The problem is not just Thorpehead,' Viktor continued. 'French Government has cancelled its contract and British have not passed the Energy Bill for next power stations. Production at factory here has almost stopped completely and workers are being laid off. President is not happy that Kyrgmanistan's international reputation has been damaged by Bicarel and now he has disgruntled workers at home in Ganirvan. That's what worries me.'

'Look Viktor. I'm sure your uncle will see it our way by the time I have worked my charms on him. And anyway, I have a new plan for Bicarel. I've been reading up on all the rare earth elements here in Kyrgmanistan. There's everything you need to become a world leader in battery production and it would be fucking simples to reconfigure the factory. If it's problematic, then we just close the fucking thing down and start up again next door.' Before Viktor could even think about whether he even wanted to engage in this new line of debate, they heard the approaching rotor blades, followed just a few moments later by the sight of a Sikorsky S-92 helicopter emblazoned with the Kyrgmanistan Government insignia, slowly lowering onto the apron in front of the terminal building.

'OK, this is us,' Viktor announced. Mark quickly downed the remains of his second glass of champagne, picked up his messenger bag and followed Viktor and the hostess outside to the waiting aircraft.

Deal, Kent

And run was what Jack had done in the weeks following his visit to Salisbury. He built a new life, living almost off-grid, starting with just the clothes he had been wearing that night and, fortunately, the roll of cash he had taken from the hotel safe when he left Holmbeach. His iPhone quickly found a new resting place at the bottom of the River Avon and was soon replaced by a pay-as-you-go. He was careful how he used public transport until he was a couple of days and several miles from Salisbury.

He soon discovered that despite outward appearances, life south of the exclusion zone was still disjointed and hand-to-mouth in many respects. Nothing functioned fully as it had before. There may have been CCTV, but it wasn't always operational. There weren't many jobs around but those employers who did need staff were not fussy where they came from. It was relatively easy to find work in return for lodgings or payment in food and occasionally cash.

By working odd days on farms or serving behind bars, Jack moved from town to town, or preferably village to village across the south of England. Just outside Chichester, he found work at a holiday park which was still being used to house people evacuated after the Thorpehead explosion. They were mainly single-parent families, as the men had almost all been forced to join the Civil Defence force. The stories related to Jack by the wives about their husbands' work were harrowing. Disposing of bodies, arresting foreign nationals on trumped-up terrorism charges and enforcing 'shoot-on-sight' policies to deter lootings or quell civil disorder. There were tales of some men taking their own lives rather than performing their duties in the Civil Defence Force. Jack found a more settled home in the holiday park in return for helping the children with English lessons. The families were forced to home-educate the children because there was either no room at the local primary school or, in some cases, resident families had objected to evacuees being taught alongside their own children because of a supposed radiation risk.

To be safe, Jack didn't use his new phone but Internet cafes to keep up with the news and stay in touch with Elodie. She'd told him that Martin Eddings had somehow made contact with her and Jack had given her his approval to share his material. She'd been able to do some research too and discovered that Claudia had been deported back to Italy, supposedly for overstaying her visa. He wanted to contact his parents but worried that even their activity could have been monitored by now, so he wrote them a letter explaining that his phone had been stolen and he was waiting for the insurance company to provide a replacement. The lady in the village post office said that mail was getting through from one side of the exclusion zone to the other but there was no guarantee how long it would take. But it was while he was online one day that Jack noticed an advert pop up on social media offering 'quick and easy' escapes to continental Europe. He knew, even before responding to the ad, that this was no organised excursion but a clandestine departure on a motorised dinghy and an illegal entry into France or Belgium. Criminal gangs were behind the traffic, which until only recently had been entirely in the opposite direction. The current government had swept to power on a promise of ending the small boat arrivals of immigrants along the Kent coast. Little did anyone know at that election that the flow would be stemmed by a nuclear explosion.

But the risk of arrest on the French coast was, in Jack's view, the lesser of two evils compared to what probable fate awaited him if apprehended by the British security services. He was aware that by this stage, diplomatic relations between the two countries had reached an all-time low. As if the fear of radioactive fallout reaching the French coast was not enough, Jack had read the previous week that the President accused Prime Minister Starthyre of imposing martial law. If he were arrested in France, he figured it would be easy enough to claim asylum and demonstrate a fear for life if returned to Britain. And perhaps, just perhaps, from France he would be able to find his way to Italy and wherever Claudia might now be living.

Ganirvan, Kyrgmanistan

Back in the departure lounge of Ganirvan International Airport, the passengers waiting for the KLM flight to Amsterdam enjoyed a grandstand view of the runway. They had seen the arrival of their inbound flight as well as an Air France jet taking off and rising against the backdrop of the Lesser Caucasian Mountains. While the airport sat on a plateau, the mountain range filled the full width of the departure lounge window like a theatre backdrop. The granite and limestone rock formations were topped the whole year round with a layer of snow. In winter, Ganirvan's boast was that its residents could go skiing simply by taking the funicular directly from the city centre to the slopes. Today. The white snow glaze contrasted with the deep blue of the sky beyond.

The passengers watched as the government helicopter emerged from that blue sky and descended steadily to land on the far side of the runway. With its rotors still running, a small group of people emerged from the building and climbed aboard before the helicopter was airbound once more. The grey of the fuselage stood out against the white background as it rose and the sun glinted off it as it continued its climb before disappearing behind the mountain peak. It was the explosion they heard first, followed seconds later by a cloud of black smoke rising above the horizon. President Alexander Baliyashvili always had a simple way of dealing with problems.

Deal, Kent

So here he was, at the end of a journey which had begun a mere six months earlier in the lounge of the Boar's Head in Holmbeach, serving coffee before hearing the loud explosion. As he walked back along the seafront towards the Deal Castle, Jack noticed through the twilight that a small group had gathered on the shingle beach. As he approached, his mobile pinged with a text message from an unidentified number. It read "New RDZ" followed by a map reference. Jack keyed the reference into Google Maps and the red pin was showing about a mile further north along the beach on Sandwich Bay. As he turned to walk back towards the pier, the people assembled on the beach started moving in the same direction. His fellow passengers had obviously received the same message. By the time he reached the rowing club, Jack had been caught up by one of the group.

'You off on the trip then?' he said as he approached. Jack didn't know whether to respond.

'Let's hope it's better than last time,' his new companion said again as he drew level. He was a short man wearing an anorak and waterproof over trousers. Like Jack, he was carrying no rucksack. They had all been given strict instructions to bring nothing with them, not even passports or ID. Just the necessary cash for those who had not been able to make payment by Bitcoin in advance. In Jack's case, that cash would more or less use up the last of the roll of notes in his security belt. He looked across at the man, whose blond curls he could see poking out from underneath a woolly beanie hat.

'What do you mean, "last time?" You've done this before?'

'Yeah, ten days ago. Up near Ramsgate. They turned up with this dodgy-looking Zodiac. Didn't look anywhere big enough for the number of us waiting. But they forced us all in. Then one of them asks if anyone has experience of GPS, some poor sod says "yes" and they tell him he's in charge. They push us off, motor starts up and we're off. It's fine at first. Do you know Pegwell Bay? No? Well, anyway, it's pretty smooth until we leave the shallows. When we're out in the Channel, the waves are getting bigger. Then they start breaking over the bow and we've got a foot of water inside the boat. It's slowing us down and we're lower in the water. Then the bloody engine dies. Don't know if it's the water or ran out of fuel but the only direction we're travelling in is downwards. Lucky for us, there's a fishing boat going back into port. Nobody even had a life jacket. They scooped us up just as the Zodiac is about to sink completely. Got a lift back into port, and the skipper says we're lucky the navy patrol didn't pick us up or we'd all be straight to prison. So we lived to fight another day.'

'Did you get your money back or is this your replacement trip?' Jack asked.

'Give over. It's not DFDS Ferries, mate. These guys are crooks. Once they've got your money, they're not bothered whether you make it across the water or not.'

'So what, you've paid again and taking the chance all over?' There was exasperation in Jack's voice.

'No choice, mate. Had to do a bit of grifting to find the money. Different crowd this time. Or at least it seems like it. To be honest, even if we don't make it, I'm better off than staying here. Deserted from the Civil Defence Force. Death penalty if I'm caught. There's only a chance I'll die in the boat, but a certainty if I stay. What about you?'

'Oh,' said Jack, thinking quickly. 'Meeting up with my girlfriend. She's been deported. Do you really think we could die out there?'

'Happens enough times. Not always reported though, and not just because of the shitty boats. The French aren't exactly pleased to have refugees turning up on their beaches. There are stories of them not coming to the rescue when boats get into difficulty.'

Before Jack could take that last comment in, one of the group called out. 'Over there!' They'd now left the seafront buildings of Deal behind and only marsh grass lay on the land side of the road. Ahead on the beach, they could see dark shapes and the flashing of a torchlight. When they approached, they found three men standing around a six-metre RIB, large enough for the dozen or so people who now stood alongside Jack and his new companion. One of the gang was looking at a phone with a list of what cash he needed to collect and he began to do this while the other two handed out life jackets.

'Life jackets,' Jack's companion said from the side of his mouth. 'I told you we would be travelling Club Class!' With the financial transactions complete, the three men dragged the Zodiac into the water. Two of them held it while the third climbed in, started the motor and programmed the GPS navigation. They then called the group forward, motioning Jack's enthusiastic companion into the bench seat.

'It's set for Loon Plage and the sea is like a mill pond today. Enjoy your cruise.' The three men stepped out of the shallows and disappeared back up the beach, leaving Jack and his fellow travellers to start the next stage of their journey in the hands of a fatalistic military deserter who would rather die at sea than be captured on land.

35 - One year later

World Review Magazine, Sydney

NUCLEAR FALLOUT ZONE – A TYPICALLY BRITISH AFFAIR

Comment by Martin Eddings, former editor of News24.com

One year ago, the Great Britain that I knew and loved and was respected almost all around the World, simply blew apart. A catastrophic nuclear accident, a result of the inherent cronyism and corner cutting which has plagued the country for generations, sent a radioactive cloud billowing from one side of the country to the other, rendering the land below its path uninhabitable for hundreds, even thousands of years.

To dig deeper into the 'how' and the 'why', we need to look at 'Great' Britain today. In doing so, we will then be forced to consider another key factor – how that nation's leader has put holding on to power ahead of so many other considerations, beginning with the wellbeing of its citizens. While reading what follows, you should also keep in mind why I, a previously well-known British news editor, am writing this article for a publication on the other side of the World – far beyond the reaches of my Government's control of media.

So let's begin by looking at Britain as we know it today. Although the correct appellation is 'Great Britain and Northern Ireland', we'll just stick with Britain. The unification referendum six months ago returned a 90% majority in favour of the island of Ireland becoming one nation, and as of yesterday, the residents of the six northern counties are now members of the Republic of Ireland and the European Union. They will be joined shortly by their neighbours in Scotland following the completion of turbo-charged accession negotiations – something previously unheard of in EU parlance. Within the coming months, a proud and independent Scotland will also take its place in an expanded European Union. That leaves just England and Wales, the latter still suffering severe transport disruption in the previously commercially active south of the country. And then there is England, which is actually two Englands with a 15km strip across its centre where nobody lives and nothing can grow in the fields. The North, so often overlooked for investment in favour of the South and South East, is now the closest thing the country has to a powerhouse. What jobs and industries remain are based there and the mayors of cities such as Birmingham, Manchester and Liverpool govern almost autonomously. Meanwhile, south of the exclusion zone, the forgotten and the left behind struggle with daily life. Many of the people initially displaced from the radioactive fallout zone live there, most still in temporary accommodation. There is no industry to speak of; it's still difficult to get farm produce to market and the only real job opportunities are administrative, usually in roles dealing with the evacuees. Criminal gangs have proliferated, controlling anything from logistics and the sale of black-market goods to the rapidly growing enterprise of small boats, taking fleeing Brits across the Channel to land illegally in France or Belgium.

But also in the South lies London, capital city and the seat of Government, if government is indeed the correct word. It's certainly where Prime Minister Gordon Strathyre lives and from where he issues orders which are in the main implemented by Field Marshal Leighton Parkes,

Chief of Defence and commander of the Civil Defence Force. But the iconic Houses of Parliament, alongside the River Thames sit empty. Westminster was prorogued just days after Thorpehead blew up, and Members of Parliament have largely been sitting at home twiddling their thumbs while the Prime Minister governs using emergency powers granted under an earlier act of Parliament. But who is there to check that those emergency powers aren't being abused? Parliament is no longer sitting and the media has been silenced. That's not just a wild or ideological accusation. This is a fact that I can relate to from personal experience. While much, too much in fact, of the British media was already pro-government, News24.com, where I previously worked, was a beacon of impartiality. Where many news sites bolstered clicks and subscriptions by simply posting what their audiences wanted to read, News24.com told the stories as they were and we spoke truth to authority without fear for any consequence. When News24.com started asking the wrong questions about how the unimaginable horror of Thorpehead came about, things began to change. Suddenly there were consequences. At first they were financial, advertising contracts cancelled. Then came the threats and journalists arrested for refusing to reveal their sources. Finally, the plug was pulled, literally. In scenes more akin to a Third World military junta, armed soldiers turned up at the office one morning and physically closed News24.com down. And what were we doing that upset the "government" of Gordon Strathyre? It wasn't just digging into the background of the Government's nuclear energy strategy and the contract awards. News24.com had a reporter embedded in the campaign group of environmentalist Mike Danvers which had discovered just how many people had been killed following the Thorpehead explosion. And not just that, they found evidence that the bodies of victims were simply being taken back inside the nuclear exclusion zone and dumped. In the course of those investigations, that journalist was killed by a Civil Defence Force patrol. I carry that guilt with me every day since and in publishing this article, I hope I can honour the work and dedication of Rashid

Bhati. That attack, and a subsequent raid on Mike Danvers' estate (from which another News24.com journalist escaped) were described by Prime Minister Strathyre as counter-terrorist actions. Mike Danvers was no terrorist. What he was trying to do was show the British public what really happened at Thorpehead nuclear power station and the lengths Strathyre's government went to conceal the truth.

Some of the images on these pages are graphic enough but for the first time, I can share some of the cache of material News24.com had gathered before it was forcibly closed down by military force.

You can see footage of the immediate aftermath of the Thorpehead explosion here: http://quiklink/news24/thorp

For evidence of how bodies were disposed of (warning, these are distressing images): http://quiklink/news24/excl

Film of the military attacking the Danvers estate: http://quiklink/news24/Danv

And so the charges against Prime Minister Gordon Strathyre are quite straightforward: more than 30,000 deaths, 2.5 million people displaced from their homes and the break-up of the Union. Whether he will ever stand trial to face these charges in a courtroom is unlikely while the judiciary is under the control of the military. But the facts behind those accusations need to be placed before the court of public opinion. Let's start at the beginning with the Nuclear Energy and Future Strategy Bill. The Government's flagship policy, driven by Roland Jones in the newly created role of Minister for Energy, was supposed to be the antidote to decades of fluctuating oil and gas prices impacting on consumers and the pathway to Britain's future energy security. No longer would the country be at the mercy of unstable foreign regimes for its supplies or the victim of conflicts in other parts of the World. The only problem was that the Bill was designed around nuclear energy alone and as such, was seriously flawed. First, the Green Party, and latterly the Opposition had been asking two questions during the Bill's ultimately stalled passage through Parliament.

The first was about water. Even the proposed new generation of smaller, modular reactors required millions of gallons of fresh water to operate. In the last decade we have at last come to recognise that drinking water is a finite resource for which there is an ever-increasing demand. We all take artificial intelligence for granted today but all that data mining and storage doesn't actually occur in real 'clouds'. It happens at giant data processing sites the size of small villages, and they are all cooled with water – masses of it. A large date data centre uses around five million litres a day! That the British Government should be asked to consider the impact of a dozen or so new nuclear power stations using three-quarters-of-a-million litres of water a day, is a reasonable request in the current climate.

The other question is what to do with the by-product of nuclear fission. Britain is still living with the legacy of its previous nuclear energy projects. Almost five million tonnes of nuclear waste from its first and second-generation power stations are still being stored in precarious conditions in the northwest of the country while a solution is sought for longer-term disposal. Successive governments have kicked the can down the road for the last five decades and now, without a solution, this Government wanted to add to that stockpile.

But how did the Energy Minister react to these questions? Well, he didn't. Opposition in both the Commons and the Lords was dismissed as the incoherent babble of fanatics. Roland Jones signed the Government's first contract to build a new generation reactor at Thorpehead. The company that won that contract had little or no track record and just happened to be owned by two of Minister Jones' chums from university. Sound familiar? Yes, despite concerning noises coming out of France, where the firm's only other nuclear project was located and vociferous resistance at Thorpehead itself, Britain's first steps towards energy security were taken just over two years ago this week. The rest is history, except for the fact that no one is ever likely to know what really went on. Why? Because any opposition was forcibly or violently shut down, whether the campaigners at Thorpehead prior to the station opening or the abhorrent reaction to what Mike Danvers was trying to achieve – disgracefully portrayed by the Prime Minister as a terrorist. Alas, the Minister for Energy will not be available to give evidence at any public enquiry (if there ever were to be one) as he is dead. Took his own life by a heroin overdose, or so said the Coroner at the military inquest. And as for his two Oxford buddies who ran Bicarel, the company which built the flawed power station? Both dead in a helicopter accident in Kyrgmanistan. What more needs to be said?

Having already established that Gordon Strathyre now presides over a deeply divided country (and not just physically) using what the French President first called out as martial law, the other burning question is, who's paying for it? Here is a country with a gaping hole where some of its most productive towns and cities once stood. Millions are displaced, living in temporary accommodation provided for them, unable to work and receiving furlough payments in lieu. After years of Government cutbacks, Britain's military capability now numbers more than one million – almost ten times its size in 2024. So where is this money coming from? Not from taxation, that's for sure. Notionally, the British Government still has a Chancellor of the Exchequer but there is no chance he will be presenting a Budget to Parliament anytime soon. But the country's GDP is all but non-existent and Revenue and Customs is struggling to recover what taxes may actually be due. Yet the troops still get paid and the displaced receive their benefits. So what else is Gordon Strathyre concealing?

Well, here I believe I may have the answer. For the last six months, financial journalist Jack Makepiece has been conducting a forensic investigation of the British Government's income and expenditure on behalf of World Review. Once of Finance Matters, Britain's leading financial daily, Jack was also the local reporter in the West Country when the Thorpehead power station was being built. After the explosion, he also covered the story for News24.com before our untimely forced closure. Like me, Jack is heavily invested in this story, but unlike me, he is a first-rate financial investigator. And it would appear that the British Prime Minister is not spending beyond the means of his tax receipts, nor borrowing excessively. He is simply enjoying the largesse of a foreign power. And not any foreign power, but one of the largest and most influential petro-states in the Arabian Gulf. Why, and what does the Sheikh expect in return? That, sadly, I cannot answer yet. It could simply be a commercial opportunity to rebuild a broken country with a busted nuclear policy, using cheap and plentiful fossil fuels that the rest of the World appears to be shying away from. Or it could be that the Arabian Gulf will be unable to support human life in two decades' time due to global warming, prompting a move to more temperate climes. Jack's work has proven the link and tracked the flow of monies between the Gulf and Gordon Strathyre in Downing Street, but it has not uncovered the motive.

World Review will be publishing the information Jack has obtained in the coming days but my challenge to the British Prime Minister is this: come out from your military bunker and level with your citizens and the rest of the World about what has happened in the last twelve months; publish the details of the agreement you have reached with the Gulf States and its implications for the people of Britain; recall Parliament, reinstate the judiciary and agree to a Government of Unity to lead the country through the next stage of its recovery from Thorpehead disaster.

I grew up in the Cold War era when the single greatest threat to our future was nuclear war. There haven't been any ballistic missiles but Britain has suffered a nuclear armageddon with the fallout reaching far beyond its exclusion zone. Life in Britain will never be the same, but unless the British Prime Minister starts looking beyond his personal pride and safety, the rest of the World will be dragged into the contagion.

Fiordland National Park, New Zealand

James Whitleigh-Howse finished reading the article, put his copy of World Review down on the desk and stared out across the waters of Lake Manapouri and the Hunter Mountains beyond. He always found it the most informed journal on matters concerning Australia and New Zealand but, true to its title, it frequently carried insightful articles on American and European politics. But the piece from Martin Eddings was the first he had read which hit so close to home. He and Robert had not long returned from Te Anau where they had done their usual weekly shop and picked up the mail. His subscription to the World Review always arrived with Friday's mail at the post office which doubled as the local store and pub. The trip to Te Anau had become a weekly ritual since James and Robert arrived in New Zealand almost nine months ago.

Totally unbeknownst to him at the time, James' father had purchased a plot of land in the far southwest of New Zealand's South Island almost forty years earlier. He only became aware of this fact eighteen months ago after his father's death, discovering it had been bequeathed to him in the will. James' mother inherited the rest of the estate, but, she explained subsequently, she had no interest in what she described as her husband's obsession with nuclear apocalypse and desire to find a new home far removed from the most likely theatres of war in the northern hemisphere. She had told him she wanted nothing to do with it and had never visited the place, but James' father did initially spend time here, overseeing the conversion of an old hut, most likely used by fishermen, into a comfortable living space with electricity and running water. By the turn of the century, the World appeared to be moving on from Cold War mentality to other existential threats, and his father seemed to lose interest in New Zealand. But he was still able to offset the cost of expanding the shack with new bedrooms and a panoramic lounge overlooking the water against some of the obscene profits he was making from his fund management business.

Since discovering his inheritance, James similarly had not taken the opportunity to visit. All that changed after Thorpehead. Despite his longstanding affair with Robert, he did have feelings for Charlotte and loved their two girls. Losing all three of them following the explosion had affected him severely and Robert had struggled to keep him focused on his work. But, in reality, he no longer had constituents to look after and high-net-worth individuals looking to park excess earnings were fewer on the ground in the weeks immediately following the explosion. Roly Jones had warned that the Prime Minister and Home Secretary were looking to set the Minister up to take the fall for Thorpehead and warned that their university connections were likely to come under scrutiny. It was this that finally brought James back to earth and to realise what it was that he cared most about. Not his family, not his career and not even Robert. It was himself. Roly's warning was the final piece in the jigsaw and the decision was made. He resigned as an MP, let out his Chelsea flat, mothballed his business and bought two one-way tickets to New Zealand.

For Robert, the dramatic lifestyle change that Thorpehead brought about had been far easier to accept than he could have imagined. Although he spent precious little time at his flat in Chiswick, when he was there he was surrounded by his one joy outside of politics – his paintings. While his employer cum partner might have been able to actually purchase the Modernist and Fauvist paintings that he so loved, Robert had to make do with prints, expensive nonetheless, of Matisse, Derain and Dufy. But the exaggerated colours and bold brushstrokes both brightened his small space and energised Robert's thinking process for work. But now, he not only had the time to try and emulate the work of his heroes, but a perfect location to interpret the majestic landscapes which lay on all sides of his new home.

It was surprising how quickly doing very little took up most of the day. They lived in an isolated location but not entirely cut off from civilisation. In summer, there were hikers following the Kepler Trail through the dramatic fjord and mountain scenery as well as bird watchers in search of the endangered Takahe. In fact, it was when the twitchers weren't around that James and Robert occasionally saw the blue-tinged flightless bird strutting around on the lawn in front of the house. Te Anau was only a short drive in reality but they limited their time there. The locals were friendly enough but also seemingly quite happy to let James and Robert lead their lives with the privacy they sought. James had begun work on a series of books he had always wanted to write on 'Great Britons' through history and had even managed to win a two-book contract from an American publisher. Robert, meanwhile was quickly proving to be a more than capable exponent of the simplified structures and flattened designs which typified post-Impressionism. But Robert was not sitting in front of his easel at the moment. He was at the smaller desk in the study, scrolling on the computer.

'Old Gordon has just had a total defenestration from

Martin Eddings in this week's World Review,' James said as he turned his gaze away from the lake and towards Robert.

'I always used to like his comment pieces on News24.com, even if I didn't necessarily share his politics.'

'Yes, I used to get on with him,' James answered, but clearly not distracted from his mission.

'What are you up to other there?'

'Looking at properties.'

'Why, something wrong with this place? We've only been here five minutes.'

'No, nothing like that,' Robert said as he looked up. 'I've had a message from Archie Wilkes which makes sense now that you've mentioned the article. He's asking if we can recommend any places down here. Seems like the Gordon Strathyre might be looking for a bolt hole.'

Printed in Dunstable, United Kingdom